Windy City Knights

Other Five Star Titles
by Michael A. Black:

A Killing Frost

Windy City Knights

A Ron Shade Novel

Michael A. Black

Five Star • Waterville, Maine

This novel is a work of fiction. Names, characters, places and incidents are either the product of the author's imagination, or, if real, used fictitiously.

First Edition
First Printing: April 2004

Published in 2004 in conjunction with Tekno Books and Ed Gorman.

Set in 11 pt. Plantin by Ramona Watson.

Printed in the United States on permanent paper.

ISBN 1-4104-0190-1 (hc : alk. paper)

For my first readers
Julie, J. Michael, and Len

For my favorite editors
Debbie Brod and Mary P. Smith

And to the memory of Officer Eric DeWit, M.P.D.
Rest in Peace, Brother

Chapter 1

Sure, Christmas comes but once a year, but really, who would want to go through it any more often? I pondered that and other such lofty matters, like old acquaintances best forgot, as I entered the ground floor stairwell and methodically climbed upward. Six floors, with twenty stairs between each one. Ten stairs to a flat landing, then ten more steps up on a diagonal stairway. That made one hundred twenty stairs to the top. Multiply that by four, and you have four hundred eighty—the number of steps I climbed every hour. Good leg training if nothing else. I thought about that as I pushed open the door and walked across the carpeted sixth-floor hallway.

It was the Wednesday after Christmas. The hotel was booked solid, but the halls were empty, except for numerous room-service trays left for housekeeping to pick up. I strolled to the elevators and checked the vending machines, ice-maker, and the ubiquitous Christmas decorations. A sagging tinsel garland drooped sadly from the top of the doorframe. I peeled the rest of it off and set it in the corner between the ice and pop machines, then went down the second corridor to the south stairwell. As I was descending to the fifth floor, I heard the desk call me on the radio.

"Ron, looks like the airport bus is arriving early," Marsha, the manager-on-duty, told me. The husky resonance of her voice reinforced the image in my mind's eye of her square face, short dark hair, and tomboyish walk. "In case you're interested."

"Roger that, babe," I said, knowing that being called "babe" really bugged her. And I enjoyed bugging her. It was one of the few small pleasures I got working this gig. Besides trudging up and down stairways all night, that is. She had a way of scrutinizing me any time I was talking to some nice-looking girl. And afterward, she'd invariably come up with some smart-ass comment. Like she was jealous, but of whom I wasn't quite sure.

But being a good manager-on-duty, she usually informed me of the comings and goings of various things, such as the shuttle bus to and from the airport, any VIP arrivals, and any problems in the two hotel bars.

The hotel was a six-story, two-wing structure with an adjacent office building on the other side. Security duties included doing door checks to both buildings periodically, and locking up at eleven. We were also expected to act as informal bouncers for the two bars during the week, when the regular bar security was off. Most of the security staff was composed of off-duty coppers. I was the only private investigator. Things usually went pretty smoothly, so there wasn't much for me to do besides hike up and down the stairwells and shake doors. Like I said, good leg training. My friend, manager, and trainer, Chappie Oliver, approved.

"It's 'bout time you got a regular job," he'd said when I told him about it. "Something that'll keep you off the streets at night, so you can get up early and run them extra miles."

Chappie had grinned when he'd mentioned the running. He wanted me to do at least five miles every morning to get in shape for the title fight that I had coming up on January 12th. And I'd kept at it faithfully. I'd had two previous fights set for the World Heavyweight Full-Contact Karate Championship, but both had been cancelled due to work emergencies. I knew that this would most likely be my last shot.

Marsha called me on the radio again.

"And what is it this time, my dear?" I asked.

"Looks like there's some kind of problem in the piano bar."

The piano bar was near the main entrance, three steps down from the ground-floor level. The bar area was recessed into the underside of the stairway that led to the upper levels. It had an angular counter, soft glowing lights, and extended partitions that allowed for a cozy atmosphere. We usually didn't have too many problems in that one. The upstairs bar was bigger and catered to a younger, more boisterous crowd.

I hit the crash bar on the door and left the stairwell, hurrying down the aisle toward the elevators. No sense running down four more sets of stairs and being winded when I got there. Luckily, the elevator opened with the push of the button, and I got in and punched "one." The rear wall of the shaft was transparent and looked out over the parking lot. On the other side of the glass, the night looked cold and dark, despite the yellow illumination of the parking lot lights. Piles of plowed snow sat in dirty bunches, forming a barricade-like perimeter around the rough black asphalt. I had the urge to go out there and take a couple of deep breaths of the frigid air before I hastened to the smoke-filled bar area.

But Marsha's voice came back on the radio with a sudden urgency as the elevator stopped at the first floor. "Ron, they need you at the piano bar right away."

"What you got?" I asked, turning and moving down the hall.

"Looks like a man beating up a woman."

Great, I thought. A domestic probably. The perfect end to a quiet night. I began a slow trot past the section of hotel offices. The piano bar was just on the other side of the winding staircase that led to the upstairs bar. As I drew close, a red-haired guy in a black leather jacket dragged a squirming blond girl up the three steps and moved toward the front exit. She was crying, and when he jerked her roughly, she screamed. He paused to pin both her arms behind her back, wrapping one arm around her waist. She kicked and flailed with frantic desperation. Quickening my pace, I intercepted them before they got outside.

"You didn't think I'd check out here and find you, did ya, bitch?" I heard him say. The guy's voice was an angry rasp. "Now where they at?" He cocked his arm back, balling up his fist. The thought of his hand smacking into her flesh tightened my gut. Women, kids, and animals— none of them would get abused if I had anything to say about it. Moving forward, I grabbed his wrist.

"Isn't she a little out of your weight class?" I said, just hoping that he'd take a swing at me so I could set him on his ass.

"Get your hands off me, asshole," he growled.

"Hotel security, Red. What's going on here?"

He straightened up and released the girl. She fell down, landing on her knees, her blond hair spilling forward, obscuring her face. The guy was almost as tall as I was, but a bit broader through the shoulders. He appeared to be in his early thirties with the bulky build of a weightlifter. His face had a smug look to it. I released his arm. It had felt solid and hard.

"Don't you ever put your hands on me again," he said, his finger jabbing out to poke my chest.

"Just tell me what's going on, pal," I said. Then, into my

radio, "Marsha, call the cops."

The mention of the police seemed to shake him.

"Hey," Red said, hesitating. "No need for that." He rotated his head slightly, as if trying to loosen his thick neck, then forced a grin. "It's my girlfriend, man. She gets like this sometimes. Too much to drink. I didn't want her to drive."

The tension in him subdued, but I didn't drop my guard. He was like a sharp spring that hadn't uncoiled all the way.

"How 'bout it, Miss?" I said. "That what it's about?"

"No, he ain't my boyfriend," she said, her hands wiping at her face. "I don't even know him. Help me. Please help me."

"Shut up," the guy said. He reached down and seemed to effortlessly pick her up, squeezing her upper arms so hard that his fingers dug into her soft flesh. She raised up on her tiptoes. Then his mouth contorted into a half-smile. "Like I said, she gets like this sometimes."

"It sounds like this is a bit more complicated," I started to say. The woman twisted her head around as she struggled to get out of his grasp and I got a brief look at her face. Smooth, even features with a slender nose that ended with almost perfect symmetry. But the smeared lipstick made her mouth look like an open gash. Still, the faint glimmer of something akin to recognition hit me. Like someone you've met before, but couldn't quite figure out where.

"Look, buddy, why don't you just let her go for a minute?" I said.

The redhead's face turned ugly again. "Awww, get the hell outta my way."

He tried to push past me and I held out both hands to block him. Suddenly he shoved the woman violently and swung an overhand right at me. Out of the corner of my eye I saw her go down in a heap. Red's punch was quick, but looping. I stepped back slightly and let it sail by me. Instead of following up with a left hook like I should have, I just pushed him and held up my open palms.

"I don't want to hurt you, so back off," I said.

"You? Hurt me?" he muttered, flashing an incredulous smirk as he moved forward with balled-up fists. "Now I'm gonna really kick your fucking ass."

The corners of his mouth turned down and a glint of anger shone in his eyes. I smashed a roundhouse kick to his left thigh as he stepped forward, then moved back. I didn't want to go to the floor with the guy and mess up my good clothes. But I had no desire to get splattered with his blood either, if I busted him up. His pale face had the look of a born bleeder. Not to mention the risk of breaking my hands on his hard head. Chappie would love that with the fight so close.

No, better to just end it clean and fast, I thought.

I raised up my hands and let him lurch forward again, figuring he'd throw that same looping right. He didn't disappoint me. This time I stepped inside and blocked it with my left, then drove a right into his gut. The air whooshed out of him, and he staggered back a step. I stepped in and hammered a left hook to the liver, then a right to the other side, and finished off by dipping one south of the border. The combination caused him to freeze, do a little stutter-step backwards, then fold to the carpet. Body punches can do that to you. Not to mention the low blow.

"You want some more?" I asked.

Red shook his head, gasping for breath. Two of the young bellmen, who had been off to the side watching, dragged him to one of the big cushiony lobby chairs. Somewhere in all of this I'd dropped my radio. One of the hotel kids reached down and picked it up. I glanced around at the faces of the people in the lobby. Their expressions seemed to be a combination of fascination and fear. Like they'd just witnessed a clashing between two big jungle cats.

"Man, that was awesome, Ron," one of the kids said, handing me my radio. The other was helping the blond to her feet now. She struggled to steady herself, obviously tanked to the gills. After taking in a deep breath then exhaling half of it, she said, "Wow, you are pretty terrific." Something seemed to click for her too as she looked up at me. She squinted slightly, then said, "You . . ." The space between her eyebrows creased slightly.

"Don't I know you?" I asked.

"Why, would you like to?" she said, stumbling forward into my arms. Her breath had that heavy, sickeningly sweet smell of fine booze. "My name's Paula. What's yours?"

I think it was hearing her say the name that did it. Or maybe it was seeing her up close, even though she looked a lot different than she had twelve years ago. Either way, it was like getting struck by lightning. The blond hair threw me, too, and her nose was a little different than I'd remembered it. Her skin looked flawless and her cheekbones were more pronounced. But the expression, the quizzical glance . . . that hadn't changed. And somehow, it even made her look younger for an instant, bringing back the vision that I'd tucked away somewhere in the back of my memory, so long ago.

"Paula?" I said. "Paula Kittermann?"

"Yeah," she said slowly. The space between her eyebrows furrowed again. "Who are you?"

"It's Ron. Ron Shade."

She jerked back and stared at me, then smiled and put

both her arms around my neck, hugging me close, whispering, "Oh, Ron. It's so good to see you." She pressed her soft body tightly against me.

I didn't know if I should hold her, or what. I raised my arms, but they sort of just hovered there awkwardly, before finally settling around her.

Marsha, who had come from behind the desk to check on things, came walking over. The smirk was already spreading across her boyish face, and her head canted slightly with that familiar, patronizing little lilt.

"A friend of yours?" she asked, flashing the cynical smile that she did so well. "Or just another recent conquest?"

"No," I said. "Believe it or not, we're old friends."

"Well, hero," Marsha said. "What's your pleasure? You want me to cancel the cops? And George is on the phone."

"Tell him I'll call him right back," I said, casting a quick look around to make sure my buddy Red wasn't coming off the mat for Round Two. But by the time I got Paula's arms untangled from around my neck and helped her over to the front desk, the red-headed guy had disappeared. I asked one of the bellmen if he'd seen him.

"Man, I don't know, Ron," the kid said. "I was too busy watching you and the babe." He nodded toward Paula.

She was dressed to kill. A tight-fitting black skirt showed the contour of her hips and the shape of her thighs. Her jacket was dark leather, and under it her purple silk blouse was unbuttoned, showing the edge of a black lace bra.

"So you want me to cancel the cops or not?" Marsha asked.

I looked around again, scanning the area once more for Red, but he seemed to have vanished into the crowd. Figuring maybe he'd snuck up into the upstairs bar, I sent the two bellmen looking for him and told Marsha I'd talk to the coppers when they got there. I didn't want Red going over to the station later and swearing out a battery complaint on me. This way my version would already be on record, and I had Paula here in case she wanted to press charges too.

Marsha handed me the phone across the counter. "It's George. I called him back for you. You can thank me later."

I smiled at her and grunted into the phone.

"What's the matter? You sound winded," George asked.

"I was in a hurry to take your phone call," I said.

"Yeah, right."

"Actually," I said, taking a deep breath, "I had to mix it up with a guy."

"What?"

"Just a minor problem in the bar."

"Oh, great," George said. Although his regular job was a detective in Violent Crimes, Area One, he and his partner had started the fledgling security company for which I was sort of a silent third partner. "You didn't go busting anything up, did you?"

"Ain't you even going to ask if I got hurt?"

"Nah, I'm only interested in the important stuff," he said. "Like did you bust anything that I'm going to have to pay for?"

"Everything's fine," I said. I took another deep breath, feeling my respiration edging back to normal.

"Well, anyway, buddy," George continued, "I just wanted to remind you about that interview tomorrow morning. Don't be late now. Me and Doug are counting on you to make a good impression. This guy could send a lot of work our way."

"Yeah, yeah, I know." When I'd been growing up, George had always been an inspiration to me. Sort of an unofficial big brother, even though he'd been friends with

15

my older brother, Tom. Now we were closer than family.

"I'll try not to let you down, Big Guy," I said, seeing the oscillation of the red-and-blue lights through the front doors. "Look, I got to go talk to the cops. I'll call you tomorrow."

"Okay," he said. "Beep me afterwards and I'll meet you at Cassidy's for lunch." I told him I would and handed the phone back to Marsha. The two uniformed cops were just coming through the front doors.

Chapter 2

I waved and the two cops sauntered over to the front desk.

"What've you got, Ron?" the older one asked. Most of them were familiar with me from my work at the hotel, and they all knew and looked up to George.

I gave a brief summary and they asked Paula if she knew who the guy was. She gave them a wide-eyed innocent act with an exaggerated, "Huh-un." But I wondered. I thought I'd detected some sort of familiarity between her and Red. Both of the bellmen came back and told me that Red wasn't in either of the bars.

"We checked all the washrooms and everyplace," one of them said.

I nodded.

"Probably had enough of you, Ron," the younger copper said. "Maybe he seen one of your kick-boxing matches on ESPN."

The other officer considered his partner's comment and asked if I wanted to sign complaints.

"At this point I'm willing to let it go if he is," I said. "If he even shows up, that is."

The cop glanced at Paula.

"You want to make out a report, Miss?" he asked.

She shook her head and muttered something. The cop looked at her a moment longer and then back to me.

"You ain't gonna let her drive, are you?"

"I'll make sure she doesn't."

He nodded and they left, assuring me they'd check the

parking lots for Red. I turned and asked Paula again if she was sure she didn't know who Red was.

"He's just some creep that followed me out here on the bus," she said, shrugging. "I mean, I had a couple of drinks with him at the airport, and he tried to pick me up."

Her tone sounded matter-of-fact. Like getting pushed around and almost beaten up was no big deal. It didn't sound right to me, but I decided not to push the issue. Still, the underlying violence of the incident was disturbing as I went to the desk and asked Marsha to call a taxi for Paula.

"You think that's a good idea with that guy looking for her?" she asked. "I mean, what if he's a stalker or something?"

"Well, she's in no shape to drive, and we're booked up, right?"

"Let me check with the Hampton and the Budgetel," she said, picking up the phone.

I turned back to check on Paula, but found her wandering toward the piano bar, the tight dark skirt hugging the tapering sweep of her hips. She managed to make it to a stool and was talking to Sue, the bartender, when I got there. Sue glanced up at me questioningly.

"Can you see that she gets a cup of coffee?" I said. Sue smiled at me and nodded. Paula grabbed for my arm and said, "Ronnie, come 'ere and sit with me. Let's have a drink."

"I'll be back in a couple," I said. Then added, "Ah, your blouse is unbuttoned."

"Oh," she said. "Thanks." Her clumsy fingers began fumbling with the buttons.

"Coffee," I mouthed to Sue. She nodded.

When I got back to the desk, Marsha shook her head.

"They're both full, too," she said. "You don't want me

18

to call some of the no-tell-motels, do you?"

I rubbed my temples with my thumb and forefinger and tried to think, wondering, how much do you owe a past love?

"Why don't you just drive her home?" Marsha asked.

"What if Red's lurking nearby?" I said.

"So take her to your place then," Marsha said. She grinned at me suggestively. "I know I would."

"Yeah, right."

I went back down the steps toward the piano bar. The singer, Kathy Daniels, was closing up her equipment.

"You okay?" she asked. "That was quite a performance."

"I needed to get in some extra sparring anyway."

"So who is she?" Kathy asked, nodding toward the bar. "I got the impression you two knew each other."

I sighed. "Just somebody I used to know."

"That's a line from a song," she said, smiling. "Next time you're here I'll sing it for you."

I glanced over and saw that Paula was drinking a glass of dark wine. I strolled over and saw the full cup of coffee sitting in front of her on the bar. She smiled at me over the rim of a wine glass. I looked at Sue, who shrugged and pointed to a middle-aged businessman-type in a brown suit who was sitting next to Paula trying to keep a one-sided conversation going. I sat down next to her and glowered rather sardonically at him. She immediately turned toward me and smiled.

"Ron, it's so neat to see you again, after so long," she said, reaching up and touching my cheek. "How are you?"

The guy's face stiffened, and he got up and left.

"Oh, getting along," I said. "Say, they're ready to close up here. Why don't you let me drive you home?"

She ran her tongue over her lips, and those green eyes

that I used to love so much did a slow scan of the room, then settled back on me.

"Okaaay," she said, slowly. "But I've got to go visit the ladies' room first."

I escorted her to the ladies' washroom and stood outside. Big Doug Percy, George's partner, was standing over by the desk talking to Marsha. He smiled and gave me a small wave, then ambled over, holding out one of his huge hands. We shook, and he said, "Marsha was telling me you had to deck some guy, huh?"

"Just a minor disagreement," I said. "You my relief tonight?"

"Yeah, George couldn't get nobody else."

I nodded and told him that I hadn't had time to lock all the perimeter doors.

"That's okay," Doug said. "It'll give me something to do. Go ahead and take the babe home." He smiled.

About that time Paula came out of the washroom and moved up against me. She put her mouth close to my ear and said in a husky whisper, "I'm ready, Ron."

Doug grinned broadly, and I could feel myself blushing. After thanking him I walked out to the parking lot with Paula. It was always a habit of mine to scan the lot, especially after I'd had a run-in with somebody. But it looked tranquil. Just piles of snow and unoccupied cars. At least in this section of the lot anyway, which was reserved for employees. My old '79 Pontiac Catalina, which I affectionately referred to as "The Beater," was parked pretty close to the doors.

"There's my car," I said.

"That's yours?" she said.

"Yeah, my Rolls is in the garage."

"Over there, that's my baby. The red one," she said, pointing to a new Pontiac Firebird a few aisles over. The windows looked completely frosted over, like it had been sitting there for a while.

"I can still leave it there, right?" she asked. "I got some suitcases in the trunk."

"Sure. I'm sure the night crew will keep an eye on it."

I opened the door for Paula, and she slid into the seat. As soon as I got in, I fired up the motor and turned the heater to high.

"It'll be a few minutes before it warms up," I said.

"Brrrr, I'm cold," Paula said, sliding over to curl up next to me. I put my arm around her and asked her where she lived. I wondered if the tentativeness of my movements transmitted the reluctance that I felt.

"Oh, Ron, I don't want to go home," she said. "I just want you to hold me for a while, okay?"

She buried her head in my shoulder, and I thought she was going to fall asleep. As gently as I could, I extricated myself and got out with the scraper. By the time I'd finished the windows and got back inside, the car had warmed up a little. Paula sat in the passenger side now, her head back against the headrest, her breathing slow and sonorous. I shifted into drive.

Ah, what the hell, I thought. Might as well head for Shade Central.

Paula didn't wake up as we got on the expressway. Under the flashing glow of the overhead lights, I caught a glimpse of her thigh where her skirt had ridden up. It looked opalescent in the momentary light. Her face had changed, but her hair had sort of spilled over the seat, looking darker somehow in the dimness of the shadows. More like the color of the Paula that I remembered. Back, way back . . .

I glanced again at her profile, trying to judge exactly how

much it had changed in the intervening twelve or thirteen years since I'd last seen her. Back when she had been "my Paula." But despite the years, and some obvious mileage, she still looked beautiful. Or was it just that the face was tinged with memories? Too many memories of that first summer after high school . . .

Paula had been the homecoming queen, and I'd been a successful, but rather shy, jock. A football, wrestling, and track star headed for the University of Illinois on an athletic scholarship. We'd been in some of the same classes the spring semester, and sort of hit it off. She came to a few of the meets, and I went to see her in a couple of school plays. When I asked her to the prom I never thought she'd accept, but she did. And when we made love in the back of my dad's station wagon a week later at the forest preserve, it had been my first time. She led me through it. It hadn't been hers, but I didn't care, thinking that whoever had gone before me just didn't matter. It was what we had then, at that moment, that counted.

I practically lived at her house that summer, eating dinner with her family on Sundays, and teasing her cousin Laurie, who lived with them. Mr. Kittermann seemed to like me initially, but that cooled quickly as he sensed how Paula and I felt. The feelings ran deep, but there's a lot of wisdom in that old saying about how nobody's first love ever works out.

We grew careless and bold, but we were in love. I still remembered being with her at a cheap motel, watching *Casablanca* together, naked and entwined in each other's arms. At the end of the movie when Bogey says to Ingrid, "We'll always have Paris," we made love again, not even concerned anymore about taking precautions. It had seemed so beautiful that I didn't feel the incipient panic until a few weeks later when she told me she was late. Then reality set in, cruel and hard, with the anger of our parents for our stupid recklessness. And the pressure to "do the right thing." But nobody could agree on exactly what that was. Her parents had always planned for her to go away to college, and I had my full-grant athletic scholarship to think about. But Paula and I just wanted to get married.

The debate dragged on endlessly, causing a lot of strain at her house and mine. Then, in August, her father, who was a teacher, took the whole family up to their summer place in Michigan. I found out later that they made her get an abortion up there at some hospital, and then they wouldn't let her see me. I kept hoping they'd change their minds, that they'd allow us to be together when they came back. I didn't even have an address to write her a letter. Crushed, I kept my summer job and, after a major fight with my parents, let the scholarship slip through my fingers as September came and went. It was the first time in my life that things had totally fallen apart. George, who'd been in the Marines in Vietnam with my older half-brother Tom, was just a regular uniformed patrolman back then. He sort of took me under his wing.

"You need to get away," George told me. "Have time to think."

A week later we were talking to an Army recruiter, and four days after that I was on a plane down to Fort Polk, Louisiana, to "be all that I could be." Six months or so later, when I finally got back on leave from Basic Training/AIT, I found out that Paula's family had sold their house and moved up to some place called Ludington, Michigan. Paula, people told me, was engaged to some rich bastard up there.

I applied for jump school and ranger training when my leave was up.

* * * * *

The exit popped up on the expressway and I moved over
to the right. About ten minutes later we pulled up in front
of my house. She snapped awake.

"Ron, where are we?" she asked with surprising alarm.

"We're at my place," I said slowly. "You can sleep on
the couch, unless you want me to take you someplace else."

"No," she said, turning to look at me. "This is cool."

We got out and went up the walk, with her hanging on
my arm for balance. I had my lights set on timers, so the
house was bright when we entered. My two cats, Georgio
and Shasha, were curled up on the sofa, sleeping. Paula
asked where the bathroom was and I showed her. She set
her big, black leather purse on the floor by the couch. Her
walk seemed a little steadier now. I took both cats and
transplanted their protesting bodies to their baskets in the
bedroom. The baskets rest against the heating vent and they
both love it there. Then I quickly pulled out a pillow and
two blankets for the couch. I'd transformed my one guest
room into a makeshift office, which contained the tools of
my trade, my computer and file cabinets. Since the upstairs
section was unused and full of dust motes, I usually kept it
closed off.

One of the benefits about living alone is that you can
leave your rooms any way you damn well please. But it
catches up to you whenever you get an unexpected guest.
The living room was strewn with clothes, old newspapers,
and magazines. I glanced around and realized it was futile
to even attempt to clean up, but what the hell, I wasn't exactly entertaining the Duchess of York, was I?

I heard a rhythmic ripping sound and turned in time to
see Georgio's big paws dancing on Paula's purse. I grabbed
his outstretched little arms and carefully extricated his

claws from the dark leather. The purse spilled open, revealing her wallet, keys, and two pairs of matching airline luggage tags. The two larger tags had plastic loops attached indicating they'd been sliced off the suitcase handles. I stuffed everything back in and set the purse on the coffee table away from the cats. At least temporarily.

In the bedroom I hung up my coat and sport jacket. As I was stripping off my tie, I heard the toilet flush. Paula came out, and I asked her if she needed anything.

"No, I guess not," she said, smoothing back her hair and looking around. "So this is your place, huh? Kinda messy, but kinda cool too."

"I guess it does have that lived-in look," I said. "But that's one of the problems of living by yourself. There's no one to pick up after you."

"You're single, huh?" she said, licking her lips. "Funny, I always pictured you with a wife and ten kids. So what have you been doing with yourself all this time?"

"I'm a private detective," I said. "And part-time hotel security," I added with a smile. "How about you?"

"Modeling," she said, smiling alluringly. She seemed to have sobered up slightly. Her tongue traced over her lips again as she stared at me. "You look good, Ron."

"You too," I said, not wanting to say I didn't recognize her at first.

She seemed to sense it anyway.

"I know," she said. "I look different, right?"

I smiled and nodded.

"It's probably my hair," she said, then added somewhat defensively, "you don't have to be nice. Everybody knows it's dyed, but I figured Madonna used to get away with it, and that girl from Chicago that was Playmate of the year and went to MTV—Jenny McCarthy. She wasn't a natural blond either, and it didn't hurt her. She's doing movies now."

"Yeah, I've seen a couple of them."

She stared at me for a moment, then let her eyes drift away.

"Well, in any case, it's great seeing you again," I said, thinking that it was more than just the hair. She looked different facially, like she'd had some cosmetic surgery or something. But that wasn't any of my business. In fact, none of it was. "Look, I've got a job interview early in the morning, so . . ."

She looked around.

"Oh, okay," she said.

"I'd offer you the guest room, but there ain't one," I said. "I been meaning to remodel, but . . ."

She dropped her jacket on one of the chairs and sat down on the couch.

"This is fine."

"Okay. Good-night. Just call me if you need anything."

I went into my bedroom and stripped off my shirt and T-shirt, throwing them into my already full laundry basket, then took off my shoes and socks. When I stood to undo my belt I glanced in the mirror. It reflected Paula standing in the doorway, her blouse open down the front, the tails brushing against her bare thighs.

She had on white panties, and I could see the darkness of her pubic hair through the thin sheen of material. Her body was tan and firm; better than I'd imagined it so many of those lonely nights, a lifetime ago in an Army bunk down in Louisiana. I looked at her, and she moved toward me, her hands feeling almost electric as they brushed over my skin.

"Oh, Ron, I don't remember you having so many big

muscles," she said, pressing against my back. I felt the softness of her breasts push against me.

"Yeah, well, Santa was good to me this year," I said.
"Last year all I got was coal in my stockings."

"Did you miss me, Ronnie?"

When she asked me, something flipped in my mind, and
it was like I was transported back all those years ago.

"Hold me, baby," she said, encircling me with her arms.
"Please."

As if signaling some sort of divine complicity, the timer
snapped the living room lights off. I turned around and put
my arms around her, letting my hands creep under the fine
silkiness of her blouse. My fingers worked their way up to
the snap of her bra, and, as our mouths met, I undid the
hooks.

"Ohhh, baby," Paula whispered. "It's so good to feel you
close again."

Chapter 3

Does the body respond to dormant stimuli from a long ago lover? I wondered as we lay there, Paula's cheek pressing onto my shoulder, the slow, steady rhythm of her breathing indicating to me that she'd fallen asleep almost immediately afterwards. Or did she just pass out? I could smell the booze on her breath. When I finally did doze off, it was fitful. I kept waking up throughout the night with Paula on one side, and the two cats curled up on the other. Finally, I woke up again at five a.m., just scant minutes before the alarm was set to go off, and reached over to deactivate it. Her breathing sounded heavy, so I assumed she was still asleep. Picking up Shasha, who was up closer to my chest, I moved her down near the slumbering golden boy, Georgio, then extricated my legs from under the covers.

The linoleum floor felt cold under my bare feet as I padded to the bathroom and urinated. The stream was dark and yellow. A sure sign of too much coffee last night. I was nearing top condition and it should have been practically clear. At the sink I rinsed my mouth and splashed some water on my face, then glanced up at the calendar: I'd run for one hundred twenty-five consecutive days preparing for this match. I had sixteen more to go. Fifteen, actually, since the day of the fight I was supposed to just rest.

Chappie, in his typical superstitious fashion, expressed concern about the fight being originally scheduled for the 13th, so we'd had it changed to Friday the 12th. But I didn't care when it was, just so it got here. In the square for today's date I'd written: job interview 0900 HRS.

Oh shit, I thought, remembering George's call.

The hardest thing about getting up early to run in the winter is taking those first few steps after you get out of bed. I was tempted to go back into the bedroom and lie down next to Paula's warm body again, but then I knew that I'd never get to my run, much less that job interview. Then I'd have to contend with both George and Chappie being pissed at me. I went downstairs to the basement and retrieved my sweat clothes from the make-shift clothesline. I dressed silently and quickly, with the rote skill developed through many previous morning rituals.

As I ascended the stairs, I thought about Paula. I wasn't crazy about leaving her alone in my house while I went out for a forty-five-minute run. After all, what did I know about her? We were old lovers. We'd slept together last night. And, for some stupid reason, like the old days, we hadn't used protection—necessary for more than preventing pregnancy these days. She probably wouldn't have blinked an eye if I'd taken out some rubbers. . . . But I hadn't had any. And the moment had seemed so spontaneous. When I'd held her in my arms, felt the electricity of her fingers on my skin, it was like we'd been transported back through some magical window in time to reclaim something that had been ours long ago.

Dumb. Very dumb. We both knew that there'd been a lot of water under the bridge. Or at least I should have known. Could I even be sure who she was anymore? But last night was now water under the bridge too.

And as far as leaving her alone while I went for the run, at this point I didn't really have a lot of options. I figured I'd wake her up and let her know I was going out running, and that I had an appointment to get to. Then maybe I

Michael A. Black

could take her out to breakfast, and drop her somewhere
afterwards. We could decide if we wanted to see each other
again. But I was feeling the pangs of regret now and wasn't
sure if I'd want to.

After turning on the nightlight, I leaned over the bed and
kissed her gently on the cheek. She snapped awake, then
smiled and reached up for me.

"Why are you dressed like that?" she asked, her fingers
curling around my hooded sweatshirt.

"Remember I told you last night I was training for a
fight?"

"Ohhhh," she groaned. "It hurts just to think about last
night."

The words stung me. Was she having the morning-after
regrets too? Did she feel it was all a big mistake?

"I have to go for my morning run," I said. "I'll be back
shortly, then I can take you for breakfast and drop you off
at home if you want, but I've got an appointment at nine.
Okay?"

She smiled, yawned, and said, "Sure, baby."

I stood and went toward the door. Just as I got there she
called out to me.

"Ron."

I paused.

"It was . . . nice seeing you again," she said.

I smiled and muttered, "Yeah. Same here, babe."

At five-fifteen I headed out the door, almost six minutes
later than my planned starting time. Closing the gate, I
slipped the bag gloves on my hands and began a quick trot.
The side streets were deserted, and it was still as dark as
night. I had to really watch my step because a slip on a
patch of ice or a trip because of a pothole might set me back
training-wise. Once I warmed up after the first half-mile or

so, I didn't worry about it so much because I'd be loose. Luckily, I hadn't taken any spills yet this winter.

None until last night, I thought.

You know what they say about seeing old lovers: like *déjà vu* all over again. But this particular reunion had been so long in coming, it had seemed eerie. Like meeting someone you knew for the first time again. Things familiar, yet different. Very different. We just weren't the same two people any more. Intersecting lives shaped by separate experiences. Separate lives. Separate lies. The experiences that you carry around with you and bring into every new relationship were there, but sort of like lost luggage. Every touch, every caress, every breath had been tinged with old memories, old delights, old pain. Remembering myself thirteen years ago, but suddenly thrust into a slightly off-key present with a stranger I knew, but didn't know. Things familiar, yet different, all colored with a lingering and overwhelming feeling of regret for what might have been.

Chappie continually preached the virtues of abstinence to me when training for a fight. He'd tell me this story about how he was duped by an unscrupulous promoter into spending the night with a prostitute before one of his big fights. "Women weaken your legs," he'd always say. "So don't be layin' up with some 'hoe when you in training, or you be paying for it in the ring." As I tried to settle into my comfortable pace I heard his words ringing again and again in my ears.

Finally, after the better part of a mile, I started to shake off my fatigue and let my mind wander. One of the side benefits of these early morning runs was they gave me time to think. The traffic was usually sparse, the air clean. Virtually no other people around. The darkness still cloaking everything, bathing it all in shades of neutral grayness. The only variations were the lighted business signs and stop lights, which introduced sudden bright flashes of rainbow colors into the predominantly gray world. Red, yellow, green, blue, and an occasional twisted pink neon shining like beacons at various points along the way.

Unfortunately, my thoughts just kept coming back to Paula. My mind did a mock Bogey imitation: *Of all the gin joints in all the world . . . Why did she have to step into mine?* Glancing at my watch, I decided to concentrate more on my pacing. I was running behind schedule, especially in view of the fact that I had to drive downtown for that interview. Maybe Paula and I would have to hit McDonald's for breakfast on the way.

As I turned a corner I began running directly into the cold wind and struggled to pull the ski mask down over my face. In Chicago they call it "The Hawk," and on cold winter days there's no escaping it. Running in the winter was like fighting a war against an indomitable adversary. Each day was a new battle. I finally had to slip off one of the bag gloves so that I could adjust the eyeslots of the mask. Packs of cars, their headlights shining in the darkness, were growing thicker on the main streets now.

I approached Agony One, the first of the three hills on my course. My breath was a steamy vapor cloud in front of me. Droplets of moisture became frozen chips on my eyelashes, and my feet seemed to weigh fifty pounds each. By the time I crested Agony Two I felt the fatigue seeping into my legs and gut.

Too much sex and not enough sleep, I told myself as I tried to fight off the creeping exhaustion. This was the time to push harder. When I got to the park I knew I had just a little over a mile to go, and one more hill left: Miss Agony. But instead of feeling renewed, I felt half-dead. Breathing through the mask only made it harder, and the part of it over my mouth was covered with solid ice. Even though the wind was blowing from behind me now, it sent a deep chill through my body. I lifted the bottom of the mask so I could spit, and proceeded across the frozen white expanse of the park. The brittle crunching of my shoes through the snow was the only sound I heard.

When I got to Miss Agony I realized that somehow I'd made up some time. The chartered bus that always passed me near the last set of tracks rumbled by. That meant I wasn't too far off my regular time. Or maybe the bus was late. I knew I couldn't relax on this part of the run because I had to get across the tracks before any freight trains trapped me. A wait of fifteen or twenty minutes would just about kill my timetable, not to mention give me a cold.

Then I heard it: the distant whistle. I knew I had no choice but to pick up the pace. Another adversary. Whenever this happened I tried to liken it to being behind on points going into the last few rounds. You had to dig deep and really come on. Go out there swinging and give it everything you had. That was why I sort of liked the unexpectedness of these early morning runs: there was an element of pressure that sometimes exerted itself and kept me sharp. I quickened my pace and headed for the tracks.

The whistle sounded again, louder this time. Then the red warning lights and bells came on, and the long wooden arms began to lower over the street. I was about a hundred yards away and started an all-out sprint. My feet skipped over the two sets of tracks as the train whistle blared again. It was a relatively safe two hundred feet away, but the engine light still looked like an approaching fireball.

My pace slowed after I crossed the tracks, and by the time I rounded the corner of my street I knew I didn't have anything left for the ending sprint. Have to make up for it tomorrow, I thought. When I pulled off the bag gloves, the steam clouds rose up from my hands as if they were smoldering. Instead of going directly downstairs to hang up my clothes, I decided to check on Paula. I went into the bedroom, but she wasn't there. Nor was she in the bathroom or kitchen. Then I saw the note sticking up on the telephone. I picked it up.

Ron, thanks. It was nice. Had to go. Call me. P.

Her phone number was under it. The yellow pages lay open to the taxi section. She'd left without saying good-bye again, but at least this time there was a note. And a way to contact her. If I wanted to.

I set the note back down by the phone and wondered if I should maybe check my wallet. No, now I was being paranoid, but an ironic thought hit me. Was this what women felt like the morning after inviting a stranger to spend the night?

I realized that I had tracked a lot of dirty snow in on my shoes, so I stooped over to unlace them. A thin stream of sweat began to pour out of my ski mask and onto the rug. I hoped this wasn't an indication of how the rest of my day was going to go. When I went down to the basement to hang up my wet clothes, I couldn't help but wonder why Paula had taken off so abruptly without even so much as a quick good-bye. I pulled the light chain and the radio that I have hooked up to the same switch came on, blaring Melissa Etheridge's "I'm the Only One." Just what I wanted to hear at that moment.

Yeah, right, babe, I thought as I stripped off my sweaty clothes in time to the music.

After my shower I heated up a cup of coffee in the microwave and slipped the two halves of a bagel into the toaster. But I kept coming back to the note by the phone. She'd used paper from my pad. As I looked at it I saw a faint impression of some unfamiliar writing. I held it obliquely toward the light and studied it. A flourishing script style, very different from mine. It matched Paula's writing, so she'd written another note after the one written to me. Always the detective, I found a pencil in my desk and lightly shaded the paper to distinguish the imprinted writing.

What looked like *8AM* became visible, with another phone number underneath. I scribbled the number on my pad, thinking that I could run it through name and address later. But instead I crumpled the shadowed page and dropped it back onto the desk. She did have a right to her privacy.

After a moment's hesitation I picked up the phone and dialed the number Paula had left in her note. It rang three times, then an answering machine picked up.

"Hi, this is Paula. Leave a message after the beep, please, and party hearty."

I thought of what to say as the recorder clicked on.

"Paula, it's Ron. It was . . . nice seeing you last night. Maybe we can do it again. Give me a call." I paused. My home number wasn't on my phone, but there was a chance she'd get it if she had caller ID. Did I want her to have it? I just gave her my business phone, which is handled by my answering service, and my beeper number. At least until I decided if I really wanted to get involved with her again. Once burned, I thought.

When I hung up I smelled something, then suddenly realized it was smoke. The bagel! I ran into the kitchen and pulled the plug on the toaster as the black cloud rose like a miniature three-alarm fire, and the ear-splitting sound of the smoke detector stung my eardrums. After extracting the two burnt halves from the toaster, I smeared them with cream cheese and munched them down anyway as I finished dressing.

Now it was twice burned . . . in one morning, I thought.

Chapter 4

I saw the kitten as I came out of the underground parking at Michigan and Monroe. The flood of people were doing their best to ignore its peril as they trampled across the intersection, seemingly oblivious to the tiny gold bundle of fur, with its tail straight up, walking in an ever expanding circle, closer and closer to the traffic flow. The light was about to change, allowing the halted drivers on Michigan to make the turn on the green arrow. That was when I broke into a quick trot. I was afraid that my sudden movements would startle the kitten, causing it to run into harm's way. But it was too late to wait.

I got to the curb as the first cars made the turn. Some guy in a van seemed almost to aim for the cat, but miraculously, when the back bumper passed, the little thing was standing right between the tires crouching, its tiny ears flattened. I was there in two more steps, bending and reaching. As I scooped it up, some asshole sounded his horn and I heard the screeching of brakes. The kitten's claws dug into my hand like ten tiny needles. Glancing up as I headed for the next curb, I saw the driver giving me the finger. I smiled and nodded back. Then, holding up the kitten, I admonished it.

"You've only got eight lives left. Use them wisely."

The little thing was so small it fit in the palm of my hand. My guess was that it couldn't have been more than a month old. But then again, it may have been stunted, too. The soft fur was gold. Almost the same color as my other cat, Georgio. The little mouth curled open in a pitiful whine exposing a pink tongue.

I glanced around, wondering what to do with it. I didn't see any officers directing traffic. Just like the old saying, there's never a cop around when you need one. Not that I wanted to give the kitten to some traffic cop, who'd probably just dump it in the nearest trash barrel. But I was already close to my interview appointment time.

George was really counting on me to impress this guy, Tom Russell, who owned Securitec, one of the largest security firms in the city. If things went well, Securitec would agree to field out some accounts to our fledgling firm. It meant bigger contracts, and lots more dough for them. And me, too. George was fond of saying that he was on "the back nine" of his career on the PD, and if this company took off, it could mean good things for him. I should have felt lucky to be a part of it. At least that's what he kept telling me.

And if I owed anybody in my life, it was George. I didn't want to let him down.

A cold blast of wind sent a shiver down my spine and brought another mew from the cat. I carefully stuck the hand with the kitten in it in my overcoat pocket. It seemed content to get out of the wind, and I quickened my pace toward the office building.

As I pushed through the revolving doors, I could feel the little bastard purring away. Obviously it felt it had found a new home. I consulted the legend on the wall and saw that Securitec was on the eighteenth floor. Some elevators opened up near a guy standing by the monitoring panel with a security badge on his belt.

"You allow animals in here?" I asked.

"Only seeing eye dogs," he said. "Why?"

"Just wondering," I said, figuring that asking him to hold

the kitty while I went upstairs wouldn't go over too well. Besides, after effecting such a great rescue, I certainly didn't want to trust the little thing to just anybody. The purring in my pocket continued as we rode up to the eighteenth floor. I paused in the hallway to take off my overcoat and drape it carefully over my arm. With the kitten in my right coat pocket, I could keep it secured with my left hand and not look too peculiar.

SECURITEC, INC. was stenciled in gold block letters outlined in black on the frosted glass door pane. I twisted the knob and went into a small waiting room. A secretary sat behind a large metal desk that looked exceptionally well organized. She did too: a prim-and-proper-looking woman in her mid-to-late forties. Her hair was pulled back into a bun, and she wore a conservative tan suit. A metal plaque on the front of her desk said Ms. Winston.

"Hi. I'm Ron Shade. I have an appointment to see Mr. Russell."

She flipped open an appointment book and glanced at the page.

"Have a seat, sir," she said. "I'll let him know you're here."

I rolled my head slowly from side to side, surveying the scene as I sat in one of the padded chairs. The walls were decorated with framed pictures, certificates, and letters, mostly from prestigious firms and clients expressing their gratitude for the great assistance of Securitec. After about five minutes, the little cat started to become somewhat agitated and began trying to claw its way out. Ms. Winston stared at me. I compressed my lips momentarily, wondering what I looked like sitting there with my hand in a squirming overcoat on my lap. The phone buzzed, and she picked it up, smiled, and told me that Mr. Russell would see me now.

"I wonder if I might ask a favor of you," I said, trying to turn on my most ingratiating smile.

Ms. Winston's eyebrows raised slightly.

"You see, I found this tiny kitten wandering around in traffic on my way here," I said, taking the little thing out of my pocket and holding it toward her. "I was wondering if you'd hold it for me while I'm in the interview?"

She recoiled in horror, her hands shooting up in front of her like a boxer.

"Allergic!" she said, cowering away from me.

"Oh," I said, stroking the cat and sticking it back into my overcoat pocket. "Sorry."

As I walked into Mr. Russell's office I was impressed at the decor. He had a large wooden bookcase along one wall, containing a comprehensive selection of leather-bound volumes of all the state statutes. There were more pictures and certificates on the wall behind him, including photos of him shaking hands with the mayor and the former and present governors. His polished mahogany desk looked large and foreboding. Russell himself resembled a college professor. Or at least what I'd imagine a college professor should look like. He appeared to be in his late fifties with medium brown hair sporting an artful streak of gray in the front. His suit was brown tweed, obviously tailored to accommodate his heavy build, and his tie was a set of horizontal stripes. The kind they call a power tie in those *Dress for Success* books.

"Mr. Shade, Tom Russell," he said, standing and extending his hand.

I gripped it, keeping my left hand in my overcoat pocket.

"Sit down," Russell said, holding his palm out toward the chair in front of the big desk. "You can hang your coat up over there if you like."

I pretended I hadn't heard him and just grinned as I sat down, keeping my hand clamped on the pocket. The kitten arched its back slightly, but then seemed to curl into a passive position.

Russell reclined slightly in a padded swivel chair and spun a humidor on his desk top, extracting a pipe. But like most pipe smokers, rather than lighting it, he just played with it for a while first. "George Grieves has told me a lot about you," he said, twisting the stem of the pipe in his fingers. "And I must admit, I was impressed at the notoriety you've achieved with some of your cases." He licked his lips. "That was you I read about with that illegal dumping thing last year, wasn't it?"

"Yes, sir," I said. "I got lucky on that one." I felt my tiny buddy getting restless.

Russell smiled. "Don't be modest. I read the account in the papers. That was good work. I like a man who can get the job done." He took out a tobacco pouch and began to pack the bowl of the pipe. "So how long have you and George had this little security firm of yours?" he asked. He seemed to put emphasis on the word "little." Zipping the pouch closed, Russell took out a silver pipe-lighter and held the flame over the bowl.

"Well, we more or less just started it up," I said. "I've been in business for myself for a few years, and George and Doug are still working at the police department." The kitten began to try and squirm out of the pocket. I adjusted my grip.

"Yes, I know," Russell said. He flipped open a tan file folder on his desk. "I see by your résumé that you're a former police officer, too." The pipe was going strong now, the smell not too unpleasant, but it still caused my throat to tighten up. "Former military, combat experience, SWAT

41

training . . . Quite impressive." He closed the folder and stared at me rather intently. "Now, Mr. Shade, I'd be interested in hearing just how you could be an asset to Securitec. As you're probably aware, we are the largest, and most prestigious organization of our kind in the Chicagoland area."

I was set to go into the spiel that I'd practiced about our security company when the cat began clawing and meowing its way out of my pocket again.

"Well," I said, trying to cover the sounds of the cat. But Russell was already looking at me a little strangely. "As you mentioned, I've got quite an extensive network of contacts around the city myself." Another tiny meow. I tried to use my fingers to soothe the little beast, but it just dug its claws into my hand. I grimaced suddenly. Russell sat back in the chair, his mouth puckering slightly, holding the pipe in front of him like some sort of weapon.

"Is something the matter, Mr. Shade?"

I forced a grin.

"Well," I began. Just then the little cat managed to scramble out of my grasp, and it dashed up the lining of my coat, down my leg, and onto the floor. I stood abruptly. Russell seemed to jump back in his chair.

"What was that?" he yelled.

"Ummm . . . it's just a little kitten I picked up on the way over here," I said, stooping and trying to grab it. But the little bastard shot under Russell's desk and made a hissing sound. "I tried to get your secretary to hold it while I was in here, but she's allergic."

"You idiot," he said, pushing back his chair and stepping gingerly toward the bookcase. He leaned over and peered under his desk. "What the hell's it doing under there?"

★ ★ ★ ★ ★

George was nowhere near as big as his partner, Doug, but he was still a good-sized man. Rugged looking, almost handsome, I always told him he reminded me of a young Robert Mitchum. And he did. Well, maybe not exactly young . . . perhaps Mitchum at fifty. His once black hair was now streaked with gray, and he had deep set lines framing his mouth and fanning out from his dark eyes. Those same dark eyes glanced at me with anxious anticipation as he slid into the booth across from me in a greasy spoon called Cassidy's on Wabash. He leaned forward, resting his large arms on the table, and seemed just about to speak when the waitress set two cups on the table in front of us and filled each with hot, steaming coffee.

"You guys need menus?" she asked.

"Eggs over easy for me," George said. "And I'll need catsup."

"You want meat with that?"

"Yeah," he grunted as he ran his hand over his face, rubbing his eyes. "Sausage. And orange juice."

She turned to me.

"I'll have mine scrambled, no meat, rye or whole wheat toast, and . . ." She scribbled dutifully, then looked at me. I smiled. "A glass of milk, too. And may I have a saucer for my coffee, please?"

The waitress nodded without batting an eye, then was off.

"You look like you had a rough night," I said. I was hedging, but sooner or later I knew I'd have to tell him about the Securitec disaster. I felt the kitten stirring in my pocket again.

George shrugged. "I just need some coffee real quick." He raised the steaming cup to his lips and took a long sip.

"Hey, guess who I bumped into the other night at the hotel?" I said.

He raised his eyebrows.

"Paula Kittermann."

He squinted momentarily, then smiled. "Oh, Paula. Jeeze, talk about a real blast from the past, huh? What's she been up to?"

"Modeling I guess. She's a blond now."

"She is?"

"Well," I said, "not completely."

He flashed a grin. "Yeah, Doug told me you left with some sharp-looking babe. But I figured that it was just standard operating procedure for you. So tell me, how did it go?" George asked.

"You mean with Paula?" I said, still trying to stall.

"No," he said, setting down his now empty cup. "I got more things on my mind than your sex life. How did it go with that guy Russell at Securitec?"

I heaved a sigh. It was now or never.

"Well, it could've been better."

"Huh?" His smile started to fade. "What's that supposed to mean?"

"It means," I said slowly, "that I blew it."

"What? How?"

The waitress came streaking back with the milk and a saucer. She set them down without missing a step. When she'd gone, I poured some of the milk into the saucer, took the little cat out of my pocket, and set him on the table. Closer inspection revealed the kitten to be male.

"What the hell is that?" George asked.

"A kitten. I rescued him on Michigan on the way to the interview." The pink tongue repeatedly darted into the puddle of milk. George's eyes narrowed as he looked at me.

"What the hell are you trying to tell me, Ron?"

"Well, I was running a bit late, and I found the cat . . ." I paused. "There was no place to put him during the interview. I tried to give it to that damn secretary, but she said she was allergic."

George's jaw muscles tightened as he listened and his head began to rock slowly.

"So, I had him in my pocket and, the cat sort of got out during the interview," I said. The kitten drank some more milk, then hissed as my hand got too close.

"Aww, Christ," he said. "You ain't telling me that you took some damn alley cat to the interview, are ya?"

"Shhh," I said, looking at the kitten. "Don't say that. You'll hurt his feelings."

"Aww, shit, Ron," he groaned. "What did Russell say? Was he pissed?"

"In a manner of speaking," I said trying to repress a grin.

George stared at me intently.

"How much?"

I shrugged again. "Him and me just didn't hit it off."

George's eyes shifted to the tiny cat again.

"It was a personality conflict," I said quickly. "And then, the kitten sort of got loose in the office and . . ."

"And?" he asked.

"And Russell sort of got kind of upset."

George frowned.

"You're holding out on me," he said. "Come on. Give me the rest of it."

"The cat peed under his desk." I looked down again. "But that guy Russell's an asshole. Trust me, it wouldn't have worked out anyway."

He gave me a baleful stare.

"Maybe not for you, but Doug and me are trying to start something up here."

"Well, like I said, the guy's an asshole."

I saw the waitress coming back with our orders and cupped my hand over the little cat. He hissed again. She set the plates down and scrutinized me.

"I'm sorry, sir," she said. "But we have a policy against bringing pets into the restaurant."

I smiled up at her. "I won't tell if you won't."

She turned abruptly and strode away.

"She must not want a tip," I said.

George shook his head as he began dipping his toast into the yellow egg yolks. I'd just taken a bite when I noticed the waitress talking to some slender, swarthy-looking guy in a suit. She pointed toward us, and the guy walked over and stood by our table. The ends of his mustache turned downward as he spoke to me.

"Sir, we have a strict policy against people bringing animals into this establishment," he said. His speech was laced with a foreign-sounding accent. "I'm afraid I must ask you to leave."

"Aww, come on," I said. "You allow seeing-eye-dogs, don't you?"

"That is not the point."

"Well," I said. "I'll just keep him in my pocket till we've finished. How about that?"

"Maybe you do not understand," he said more forcefully. "You're both leaving. Now."

"Both?" George said. "What did I do?"

"You," the manager said, turning his gaze slightly, "are with him."

"Look," George said. "I just want to eat my eggs." He dipped a piece of toast into a yolk. "I've been having a rough morning, and these eggs are the only thing that's gone right for me." He popped the crust into his mouth.

"No," the manager said. "You both get out now, or I'll have you thrown out."

"Well," I said. "I wouldn't advise you trying to throw my buddy here out. Not only is he big enough and bad enough to kick anybody's ass in this whole joint, but he gets in a real foul mood if anybody gets between him and his egg yolks." I shoveled some more of the eggs into my mouth.

The manager seemed to consider George's size, then mine.

"You'll both leave at once or I'll call the police," he said, his voice rising a few octaves.

"We'll be out of here in just a couple more minutes," George said.

"I said now."

George sighed heavily, then pulled out his badge case and flipped it open, showing his Chicago star.

"Take it from me," he said without looking up. "The best way to handle this is to just turn around and forget you ever saw any god-damned cat. That's what I'm doing."

"What's your badge number?" the manager said, leaning down to stare at the star.

"Hey," George growled suddenly. His voice twisted into a harsh whisper. "Maybe I'll just have my friends in the building and health departments come over here and go over everything with a fine-tooth comb. You'll be closed up till next Christmas making all the necessary code corrections. *Comprende,* asshole?"

The guy's face flushed and his lips drew together. Then he turned and walked slowly away.

"Pretty impressive," I said. "I didn't know you were bilingual."

"Ha, ha," he said with slow deliberation. "That bastard ain't the only one that wishes he never saw that damn cat today."

"You shouldn't talk that way about little George here," I said, stroking the kitten's back.

"Oh, Christ. You're not gonna name another one of them fucking things after me, are ya?"

I grinned. "Actually, I haven't decided yet. You got any suggestions? I'll make you an honorary uncle."

He frowned.

"You know what your problem is, Ron?" he said.

"No, but I'm sure you're gonna tell me."

"You're a god-damn crusader," he said. "You know, when I was in 'Nam, every time a bunch of us used to get into the village to get laid, there was this half-breed gook kid that used to stand on the corner trying to sell us flowers."

"So?"

"So," he said, "I used to feel sorry for him. Even bought some from him once to give to one of the whores. But that was it." He picked up his cup and drank down a large swallow of coffee. "I felt sorry for him, but I didn't try to adopt him or anything."

"I think there's a moral lurking in this story some-where," I said, finishing off the last of my eggs.

"Yeah, there is," he said.

"So tell me."

"When I stopped to buy the flowers, a bunch of the little bastards came running along and one of 'em ripped my watch off." He chomped down hard on a piece of toast, then used the rest of it to point at me as he talked. "Like I said, it don't pay to be a crusader. And you got a crusader complex. You're always picking up strays. You just don't know when to leave things lay, even for your own good."

"Say, that was very professorial," I said. "Forget the security business. Become a pop psychologist instead. Maybe we could get you on *Oprah*."

He grunted and popped the rest of the toast into his mouth.

"Hey, I just thought of something, Dr. Grieves," I said. "Wasn't there some kind of cartoon show you and Tom used to tell me about when I was a kid? You guys used to make me pretend I was a rabbit or something . . . a rabbit who thought he was some kind of a knight."

The space between his eyebrows creased.

"You mean Crusader Rabbit?" he asked, his jaws bulging with the food.

"Right," I said. "Didn't he have a big tiger for a partner?"

"Rags," he said. "The tiger's name was Rags."

"So is this one's," I said, picking up the kitten. "What do you think?"

He snorted and shoved the last piece of toast into his mouth.

"I guess it's better than another George," he said.

Chapter 5

On the way back to my car I stopped and got a box from a sympathetic bookstore owner on south Michigan. Rags was so small I didn't want to let him loose on the floor of The Beater in case he wound up hiding behind the brake pedal or something. Nor did I want to leave him in my pocket, lest I risk him repeating the gesture he made on Russell's carpet. The box was plenty big enough for him, and he even seemed to like it. The wind had kicked up real bad. I folded my scarf in the bottom so he'd have something to lie on and proceeded to my car. By the time I got to the underground entrance tiny slivers of snow were stinging my face.

Grant Park Underground Parking was a massive parking area beneath the streets and sidewalks of the Loop run by the Chicago Park District. I went down the hooded entrance that sprang up on Michigan at Monroe. The cement stairs ran parallel to the up escalator. I moved down them gingerly, not wanting to disturb my little buddy, and handed my parking stub to the woman behind the thick bulletproof glass and she rang me up. Things looked pale and dingy down here in the artificial light. It smelled like a musty urinal.

I went down another set of stairs, this one an escalator, and walked into the underground parking area with the box containing Rags tucked safely under my arm. Huge mercury vapor lights hung from the cement ceiling, casting a yellowish light. The ceiling itself appeared dangerously close to collapsing in various places where the cement had eroded away, leaving a skeletal metallic net embedded in the stone. I managed to find my car after only about five minutes of searching. Turning in my receipt at the exit, I headed up the ramp and back into the open air. The day had started out sort of overcast and cold, but despite the snow, the sun seemed to be peeping out from behind some gray clouds overhead. As I headed across Congress and back to Lake Shore Drive, it was almost sunny.

Perhaps it's an omen, I thought. Better times are coming. But the interlude with Paula, which I was already starting to regret, and letting George down continued to gnaw at me.

The ride back went rather quickly. I got off at 111th Street and headed for the veterinarian's office, figuring it would be wise to get Rags checked out before I put him in "general population" with my other cats. As I pulled up to the animal hospital, my beeper went off. I checked the number, figuring it was George asking me to work at the hotel tonight, but it was the number of my answering service. I took my cellular phone and the box inside. After signing in and settling down on the "cats only" side, I unlocked the cellular and dialed the number. The receptionist answered promptly.

"This is Ron Shade. You beeped me."

"Oh, yes, Mr. Shade," she said. "I have a message from a Mr. Webber. He requested you call him as soon as possible." She gave me the number.

"He say what he wanted?"

"He asked if you were the private detective, and mentioned your name specifically. He said it was, what was the word he used?" I could almost sense her straining her memory. "Imperative. He said it was 'imperative' that he speak with you right away."

I thanked her and hung up. The number looked unfamiliar, but it did have a Chicago area code. I glanced over at the lady sitting across from me, holding a very fat white and black cat on her lap. The beast's green eyes roamed over me languidly. Ah, the life of a pampered cat, I thought. I've often wondered what goes through their minds as they seem to benignly tolerate our ownership of them.

The pretty veterinarian opened the door and smiled knowingly at me, which wasn't surprising. When you've got more than one cat, people remember you. The woman with the fat cat stood and went in. I dialed the number to check the name and address, and punched in the number the answering service had given me when the computer-voice instructed me to do so. The voice repeated the number and told me it was not listed. I hit the END button, but didn't immediately re-lock the phone. I usually kept it locked. There were too many pirates out there scanning for frequencies to clone to leave it turned on.

Rags scratched intermittently at the box. I opened it and rubbed his head. He closed his eyes and began to purr. The area behind the receptionist was an open corridor, and I could hear dogs barking. Not the best background noise for a prospective client to hear, but maybe he'd think I owned a guard dog service as well. I shrugged and dialed the number. It was answered after three rings with a quick hello.

"May I speak to Mr. Webber please," I said.

"This is he," the voice said.

Hmm, proper grammar, I thought. Obviously someone with some education.

"Ron Shade here, returning your call."

"Oh, yes, Mr. Shade. How good of you to call me back so quickly." The voice had a distinctive, clipped inflection to the words. Short, abbreviated tones. Possibly a British accent.

"What can I do for you, Mr. Webber?"

"Well," I heard a sigh. "I'm in a pickle. How about I cut directly to the chase? I own a company on the north shore, and I believe one of my employees is pulling a bit of a game with me. He claims to have been injured on the job, so that he can't work. But I've been getting reports to the contrary. Tell me, do you do that type of investigation?"

"Sounds like it's right up my alley."

"Good. Could we meet this morning and discuss it?"

"Sure. Where are you located?"

"My company is in Wilmette. But I'm heading to my office right now. It's in Winnetka. I expect to be tied up there most of the day."

I glanced at my watch. Eleven thirty-five.

"I could be up there around one, or so," I said, trying to anticipate how long the drive would be. "I'm with another client at the moment."

"That would be fine. I am interested in getting this matter attended to as quickly as possible. Whatever your standard fee is, it will be no problem. I'd even be willing to discuss a bonus if it could be handled expeditiously."

"All right." It was refreshing to have a prospective client bring up money with a positive note. "I'll see you at one then. What's your address?"

"I'm a bit concerned about meeting you where my other employees might see you. I believe the culprit may have several confederates." He paused. "There's a restaurant on Green Bay Road called Saravan's. Could we possibly meet there?"

"Sure. No problem."

"Excellent." He gave me the address. "I'll reserve a table

for us, and leave your name with the maitre d'."

"If you don't mind my asking, how did you hear about my agency?"

He paused again, then said, "From an associate of mine. I prefer not to mention whom over the phone, but I will say you came with the highest recommendation."

That piqued my curiosity.

After he hung up, I glanced down at little Rags. He'd settled back to sleep curled up on my scarf again. A paying client, I thought. Maybe this cat would bring me some luck after all.

My fourth refill of Saravan's coffee was tasting bitter and cold. After leaving Rags at the vet's, and fighting the burgeoning expressway traffic for a solid hour, I'd sat on my ass waiting for another sixty minutes hoping against hope that the prospective client would show up. The maitre d' had told me that Mr. Webber had called to say he was running late, but he begged my indulgence and expected to be there shortly. I'd called the phone number several more times, but all I got was the computer-voice telling me that the cellular customer was unavailable or had traveled beyond the service area. A cell phone . . . Not that unusual for a businessman to give out that number, but, hell, why'd he force the quick meeting in the first place if keeping the appointment wasn't that urgent?

Maybe he'd gotten cold feet thinking about the bonus he'd promised, I thought. I mentally kicked myself for not getting more information—like the name of his business—but I'd been thinking about my own cellular bill as I'd been talking to him. And that possible bonus. But getting stiffed occasionally by prospective clients was just an unfortunate fact of life when you owned your own business. I glanced at my watch and decided enough was enough. I still had my pride. If this guy Webber re-contacted me, I'd charge him extra for standing me up.

After paying for my coffee, I went outside, fired up The Beater, and headed down to Willow Road. It was the fastest route back to the South Side, but at this hour I knew that any way I went was going to be hell. To make it worse, a light snow had fallen and the big plows were starting to circulate. When I got to the expressway it was smooth sailing heading south until I got to the outskirts of the Loop. The rush-hour was just beginning, and people were moving slower than normal because of the snow. I crept from one traffic jam to the next, swearing at the gawkers who slowed to get a good look at the numerous accidents. By the time I got home it was close to five-thirty, and already dark.

I parked in front, undoing my tie as I walked. The temperature felt like it was dropping so I knew that I'd have to fill the tank on my way back from my evening workout. God, I hated winter. A thin dusting of white covered my previously shoveled walk, and I noticed some strange tracks leading up to and back from my front door.

Could have been the mailman, I thought, until I saw them branch out and cut across the lawn. The footprints went along the walk toward my back door. Since both the electric and water meters are outside, I still didn't think too much of them. But as I opened the gate, I saw the tracks continued all the way to my back porch. That was when I pulled out my gun.

Pausing at the corner, I studied the imprints in the snow. A wide shoe with a slick sole. Standard heel. Not the gym shoe of your typical teenage burglar. No, these were tracks of an older individual. And they went right up my back steps. The stride seemed to be less than mine, but that really didn't mean much unless you were Sherlock Holmes or the FBI.

Walking gingerly, so I didn't mess anything up, I took out my keys. Holding my gun in my right hand, I pulled open the screen door and tried the knob. It was locked. My rear door was solid, with just a peep-hole set at eye level for my six-foot-one. But I noticed some heavy-duty gouges in the wooden jamb next to the knob. Like somebody had used a pry-tool there. I slipped the key in the lock and twisted. Closing the door behind me, I stepped over to the one between the porch and the house. In the summertime I normally left this door open when I was out, but I always kept it closed in the winter to conserve heat. Dropping my keys in my pocket, I twisted the knob. The back door opened and I rushed in, keeping the Beretta leveled in front of me. I saw a quick darting movement on the floor—one of the cats startled by my quick entrance.

I moved through the kitchen, scanning as I went. The place was a shambles. Papers and drawers dumped everywhere. I methodically checked each room, but found no one. Then I did the basement and the upstairs. All empty, but definitely messed up. The room I'd been using for an office had been completely ransacked. My files lay scattered about on the floor. The drawers of my desk were all hanging open, their contents strewn about. My dresser drawers had been emptied out too. But nothing of obvious value seemed to be missing. My TV and VCR were still there, as were my check book and microwave. The place had been given a complete, but selective, going over. But not by some junkie from the neighborhood, that was for sure.

After satisfying myself that I was alone in the house, I went around calling and coaxing for the cats. I wanted to make sure they were okay. I knew at least one of them was, from the speedy retreat before, but I wasn't sure which one that had been. I looked behind the couch, then under the bed. My mattress had been up-ended, too. Whoever had done this had been thorough and expedient. The open drawers told me that.

A professional burglar will go through a house looking for valuables in such a way that he wastes no movement. Going through a series of drawers, you save time by starting at the bottom, then leaving the drawer open and searching the next one above it. You don't have to waste time closing them. And the back door had been pried open and not just kicked in. Less noticeable. The same way I would have done it. Little things, but they told me it was a pro. Or someone who moved like a pro.

But what the hell had he been after?

Something else was obvious too. The search had been slow and methodical, like somebody was taking his sweet-ass time, certain that I wouldn't be back for a while. . . .

Like somebody who knew I'd be on a wild goose chase up to the north shore? The red light was still flashing on my Caller ID. Two calls since I'd left. One at eight-forty-five a.m. from a pay phone with a Lincoln Estates exchange. The second was at twelve-forty-five p.m. and listed a cell phone with a number that hit me like a kick to the head. It should have. I'd dialed it at least half-a-dozen times when I'd been sitting in the north shore restaurant trying to get a hold of "Mr. Webber."

And that was why he wasn't worried about me coming home unexpectedly and catching him. I sat on the couch and thought of all the burglary reports I'd taken as a cop, and how the victims had all seemed to share that same sense of frustrated outrage. Now I understood that feeling.

It was as if I'd been violated in some way, by some un-known force. A feeling of anger and despair, made more se-vere by the anonymity of the perpetrator. But this guy wasn't totally anonymous. At least I knew he sometimes used a British accent.

I looked over and noticed that the red light on my an-swering machine was blinking. I pressed the button to re-play the last two messages. The twelve-forty-five p.m. message just had blank tape. I played the eight-forty-five a.m. call.

"Hi, Ron, it's Paula," the voice said. "Sorry I left while you were running, but I had to go get my car." She paused. "Ron, I'm in kind of a jam. Would it be okay if I stayed at your place again tonight?" Her voice suddenly sounded more hurried. "I'll call you back later. Bye."

I rechecked the caller ID box. No other calls besides those two.

Maybe she changed her mind, I thought, feeling silently relieved. The chapter of my life with Paula in it was ancient history now, and after the miserable day I'd had, I didn't feel like trying for a rewrite.

I finally found Georgio hiding in an upstairs closet, and Shasha under one of the living room chairs. At least they were okay. I petted each of them in turn as I dialed the po-lice.

"I guess I should have invested in a dog," I said to Georgio as he rubbed up against my leg. But even a big guard dog wouldn't have prevented me from falling for the old wild goose chase ruse. My own stupidity was to blame for that. I sat down on the couch and picked him up as I waited for the cops.

Chapter 6

"So what'd they take?" Chappie asked me as he helped me on with my gloves.

"Just a gun and some money from my dresser drawer," I said. "But it wasn't my stash. Only about a hundred dollars."

His brown brow furrowed slightly. "It wasn't that gun that your friend Paul left you, was it?"

"No, but it was just as valuable to me. It was a two-shot .22 derringer that my Uncle Gordon gave me."

Chappie shook his head. "You can kiss that one goodbye. The police find any fingerprints?"

"Are you kidding? They hardly checked."

He shook his head.

"I had to rush them out of there so I could make it over here for my workout." I grinned. He didn't. The overhead lights reflected off of his dark, shaved head.

"And you was still late," he said, standing up. He'd finished tying the glove. He was a bit shorter than me, and technically past his prime, but the corded muscles of his forearms still bulged with each movement. Chappie had been a perennial middleweight contender when he was young, but he never got the big break. He had made enough to buy this building in the Beverly section of Chicago and open the best boxing, karate, weightlifting gym in the city. He called it simply, The Beverly Gym.

Beside being my manager/trainer since I got back into kickboxing, he also managed and trained several boxers, and was always on the lookout for new talent. He had a couple of youngsters set for the Golden Gloves, and numerous journeymen boxers regularly trained there. Beside me, the only other kickboxer of consequence at the gym was Raul Sanchez, who'd won a cruiserweight title. Chappie'd put a sign up in the window advertising that he had a world champion fighter at his gym. Unfortunately, Raul had lost his title in a big-money fight in Las Vegas about six months later and it had broken his heart to see that sign come down. Almost as much as giving up the belt. I hoped that in a couple more months Chappie might put up another one saying: Ron Shade, Heavyweight Full-Contact Karate Champion, Trains Here.

But first I had to beat Elijah Day, and the way to that was to get through tonight's workout. I knew before we started that it was going to be a ball-buster. We were in that phase of the training.

I did a quick warm-up on the heavybag, then shadowboxed for a round.

"You ready?" Chappie asked, walking up the steps to the ring apron.

I nodded and stepped up into the ring that occupied most of the floor in the boxing section of the gym. There was an electric lighting system on one wall with three bulbs: one for each minute of the round. That way you learned to pace yourself to work hard that last minute. And even though the kickboxing rounds were only two minutes long, Chappie always made me go the standard boxing three minutes.

Chappie brought out the focus pads and we worked all the combinations we'd discussed. He'd watched the tapes of Day's last few fights and had come up with a plan to beat him. It was based on endurance and counters. Day was bigger than I was, and even though I'd managed to knock him out the last time we'd fought, it was obvious that he'd taken me lightly and hadn't trained.

"This time he gonna be in shape," Chappie said as he held up the focus mitt for me to do a three-punch combination followed by a hook kick. "I want you stickin' and movin' these first rounds. Make him reach. Make him miss. Don't trade punches."

The round bell rang and I leaned forward with my hands on my knees.

"You tired already?" he said.

"A little."

Chappie shook his head. "You better get with it."

As I waited through the minute's rest, I suddenly wondered if Paula had tried to call me back like she'd said.

Put it out of your head, I thought. Concentrate on the fight.

Chappie'd lined up two sparring partners for me and they alternated rounds. The first one was a lumbering white guy named Jack Pater. He was big, and he packed a lot of power. The second one was a younger, quicker black kid named Lucander. He was about the same size as Elijah Day, but I'd sparred with both of them so much in the last few weeks that I practically knew all their moves.

Big Jack climbed in the ring after me, slipping in his mouthpiece. I bit down on mine, and Chappie came over and smeared Vaseline on my face. Then he did the same to Jack. The Vaseline helped deflect the blows, making you less susceptible to cuts. Plus, we both wore headgear in training. Chappie stepped over, activated the timer, and rang the bell.

Jack and I waltzed for a quick three minutes, with him trying to load up with his looping power shots, and me dancing and peppering him with punches and kicks.

Between rounds Chappie gave me a quick critique of my work.

"What the fuck's the matter with you?" he asked.

I shrugged as he attended to me. Lucander stepped in the ring and we slapped gloves. This round went faster, and Lucander seemed to sense my incipient fatigue and picked up the pace a bit.

Midway through the round I began to feel the lack of sleep from my misspent night. Paula's face suddenly loomed large in my memory as we clinched and spun. Then Lucander caught me with a left hook to the abdomen, and followed up nicely with a right that made my head ring. Luckily it erased her face from my mind's eye, too. The bell sounded, ending the round. Chappie tore into me again.

"What the fuck you doin' gettin' caught with a shot like that," he said, grabbing the edges of my headgear. "You do that with Elijah Day and he gonna take your head off."

He smeared some more Vaseline over my face and then went over and tended to Lucander. I wished I had a stool to sit down on, but we seldom used them in training. When the bell rang again I was mad. But as Chappie always said, don't get mad, get even.

It was Big Jack's turn again. Even he was chasing me now, smelling blood. I continued dancing, circling, letting him move forward, then peppered him from long range with the jab and snapped a couple of kicks in on his gut. That backed him off slightly, and I began timing his punches. He was dropping his guard slightly after throwing a right. Like I said, I knew their moves like the back of my hand. I let Jack push me, timed his next punch, and then sent a counter right smashing into his face. The punch stunned him. I followed and trapped him against the ropes. Now it was my turn to work his body. He covered up real well, but I dug several good hooks into his liver.

The round ended and we went back to our respective corners. We were both breathing hard now, but I was really feeling winded. The amorous activities of the previous night, coupled with little sleep and a long, hard day, were starting to weigh on me. Chappie looked at me and shook his head.

"You doin' a little bit better, but you still messin' up," he said, smearing more Vaseline on. "You ain't been doin' your roadwork, or what?"

"I met an old girlfriend last night," I said after blowing out a quick breath.

He smirked and said, "I shoulda knowed." He turned and went over to the other corner as Lucander was stepping through the ropes. "Last round," he shouted.

The bell rang and each of us came out intent on taking the other one out. I kept on the move for the first minute, popping out my jab. Lucander caught me several times with body blows, and I smashed counter hooks in return. The bulb lit up, indicating the final minute. We both seemed to know this was it, so we poured it on. He dropped his guard as he tried a hook kick, and I pushed out a right that had everything behind it. He went down, rolled, and got back up again. Chappie went over and held up his fingers, ticking off an eight-count. He looked into Lucander's eyes and asked him if he was okay. The kid nodded, and Chappie wiped off the gloves.

He came after me like a man possessed, swinging wildly. I sensed that his legs weren't all the way back, but I danced away, not following up as I would have in a real fight. I've never been a believer in gym wars. Especially in a routine sparring session. So I let the kid chase me until the bell rang, just using the light counters to keep him off. At the end of the round Chappie looked at me with a mocking smile.

"You gonna let Elijah Day off the hook too?" he said.

"Remind me not to when we get there," I said. In my heart I knew that I hadn't been at my best, but after all, this was just training.

Phil Brice, our resident bodybuilder and Chappie's assistant manager, came ambling over, his massive arms and distended lats stretching the fabric of his thin nylon shirt.

"Chappie, you want me to untie them for you?" Brice asked.

Chappie nodded and headed toward the office where he kept his notebook. He made comprehensive notes on each training session. Knowing that I'd meet with him later, I concentrated on getting my breathing back to normal.

"You only went four," Chappie said over his shoulder. "We should be doing at least six at this late date."

I wanted to remind him that it had been four three-minute rounds, which translated to six kickboxing rounds, but I was too beat. I just lowered my head and stared at the drips of sweat dotting the canvas. I'd been a couple of steps behind all day.

Brice hopped up onto the ring apron, undid our gloves, and helped pull them off. All I could think about was getting something to drink and hitting the steam and showers.

I nodded a thanks to Jack and Lucander and headed across the boxing area, past the weightlifting section, where several muscleheads pumped iron, grunting noisily. Chappie's daughter, Darlene, was leading her nightly aerobics class to the beat of some Whitney Houston song. She smiled at me and managed a quick wave. I stared at all the leotard-clad girls bouncing around and could barely manage to smile back.

After drinking huge amounts of water, I took ten in the steam room, got under the shower, and just let the warm spray wash over me.

I stretched and reflected on how good I felt, despite my lousy luck: first the ill-fated reunion with Paula, then the disastrous job interview, the wild goose chase, and finally the damn burglary.

But the hell with it all, I thought. Especially with that asshole Russell and his god-damn security company. Pretty soon I'd be the heavyweight kickboxing champion of the world. Yeah, I thought, there's nothing like a good workout to put things in perspective and leave you feeling on top of the world.

As I was drying myself, my beeper went off. I checked the number. It was a Chicago exchange, but it had George's badge number after it, followed by a 911. I figured that he needed me to work the hotel job tonight, and I wasn't really up for it. I fished out my cell phone. He answered on the second ring with a gruff-sounding, "Detective Grieves."

"Yeah, it's me calling you back, and I ain't gonna work at the hotel tonight 'cause I'm too damned tired, okay?"

"Huh?" he said. "What the fuck you talking about?"

"What the fuck am I talking about?" I said playfully. "You beeped me, remember?"

When I heard silence instead of his usual wise-ass comment I knew something was wrong.

"Ron," he said slowly. "Remember this morning you told me that you'd bumped into Paula Kittermann last night?"

"Yeah. Why?"

I heard him blow out a heavy breath before he spoke. "I'm down at the Harrison Street Morgue," he said. "We got a body of a female, and I think it might be her. Had one of your cards with your beeper number on it in her purse. Can you come down here right away and make the ID?"

Chapter 7

I got to the morgue fast, but it was like I was on automatic pilot. I didn't remember the trip. It just seemed like all of a sudden I was there. George and Doug met me in the receiving room next to the loading dock, which was around the back. They kept the front entrance locked after regular business hours. George looked solemn as he set the paper cup of coffee down and came over to me.

"It was a hit-and-run," he said. "Looks like she wandered out between two parked cars." He spoke slowly and his eyes scanned my face as he talked.

"Are you sure it's her?" My voice cracked as I talked.

He shrugged.

"I remembered what you said this morning about Paula being a blond now, and figured you could tell if it was her. It's been so long since I seen her, I ain't sure."

"Okay," I said. I wasn't anxious to go look. Some part of me was still holding out hope that it wasn't true. Maybe it would just turn out to be some other girl that sort of looked like her. God, how I was hoping. I remember whispering a silent prayer as Doug stood up and slapped me on the shoulder. We moved down the hallway to the viewing room. The walls were made of heavy cinderblock and painted a putrid green.

"Think you can tell from the TV, Ron?" Doug asked. It was the morgue's standard policy to first attempt an identification by closed circuit television viewing.

"I don't know," I said.

"Christ, you told me you slept with her last night," George said. The anger in his voice was almost palpable.

What the hell was he so pissed off about?

I just stared back at him.

He grabbed my shoulder with an uncharacteristic roughness and hustled me through the interior rooms to the last viewing area. It was a small room with three large windows. On the other side of the glass the same blond hair that I'd caressed the night before now lay spread out against the blackness of the plastic bodybag. Her face was swollen and discolored, lips curling back in an almost ludicrous grimace. Dark blood had coagulated over her teeth, and I could see her eyelids were caked with it too, but her glazed eyes stared straight up at the ceiling. I clenched my jaw and looked away.

"Well?" George said.

I nodded.

"Shit." He turned to Doug and said, "You wanna give us a minute?"

Doug nodded and left us alone.

"You're sure?" he asked harshly. "You're absolutely sure?"

"Yeah," I said. "What the fuck's your problem, anyway?"

His lips drew together and his head jutted forward.

"What the fuck's my problem?" he said. His index finger shot forward and beat a staccato rhythm on my chest as he spoke. "You're my fucking problem. You go jumping into bed with some broad you ain't seen in a dozen years, and now she turns up dead. And guess what? Know what we found in her purse? Besides your fucking card, that is?" His big index finger kept jabbing me. "A fucking kit. Syringe, cooker, and a couple pony packs of smack." He glared at me. "Yeah, that's right, she was a junkie."

I was too stunned to speak.

"Thinking with your dick again," he was saying. "You ever hear of AIDS?"

His voice sounded distant. Like we were suddenly shouting through a tunnel.

"Well, have you?"

"Yeah," I said slowly.

"Now tell me that you were at least smart about it."

I was still thinking about seeing Paula's face, so I didn't understand what he meant.

"Tell me, dammit."

"What?" I yelled.

George reached out and grabbed my jacket with both hands and shoved me against the wall.

"Did you at least use a rubber?" His face was inches from mine.

I stared into his eyes for a moment, then looked away.

"Aww, shit," he said. His fingers slackened and fell away from my coat. George turned slightly and suddenly smacked the edge of his fist against the wall. "Are you ever gonna start acting like a responsible adult, for Christ's sake?"

A vision of Paula's face, smiling and laughing, danced through my memory . . . the sight of her reflected in my bedroom mirror, the tails of her blouse brushing the tops of her thighs . . . the electric touch of her fingers on my skin.

George stared at me and licked his lips.

"Is that all?" I asked. There was a certain detachment that I strained for. A distancing that would let me get through this without breaking down. I tiptoed on the edge of it, struggling to seize control of myself, but it was like trying to catch smoke. Like someone had used a big monkey wrench to pinch off part of my gut. I felt the tears rush up behind my eyes, but I knew I couldn't lose control. No, not in front of him. Not now.

"No, it ain't," he said, his face looming closer to mine. "You want to keep on working for me, you better start keeping your peter in your fucking pants from now on."

I started to tell him to go to hell, but I swallowed it instead. I'd seen George lose it before with arrestees and street punks, but never with me. It was almost like he was trying to bait me or something. Then I saw his eyes starting to mist over and I looked away. He shifted around next to me and braced his back flat against the wall.

We stood there side-by-side for a few moments more, each of us staring straight ahead at the three-by-five Plexiglas panes, neither daring to glance at the other. Then he blew out a long, slow breath. "You probably ought to get tested right away."

"Yeah," I said. "I will."

A morgue attendant in green scrubs appeared on the other side of the glass and was adjusting the edge of the black plastic over Paula's face.

Please, be gentle, I thought.

"I'll see if I can pull some strings with the lab here. Maybe they can run a quickie HIV scan on an extra blood sample from the autopsy."

"Okay. Thanks." The attendant began pushing the gurney away.

Out of the corner of my eye, I saw George reach up and wipe a solitary tear from the side of his cheek.

"How'd this happen?" I asked, still looking straight ahead.

He pursed his lips before he spoke. "Looks like she just finished shooting up and walked out into the street while she still had the nods. The car appears to have been stolen. Peeled ignition. Abandoned about a block away from the scene."

I felt numb. Like I was trapped in some god-awful dream.

"You know where she was living?" he asked. "We found her driver's license and IDs. Don't know if it's current or not. Address is south of the Loop."

I shook my head.

"I think I've got her phone number at home," I said. "It was a 773 area code. I left a message on her machine this morning."

"Well, hold on to it for me, just in case," he said. "What was the name of that town her parents moved to up in Michigan?"

"Ludington."

"They still live there?"

I shrugged.

"You know their number?"

I shook my head. "You want me to try to find out?"

"Nah, we'll handle it," he said. "It's not your job." He ran his tongue over his teeth, then added, "Look, Ron, I'm sorry I yelled at you like that. It's just that, dammit, you've always been sorta like a kid brother to me, and . . . Aw, hell, I'm just worried about you, that's all. These days, you just never know. I mean look at that young boxer a couple of years ago . . . Tommy Morrison. And Magic Johnson. And who was that Olympic diving guy that got infected?"

I nodded, too upset to say anything. Finally, I was able to speak after swallowing the lump in my throat.

"You need anything else?" I asked.

"No, you might as well take off," he said, putting his arm around my shoulders. "Doug and I will take a run over to her apartment and then try to get a hold of her parents up in Michigan."

"Okay," I said. That was one task I didn't envy. "Let me know about their address. I'll send some flowers."

The next day I picked up the little cat. All his tests had come back negative for feline leukemia, but he was infested with worms and fleas. The clean-up bill was hefty, and I decided that with all the money I'd invested, I might as well keep him. After fashioning a make-shift bed in the cat-carrier, I put him by a heating vent. Georgio and Shasha went to inspect him regularly, but kept a respectful distance. I prepared a second litter box and stuck him in the workout section of my basement. He was so tiny that I worried he'd get lost running around unattended. I solved the problem by going out to the garage and pulling down a bird cage I'd picked up for my former girlfriend at a garage sale. We'd broken up before I could give it to her, and I'd kept it, figuring to put an ad in the paper or something.

It's a good thing I'm such a pack-rat, I thought as I re-did Rags' temporary living quarters.

With the trapdoor to the basement closed, he would be segregated from the other cats. The vet had cautioned me not to put him in "general population" until he was rid of the worms.

Paula's death cast a pall over the rest of the holiday week for me. I kept seeing her face, and recalling memories of when we'd first gone out that I hadn't thought of in years. Death seemed so final, so harsh, so brutal. Still, I went through the motions, doing the tasks that I had to get done. George called with the information on Paula's parents. He said they were pretty devastated, and he'd helped them with the arrangements to have Paula shipped back to Michigan. Better him than me.

I thought about calling them . . . maybe even going up there for the funeral. But ultimately I decided against it. Funerals, after all, are for those left behind, not for the dead, and I had no desire to talk to her parents. What would I say to them? Yeah, I met your daughter again and we went to bed right before she was run over. Real classy.

I called information and got hold of the funeral home up in Michigan that had claimed the body so I could send flowers along with a sympathy card. I used my office address, which consisted of my P.O. box.

Setting up my blood test didn't go as smoothly as Rags' had. It was, after all, the Friday before a holiday weekend. But when the nurse heard that I had been with someone who may have been an intravenous drug user, she told me to come into the clinic and she'd squeeze me in. When I got there and identified myself, she put on a second pair of latex gloves before she tied the plastic tubing around my biceps and patted the distended veins on my arm. I watched as the needle pierced my flesh, feeling the sharp prick, followed by the steady flow of the dark blood into the hollow glass vial. When she had enough, she deftly snapped in a second vial and let that one fill with my blood too. She carefully withdrew the needle and stuck a small wad of cotton onto the wound site and folded my forearm up over it.

This can't be happening, I thought. How could I have been such an idiot? So reckless with my health . . . my future. George had always berated me, telling me someday I'd have to grow up. Now I wondered if I'd have the chance to change. I made a silent vow that if I got through this I would.

As she labeled the vials, she gave me the mandatory lecture about proper precautions and practicing safe sex, which consisted of either abstaining or using a condom until I got the all clear. The second vial, she told me, was for testing several possible STDs as well as hepatitis A, B, and C.

"Of course there is a chance that even if the HIV test comes up negative," she continued sternly, "you could still be infected. So you'll have to have a re-test again in six months. Do you have any other regular partners?"

I shook my head. There was something about the way she'd said "partners," stressing the "s." It seemed to convey her total disdain.

"Well, you'll have to continue with all the precautions I listed until that time," she said. "Six months. Do you understand?"

I nodded, feeling to reply verbally would be somehow inappropriate.

"I'll try and get these to the lab this afternoon," she said, holding the blood-filled vials in her gloved fingers. "You can check back with us in a week for the results."

"A week? How come so long?"

"They're very busy," was all she said.

I tried to stay busy myself by putting in a lion's share of hours at the hotel for George, and keeping my peter in my pants, of course. But whenever I pulled into the parking lot, I couldn't help glancing wistfully toward the area where her car had been, and thinking of that night when she'd pointed to it and said, "That's my baby." One of the local coppers mentioned that the red Firebird had been towed from the lot earlier that day as an abandoned vehicle with its trunk punched. I remembered Paula's strange message call about going to pick up her car and being in some kind of jam. But I hadn't figured at the time that the jam involved drugs.

I called George and asked him to notify Paula's family about the car so they wouldn't have to pay a huge storage fee to get it back. He said he'd take care of it. For some strange reason I hoped her car hadn't been vandalized too badly. Somehow it seemed like another violation of her.

In the hotel people remarked at how sullen I seemed, but I kept everything to myself. Even Kathy Daniels singing my favorite song didn't do much to lift my spirits, and she seemed to notice.

"You seem down, Ron. Anything wrong?"

I didn't answer immediately, not knowing where to begin. Was anything right, would have been a question closer to the truth.

"A friend of mine was killed a few days ago."

"Oh, I'm sorry to hear that. Anyone I'd know?"

"Nah." I didn't want to go into it.

"Were you close?"

I smiled. "Yeah, once."

She nodded and asked me if I had anything special I'd like to hear.

"How about, 'As Time Goes By'?"

"From that old Humphrey Bogart/Ingrid Bergman movie? I love that one, but I'm afraid I don't have the music for it."

I told her that anything would do, and as I left to do my rounds her voice floated after me singing "Georgia On My Mind."

For the next few days the mindless shifts at the hotel and the punishing workouts at Chappie's at least kept my mind occupied, and got me through that difficult period between Christmas and New Year's. As the freezing cold whistled along with the Hawk, I was anxious to start fresh. I was ready, as they say, for the times to get better.

Chapter 8

January started out pretty rocky. The temperature took a nose-dive into the minus digits with a wind-chill to match. It was all I could do each morning to get up, get dressed, and put in my roadwork. The snow felt brittle and dry under my shoes. Like it'd be there forever. Then Wednesday afternoon The Beater wouldn't start. The engine turned over, but it just wouldn't catch. I called my buddy Bob Matulik, who owned a garage near my house. He told me he'd send the tow truck and for me to come by later about the car. When I did, it wasn't good news.

"Fuel pump's shot, Ron," he said.

"Great. How much is that gonna run?"

Bob raised his eyebrows. "Not sure," he said. "The rough part's gonna be finding one. Plus this car's so old I'll have to do it myself because nobody else knows how to fine-tune a carburetor anymore." He grinned wryly. "When I get a chance, I'll send one of the guys over to the junkyards and see what we can come up with. How much longer you gonna keep this beast, anyway?"

"Well, I was waiting for it to flip over on the second hundred thousand so I could advertise it as low mileage."

That got a laugh out of him. "A '79 Catalina," he mused. "One of the last in the era of the old muscle-cars. Big engines, carburetors, lots of torque . . ."

"When cars were really cars," I said. "My Camaro got stolen so I ended up with this one. Figured it would only be temporary, but I ended up putting so much money into it, I decided to keep it. Couldn't afford not to."

"I dunno," Bob said, shaking his head. "Car gets this old it starts to nickel and dime you to death. Hard to find parts, too."

"Guess I'd better plan for the worst, then."

Actually, I had been saving for a new car. The money I had in the bank, mostly from the insurance recoveries I'd made, was building steadily, but I had nowhere near enough to put down on a new Camaro. Unless I went with one of those deals where you put ninety-nine dollars down and drive it until it's repossessed because you're stuck with such a huge, unmanageable monthly payment. Kind of shoots your credit rating to hell, too. Maybe the extra money I was getting from helping George out at the hotel would make the difference.

I hadn't really spoken to him since that night at the morgue. Doug had been the one calling me to set up my hours. George took a few days off after New Year's and went out of town. I knew he was back, but we just hadn't tagged up. I took out my cell phone and dialed George's work number. Someone else answered, and when I asked for him the guy dropped the phone and bellowed out his name. George came on about a minute later.

"Detective Grieves, may I help you?"

"Hi, it's Ron."

"Oh, yeah, Ron. How you doing? I was gonna call you."

"You were?"

"Yeah. Just wanted to let you know that nothing came back on the latents from that car in that hit-and-run on Paula," he said slowly. "Ah, they're gonna have to put the investigation on the back burner, so to speak."

Which meant they were administratively closing it. But I'd figured as much.

"Yeah, well I kind of expected that."

"But I promise you I'll lean on some of my street contacts," he said quickly. "Something will turn up sooner or later."

"I appreciate it," I said. His voice had a conciliatory tone to it. I figured it was a good time to ask him. "So tell me something . . . You still pissed at me for blowing the interview with that Russell guy?"

"Who? Oh that asshole. Nah. I got some new plans now. Don't even include him or his fucking Securitec."

"Oh?"

"Doug and I are gonna expand our company," he said. "We might even consider keeping you as our third partner. Even got a new name picked out. Windy City Knights. What do you think?"

"Does have a ring to it. We'll have to talk it over. Say, you guys busy tonight?"

"That depends," he said slowly. Same old cautious George. "Why?"

"There's a fight card at the Riviera. I could get you guys tickets if you want."

"Hey, that'd be great. We were gonna try and blow outta here a little early, too."

"Okay. I'll leave them at the front gate. Starts at seven."

"Outstanding. Can't wait to tell Doug."

"Just one more thing," I said. "I need to borrow your truck for a couple days."

"Huh?" he barked. "My truck."

"Yeah, The Beater's fuel pump conked out. I need some transportation."

I expected him to be upset, but he laughed instead.

"Yeah, sure. I'll just call Ellen and tell her to give you the keys."

"I appreciate it, brother."

"No problem. And, Ron . . ."

"Yeah?"

"I meant what I said about trying to get a line on who ran down Paula. I want you to know that."

"I never doubted it." I thanked him again and hung up.

I was able to hitch a ride over to George's on Bob's tow truck, which was heading out for yet another in an unending stream of service calls. Maybe George should expand the business to include cold weather jumps, I thought as we wheeled through the recently plowed streets. I helped the tow truck driver with the jump he had to do, then picked up the truck from George's house. His wife, Ellen, gave me the keys and we talked for a few minutes while I let it warm up. She told me that she had to go pick up the kids. I went back out to the big Ford F-150 and got in. It was warm, but I could see the gas gauge needle dipping down toward the low red end as it idled. In this kind of weather, with the truck sitting outside, it was a necessity to keep a full tank. The sucker only got about eight or nine miles to the gallon and cost a cool fifty to top off the dual gas tanks. I checked my wallet and headed for the nearest gas station. No wonder George hadn't given me any grief over loaning it to me. He knew I'd have to fill it up for him. But beggars can't be choosers, I thought as I wheeled the big truck through the side streets. Plus, it was already close to three and I had a workout to get in at the gym before tonight's card.

After shooting home I grabbed my gear and made a quick protein drink for energy. But at the gym Chappie was standing by the ring apron tapping his foot. Raul was already in the ring shadowboxing.

"Nice of you to grace us with your presence," Chappie said. "Raul's been waitin'."

"Sorry, guys," I said. "Car problems."

Raul nodded and continued to dance around the ring. Chappie grinned and shook his head. I hurried to the locker room and started to change. Usually I like to take my time getting dressed. A personal ritual, so to speak. But today I felt pressed. Hurried. Not a good omen. I slipped on my cup supporter and laced the long, nylon fighting pants over it. Today Chappie'd said that he wanted some realistic training. That meant that Raul and I would go at it hard for at least four rounds. Or until one of us got hurt. I didn't want it to be me.

I tossed my ditty bag down by the ring and started to tape my hands. Chappie came over and gestured for the tape. In his capable hands the task was done in about a minute.

"You warmed up?" he asked me.

I shook my head.

"Get in there and shadowbox some," he said. "Raul's done been waiting for too long now."

I stepped up through the ropes and began a quick bouncing around the ring. Occasionally I stopped and stretched, but I was always pretty limber from my daily stretching routine. On the other hand, knowing today that we'd be going for broke, I did a little more stretching than for a regular sparring session. As I did this I reflected on the upcoming fight. Nine more days. Then I'd have the belt . . . Or would I?

My ruminations ended when Chappie said, "You ready? Let's get it on before next Christmas rolls around."

I nodded, but just then my beeper, which was clipped to my bag, went off. Chappie swore and said, "I know you ain't planning on answering that."

"I am unless you want to take over paying my bills," I

said, stepping through the ropes. I reached down for it, but the big boxing gloves made it impossible for me to press any buttons. I flashed an exaggerated grin at Chappie, who grabbed the beeper and pushed the button. The number of my answering service flashed on the screen. She'd put a nine after it, which indicated that it was a low grade emergency.

"Sorry, I gotta make a quick call," I said.

"Fine," Chappie said, grabbing some focus pads. "Me and Raul gonna do some real work, like I'm sure Elijah Day be doing."

I went into the office and had Brice dial the number for me since I was still wearing the boxing gloves. Chris, my service operator, came on the line.

"Yeah, babe, what's up?"

"Oh, Mr. Shade. Sorry to bother you but this girl keeps calling for you. She says it's no emergency or anything, but I can tell she's pretty nervous."

"She give a name?"

"Yeah. Laurel Kittermann."

"Laurel?" I said. Visions of Paula's cousin danced through my mind, all freckles and pigtails. Laurel's mom and dad had both died in a car crash when she was very young, and Paula's parents had taken their niece in to raise as their own. "She leave a number?"

"Yeah, she did." She read off a Chicago-area exchange. "I already checked it through name and address for you. It's a Denny's in South Holland."

"What's she doing there?"

"I got the impression she's lost," Chris offered.

"Oh, great," I said. "I'd better give her a call. Thanks."

After she hung up I had to call Brice in to dial the phone for me again. A nasal, feminine voice answered with a

"Denny's, may I help you?"

"Yeah, I hope so," I said, trying to sound ingratiating. "I'm Detective Ron Shade, and I'm trying to get hold of a Laurel Kittermann. She's supposed to be at the restaurant now."

It was the "detective" part. Got 'em every time. I heard the nasal voice call out, then heard another.

"Ron, it's Laurel Kittermann," she said. "I'm not sure if you remember me."

"Of course I do. You're in Chicago?"

"Yes. I came down to take care of Paula's affairs." She let her voice trail off.

Affairs, I thought momentarily. Was that why she was calling me?

"I'm very sorry for your loss," I said.

"Thank you," she said. "Oh, the flowers were very lovely. My family really appreciated your thoughtfulness."

"I wish I could've made it up there," I lied, hoping my tone sounded convincing. "But I was real busy on a case."

"Yes, Detective Grieves told us. You're a private detective?" She paused, then added, "I was hoping we could get together."

"Yeah, sure." I heard Chappie's angry shouting, asking if I was going to spend all day tying up his phone.

"Look, Laurel, I'm kind of pressed for time right now. Where are you?"

"That's just it. I'm not real sure. I haven't been down to Chicago since we moved up to Ludington, and I'm kind of lost."

"Okay. What's the address of the place you're at now?" I heard her ask the waitress. She repeated it back to me. "You're not that far away from where I am. Just take Halsted, that's the street that runs north and south to

127th. Then turn left and go to Western."

"Wait a minute. Which way did you say was north?"

Chappie bellowed again, but I had to go through the directions two more times before she finally had them down.

"I'm working out at a place called The Beverly Gym at Ninety-Ninth and Western," I said. "Just park in the lot in back and ask for me when you get here, okay? I'll get you up to Paula's from here."

"Okay, Ron. I'm looking forward to seeing you again after all this time."

"Me too."

When I did get back to the ring, I had cooled down, but Chappie was so angry that I immediately said I was ready and shoved in my mouthpiece. Raul was covered with a fine sheen of perspiration, and he nodded at me as we tapped gloves. Chappie smeared some Vaseline over my face, laced on the helmet, and rang the bell, and I moved to the center of the ring. I'd cooled down way too much, and felt it.

Raul sent his quick jab out to meet me. Several times. At around a hard 184, he was a natural cruiserweight, and hence about thirty pounds lighter than I was. Naturally he was a tad faster, too. Part of our training game plan was for me to do a lot of sparring with Raul, figuring if I could get used to slipping and blocking his lightning-like punches, I'd have no problem making Elijah Day miss. But today I wasn't dodging very well. Raul stung me with several more jabs, then smashed a hard front kick into my chest.

"Show me some kicks, Ron," I heard Chappie's voice say. He continued with his gentle prodding: "Or is you sleeping? Maybe you be catching, 'cause you sure getting tagged with everything he throwing."

It was true. I couldn't seem to find my legs. Or my arms for that matter. The distractions of the phone call, coupled with the cool down, made me feel bulky and slow.

I zoomed a couple of jabs of my own, but Raul's head snapped out of the way. My kicks swept up, connecting with nothing. At the end of the round Chappie sprayed some water over Raul, then me. His voice held the bitter chastisement that he reserved for such occasions.

"You leave your head in the locker room today, Shade? Or are you plannin' on wrappin' it up so you can give it to Day yourself? 'Cause you get in that ring with him doing what you doing today, he gonna hand it to you."

I let him talk, knowing it was just his way of trying to motivate me, and concentrated on getting my breath back. Slow deep breaths. Chappie left me and went over to Raul, administering to him. When the ten-second buzzer rang I slipped in my mouthpiece and moved to the center of the ring.

The second round was pretty much even. Raul continued to dance away from me, but every time he came in close I managed to get in at least one or two body shots. You can move your head easier than your body, so it's easier to hit, and it pays long-term dividends by slowing your opponent down. Between rounds Chappie quieted down some. He told me to pick up the pace. In the third Raul seemed to find his rhythm and began catching me with hooks and right hands again. One of them at the bell stung me so hard my head was ringing.

"Look, if you want me to just cancel the Day fight, tell me now," Chappie said. "I don't know what the hell you doing in there."

But by the fourth I was finally starting to get really warmed up. We were going at it pretty hard. The closest I'd been to a gym war in a long time. I stopped trying to chase Raul and began concentrating on cutting off the ring. More body shots slowed him down, and that allowed me to get in a few shots to the head. Kill the body and the head will die, an old boxing proverb said. It was very true, which was why Chappie always advocated a strong body attack. Raul's knees buckled slightly at the bell, and Chappie went to his corner first. I stood with my arms resting on the ropes trying to regain my wind. When Chappie came up next to me, he sprayed some water over my face and let me rinse.

"Now you starting to look like a fighter again," was all he said.

In round five Raul seemed to have regained some of his energy. He smashed a couple of kicks to my body and arms, but left himself open when he dropped his leg back down. Elijah Day had done the same thing during our first fight. I tagged Raul with the wickedest left hook I'd thrown all night. He backed off, and when I came forward he tried a spinning backfist. It was a full-contact karate move and could be devastating if properly delivered, but like every technique there was a counter. As he stepped around, I moved in and threw an overhand right that smacked into the side of his head. Raul went down to the canvas, Chappie watching and tolling off an eight count.

Raul jumped up and began kicking his legs to keep the circulation going. Chappie checked his eyes and asked him if he was all right.

"Yeah," Raul said. "No problem. Good shot, Ron."

But his eyes were glassy and I knew he was still on what they call "queer street."

We tapped gloves and began again. One thing for sure, there was no quit in Raul. He immediately started to come after me, throwing punches and kicks, but it was my turn to dance away this time. I spent the rest of the round moving and slipping, instead of trying to follow up on my advantage. We both knew I could have taken him out of there if

85

I'd wanted to, but it was no challenge for me to knock out a man who was thirty pounds lighter than I was. My challenge would come when I stood across the ring from Elijah Day.

When we finished the round, Chappie came in and sprayed us both with water. He slipped on a pair of focus mitts and told Raul he could hit the showers. Raul nodded and slapped my outstretched glove.

"Good workout, champ," he said.

I was about to say that I wasn't champ yet, but Chappie said it for me. Then, turning to me he said, "We still gots some work to do. Otherwise you might end being chump instead."

He kept me throwing punches, kicks, and practicing combinations for the better part of fifteen minutes. By the time the bell rang, I felt like I could barely move.

"Maybe we do some sit-ups and work the bag a little more now," Chappie said with a sardonic grin.

"Ohhh, you missed your calling," I groaned. "You should have been the mean sergeant in that French Foreign Legion movie."

"Which movie was that?"

"*Beau Geste*. It's French for gallant gesture."

"Well, we gotta few more gallant gestures of our own to work on." He grabbed his scissors and cut loose the tape around the gloves and started undoing the laces.

"Hey, Ron," I heard Brice call. "Somebody's here for you."

I looked over and saw him ushering in a tall, slender, brown-haired girl in her early twenties. She was dressed in jeans and her coat was open, revealing a black University of Michigan sweatshirt. Her eyes narrowed as she stared at me.

"Ron?" she said.

"Laurie?" I asked. My mind had been fixated on that image of the pubescent teenager in pigtails and braces. The young woman who stood before me now was sleek and sophisticated looking, even in blue jeans. Her face had narrowed and her sharp features were perfectly accentuated by her make-up. The only remnant of youth was the dark spray of freckles over her nose and cheeks.

Chappie had pulled off the right glove and I moved over toward her. We shook hands tentatively. She stared at the gauze wrapped around mine.

"I didn't know you were a fighter," she said.

"Sometimes he don't know it either," Chappie said.

Laurie looked suddenly embarrassed.

"I'm sorry to interrupt your workout."

"That's okay," I said quickly. "I was just finishing up. Let me grab a shower and we'll go for a cup of coffee."

"All right. Is there a ladies' room here?"

"Sure." I pointed to the doorway. "Just go through there and turn left. It's all the way in the back."

I watched her walk away, then held out my left hand for Chappie to cut the tape and unlace the glove.

"Well, looks like we gonna have another weak leg workout tomorrow too, huh?" Chappie said.

"Hey, it's not like that at all," I said defensively. "She's the cousin of a girl I used to go out with a long time ago."

"Yeah," he said, pulling off the big, sixteen-ounce glove and leaning in close to me. "Well, in case you ain't noticed, she done growed up. And the title fight is only nine days away."

Chapter 9

I showered and changed in about fifteen minutes flat, and when I came up front from the locker room I saw Laurie standing in the doorway watching Darlene lead a group of girls through an aerobics workout. She smiled as I approached her.

"Wow, Ron, you look so different," she said. "Are you a professional?"

"Well, I try to be," I said.

"That's true," Chappie said, walking over to us. "But sometimes he tries harder than others. By the way, I'm Chappie Oliver, Miss. I own this place."

"Laurie Kittermann," she said, shaking hands.

"In addition to being my trainer and manager," I said, "Chappie also routinely substitutes as my best friend and surrogate father as needed."

"Yeah," he said. "And as all four of those, you just remember what I told you before. About your legs." He shot me a glaring look and rolled his eyes surreptitiously at Laurie.

I gave a quick nod. Laurie looked at us quizzically, then Chappie said, "Don't forget about tonight. We be counting on you."

"I'll see you there," I said. He and Laurie exchanged amenities, and he walked back into the gym.

"You two seem really close," she said.

"George is like my big brother. Chappie's my surrogate father. That's his daughter leading the class."

"Wow, she's gorgeous," Laurel said, glancing at Darlene's milk chocolate limbs extending from her spandex suit.

"So, you mentioned that you were down here to take care of Paula's affairs?"

"Yeah. My aunt and uncle were just so devastated that I didn't think they could handle it. I'm on semester break anyway."

"Oh really?" I pointed to her University of Michigan sweatshirt. "That where you go?"

"Yes, I'm in law school there."

"Great. Say, you want to grab a bite to eat? There's a hamburger place right across the street."

"Okay."

We went across to Jensen's, a non-franchised hamburger and coke place that had survived unchanged there for several decades. I let Laurie walk ahead of me down the narrow strip of sidewalk with the grayish snow piled high on each side. Her dark blue jacket ended just below the beltline, allowing me to admire the contour of her legs in the tight jeans. Funny how people change so little in your memory sometimes. I couldn't believe that this dynamite-looking babe was the same little girl that I remembered with freckles and pigtails. But then, she was seven years younger than Paula, which was almost, but not quite, as bad as the eighteen years that separated my older half-brother Tom and me.

She still had the freckles, I noted again as we took our trays through the line. A dark spray of pigment over high cheekbones. But instead of making her look younger, they sort of cast an exotic look over her face. She ordered a jumbo burger, fries, and the inevitable diet soft drink. As much as I would have liked to have gotten the same, I could almost feel Chappie's reproachful glare, so I just had a regular burger and coffee.

She'd lit up a cigarette on the way over from the gym, but then tossed it into a snowbank before we'd entered the restaurant.

"You don't smoke, right?" she asked.

I shook my head.

"Yeah, I figured you'd still be into all those healthy practices just like when you used to go out with Paula," she said smiling.

Not all healthy practices, I thought.

We moved to a non-smoking section by the windows, and I watched her wolf down part of her jumbo burger and fries while I just sipped my coffee. The girl was hungry, that was for sure.

Midway through, she stopped and wiped her lips with the paper napkin and looked at me.

"I feel like such a pig," she said. "Eating all this in front of you. But the trip down was so long, and I'm just famished."

"Don't worry about it. It's nice to see a girl with a healthy appetite for a change. Usually all you gals eat are salads."

"Ohhh, tomorrow that's what I'll wish I'd eaten," she said with a smile. Her eyes sort of crinkled when she smiled. Paula's eyes had done that too.

I finished off my own burger and glanced out the window. The traffic going away from the city was edging toward the normal late-afternoon rush. A big CTA bus sloshed through a wedge of dirty snow as it pulled away from the curb. Laurie set the remainder of her burger down and wiped her mouth again. In typical girl fashion, she'd left at least half her fries. I stared at them lustfully, then looked away.

"Want some of these?" she asked.

"No thanks. I'm on a special training diet. And Chappie would kill me if he found out I was eating junk food this close to the fight. Like I said, he's sort of like a surrogate father. And George is my big brother."

"That's nice," she said softly. "And how is George? He was so sweet to us."

"He's fine," I said. Then, after a beat or two, "So how are your aunt and uncle doing?"

"Well, I'd be lying to you if I said they were all right. It's got to be the worst nightmare for a parent to have to bury a child." She paused. "And, like I said, that's one of the reasons that I came down here."

I managed a quick nod of reassurance.

Laurie took a sip of her drink. "Detective Grieves mentioned that you were a private detective," she said. "What's that like?"

"It's a lot less glamorous than it sounds. Lots of long, boring work, with little pay. Besides my fighting, I'm working for George's new security company to make ends meet. I've got to pay my own insurance, do my own billing, my own collecting, and run my office out of my house and car. But the worst part is I have to listen to George tell me all the time how lucky I am to be my own boss."

She smiled again. "So how much do you charge for an investigation?"

"That depends on the case," I said slowly, suddenly not liking the way the conversation was going. "Why?"

She blinked twice and set the glass down before answering me. "Because I was thinking of hiring you. To look into Paula's death. The police said it was a hit-and-run."

"That's what George told me too." I paused and took a deep breath. "And they're a lot more adept at running that type of investigation than I am. Something like that requires lab work, informants, interviews, and a lot of leg work. Besides, I'm training for the biggest fight of my career right now."

"But how much time are the police really going to devote to it?" she said. Her hazel eyes flashed momentarily, and I sensed the pent-up emotion roiling just beneath the surface.

"Be honest with me, Ron. I mean, it's been almost a week and they haven't done anything, have they?"

"Well, I don't know about that."

"Please, just think about it, okay," she said, reaching forward and touching my hand. "And I can afford to pay you. I've got some money saved up, and my aunt and uncle want to pay too."

It suddenly hit me as to why they hadn't come down themselves. Perhaps, even after all this time, they were still afraid to face me after what they did to me and Paula so many years ago.

"Why don't we hold off on that till you've had a chance to talk to George and read the police reports so far," I said. "In the meantime, I'll be glad to help you go through Paula's stuff if you want."

"Okay, that would be great," she said. "I'm not even sure how to get there. I was planning on staying at her old place while I was back here in Chicago. I called the landlord and he said the rent was paid up until the end of the month."

"I've got to go up to Uptown for a fight tonight," I said. "That's what Chappie was mumbling about before. One of our fighters has a match there, and we've got to work the corner."

"Oh, is that what he was talking about when he mentioned your legs?" she asked.

"Sort of. But anyway, if we leave now, you can follow me up to Paula's and I'll show you where it's at."

"You've been there?"

"No, George told me the address before. I don't know exactly where it is. But I'm sure I can find it."

"I was just wondering," she paused and bit her lip softly, "if you two were seeing each other again after she moved back down here."

"Actually I sort of bumped into her right after Christmas for the first time since we were kids," I said.

Laurie smiled slightly. "Fate is funny sometimes, isn't it?"

"Yeah," I said. And sad, too, I thought.

Paula's apartment was almost in the south Loop area, so I led Laurie over to the expressway and told her to follow me to Chinatown. We got off at Cermak and took Clark north. When we found her address on Polk, the street was cold, dark, and full of parked cars. I pulled George's pickup into an alley and got in Laurie's car. She had a small blue Nissan with a five-speed.

"Aren't you worried about your truck getting a ticket?" she asked me as we pulled away from the alley.

"Nah," I said. "George will take care of it if it does." We drove around for a good ten minutes more, then finally found an empty parking space about a block away from Paula's building. I jumped out and fed several quarters into the meter.

"How long is it good for?" she asked me.

"Not long," I told her. "Only two hours. You'd better plan on finding a lot somewhere close if you're going to be staying at Paula's place."

"I guess so," she said.

The cold wind seemed to cut right through our clothes as we walked up the block toward the address. It was one of those moderately tall brick apartment buildings with twin tiers going up, leaving a courtyard in the middle. In the early winter darkness, the courtyard area looked like a black hole.

George had sent the family the contents of Paula's purse, including the keys to her apartment. According to Laurie, all we had to do was ring the super, a Mr. Turner, on the second floor and inform him that we were going to be in the place tonight. She'd already told him on the phone that she intended on staying there for a while. He turned out to be an older guy in his sixties, wearing two cardigan sweaters and a pained expression on his face. He eyed us suspiciously behind convex glasses.

"Fine," he said. "Like I told you when you called, Miss, the rent's been paid, till the end of the month. Then it'll go against the security deposit if all the stuff's not outta there. I'll have to inspect the place prior to the deposit being returned." He ducked inside and reappeared with a large stack of papers secured by two rubber bands. "Here," he said, shoving the stack toward us. "I been holding her mail since your call. Better notify the post office right away about the change of address though."

"Thank you, sir," Laurie said.

I marveled at her politeness. But then again, she wasn't a full-fledged lawyer yet. "Say, you wouldn't know where Paula usually parked her car, would you?" I asked.

"There's a lot across the alley," Turner said. "Most of the tenants that have cars pay the guy a monthly fee."

"You know if she could park her car over there?" I asked, indicating Laurie.

He shook his head. "I don't get over there much," he said and closed the door.

We went over to the elevator and punched the button. I would have rather taken the stairs, like I normally do, but waited in deference to Laurie. I'd noticed, much to my dismay, that she'd taken out a cigarette and lit up as soon as we'd left the restaurant, so I wasn't sure if she'd be ready, willing, or even able to walk up five flights. I looked at my watch as we waited for the elevator and she must have picked up on my impatience.

"Ron, what time do you have to be at your fight?"

"It'll start about seven, or so, but our guy doesn't fight right away," I said, thinking all the while how much money I'd be losing if I didn't make my appearance and pick up my SECURITY T-shirt from Saul. "I've still got some time."

"I really appreciate all you've done for me, but you can leave if you need to," she said. "I think I can manage alone from here."

"That's okay. I'll feel better if I can help you get settled. Say, I meant to ask you, were her car keys on that ring that George sent you?" She held it up for me to look at. Pontiac keys. That meant that we'd have to go pick up Paula's car at the tow yard sometime. Laurie smiled as the elevator door finally slid open.

When we got in, I focused on the real reason I wanted to go up there with her. I was kind of curious to see Paula's old place. Curious to see if it would afford me a glimpse of what her life had been like between the time she'd exited mine so abruptly when we were young, and when she'd briefly re-entered it. The elevator was a small, coffin-like box and I felt cramped with just the two of us inside. The doors remained open for what seemed like an inordinate length of time, then closed with a whispering clamp. After a starting jerk, we rode upward without pause.

There were two apartments on the fifth floor at opposite ends of the hallway. Neighbors far enough away so as not to be a distraction. The carpeting on the floor showed little wear, and the walls were a placid green with a floral mural near the elevator. Unlike a lot of other apartment buildings in the city that have a gritty feel, this one seemed fairly pleasant and well kept up.

We went down to Five-B. Paula's place. I felt a sudden weird sensation, going to the apartment of a former lover, a place I'd never been to, with her younger cousin, who wasn't so little anymore. Everything seemed slightly off-key. Like I'd stepped off the elevator and into the Twilight Zone. Laurie put the key in the knob, twisted, then tried the door. Still locked. She inserted the key into the deadbolt lock and turned it. My curiosity burned at what we'd find on the other side of the door. But when Laurie stepped in and switched on the light, she jumped back.

"Oh my God," Laurie said. Clutter was everywhere. Tables had been turned over and the bottoms of the chairs and sofa had been cut out. The cushions had been sliced open too. Stuffing was scattered like remnants of phony snow left over from some partially dismantled old Christmas display. The television set had been destroyed and the coffee table had been split apart. Metal lamp trees lay in piles of shattered ceramics.

I told Laurie to wait outside as I drew my Beretta and went in. The door had been locked, so that meant there was a chance that the offender might still be inside. With the gun extended I swept the whole apartment. In the bedroom I noticed that the drawers had been left standing open. All the rooms were in a similar state of chaos, but whoever had done it was long gone. It had all the earmarks of a thorough, systematic professional search. Like my place had looked when

96

I'd found it. Sort of like *déjà vu* . . . all over again.

But there was a more vicious tone to this one. Chair and sofa cushions slashed open, their stuffing strewn about, the TV screen kicked in, VCR and CD players trashed. If they didn't want them, why wreck them? After I'd holstered my gun I went back to the living room and told her it was all right to come in.

"Ron, what happened?"

"Burglary, from the looks of it," I said, bending over to check the doorjamb. It looked free of scratches or pry marks. "We'd better call the cops. Try not to touch anything."

It took the coppers a good forty-five minutes to arrive. The uniforms came first, to make sure it was bona fide. The Evidence techs would be dispatched, the officer told us, but he wasn't sure just when they'd get here. I tried to glance surreptitiously at my watch, but I felt Laurie squeeze my arm.

"I know you have to go. I'll be fine."

"Are you sure?"

She nodded. "Thanks for everything, Ron."

"You aren't still planning on staying here tonight, are you?"

"Yeah. Why?"

"Well," I said, trying not to alarm her. "The place is a mess. Where will you sleep?" I hesitated to tell her that my place had been burglarized in similar fashion a week prior. But in this one I'd checked both doors and found no signs of forced entry. That meant that the guy had to either be a human cockroach, or that he had a key.

"Oh, I'll manage," she said. "I can clear a place in the bedroom. I've even slept on a floor or two in my time," she added with a smile. "Now go to your fight."

"Okay, but call me later. You have the number?"

"I've got it written down." She got her address book from her purse and read it off to me. "And I've got your beeper number here too."

"Great. I'm not that far away tonight, so if there's any problems, anything, you beep me right away, okay?"

"Okay," she said, holding up three fingers in a mock salute. "Girl Scout's honor." I left her there and trotted down the stairs. Against my better judgment, I stopped in and told old Mr. Turner about the burglary.

"Yeah, figured as much," he said. "Saw the cop car pull up. I try to keep an eye out, but hell, it's hard."

"Well, Paula's cousin's staying up there," I said. "I'd appreciate it if you'd kind of keep a special watch on her."

"Hell, sonny, I ain't no security guard," he said, his lower lip curling down tremulously.

I thought of a bunch of smart replies, but held my tongue. It would serve no purpose to piss the guy off. Instead I just nodded politely and left. When I got outside, the cold wind hit me like a stiff body punch. I zipped up my coat and rolled my stocking cap down over my ears as I made a quick run to the alley where I'd left the truck. When I finally got there I found a parking ticket stuck on the windshield wiper. It was gratifying to know that, even in this subzero cold, an eagle-eyed civil servant had observed the egregious transgression and taken appropriate action in dedicated fashion.

The pick-up started with a quick turn of the key, but the engine seemed to moan and squeal with the cold. I shivered behind the wheel and let it warm up before I started driving. When I did pull out, I made a wide turn and drove back past Paula's building before getting on Clark and heading north. The lights seemed to be burning brighter on the fifth floor.

Chapter 10

I got to the Aragon in about fifteen minutes, and pulled the truck into the big parking garage right next door. During the drive I'd been ruminating about how much I disliked this second, coincidental burglary. One thing my experience in the field had taught me is that a true coincidence usually comes around about as often as Halley's Comet. I crossed the alley and bypassed the line standing in front at the ticket booth. Hirum, the old security guard at the door, nodded and smiled. He knew me by sight from the many times I'd worked and fought at the place. When I walked down the hall I saw Chappie pacing by the stairs. "Hey, boss," I said. "What's happening?"

"You seen Alley?" he asked me. Alley was his nickname for a young Russian kid Chappie was training. From his expression I could see he was worried.

"He ain't here?"

"Nope. I asked him last night if he needed a ride, but he told me he already had one. I thought you was taking him."

"He never said anything to me." I glanced at my watch. It was already closing in on seven.

"Shit," Chappie muttered. "We got forty-five minutes to show time. The first cards are already warming up. I better go find Saul and talk to him."

Saul Bloom was the promoter and a hell of a nice guy. He'd gone the extra yard numerous times, putting on some of the kickboxing matches as a favor to Chappie and me, even though they weren't as big a draw as a straight boxing card. I was just about ready to tell Chappie that I could go look for Alley when I heard some kind of ruckus by the front doors. We looked over and saw Alley and a crowd of people arguing with Hirum. He was raising his radio to his mouth when Chappie and I ran over there.

"Alley, where the hell you been?" Chappie asked. The kid smiled broadly and said something in Russian to a bearded, barrel-chested guy standing next to him.

The big guy smiled, spoke back to Alley, then said to us in a deep baritone, "Ah, you are the people that Allyosha has told me about." He extended a big hand. "I am Father Boris Dilousovich."

"Ron Shade," I said. "Glad to meet you."

"And this must be Mr. Oliver," Big Boris said. He looked to be in his fifties, his dark beard flecked with gray, but I figured that in his younger days he could have given George's partner, Doug Percy, a run for his money.

"Alley, where the hell you been?" Chappie repeated, after shaking Boris's hand briefly. "We got a fight in about forty minutes, maybe sooner." Alley flashed a sheepish smile.

"Perhaps I can explain," Boris said. "I am the minister for the Russian Orthodox church on Diversey. Allyosha wanted to light a candle for his loved ones in our homeland before the contest tonight." He grinned broadly. "You see it is Christmas."

"Christmas was last month," Chappie said, tugging on Alley's sleeve. "And he don't get warmed up, he gonna get more than coal dumped in his stockings."

"Oh, but today is our Christmas," Boris said, his broad smile never faltering. "Russian Orthodox Christmas." He laughed heartily, said something in Russian that started the crowd around him laughing and singing. "Merry Christmas, Mr. Oliver."

"Da, Chappie," Alley said. "Merry Christmas." He leaned forward and grabbed Chappie's shoulders and kissed him twice, once on each cheek. Chappie jerked away and scowled.

"Cut that out, you crazy Russian," he said. But he saw me laughing and cracked a slight grin. "What the fuck you laughing at? He probably gonna do you next."

"Not on your life," I said. "I was ready for him. I saw *Casablanca*."

"Good," Chappie said. "Now take him upstairs and start getting him ready. I'll square the Red Army here with the ticketman."

Saul always kept a stash of guest passes at the front booth in case we had any special VIP's, like reporters or friends, show up. That way we could just slip them in with no fuss. I motioned for Alley to follow me and we headed toward the long hallway. I heard someone call my name and turned to see George and Big Doug walking down the stairs.

"We got here earlier," George said. "Been looking for you. Thanks for leaving them guest passes at the booth for us."

"No problem," I said. "Where'd you park?"

"In the alley," Doug said. "We took the unmarked. In case we might want to serve a warrant later." He chuckled. I knew that meant that they were still on the clock technically, subject to call. I introduced them to Alley and they shook hands.

"Watch him tonight, guys," I said. "You're seeing a future champ."

"When you fightin' again, Ron?" Doug asked.

"Next Friday night," I told him, trying to make it seem farther away than it was.

"For the title," George added. "And this time nothing's gonna stop him. I might even bet on him if the odds are right."

"Your confidence is inspiring," I said, grinning. "Oh, by the way, I need a favor."

"Don't you always?" he said. "What is it this time?"

"You still got your Chinaman in traffic division?"

"Yeah."

"Can you get a parking ticket pulled for me?" His expression soured and I quickly added, "It's for Laurie Kittermann."

"Laurie?" George said. "Paula's cousin?"

"Yeah," I said. "She came down here to get Paula's stuff and she got tagged by some meter maid. Poor kid's lost. She wants to come by to see you regarding the progress of the investigation, and to thank you, too."

"All right, god-dammit," he sighed. "Give it to me."

"Oh, I'll have to get it from her," I said, wondering how I could erase the license number of his truck without him getting suspicious before I gave him the ticket. "Say, do you know that Paula's apartment was burglarized just like my place?"

"That so?" said George.

"Well," I said, "do you think there could be a connection?"

He frowned. "Ron, do you know how many burglaries there are in this city? They got a regular cottage industry reading the obits and then burglarizing the house during the funerals." He paused and sighed. "So, you call it in?"

"Yeah," I said, thinking that Paula's obituary wouldn't have been in the local papers. "I was just hoping you'd keep it in mind or something."

"Sure thing," he said. Then to Doug, "Let's grab a

couple of brewskis before things get started."

"We gotta go upstairs to get ready. See you two ring-side."

"Knock 'em dead, kid," Doug said, raising a ham-like fist.

Alley grinned and said, "Da."

On the way to the locker room I reflected on how low it was of me to lie to George about the ticket, but I rationalized that the thing really was for Laurie. Sort of. I mean, I wouldn't have parked in that alley in the first place, if I hadn't been helping her. And anyway, I thought, that's what friends were for, right? Besides, I knew he'd do the same to me if the positions were reversed, especially if it was still his truck.

Inside the locker room Alley changed into his protective cup and trunks and draped his robe around himself to keep warm. I let him put on his socks and shoes and lace them up so they were comfortable. Then I got out the gauze and tape and waited to start wrapping his hands.

"Need any help with that?" I heard someone say. I turned my head and saw a grizzled old face that went with the voice. It was Vic Roddy, our cut-man. Vic, who'd been around boxing his whole life, had worked the corners of some pretty big names. He'd also been Chappie's cut-man when he'd been a contender. Since he lived in Chicago, he'd pretty much been available for us whenever we needed him.

"Far be it from me to pass up an honest buck," he always said with a lopsided grin. "Or to see a good fight either."

His white hair stuck out from beneath a wool stocking cap and his cheeks were still flushed from the cold wind.

"I think I can manage," I said. "Vic, this is Alley, our fighter tonight."

"Pleased to meetcha," Vic said.

"Da," Alley replied.

Vic shot me a quizzical glance.

"Not too much English," I said.

Vic nodded. "Polish?"

"Ruskie."

Vic grunted an approval. He took off his coat and hung it in an open locker, then sat stolidly on the end of the bench while he checked his kit.

Presently Chappie came in with the officials and said Nate Ross's cornerman would be in shortly. Chappie and Vic shook hands warmly, and Chappie thanked him for coming.

"I'm always available for you, Champ," Vic said.

I went to the other locker room to watch Nate get taped up. The rule about having the opposing camp in to watch this part of the preparation stemmed back to a tradition from one of the great heavyweight fights of the early twentieth century. When Jack Dempsey had knocked out Jess Willard to win the heavyweight championship, Willard's manager had cried foul, and alleged that Dempsey had put plaster of Paris powder on his taped hands, making them extra hard once his sweat moistened the tape. Willard, who suffered a terrible beating, was barely able to get up. He probably never even should have been in the ring with Dempsey in the first place, anyway. But out of that fight the regulation came, and probably for the better, too. I doubted that the Manassa Mauler had needed any extra help to pulverize the lumbering Willard, but many other unscrupulous managers had tried various games through the years in this vicious and dirty sport. Anything to help safeguard the fighters was all right in my book.

I nodded to Nate Ross as he sat on the steel table in his

purple and scarlet robe. We knew each other slightly, having met at previous fights around the area. He lived in Whiting, Indiana, and worked full-time as an automobile mechanic. In the evenings he trained himself as a fighter, and he'd developed into a pretty good journeyman. Tonight's bout was listed as a cruiserweight, which is just below the 200-pound level. I knew Alley was about 190, but Nate looked a lot heavier. A roll of fat, visible between the open lapels of his robe, looped over the top of his trunks, and he made no effort to hide it. But in shape or not, he could be one rough son-of-a-bitch, and usually gave as good as he got. I hoped that Alley hadn't been overmatched in his first pro fight.

After the gloves had been initialed, I went back to our locker room. Chappie was holding the focus pads for Alley, who was throwing a series of quick punches. The worst thing for a fighter to do was to enter the ring cold, which increased the susceptibility of being knocked out. Ideally, a thin layer of sweat was best as you stepped through the ropes. The ref came in and gave us the abbreviated pre-fight instructions. The first fight had only gone three rounds before ending in a knockout, so we were up next. Chappie nodded and slipped Alley's robe back over his shoulders. He still looked a little dry to me.

The trip from the locker room to the ring has been described as the longest walk in the world. And, from experience, I knew that it really was, too. Next week it'll be my turn, I thought, as we entered the main auditorium. The sounds and smells washed over us like an incoming wave. Cigarette smoke hovered in the air, and the pervasive stench of beer and sweat seemed to be everywhere. Hundreds of indistinguishable voices buzzed in a discordant drone. Some heads turned to watch us, but most seemed oblivious. Unless you were a big name, or the main event, all you were to these people was a human punching bag, a face to get bashed in, or, as Jack London once said, a piece of meat.

We went up the ring steps and I held the ropes for Chappie, Vic, and Alley to step through. The judges were seated at the center of three of the ringsides, and the two cable TV announcers were at the fourth. A cameraman holding a camcorder on his shoulder moved deftly on the ring apron. The announcer shuffled through his cards, then began his spiel. After "Ladies and Gentlemen . . ." the crowd quieted. He murdered Alley's name, introduced him as "The Mad Russian," and then did the same for Nate Ross, whom the announcer called "The Fightin' Mechanic." We moved to the center of the ring, and I saw Chappie's eyes dart to the roll of fat around Ross' waist. The ref tightened up his instructions and Alley and Ross tapped gloves. As we stepped back to our corner, Chappie said, "Work the body," as he smeared a tad more Vaseline over Alley's eyebrows.

The bell sounded and Alley moved out of the corner and began circling to his left. His jab snaked out beautifully and caught Ross on the forehead. He repeated the jab several more times, then stepped inside and hooked to the belly. Ross clinched and pushed. He was using his guile to survive. The fat around his waist jiggled like Jell-O as Alley smacked his gloves to the rib cage while he waited for the ref to break them.

After the first round I figured we were out of the woods. Alley looked pretty much warmed up, and his body attack had slowed Ross visibly. Chappie gave him some water to rinse out his mouth while I massaged his shoulders, arms, and neck. I couldn't help thinking again that next week it would be me on that stool gasping for breath between rounds.

"You doin' great, kid," Chappie said. "Keep jabbing your way in, then punish that body."

Alley nodded. His face looked flushed from the effort as Chappie smeared on more Vaseline. The timekeeper called for "Seconds out," and Chappie and I stepped back through the ropes. When the bell rang, Alley stood and I grabbed the stool. Alley continued to work the jab and then hook to the body. But Ross was able to tie him up when he moved inside. By the middle of the round Ross seemed to have warmed up sufficiently to start firing off counter punches that caught Alley as he tried to move in. They clinched and Ross spun Alley into the ropes, threw a combination, and tossed in an elbow at the end of his last hook. "Damn him!" Chappie yelled.

But that wasn't the worst of it. At the end of the round Ross came in again with a looping right and hit Alley low. The ref ignored it, and Alley glanced over his shoulder as he limped back to our corner. We were in the ring in a flash, Chappie holding the kid's trunks and protective cup away from his stomach to let him breathe easier, and me slapping the ice bag against the back of Alley's neck. Chappie told him to stay outside and work the jab more, then look for an uppercut.

"You know, uppercut," Chappie said, mimicking the punch. The ref strolled by and Chappie's head whirled as he called, "Hey, ref, you gonna keep lettin' him hit low like that?"

"It looked borderline," the ref said.

Chappie scowled and said, "Like hell." But at least he'd planted the seed. Maybe the ref would call the next one. The minute was up and the timekeeper called for us to vacate again. As Alley stood, I grabbed the stool and jumped off the ring apron. Alley kept shooting out the jab, and was catching Ross with an occasional hook to the body. Chappie had wanted him to coast slightly this time so he could go all out in the last round. Things were going pretty well until, with about thirty seconds left, Ross moved back against the ropes and Alley came in trying to follow up. Ross grabbed for him and they clashed heads. When the ref broke them from the clinch, a stream of blood snaked its way down Alley's face. It looked to be over the right eye.

"Shit," Chappie said. "He butted him."

The cut looked bad enough for the ref to call a time out and he escorted Alley over to the ring edge. The doctor stepped up on the apron and took a look, then motioned for them to resume. The sight of the blood sent my own thoughts darting back to my recent blood test, with all its horrible implications. Maybe I wouldn't be fighting next week after all . . . Maybe . . .

But that wasn't something I was going to think about until I knew for sure.

At the sight of his opponent's blood, Ross stepped up the pace, but Alley wisely got on his bicycle and retreated behind the jab until the round ended. He kept wiping at his eye as he walked back to the corner. Vic was already on the apron with his magic bottle out and a Q-Tip between his teeth. He swabbed the cut quickly then squeezed it shut between his fingers. I held the ice pack against the back of Alley's neck again from outside the ropes. Chappie's dark face, shiny with sweat, leaned close to Alley. "Last round. Last chance. He ready to go. Use that jab and watch when he throws that right. He steps forward. Use the uppercut. That's the key. You got to win this round, understand? When he throws the right, you use the uppercut."

Alley nodded, his breath coming in ragged gasps. The ref circled in front of us and said, "Last round. How's the cut?"

"He's okay," Chappie said.

At the timekeeper's warning, Chappie and Vic stepped between the ropes. Vic had closed the cut and smeared it with a Vaseline mix. I wondered if it would hold. An old pro like Nate Ross would surely attack the cut to try to open it up. Chappie and I both knew that this round would be the test. As an amateur, Alley had been used to only going three rounds. We'd been working four, five, and sometimes six in the gym, but being in a real fight was a different story, much less a war like this one had become. Chappie kept calling his instructions to Alley from ringside. I remembered the times that I'd fought; somehow Chappie's voice had been discernible through all the noise. I hoped that it would be the same for Alley. The kid was giving it everything he had.

Ross kicked it up a little too. He was throwing heavy, looping punches whenever Alley tried to follow up, and managed to connect with a powerful right that backed Alley up. The cut had opened again, and the kid took two steps back, blinking quickly. Ross, sensing that he had him hurt, moved forward, poised for the kill. He fired off a left, then stepped in with a right cross. That's when Alley pivoted and threw the uppercut. Ross was down on all fours as the ref pointed Alley toward the neutral corner and picked up the count. Ross got up at eight on rubbery legs. Alley moved in and slammed home a good body shot behind a jab before Ross grabbed and tied him up. The ref practically had to pry Ross's arms off. Alley moved forward, the blood streaming down his face, as Ross backed up to the ropes and covered up. Alley managed to smack a few hooks to the body before Ross clinched again, and when the ref finally broke them, the bell rang. Alley turned and walked back toward us. Vic immediately started administering to the cut again, and Chappie grinned and draped a towel over Alley's shoulders. Nate Ross stared at us from across the ring, and, after blinking several times, gave us a nod of respect.

"Welcome to the pros," Chappie said.

Chapter 11

Not surprisingly, we won the decision on all three cards. One of the announcers from the cable station broadcasting the program came over with a cameraman and started interviewing Chappie and Alley. When it was obvious how little English Alley spoke, the guy focused his attention on Chappie, who called Alley "the strongest 190 pounder" that he'd ever seen. Nate Ross even came over and congratulated him, but Chappie gave him a look of disdain for the butting, and Nate quickly retreated. We got out of the ring and went back to the locker room. Chappie told Alley to take a quick shower and get dressed.

"We gonna go for stitches," he said. "You want to come?"

"I told Saul I'd work security for the rest of the cards," I said. "I'd like to pick up some extra bucks."

"Make sure that's all you pick up," Chappie said.

"Now what's that supposed to mean?"

"It means that you promised me you ain't gonna be skipping no more runs in the mornings," he said. "That means goin' home and gettin' some sleep, and not stayin' up all night gettin' some leg."

"You know, if I got half as much leg as you seem to think I do, I wouldn't be able to walk for a week."

"Just the same," he said, "remember your fight's coming up next week. Don't run the well dry now."

I told him not to worry. The door opened and Saul Bloom came in. Right behind him was the squat figure of

Alley's manager, a sleazy guy named Smershkevich. He nodded to us and put a fresh cigarette between his lips.

"Chappie," Saul said, "the kid put on a great fight. Mr. Smershkevich told me that he was good, but I didn't expect that he'd look this polished in his first pro fight."

Smershkevich let some smoke leak from between his teeth as he flashed what passed for a smile at us. "How bad's the cut look?" Saul asked.

"I seen worse," Vic said. "Get him stitched up right and he'll be fine inside of a month."

"Good, good," Saul said, smiling. "Too bad we couldn't run him again on your card, Ron. Ah . . . you're going to stay the rest of the night, right?"

"Yeah," I said. I opened my locker and got out the black SECURITY sweatshirt and slipped it on. Saul told me he'd talk to us later. Smershkevich glanced around, then walked over by the shower room and started talking to Alley who was toweling off. Although I couldn't have understood them even if I could have heard them, I watched the interplay between the two. Alley seemed frozen as the shorter man spoke in harsh-sounding guttural tones. Smershkevich exhaled a plume of smoke then tossed the butt into the shower stalls. I guess that's the way they did things in the old country. He turned and walked off, pausing to nod to us, and then told Saul that he would call him tomorrow. Saul said that he had to speak to Chappie briefly, and they both stepped outside. Vic was staring at the door, then he glanced toward me.

"That guy gives me the creeps," I said.

"It's too bad the kid's mixed up with that son-of-a-bitch," he said.

"Who? Smershkevich? You know him?"

"Yeah. A while back he brought a couple of Poles over to

do some boxing," Vic said. "Ended up pocketing most of the dough himself. Set one of the kids up against much stiffer competition than he was ready for just to collect a fast buck, then dropped him like a hot potato when the kid got a detached retina."

"Sounds like a real prick."

Vic nodded. "He stiffed a lot of people, myself included. Now don't get me wrong. I know that if Chappie's involved, I'll get paid. What I'm saying is, be careful, or the bastard will shit all over you."

"Thanks," I said. I glanced in and saw Alley sitting on the bench with the towel draped around his neck. I went over to him and told him to get dressed. He nodded, his lips twisting into a thin line. "You okay?" I asked.

He nodded again, got up, and went to his locker. Chappie came in and told him to hurry up.

"We want to get that cut stitched up before it start to spread," he said. Vic moved over and slipped a butterfly bandage over it. I walked them to the door and then stepped back into the main auditorium. The next boxing card was already in progress and I watched two young middleweights circling each other warily. The main event was a heavyweight bout between a rising former Olympian named Shedrick Rust and a tomato can designed to provide nothing more than a quick workout. Rust was a former con who'd picked up boxing in the penitentiary. He'd made the last Olympic team almost by default, and was quickly knocked out of medal contention by a powerful Cuban. Nonetheless, because he was a heavyweight, he was given a lot of attention by the press. With a couple of rich backers, he'd been given a series of relatively easy bouts, and tonight's was no exception. The opponents were hand-picked so as not to give him too much trouble. From what I'd seen of Rust, he didn't quite have the discipline to become a top fighter. I thought about that, and Chappie's comments about not missing my roadwork, as I strode through the crowd.

After breaking up a minor fight by the bar between two drunks, I told two of the uniformed guys to escort both of the combatants outside. As I watched them go, I heard someone behind me say my name. It was George.

"You got a real flair for security work," he said, tipping his cup of beer at me in a mock toast. "Ever think of making it a career? I know a guy who runs a company called Securitec."

I grinned. At least he wasn't pissed off about it anymore.

"I think that it's most distressing to see one of Chicago's finest imbibing while on duty," I said mimicking an officious tone.

"Ah, we're off the clock for a while," he said, taking a large sip of his beer. "What's the scoop on this Rust guy? Any good?"

"Overrated. Why? Somebody trying to lay down some action on him?"

He shrugged. "Some guy's giving three to one."

"Don't take it. The guy he's fighting is a tomato can. Guaranteed to flop on his back inside of six rounds."

"Okay," he said, picking up a second cup of beer which I assumed was for Doug. "Thanks."

I started walking down the aisle with him when my beeper went off. The number didn't register at first, then I realized it was Laurie calling from Paula's. I went back to the bar and asked the bartender for the phone. He set it on the bar and I dialed the number. She answered tentatively after the second ring.

"Laurie, it's Ron. What's up?"

"Oh, Ron, I'm so glad you called." Her voice sounded tense. "I don't know, maybe it's nothing, but I was getting ready to go down and put some more money in the parking meter, when I thought I heard footsteps in the hallway. I looked out the peephole, but couldn't see anybody. I thought it was nothing, then about ten minutes after that, the phone rang and when I picked it up, they just hung up."

"You got the door locked?"

"Yes," she said. "What do you think is going on? Should I be worried?"

"Well, maybe it'd be better if you didn't stay there tonight," I said. "Why don't I come over and get you? You can follow me back south, and I'll get you set up in a hotel."

"Okay," she said. "You're coming right over then?"

"I'll be there shortly. In the meantime, don't open the door for anybody but me."

After I hung up I went up to the locker room and grabbed my coat. I gave it to Hirum, the security guard at the front door, and asked him to watch it. Then I jogged back inside and found George and Doug seated near ringside in the seats I'd gotten them.

"Hey, I need to borrow your car for a minute," I said.

"What?" George said. Doug was intent on watching the ring action and paid us little attention.

"It's an emergency."

"Every fucking thing with you is an emergency."

"George, Laurie's in trouble."

He scrunched up his face and thrust his big hand into his pocket.

"Jesus H. Christ," he muttered. "First you borrow my truck, then you want me to fix your parking tickets, and now you want my fucking unmarked. What's next? You gonna ask to take my wife to Milwaukee for the weekend?"

I withheld any smart-ass comments regarding that suggestion.

He thrust the keys in my hand. "Thanks, buddy," I said.

"Hey," he grunted.

I paused. He handed me his wallet, which had his Chicago star pinned to it.

"Anybody tries to stop you, just hang this out the window at 'em."

I nodded, smiled, and jogged up the aisle. I slowed to a walk at the entrance, and looked around for Saul. Since he was paying me, I didn't think he would appreciate it if I ran out on a personal rescue mission. But if I could get in and out without him missing me, I didn't see what harm it would do. At the door I got my coat from Hirum and took one of his portable radios.

"Hirum, can you cover for me for a few?" I asked him. He nodded and winked.

I went outside, ducking into the cold blast of wind, and pulled on my stocking hat. The unmarked was parked right where they'd said it was near the mouth of the alley. I opened the door and fired it up, letting the defrosters work on the thin layer of frost that had accumulated on the windshield. I popped the trunk and found a plastic scraper to do the windows. When I was putting it back I noticed George's briefcase sitting there next to the spare tire. I opened it up and went through it quickly, taking an assortment of official Chicago Police forms to replenish my supplies. By the time I got back in the car, I figured that maybe ten minutes had passed since Laurie had called.

As I pulled away, I set the red light on the dashboard and plugged it into the cigarette lighter. I switched on the police band radio and listened to the steady litany of calls as I proceeded to knife my way through the various inter-sections toward the south Loop. I didn't use the siren, nor did I go terrifically fast. I stopped at every red light, albeit briefly, and continued on my way. What would have nor-mally been a fifteen-minute trip, I made in seven and a half. I also left the unmarked in a NO PARKING zone at the corner and ran up to the building. Her voice sounded brittle and tight when she asked who it was over the speaker system.

"Laurie, it's Ron," I said. The door buzzed open mo-ments later. For expediency, I took the elevator again, rather than the stairs. But the damn thing was so slow, I questioned my decision. Finally, the doors popped open and I went to the door and rapped gently. She opened it moments later and reached both arms out for me.

"Oh, Ron, thanks for coming so quickly," she said. I held her as she buried her face in my chest. Despite her cig-arette habit, her hair smelled like sweet apple shampoo. Even through the security sweatshirt I felt the softness of her breasts as she pushed against me.

"Oh, I feel like such a baby," she said. "I hear a few strange noises and get one hang-up phone call and I ruin your evening."

"Hey, it's okay," I said. "And you're not being a baby. You're being sensible. I wasn't too keen on you staying here tonight after we found the place burglarized. Get your coat and you can follow me back over to the Aragon. When the fights are over, I'll lead you back south, and we'll get you set up in a room for the night."

She sighed.

"I just hate to put you to all this trouble," she said, "but thank you."

"It's no trouble. Come on."

She collected her coat and the tote bag, and I checked the hallway and the stairwells. No one was lurking in either. We had to wait for the damn elevator again, but finally it arrived. Outside the wind seemed to have gotten stronger, whipping around us and sending Laurie's hair billowing out from her head.

"Good thing you're a Michigan girl," I said. "You're used to the cold."

"This seems worse than home. Or maybe it's just that I'm not used to things down here. I feel like such a fish out of water." Her eyes narrowed momentarily, then she said, "Oh, great."

I followed her gaze and saw a parking ticket flapping against her frost-covered windshield, the red violation tag visible behind the Plexiglas of the parking meter. Must have been a slow night around the bars for the meter maids. I grabbed it and smiled.

"Let me see if I can take care of this," I said.

"No. It's my fault. I'll pay for it."

"Well. Let's not worry about that right now. Start it up and I'll pull around so you can follow me. I'm driving that black Chevy over there."

"Where's the truck?" she asked.

"It's a long story," I said. It was another long story getting back to the Aragon. Not only couldn't I use the red light this time, I had to go slow enough so that Laurie wouldn't lose sight of me and get lost. Once, I went through a yellow light and she stopped, and I had to wait in traffic with the flashers and red light going until she got behind me again. When we finally got to the Aragon, I pulled the unmarked back into the same spot in the alley and motioned for her to park directly in front of me.

"Is that allowed?" she asked, rolling down the window.

"I don't want to get another ticket."

"You're going to have to learn to trust my instincts in these matters," I said. I took the parking ticket that I'd gotten on George's truck earlier and slipped it under her windshield wiper. Then I called Hirum on the portable radio.

"Shade to Hirum. How's it looking in there?"

"Warm and comfy," came the reply. It was his way of saying the coast was clear. "How 'bout you?"

"Same here," I said. I smiled at Laurie and motioned for her to follow me. At the door I introduced her to Hirum and gave him back his radio. He told me that nothing much had happened. "Saul been down here looking for me?" I asked.

He shook his head. "He's probably upstairs counting all his money."

I nodded a thanks and took Laurie inside and found her a seat near the aisle. I thought about seating her next to George but decided to wait before introducing them. The main event was in progress, with Rust looking big, stiff, and awkward against an equally ungainly foe. George and Doug were sitting in the same two seats, and I brought them each a beer. "Thanks, buddy," Doug said. "You're all right."

"Any problems?" George asked.

"Just this," I said, handing him Laurie's parking ticket along with his wallet and keys. He frowned and stuck it into his pocket.

"All I know is that you're gonna owe me big time after this," he said.

Predictably, the main event ended in the seventh, with Rust catching his opponent on the ropes and pummeling him with a series of unanswered punches until the ref stepped in. I stuck around until the crowd had emptied out and the janitorial guys began cleaning up. Hirum and I escorted Saul to the money room and he slipped me the usual fee in a plain white envelope. George and Doug had long since departed without fanfare. Laurie stayed near me as I attended to my last minute duties, then we walked to the truck. After it had sufficiently warmed up, I drove out of the parking garage and pulled into the alley next to her car.

"Follow me to the expressway," I said. "We'll get you set up at the Holiday Inn and then we can come back tomorrow with the truck and pick some things up."

"Oh, Ron, you're so sweet," she said. "I don't know how I'm ever going to be able to thank you for all this."

I watched her hips in the tight jeans slide over the seat as she got out and thought that if I was a different kind of guy . . .

The drive south took us about thirty minutes. It was almost eleven-thirty and the traffic south was real light. I led her over to the hotel and carried her suitcase inside to register. She paid for the room with her credit card, and I walked with her to the door. Inside she turned on the light and looked around.

"Oh, that bed looks so heavenly," she said. "This was a good idea, Ron. I feel totally exhausted."

"Well, get some sleep then, and I'll come by in the morning and take you to breakfast."

"Are you sure?" she said. "I wouldn't want to interfere with any of your plans."

"That's one of the great things about being your own boss. I haven't got any plans. No money either," I added with the slyest of grins.

She smiled and came forward and gave me a quick hug. "Thanks," she whispered, and kissed me lightly on the cheek. In the hallway, I stood and watched as she smiled once more before closing the door. The deadbolt lock clicked from inside and I meandered down the hallway.

Well, I thought. Chappie will be happy. When I pushed open the doors and made my way to the truck in the cold wind, I remembered her smile as she'd closed the door, her scent as we'd briefly embraced, and I couldn't help but wonder what she would have said if I'd asked to stay.

Chapter 12

The next morning I got up early and went for my usual six a.m. five-mile run. The temperature had elevated slightly, and a thin layer of snow had fallen overnight, looking kind of pretty under the nascent sky. But I barely noticed the solemnity of the morning as I ran, my mind reviewing the unlikely coincidences of the past week. Two almost identical burglaries. Both apparently professional jobs. My place and then Paula's. Were they connected? And what was with the hang-up call that Laurie'd received at Paula's apartment? Lots of questions, but no answers.

By the time I'd looped the circle and begun heading back for the tail end of the run, the wind had reasserted itself and all but obliterated my previous tracks with a dusting of new snow. When I rounded the curb on my block, I'd decided to take Laurie up on her offer to hire me to look into things. It couldn't hurt, I figured. There were just too damn many coincidences to ignore. As I trudged up the sidewalk to my house, the neighborhood was just coming alive with people warming up their cars to leave for work. I grabbed the broom I keep stashed under the back steps and swept the light snow from the sidewalks.

Inside, I peeled off my clothes and checked my calendar for appointments. I always kept the calendar hanging right next to the toilet so I was assured of keeping track of things on a daily basis. I'd scribbled a note that Rags had to go in for his second, and hopefully final, worming. That meant I had to get him to the vet's by nine. Since it was only seven-fifteen I figured I had plenty of time. I shaved and adjusted the shower to the proper degree of warmth before stepping under it. After toweling off and getting dressed for action, I fed Georgio and Shasha upstairs and then went down in the basement to check on the little guy. He came prancing over to the edge of the cage when I whistled and shook the box of kitten chow. I felt downright bad that I had to deceive him, but picked him up and placed him gently in the cat carrier. His little head canted to one side as he looked at me through the bars in a perplexed fashion.

"Hey, I'm sorry, okay?" I said to him. "But if all goes well today, you should get to go into general population." He blinked twice and folded his paws under his chest as he sat down in regal fashion. I placed the kitty carrier by the heating vent and sat down for a nutritious breakfast of blended strawberries, a banana, protein powder, and milk. After finishing it, I allowed myself the luxury of a cup of coffee while I filled out the proper forms that I needed for the initial phase of my investigation. I sat at my desk and looked up the number for Ameritech Security in my Rolodex. At eight-fifteen exactly I dialed, and when somebody answered I lowered the timbre of my voice slightly and gave my best imitation of George's South Side accent.

"Yeah, this is Detective Grieves, Chicago Police Violent Crimes," I said. "Who's this?"

"Irwin Caufman," a male voice said tentatively. "May I help you?"

"Yeah, I hope so," I said. "I'm working a homicide case and I got reason to believe that it may be tied into a burglary that happened a week or so ago. Hold on a second, I'll give you the date." I rustled some papers on my desk and breathed laboriously into the phone. "Yeah, it was December twenty-ninth. Can you get me some MUD records if I give you the burglary victim's phone number?"

"As long as you have a subpoena," Caufman said. "Those records are confidential, you know."

"Yeah," I said, edging some petulance into my tone. "But I ain't got time to run down to the grand jury today. I gotta move on this thing. I'm at the victim's house now. How 'bout I fax you a release form, signed by him, and you fax me the records at Area One. Just put 'em attention to Detective George Grieves, okay, Irwin? What's your fax number?"

"Well," he started to say. But I detected the uncertainty in his voice.

"Come on, Irwin," I said. "You're telephone security, right? Let's cut the red tape a little bit. I mean you'll be faxing 'em right to my office, and you'll have a signed, official Chicago Police Department Release form, for Christ's sake. Gimme the number."

I heard him exhale, then he reeled it off. "Thanks, Irwin. I owe ya one. I'll make out the cover sheet to you, then I'll have my victim sign the release and I'll use his machine to fax it, okay? My fax number's on my cover sheet."

"Fine," he said quickly.

I thanked him again and said, "Okay, now I have to unplug his phone to plug in his fax machine so here goes. It's been nice talkin' to ya, and you need anything out of the Second District, you just give me a call."

Irwin assured me that he would. I hung the phone up and plugged in my fax machine. After dialing, I set the cover sheet and release forms that I'd lifted from George's trunk last night into the tray and marveled at the faceless anonymity of modern technology as the papers passed through the rollers.

Making one last pass through the house, I collected my

gun, IDs, wallet, and cell phone. I also looked through my desk and found the number I'd obtained from the impression Paula's writing had left on my telephone pad the morning she'd stayed with me. As I jotted it down in my pocket notebook, I still wondered about the significance of the *"8AM"* next to it. I picked up the cat cage, and the little guy opened his mouth and cried pitifully as I headed out the back door. I'd had to park George's big F-150 in front of my house since it wouldn't fit in my garage. I put the carrier case with Rags inside on the front seat of the pickup, started it, and used the brush and scraper on the windows. The truck had fired right up, but I thought the gas gauge needle actually descended a tad as I let it idle. Undaunted, I shifted it into drive and proceeded cautiously down the snow-covered street, knowing that George would probably kill me if I put as much as a scratch on his pride and joy.

Despite being well into winter, the light snow still made the morning drivers skittish. It was kind of nice being in the truck, because I was up higher than normal and could see the traffic conditions ahead. I mentally debated buying a truck for myself instead of the new Camaro I'd been saving for. But another glance at the descending gas gauge made me forget about that idea. My wallet would shrink so much from the gas costs that I'd probably need to stick a pillow under the left side of my ass just to keep level when sitting down.

I dropped Rags off at the vet's, and they told me to check back with them after three. The kitten had the look of dejection on his face as I handed him over. When I was back in the truck again, I called Laurie's room at the hotel. She answered on the second ring.

"Hey, babe, it's Ron. How about some breakfast?"

"Love some. Are you at home?"

"Already up and running. I should be at your hotel momentarily. Meet you in about ten minutes by the front entrance?"

"Sounds great. Say, do you think I should keep this room for another night, or would it be safe to go back and stay at Paula's?"

"Why don't we talk about things? I'm a little bit leery of having you stay alone at that apartment."

"I should be all right."

"Not to mention the parking problems," I said. I thought I sensed her beginning to weaken.

"Okay, I'll stay here. You talked me into it. See you by the front."

With the traffic being slower than normal, it took me almost fifteen minutes to get there. When I pulled up in front I saw her standing by the vestibule between the glass doors. I slowed to a stop, and she came walking out, taking one last drag on her cigarette, then tossing the butt into the snow. She wore a black nylon ski jacket and blue jeans that fit her like a second skin. A lavender scarf was wrapped around her neck, and she had one of those knit earmuff things that fitted over her head while letting her hair flow freely. The cloudy vapors traced from her nostrils as she smiled and pulled open the door.

"Brrrr," she said. "I hope my poor little car will start."

"We can check it later," I said. "I figured we could grab a bite to eat then use the truck to pick up some of the stuff from the apartment."

"Great, but are you sure you don't mind? You have the time?"

"My time is your time," I said. "I've decided to take the case."

Her eyes widened and she looked mildly shocked. "Ron, that's wonderful. I really appreciate it. But what changed your mind?"

"A couple things," I said. I told her about the "coincidental burglary" to my house right after Paula had spent the night. It suddenly hit me how that must have sounded to her, but I was past worrying about it. After all, she definitely wasn't the same little girl in pigtails that I'd remembered.

"I should be getting a hold of some MUD records that might give me a lead," I said.

"MUD records?"

"An acronym for Micro Unit Detail sheets," I said. "They're computerized printouts of the phone numbers of every call made from a particular phone."

"Wow, I didn't know something like that existed," she said. "How do you get them?"

"Ah, George is sort of helping me on that," I said.

"So will they show who made that hang-up call last night?"

"No, you have to know the number that the call originated from," I said. "But that hang-up call bothers me too. Like I said, it's a lot of little things added together that don't seem quite right."

"I'm glad we agree," she said. "On the phone Detective Grieves told me that there was evidence that Paula was using heroin." She shook her head. "I just can't imagine that. I mean, she used to smoke a little pot now and then. But heroin . . ."

We pulled into a Greek restaurant known as The Eggman's. Like most Greek places, they made sure you never got slighted with your food.

"If we eat at this place," I said, "it'll take us the rest of

127

the day to work it off. Then maybe I can buy you dinner."

"Sounds nice," she said.

Inside the hostess approached us and asked if we wanted smoking or non-smoking. Laurie glanced at me quickly and said, "Non." As we weaved through the crowded dining room, she glanced back over her shoulder.

"That was right, wasn't it?" she asked. "I know you don't like smoking, do you?"

"No. Especially when I'm in training."

We sat in a booth by the window. Laurie slipped off her black nylon jacket and folded it on the seat beside her.

"Have you ever smoked, Ron?"

"No. Not even marijuana."

"Wow." She smiled.

I noticed her hazel eyes had tiny splashes of green in them.

"I'd quit, believe it or not, for four months," she said, her eyes widening as she spoke. "Got through my finals and everything. Then," her eyes narrowed, and she blinked a couple of times, "when we got the call about Paula, I reached for my uncle's pack of Marlboros and I was hooked again, just like that." She snapped her fingers. "Like I'd never stopped. Although that first one really knocked me on my ass." She paused and took in a deep breath, as if she were reliving the moment, and let out a sigh. "Guess I'm just a nicotine junkie."

The waitress came and took our order. I got my usual high energy special. Two scrambled eggs, rye toast, coffee, orange juice, very crisp bacon, and a side order of pancakes. Laurie had an omelet and watched in amazement as I ate. Afterwards she wanted to pick up the check, but I grabbed it. She insisted on giving me a check as a retainer, however. I accepted it and told her that I'd draw up one of my standard contracts later on. We drove to a Pack-and-Send shop and bought some boxes, tape, and address labels, then hit the expressway and drove straight to Paula's old apartment. Outside, we stopped and checked with the parking lot attendant the super had mentioned. The guy said he remembered Paula's red Firebird, and even pointed out her spot. But he said he hadn't seen her or the car for a couple of weeks. I gave him one of my cards and five bucks and told him if anyone asked about the car to give me a call. He nodded as he pocketed the bill and put the card in his wallet. I pulled the truck into a vacant spot by the alley and Laurie narrowed her eyes as she looked at me.

"I hope that contract doesn't include paying all your parking tickets," she said.

"Just the ones I get in the line of duty. Besides," I said, grinning as I reached across her legs, popped open the glove box, and took out the ticket that I'd gotten on the truck last night, "I got friends in high places."

"I thought you gave that to your friend already?"

"That was the one on your car," I said. "He'll have to take care of this one. It's on his truck."

We were laughing as we made a quick trek across the sidewalk to the front doors. Paula's mailbox contained two letters that looked like advertisements. Laurie asked if we should check in with Mr. Turner, the super, but I decided to just go on up and get busy. I told her I'd touch bases with him later on to see if he'd noticed anything strange after we left. I also wanted to ask him about any boyfriends or visitors that Paula might have had in the months before her death. There was something about that old bird that rubbed me the wrong way, but I didn't want to spoil what was left of a perfectly good morning.

As we got up to the fifth floor, my beeper went off. It

was George's work number and there was a 911 after it, which meant that I was to get a hold of him pronto. I left Laurie locked inside and told her I had to go back down to the truck to get my cell phone. Actually I had the phone in my pocket, but didn't want her to hear the conversation. I was pretty sure what the call was all about, and I figured he'd be pissed. Besides, she was only studying to be a lawyer, and hadn't passed the bar yet; she might still have some idealism left.

I went into the stairwell and found a landing mid-way between the fifth and sixth floors. A filthy window provided a view of the crisscrossing streets, more high-rise apartment buildings, alleys, and a parking lot. I leaned against the wall and punched in the number. He answered on the first ring with his usual gruff, "Detective Grieves."

"Yeah, buddy, it's Ron. What's up?"

"You tell me," he said. "What's with all these faxes with your MUD records? I didn't know what the hell they were, until I looked at the number and saw it was yours."

"Ah, Sherlock, Dr. Moriarty sure ain't gonna put nothing over on you."

"Kiss my ass," he said. "Now what gives?"

"Paula made at least one call from my place the morning she was killed," I said. "I mean, she had to call a cab or something. If we can find out which company, it's a place to start backtracking."

"Ron," he said, his voice taking a harsher edge. "I told you that I've taken it about as far as I can right now. And what's this 'we' shit?"

"Well, I told you her cousin's in town, right?"

"Yeah."

"So I'm working for her," I said. "Just going over the case a little."

I heard him sigh. I was expecting a tirade, or at the very least a lecture, but all he said was, "Okay, keep me posted."

"You ain't pissed off?"

"Not at the moment," he said. "At least not until I find out how the hell you got Ameritech to fax me some fucking MUD sheets without a subpoena."

"Oh, that," I said. "It just pays to have friends in high places."

"Or low places, knowing you," he added. "So now I suppose you want me to trace down these names and addresses, huh?"

"Hey, that'd be great," I said, taking out my notebook. "Say, while you're at it, see what you can come up with for this number, will ya?" I read off the *8AM* number I'd obtained from the phone pad.

"Christ, you expect me to do all your god-damn work for you?" he muttered, but from his distracted tone, I could tell that he was scribbling it down.

"Thanks, buddy," I said. "It's great to help a friend in need. Gives you a warm feeling, doesn't it?"

"Yeah, so does wetting your pants, at first," he said. "Maybe you ought to try it sometime. The helping a friend part, that is."

"Well, actually I am. You see, I'm helping Laurie clean out Paula's old place and," I hesitated, and heaved a heavy sigh of my own that I hoped was sufficiently dramatic, "it's pretty rough on the poor kid. I mean, I'd hate to have to leave her to do it alone."

"It's a good thing you're a better fighter than you are a bullshitter," he said with a laugh. "Okay, I'll do all this stuff for you on one condition."

"What?"

"You work evening shift at the hotel for me tonight," he said.

"For Christ's sake, George, I'm training for a title shot."

"Yeah, yeah, but I'm in a super-bind," he said. "The guy who was supposed to work had a death in the family. I can't get nobody else on such short notice."

"Nobody but your old buddy Ron, huh?"

"Yeah, my old buddy Ron, who expects me to do him favors all the time," he shot back. "What the hell, you work for yourself. You make up your own schedule as you go along. You saying you can't help out after all me and Doug done for you?"

"All right, all right," I said.

Just then my beeper went off again. It was Paula's apartment number. And there was a 911 after it. I told George I had to go, hung up, and rushed down the stairs.

Chapter 13

Just as I reached the fifth floor landing, the door swung open. I sidestepped and narrowly missed running into old Mr. Turner. He was holding a cellular phone. When he saw me he just about jumped out of his skin.

"What the hell you doing in here?" he barked. He was wearing the same convex glasses that I'd seen before. They made his eyes look bigger.

"Sorry," I said and pushed past him. I ran down the hallway and knocked hard on the door to the apartment, telling Laurie it was me. I heard the locks click and the door opened. She looked ashen. "What's wrong?" I asked.

Before she could speak she raised up her arms and moved forward to embrace me, burying her face against my chest. After a couple of calming deep breaths, she told me. "I thought I heard the doorknob turning so I figured it was you coming back," she said. "But it just made this clicking sound, you know, like somebody twisting it. Then I called your name, and the sound stopped. Nobody answered." She looked at me and her eyes widened. "So I went to the peephole to see who it was, and I couldn't see. Somebody'd put something over the hole." I glanced at the peephole and saw an inch-long piece of masking tape over the opening. "Then the phone rang and when I picked it up it was another hang-up call. I was so scared, I dialed your beeper as fast as I could." She smiled slightly. "I know it by heart now."

"How long ago did this happen?"

"Not more than a couple minutes."

"Okay. Lock the door and don't open it. I'll be right back."

She nodded, swallowing hard. I sensed that it bothered her for me to leave, but if my hunch was right, time was of the essence. I carefully peeled the tape off the peephole and stuck the end of it on the inside of the door. Then I went to the elevator and punched the down button. I would have rather taken the stairs, but didn't want to appear winded when I got to where I was going. I heard the sound of the elevator, and the doors popped open with a pinging sound. After stepping in, I pressed button two. When the doors opened for the second floor, I stepped out and strode over to Mr. Turner's apartment and hammered my fist on the door till he answered.

"You don't have to keep pounding like that," he said angrily. "I heard you." He wasn't wearing his glasses, and I thought I knew why.

"I wanted to be sure you did," I said. "You just wear your glasses for reading?" I stared at him closely for a few seconds. A hard-edged stare affects people differently, but with Turner it had the effect that I'd hoped for.

His tongue darted over his upper lip. "What do you want?"

"I wondered if I could use your phone."

"What for? You ain't got a phone upstairs?"

"Yeah, we do," I said slowly. "But somebody keeps calling there and hanging up." I continued to look at him.

He drew his lips tightly together and tried to out-stare me. He lost.

"Well, I don't let anybody use my phone," he said.

I waited two more beats before continuing. "I don't think I introduced myself properly before," I said, taking out my private investigator's license and holding it up in

134

front of him. He blinked again, then reached inside his sweater and took out the reading glasses.

"I'm a private investigator," I said. "And I'm looking into Paula Kittermann's death. I'm working with the Chicago Police on it."

He took off his glasses and stuck them back in an open case clipped to his shirt. I saw the gray plastic of the cellular phone sticking out of the outside sweater pocket. My hand shot forward and grabbed it. "Hey!" he grunted. "Gimme that back."

I moved forward, putting my left leg inside on his side of the jamb, so he couldn't close the door unless he wanted to try and push me back out into the hall. And he knew better than that.

"Gimme my phone," he repeated. "I'll call the cops on you."

"Call 'em," I said as I pressed the recall button. The phone number for Paula's apartment flashed across the screen. I looked back at Turner. He sort of recoiled like he was afraid that I was going to hit him.

"I ain't gonna hurt you, buddy," I said, letting a hint of menace creep into my voice just the same. Stripping off the battery, I checked the faceplate of the cellular. The serial number had been scratched off. "This your phone?"

"Yeah," he said, trying to recover some of his false bravado. "What of it?"

"Well, for one thing, the last number in the memory is to Paula's apartment upstairs."

"So what? I'm the super here. I got a right to call to check up on things."

"Checking up is one thing," I said. "Calling and hanging up is another. Ever hear of a criminal statute called telephone harassment?"

His lower lip puckered up defiantly, and he blinked several times.

"Not to mention the piece of masking tape you stuck over the eyelet," I continued.

"You can't prove that."

"Oh no? There's a pretty good fingerprint on the adhesive side," I said. It's always dangerous to bluff, but when you have the upper hand, sometimes you just got to go for it. Besides, he looked ham-handed enough to have probably left the print anyway. "Should I have one of my police friends send it to the lab to see if it matches any of your prints?"

His eyes shot to the floor and I knew I had him. "It all adds up to some pretty suspicious behavior. You'd better come up with the truth, or you'll be explaining it all down at the station." I let my gaze settle on Turner. His tongue darted over his lips again, and he swallowed hard.

"All—all right," he said stammering slightly. "I made the call. Just wanted to see who was in there."

"Look, don't even try to bullshit me," I said. "I ain't in the mood. You made the call last night too, didn't you?"

He looked momentarily surprised, then nodded.

"Okay," I said. "Now, tell me why. And where did this phone come from?"

The question about the phone seemed to stun him. "Some guy came by here," Turner said, his gaze turning downward. "It was a few days after the cops had been here and told me she was dead. He told me he worked for a lawyer. That Paula'd been involved in some kind of a civil lawsuit. He needed to serve some papers. Asked if I'd mind letting him post a subpoena inside her apartment for her next of kin. Said he wouldn't take nothing, and I could stand right there. Paid me fifty dollars." He reached up and wiped at his nose. "Well, I let him in, and he just posted the paper like he said he was gonna do, then left. I locked the door after him."

"You watched him the whole time?"

Turner nodded. "Well, he did look around a little bit. Went to the washroom."

"Is it possible he could have unlocked the door when you weren't looking?"

"Nah," he said, shaking his head. "I checked the door when we left. Locked it myself."

"What about the back door? The one that leads to the fire escape. You check it too?"

His jaw just sagged open.

"Yeah, that's what I thought," I said. "Now why did you keep making those hang-up calls?"

He exhaled dejectedly before he spoke. "He came back a day or two later. Told me that it was important to get a hold of him if anybody, family or anything, came by the apartment. Said that there were papers he'd have to serve in person. Paid me a hundred dollars for just keeping an eye out and calling him back if there was somebody in her apartment. He give me that phone, too." He nodded toward the cellular. "Told me I could keep it just for helping him out."

"Yeah, well don't get used to it. It's probably cloned. You have this guy's number?"

"What do you mean, 'cloned'?"

"I mean that it's stolen," I said, holding up the back so he could see the scratched-off serial number. "They steal somebody's phone and reprogram it with someone else's number. As soon as that person gets his next bill the phone company will cancel this one out." I snapped the battery back in place. "Now, what did this dude look like?"

He stared up at me in disbelief. "Young guy. Real clean cut looking." His voice sounded tired and old.

"Was he white, black? Big, small?"

"About your size, I guess. Maybe a little bit shorter, but stockier. Sort of like a football player or something. White guy. Red hair."

I grinned. Red, my buddy from the hotel. "You got his name and number?"

"Yeah," Turner said. He reached in his sweater pocket and took out a card. It said Regis Phillips, with a phone number and a box address below it. I put the card in my pocket along with the phone. Turner's jaw jutted out and he said, "Hey. What you doing with those?"

"Saving you the cost of a lawyer," I said. "This is some real nasty business, and I don't think you want to get mixed up in the possession of stolen property. Do you?" He pursed his lips again, then shook his head. "Good," I said. "Now, just so we continue on this new course of cooperation, after you made the hang-up call last night, did you call this Phillips guy and let him know we were in the apartment?"

"Yeah," Turner said slowly. "He thanked me. Then he called back later and said that he'd missed you. Told me there'd be more money in it for me to continue keeping my eyes open."

"Why the tape?"

"He told me to put it over the peep-hole in case he had to come back to serve them papers," he said. "That way you wouldn't know it was him."

Yeah, I thought. So we wouldn't see the gun in his hand either. I silently thanked God that Laurie hadn't stayed there alone last night.

"So did you call him today after you saw us?"

Turner shook his head. "I was gonna, but I was kind of afraid to." He glanced up at me obliquely. "After you caught me with the phone in the stairwell, I didn't want to make it seem too obvious."

"Ever seen this guy before he approached you? He ever come over to see Paula socially or anything?"

Turner shook his head.

"She had quite a few boyfriends," he said, "but not him. I'd never seen him before."

"Do you know any of her friends?" I asked. "Her recent ones?"

"Well, like I said, she had a passel of men always going up there. Most of 'em seemed like bar pick-ups. Sometimes they'd spend the night, sometimes not. Seemed to be with this one fella past few months though."

"What did he look like?"

His lips meshed together loosely as he pondered the question. "Lots older than her," he said. "I guess about fifty, or so. Gray hair. Kind of heavyset. Sort of puffy looking. Like a drinker."

"What else you remember about him?"

He shrugged.

"Okay," I said, taking out my notebook and pen. "Start with the basics. Male, about fifty. Gray hair, heavyset. White?" Turner nodded.

"Mustache? Glasses? Facial scars?"

"He did have a mustache," he said. "No glasses, that I ever saw, but I didn't get a real close look at him. He just sort of stands out from the others 'cause he came by regular."

"Okay," I said. "Thanks. And if this guy calls you back, just tell him that the phone quit working and that you're still keeping your eyes open. Then call me. I'll make it worth your while." I handed him one of my cards. I wasn't entirely sure that I could trust him, and certainly wasn't about to give him a C-note for watching. But I figured that it was worth a shot. I went back up to the apartment.

"I was getting a bit worried," Laurie said, letting me in. "That was a lot longer than ten minutes."

"Yeah, but it was productive. I found out who was making those hang-up calls."

"Who?"

"Mr. Turner, the super."

Her eyes widened, then she said, "Why that old creep."

I explained to her what Turner had told me.

"So who is this guy with the red hair?"

"I'm not sure right now," I said. "Turner told me that he hadn't called Red today, but I'm not entirely sure we can trust him."

"So what do we do?"

"We pack up as much stuff as we can. Then I go down and do a recon to check for Injuns before we leave."

"Injuns?"

"That's what George and my brother Tom used to say when they were in Nam," I said. "It's a euphemism for hostiles."

"Not very politically correct," Laurie said, with a tone of mock rebuke.

"That's me, your Politically Incorrect Private Eye."

We packed up most of Paula's clothes in the boxes we'd brought. Her other possessions seemed fairly scarce, except for drawers full of make-up, hair dyers, and other female trinkets. We found some personal records, checkbook, credit card receipts, and bankbook. No passport, which Laurie thought was strange. Paula had recently sent a postcard from Bangkok while she was there on a modeling assignment. It was almost like it was a stage set of a girl's apartment or something. Under the dresser I did find a leather-bound portfolio. Inside were several professionally done photographs of Paula in both color and black-and-white.

"Like I mentioned, she told me that she was doing some modeling assignments," Laurie said.

"Is that how she was supporting herself?" I asked. I paged through the book. Several of the pages had been torn out of the back.

"As far as I know," Laurie said. "She just said the money was real good."

I checked an empty plastic slot on the inside front cover that looked like it had once held a business card. Taking out my pocketknife, I inserted the blade into the plastic sleeve and gently cut it loose.

"What are you doing?" Laurie asked as I moved toward the window.

"An old Charlie Chan trick." I held the clear piece of plastic up toward the light. The imprint was faintly visible: SAMUEL R. PEEPS PHOTOGRAPHY. I was able to make out a north Dearborn address and phone number. I went to the phone and dialed the number.

"Samuel Peeps Photography," a male voice said. "May I help you?" The voice sounded very British . . . It had a familiar ring to it.

"Do you do portfolios for male models?" I asked, raising my voice a few octaves.

"Sure, just pop on by," the voice said.

I verified the address and asked him what time he closed. "I'll be here till late," he said. "If you want to stop in."

I said I would and told him my name was Lewis Van

Tillworth the Third. When I hung up, Laurie tilted her head and smiled.

"That was quite a performance," she said. "I had no idea you were so talented."

"And you ain't even seen me in action yet, babe," I said. I was beginning to like the look of her smile, and grinned back.

I was looking forward to meeting Mr. Peeps.

Chapter 14

It took me several trips to get the boxes loaded into the back of the truck. I didn't even want to think about unloading them when we got back to my place. I'd told Laurie that we could just store everything in my basement until she made arrangements to have it all shipped up to Ludington. We covered the bed with a tarp and secured it with a couple of bungee cords that George always left in the glovebox. The only trouble was that with the boxes all piled so high in the bed, I couldn't see out the rear-view mirror. Not that I was totally inept at driving downtown just using the side mirrors, but I quickly realized that if old Mr. Turner had, in fact, called Red, I probably wouldn't be able to notice a tail very easily. I figured that he'd been straight with me, but I still had one of my customary uneasy feelings.

After starting up the truck and flipping on the heater to high, I snatched the parking ticket from the windshield wiper and quickly got back inside. Laurie sat shivering beside me as I took out my cell phone and made two quick calls: One to Bob Matulik to see what the prognosis was on The Beater, and the other to the vet to check on Rags. Both had good news.

"Should be ready in about an hour or so, Ron," Bob told me. "Just finishing up with the fuel pump now."

"Great," I said, not wanting to know how much the bill was going to be. "You'll be open till seven, right?"

He assured me he would, and I said that I'd be by. The vet told me that Rags had endured the second worming with exceptional aplomb. I told her I'd be by for him before six. I glanced at my watch. Three-thirty.

"Sounds like you're going to be a very busy man," Laurie said.

"After we check on this photographer, I still have to touch bases with George on something and call Chappie."

"Oh?"

"Yeah, George sort of suckered me into working at the hotel security job tonight."

"Really? At my hotel?"

"No such luck. Same chain, different location."

"Too bad. I was hoping maybe we could have dinner or something. On me."

"I'll take a raincheck," I said, smiling.

The truck had warmed up enough to actually start blowing hot air though the vents. I shifted into drive, scanned for any obvious signs that someone was watching us, and headed down to Clark Street. The pre-rush-hour traffic was just beginning to get heavy. About three cars back I noticed a black limo taking basically the same route we had, but then it turned off. Was I being too paranoid? At this stage of the game everybody looked like a potential suspect, especially if you didn't know who you were looking for.

Which was one reason why I wanted to get a look at this guy Peeps. His damn accent was another. I strained my memory trying to remember the voice of Mr. Webber, the guy who'd called me and sent me on that wild goose chase. They sounded pretty much the same, but I just couldn't be sure. Of course, the caller could have been changing his voice or even affecting an accent. But it was yet another of the many coincidences that kept popping up in this case.

The Dearborn address turned out to be one of those

nondescript gray office buildings in the Loop with an exclusive view of the El tracks. I circled the block, pulled into an alley, and inserted the parking ticket under the windshield wiper again.

"You're sure getting a lot of use out of that thing," Laurie said.

"I'm trying to cut down on your expense fees." I handed her my cellular phone as we dodged several cars crossing the street to a Starbucks Coffee shop. "Okay, any sign of trouble with the truck, like a cop and a tow truck, and you beep me 811. Any personal trouble, like some creep bothering you, use 911. Got it?"

"Roger wilco," she said, giving me a quick, left-handed salute. "That's what you're supposed to say, isn't it?"

"Yeah, but you're supposed to salute with your right arm."

"Well I'm holding the phone in that hand."

An El train clattered by overhead.

I trotted back across the street and went inside the building. The lobby was typical downtown: long marble floors and walls, with a series of elevators to the left. Several doors, with pebbled glass fronts, were opposite. I checked the rectangular legend on the wall between the elevators. White letters against a black background indicated that Samuel Peeps Photography was located in room 1207. I pressed the button again, figuring that it would be easier and quicker to ride up twelve floors than take the stairs and maybe find that the stairwell door wouldn't open from the inside. When the doors popped open on twelve, I saw more of the same pebbled glass doors, set in heavy wooden frames. I followed the numbers around to 1207 and twisted the knob. It opened into a small waiting room with several chairs and a coat rack. A buzzer sounded inside the office, which was evidently behind another door on the far end of the waiting-room wall. No pretty secretary to welcome me inside. A shadow moved on the other side of the frosted glass and the inside door was opened by a heavyset man around fifty with grayish hair and a mustache. He had, as Mr. Turner would have said, the puffy look of a drinker.

"May I help you?" he said in perfect Queen's English.

"I'm Lewis Van Tillworth the Third."

"Funny, you don't look like the male model type," he said. "Don't sound much the same either." I couldn't figure whether his voice contained alarm or amusement. He waited for my reply, his eyes scanning me, trying to read me.

"Actually, I'm a private detective," I said. "I'm looking into the death of a young woman. She was one of your clients."

"Oh," Peeps said, moving forward and taking out a pack of cigarettes. He put one in his mouth, fired up a lighter, and said, with a smoky breath, "And who might that be?"

"Paula Kittermann."

He tried crinkling his brow, then shaking his head. "Doesn't sound familiar. What makes you think she was one of my clients?"

"You did a portfolio for her," I said. "She was a model. Recently went abroad to do some shoots. Sounding more familiar yet?"

Peeps blew out a plume of smoke and leaned against the doorframe. "Not really," he said. "You say she was one of mine?" He inhaled on the cigarette thoughtfully, then said, "I'm afraid I really can't be of help to you. I do work with a great many prospective models, setting up portfolios and the like. Sometimes things take off, sometimes they don't. And sometimes they hook up with somebody else." He shrugged. "But her name doesn't ring a bell. Now, Mister . . . Van Tillworth, if you'll excuse me. I'm a very busy man."

"I can see that," I said, glancing around the empty office.

"Looks can be deceiving."

"Yes, they can." I moved forward, closing the distance between us, then smiled. "Mr. Peeps, I have a confession to make. My name isn't really Van Tillworth. It's Shade. Ron Shade."

I waited to see if the James Bond technique would cause any reaction. If it did, he didn't show it. "And I happen to know that you had a relationship with Paula and I'd really like to hear about it."

Peeps swallowed hard. Then, squinting through the smoke, he said, "I don't have to talk to you. Now get out of my bloody office."

"Didn't you ever hear that smoking was hazardous to your health?" I asked. Peeps just stared at me. I think it unnerved him that I'd violated his personal space a bit. He was as tall as I was, but not in shape, and he obviously knew it. I reached up quickly and snatched the cigarette from between his lips. "And so is lying to me."

"Get out of here or I'll call the police," he said, trying to imbue some authority into his voice. It didn't work.

"I'm gonna ask you one more time politely about your relationship with Paula," I said slowly. I felt the anger that I'd experienced with old Mr. Turner starting to resurface here. And Peeps wasn't an old man.

He must have sensed my hostility because he tried to make a move inside his office and slam the door. I caught it with the flat of my palm just as he ducked in and I shoved all my weight forward. Peeps, both his hands on the edge of the door, tried to shift his weight to push against me, but he was a couple beats too slow. My legs drove forward and shoved him back. We were in a smaller office area, with several file cabinets and a lot of photographic and video equipment.

I shoved him and he stumbled backward until his hip hit against a big metal desk in the center of the room. He picked up an ashtray in his right hand, but I seized his wrist, and slammed my fist into his substantial gut. The air whooshed out of him as he sagged forward. I pulled his arm down and outward, using my left hand to bend his elbow and apply a hammer-lock. The ashtray fell to the carpet, dumping its contents over the desk and floor.

I clucked sympathetically.

"Too bad," I said. "Looks like the housekeeper's gonna have some extra work to do. But I warned you about those cigarettes, didn't I?"

He struggled to catch his breath, his left hand holding his stomach.

"You do have a housekeeper here, don't you?" I said, then added, "Take shallow breaths. It'll hurt less."

"Let go of my arm," he said, his teeth clenching in pain.

"Not till we come to a little understanding. Now, you got a file on Paula?"

"What if I do?" he grunted. I tightened the pressure on his arm a notch. "All right! All right! I do. So what?"

"I want it. Now," I said. "Where is it?"

He managed to point and grunt at two gunmetal filing cabinets against the far wall.

I walked him over to the cabinets, still pinning his arm behind his back, exerting just enough force to keep him up on his toes. His breath was still coming in savage rasps. The oval lock at the top had been pressed in, indicating that it was locked. Peeps had one of those metal rings of keys on his belt with the retractable chain. I wedged my left arm between his forearm and back, with my hand gripping his biceps. That left my right hand free to grab the keys. "Which one opens it?"

His mouth twisted downward at the edges as he told me. I inserted it into the lock, popped it open, and let the keys snap back into the metal shell on his belt.

"Always wanted one of those things," I said. "Now, where's that file?"

"I can't get it with you holding my arm," he said.

"Pretend you're handicapped," I said, leaning forward to exert slightly more pressure. He grunted and grabbed one of the drawer handles with his left hand. He pulled the drawer open and I backed him away for a moment so I could peek inside. I didn't want him reaching in and coming out with a weapon. All I saw were files so I pushed him back. "Okay, you're a southpaw again. Get me that file." His fingers sorted through the hanging file envelopes, pulling out some, then tossing them onto the floor. That cleaning lady was going to have more than cigarette butts to pick up. Finally he withdrew a thick file and set it on top of the cabinet.

"That's it," he said.

"You're sure?" I tightened the pressure on his arm a notch.

"Yes, yes. Now let me go. Please."

"Since you were so polite." I released him then picked up the file and glanced at it. There were pictures galore of Paula in a variety of outfits, and without anything at all. Some of the nudes were tastefully done. Others looked progressively more tawdry. Some were soft-core porn shots of her with a variety of both male and female sex partners. Some were group shots. They looked like they'd been staged for some men's magazine fantasy. A video cassette was also among the sheaves of pictures.

Modeling, huh? I wondered what her parents, who thought I wasn't good enough for her way back when, would think now. But that was counterproductive. I concentrated on the task at hand. "Is this it?" I asked.

"Yes," he grunted.

"Are you sure?" I clenched my right hand into a fist. Peeps looked at it, then at my face. From his expression I could tell he didn't want any part of me.

"Yes, yes. There was some hard-core stuff, but I got rid of that." His voice sounded worn and empty, his tone deflated. "Satisfied?" he said, massaging his arm. "She was nothing but a fucking slut."

"Oh yeah? I heard you were going out with her."

"What? Hardly. It was strictly a business arrangement between us. Nothing more."

"Then why'd you lie to me before?"

"I didn't want to show you any of that stuff." The veins in his neck pulsed as he spoke. "Look at it from my perspective. For all I knew you might have been her ex-boyfriend or something."

"You ever go over to her apartment?"

"Sure. We did shoots over there sometimes."

"You ever call yourself Mr. Webber?" I asked, trying to gauge his reaction when I mentioned the name.

"No. Why would I?" I figured he was lying and thought about roughing him up a bit more, but decided against it. I didn't want him calling the cops and saying that I'd beaten the crap out of him. I'd let George do that when he pulled him in for questioning about my burglary.

"Never mind," I said. "How long did you know Paula?"

"About six months. Look, it's just like I told you before.

It was just a business thing between us. Nothing more."

I held up my fist.

"I can think of two good reasons why you shouldn't be lying to me."

"I'm not," he said, staring at my callused knuckles. I caught the glimmer of fear in his eyes. "I can see you're a pro. Look, I didn't even know she'd gotten herself killed till I read it in the papers."

"I figured Regis would've told you," I said on a lark.

"Who? Never heard of him," Peeps said.

I glanced at my watch. Four-fifteen. I still had a lot to do before I hit the hotel tonight.

"Okay. I'm taking this with me," I said, picking up the file. "Now I intend to check on a few things you told me, Mr. Peeps. And if I find out that you've been less than truthful with me, I'll be back." Peeps looked so mad I figured he wanted to spit at me. But he knew better. I walked slowly through the inner office, pausing to pick up a couple of his business cards as I went out.

We sat in the truck at the mouth of the alley with the engine idling. Laurie's reaction was about what I expected as I watched with surreptitious glances as she paged through the pictures. When she'd finished, she closed the file and sat with it on her lap. A tear trickled down her cheek.

"Oh, God," she said. "I'd hate for her mom and dad to see them." Her fist raised up and then descended, smacking the green folder. "I mean, how could she pose for some of those?"

For the money, I was going to say. But I remained silent. I'd already had a feeling that the more we found out, the less we'd like it. What I was mostly worried about was its cumulative effect on Laurie. After all, Paula was beyond hurting now. But my gut was suddenly tightening as I began thinking about the unprotected sex we'd had. Silently I wondered again what that HIV test would show. I'd been doing my best to push it out of my mind. Still, it was never far from my conscious thoughts.

"Detective Grieves said that she had heroin in her system," Laurie said. "Do you really think she was on drugs? I mean, could that have been why she'd do things like this?"

"It'd probably be better if we didn't jump to conclusions right now," I said. But I thought, it's a long way from Ludington. "Why don't you go through the file tonight and separate the pictures that you want from those you don't? Then, when this is finished, I'll help you destroy the others."

She nodded. I didn't envy her task.

"I'm not so sure I even want to see what's on this," Laurie said, holding up the video cassette.

"It'd be better not to toss anything until we've had a chance to sort things out," I said. "Sometimes you can overlook clues."

She mustered a smile. "Right. I guess that's what we're paying you for, isn't it?"

When we got to the Second District, I parked George's truck in the circular drive and went inside with Laurie. The desk sergeant sat behind the chest-high barrier with a cup of coffee and a *Sun-Times*. He glanced up idly, and went back to his reading as a young female officer came over.

"May I help you?" she asked. She had skin the color of light caramel and her black hair was pulled back tightly from her face. I told her we were there to see Detective Grieves. She asked my name, made a quick call, then told us to go right up. On the second floor I proceeded quickly to the section of offices where George hung his hat. I had to be careful because his boss, Lieutenant Bielmaster, and I were old enemies and I knew he'd take my appearance as a chance to berate George. But it went as smoothly as a commando operation, and we found George and Doug sitting at their desks doing reports. The big room was full of other detectives typing, talking on the phone, or poring over files. It almost looked like the research section of some library.

"Things looking pretty quiet this afternoon, gentlemen?" I asked as we walked over to George's desk. He looked up and grinned, then did a double take when he saw Laurie. I introduced them right away.

"You remember George from the old neighborhood, don't you?" I asked Laurie.

"Actually, I remember hearing about you," she said, smiling and shaking his hand. "I think you were away in the Army or something."

"Marines," he corrected.

"Oh yeah," I said. "Don't make *that* mistake. I was in the Army."

We sat down and George asked if we wanted coffee. I told him we did and he grabbed an eight-by-ten manila envelope from a three-sectioned plastic tray before we left for the breakroom. Downstairs he popped several quarters into the machine and said, "Pick your poison." Laurie had cream and sugar. George and I had black.

"I can't think of a finer person to look over this case than Ron here," George said as we sat at one of the tables. He held up the manila envelope. "These are the MUD records that our buddy Irwin faxed over." He winked at me, then said, "I'll have to thank him for that." Taking the MUD record sheets out of the manila envelope he ran a big finger down the page, stopping at a highlighted section. "This one here's for a taxi," he said pointing to a printed number. "Island Cab, which is about ten minutes from your house, made about five-forty. The next two are non-published." He took a sip of his coffee, then added, "I got a buddy in Ameritech security gonna call me back with that one."

I studied the numbers to see if any were familiar to me. One was Paula's apartment telephone number. Probably to check her answering machine for messages. The second one was totally unfamiliar. I took out my notebook and went through it, finding the number that I'd gotten off the impression of the note that Paula had left. But I couldn't match up the number to any on the sheet.

"Think you can find out about this number, too?" I asked, handing it to George. "And here's a present for you." I gave him the cellular phone that I'd taken from old man Turner. George raised his eyebrows then stripped the battery off again.

"Hot?"

"It's got to be cloned. The serial number's been scratched off," I said. "Some dude gave it to the super at Paula's building to keep tabs on us when we came back to the apartment. A white guy with red hair. Sound familiar?"

George squinted for a moment, then shook his head.

"It sounds like the guy I had trouble with at the hotel when I met Paula," I said. "I nicknamed him Red, for lack of a better name. Don't you see that it's all starting to tie together?"

He nodded, glanced at Laurie, and stood. "I'll see what I can find out. Well, I gotta be getting back upstairs. Ah, you are gonna be able to cover that evening shift for me tonight, aren't you?"

"Sure I am," I said, grinning. "Have I ever let you down?"

"Like I told you, Laurie," George said, patting me on the back and grinning broadly, "there ain't nobody finer than Ron to look into something like this." His face turned toward me. "I need you there by six-fifteen, okay?"

"Okay," I said, taking out the parking ticket and handing it to him.

"What's this?" he grunted. "Another one? Oh, no, dammit. I ain't gonna take care of this one for you."

"Well, that's up to you," I said. "But the guy who owns that truck is gonna be plenty pissed if you don't."

His brow furrowed as he squinted to read the license number. He snorted good naturedly and stuck it in his pocket. "Why is it every time I start out helping you, I end up with my own ass in a sling?"

"One hand washes the other," I said. "You mind if we keep the truck one more day?"

"Only if you remember to fill it up and watch where you park," he said as we walked toward the elevator. "Anything else, Mister Shade? Or would you prefer to be called Prince Ron?"

"Prince Ron does have a nice ring to it, but Mister Shade will be just fine," I said. "And, yeah, there is one more thing."

I took out one of the cards I'd taken from Peeps' office. "Could you check out this guy? He's involved in this thing in some way. And he's probably the guy who burglarized my house, too."

"How you figure that?"

"I just came from his office. He and I had a little talk. He sounds like the same dude who set me up for that wild goose chase up to the north shore the day of the burglary."

George frowned, nodded, and stuck the card in his pocket. The elevator doors opened and we rode down to the first floor in silence. Little did I know that handing him that damn card would come back to bite me in the ass.

Chapter 15

Except for the usual traffic backup where the express and local lanes merge around 71st Street, we made pretty good time going home. I kept as good a watch as I could for any black limousines, but nothing suspicious floated into either of the side-view mirrors. Getting off at 119th Street, I shot back north to the animal hospital. By the time we got there it was twenty to six, and I knew I'd be cutting it close. Rags seemed unusually subdued as the attendant brought him out in the travel case. Laurie cooed how cute he was and immediately tried to initiate some sort of conversation with him. When he failed to respond, she turned to me.

"Oh, Ron, he's a little darling. I didn't know you liked cats."

"Yeah, I just seem to keep accumulating them. This one almost got run over last week."

"Oh no. He's so tiny," she said, sticking her fingers between the metal squares of the cage door. "Do you mind if I take him out and put him on my lap?"

"At your own risk," I said. Then added, "But I guess if he gives you any trouble we can slap him behind bars again." It took them only a few minutes to bond. Rags sat on her lap purring the whole way home. I pulled up in front of my house and took him inside away from the cold. The other two cats came out to eye us suspiciously. Georgio emitted a mournful cry that told me that the supply of cat food had run out during my extended absence. I told Laurie their names and where the cat food was. She went to feed them while I made the first of several trips with the boxes from the truck to my front porch. Laurie came and helped me and we finished in record time. But the clock was edging closer to six.

"What's wrong?" she asked.

"I told Big Ed I'd pick up The Beater tonight," I said. "And I got to be at work at the hotel by six-fifteen."

"When will you get a chance to eat?" she asked.

"I'll grab something there. I need to change though." I glanced at my watch.

"Well, I can drive the truck if that's what you're worried about," she said. "I would like a chance to sort through some of this stuff. What time do you get off?"

"Midnight."

"Well," she said, placing a hand on my arm. "If you'd trust me to stay here unsupervised while you're gone, I could go through these boxes and see what I want to keep. I need to go through all that mail too. I can drop you off to get your car and I'll just wait here for you. Then you can take me to the hotel when you get back."

"Sounds like a plan," I said. I went into the bedroom and quickly stripped off my clothes, giving Laurie a quick rundown where everything was through the partially closed door. I changed T-shirts, underwear, and socks too, pausing to swipe deodorant under each arm along the way just so I'd feel civilized. After tossing on a dress shirt, I slipped on my regular jacket and grabbed my tie to put on in the car. Looping my belt through my pants, and pancake holster, I came out of the bedroom and motioned to Laurie.

"Ready?" I asked. She nodded. "Think you can find everything?"

"I'm sure I'll be able to," she said, smiling. "Aren't you going to finish dressing?"

"Nah," I said, snapping my Beretta in place and slinging my sport coat over my arm. "I'm used to doing quick changes."

Big Ed had The Beater outside and all warmed up for me when I got there. I gave him a check and told him I had to get to my second job so that I could make the deposit in the morning to cover it.

"Better make it a double shift if you want to keep driving that thing, Ron," he said laughing. "It's at the stage where it's gonna start nickel-and-diming you to death. And the parts ain't easy to find."

I conferred briefly with Laurie and gave her my extra house key. She assured me that everything would be fine. The Beater roared to life at the turn of the ignition, and I sped off toward the Lincoln Estates Holiday Inn with practically no time to spare. But I still had one last task to accomplish before I got there. And I'd saved the worst till last. As I rounded the corner and hit the expressway, I pulled out my cellular phone and hastily dialed the gym. Brice answered and I told him that I needed to speak to the boss. When he came on I said, "Chappie, it's Ron."

"Yeah. What's up?"

"Ah, I got roped into working hotel security tonight," I said hesitantly. "Looks like I'll have to skip our workout."

The uneasy silence was punctuated by static. "You there?" I asked.

"Yeah, I'm here," he said. "Don't know about you, though. You think you that good you can skip a crucial workout when that fight's right around the corner?"

"Chappie, I'm sorry—"

"Sorry ain't shit. When you be getting your ass whupped 'cause you didn't train, that be sorry. You think Elijah Day be skippin' training?" He paused to let it sink in. "You only gots a week, Ron. Where's your head at, man? Or is you lookin' to get it knocked off?"

"Look, I said I was sorry."

"You gonna be more sorry. You want me to cancel the fight?"

"No. Of course not."

"Then start acting like a fighter," he said. "A professional fighter. A champion. And in case you don't know what that is, it's somebody who gets paid to fight and win, not just show up."

"Chappie," I started to say, but he'd hung up. I pressed the END button on the phone and locked it. After blowing out a slow breath that fogged the windshield slightly, I thought about what he'd said, and why he'd said it.

As my trainer, it was his job to prepare me for the fight, and he'd basically done that. We'd already put in a lot of long, hard training sessions, and I'd never let myself get that far out of shape to begin with. My urine had been practically clear this morning before my run, which usually meant that I was in tip-top shape. Plus I'd beaten Day before, so I should have the psychological advantage. Or maybe that would make him train harder. He was the champion now, which, according to Chappie, usually added about twenty-five percent to a fighter's edge.

I kept turning it over in my mind as I drove south until it became a jangled mess. But at this point I knew that the major thing I had to battle between now and the fight wasn't conditioning or practice. It was nerves. I had to maintain my sharpness and peak at just the right time.

The closer the fight got, the more I thought about it. I'd seen Elijah Day staring across the ring at me in my dreams. I saw him beyond each street corner when I put in my morning miles. And I knew I'd see him when I left the locker room to take that long walk to the ring. The one that was the longest walk in the world.

I arrived at six-twenty-three on the dot, managing to punch-in almost on time. I dumped my heavy coat in the office area behind the front desk, draped my sport jacket over the back of a chair, and was tying my necktie in the mirror that was hung there. Marsha came up to me and smiled. "Hey, Ron," she said. "Back for more excitement tonight?"

"Yeah."

"I haven't seen you for a few. What you been up to?"

"I've been training for a fight."

"No big cases?" she asked, handing me my portable radio.

"Nah, just trying to keep my head above the water." My beeper went off and I checked the number. It was my house. I immediately went to the phone and called. Laurie's voice sounded tentative.

"It's me," I said. "Everything okay?"

"Oh, Ron, I'm sorry to bother you," she said, sounding embarrassed. "I kind of thought that I'd take a look at this videotape later on, to see if it should go in the keep or destroy pile. I wasn't sure how to operate your machine."

I gave her a quick run-down on using the small TV with the built-in VCR.

"Just scan it and see," I said. "But remember, I'll want to take a look at everything before you throw anything away."

"Right," she said. Her voice sounded wistful, then she added, "I just didn't think it'd be this hard. I keep thinking that I'll see her again, or something, or that she'll be turning up for a visit. I just wish I could sit down with her and ask her what the hell she was doing with her life."

"Yeah," I said. "Well, do what you can tonight. And there's a bunch of movie tapes in the cases by the big TV if you want to watch something else."

She thanked me and we hung up. I was beginning to regret letting her watch that tape alone, and I thought about calling her back. Knowing that Peeps had been associated with it, I figured that sleaze wouldn't be too far behind. But I decided against it. She'd already confronted part of the truth about Paula. I'd leave it up to her what she told her aunt and uncle.

After I'd slipped on my sport coat, I saw Marsha staring at me.

"You playing house with someone now, Ron?"

"Not really," I said. "Just a friend."

"Oh, sure. I know. It's none of my business." She smiled and canted her head. I rolled my eyes and walked out of the office to begin my rounds. As I passed by the front desk a woman was complaining that the bottom toilet paper dispenser in the women's washroom was empty, and the top one wasn't rotating correctly. The desk clerk called Marsha's name. I smirked and strolled leisurely away. When I got to the piano bar Kathy was just setting up. Sue, the bartender, gave me my usual club soda, and I went over to the elevated platform by the piano.

"Hi, Ron," Kathy said. She studied me for a second, then asked, "You all right?"

"Do I look that bad?"

"Just sort of preoccupied."

"Yeah, I guess I am. I've been looking into the death of an old friend, and some of the pieces I've uncovered aren't real pretty."

"Oh. Must be difficult for you."

161

"Brings back a lot of old memories."

She nodded. "I know the feeling."

We chatted for a few minutes more while she sorted through her music, then sat on the bench behind the piano. She flipped the microphone on. I set the empty glass on the bar and took off toward the office building, which was supposed to be locked up by six-thirty. At least I'll get my leg workout in tonight going up and down the stairs, I thought. That ought to count for something. As I walked through the big, expansive lobby Kathy's voice suddenly floated after me. She was singing "These Foolish Things."

The shift went by pretty routinely: an obnoxious drunk in the upstairs bar and a rowdy group of college kids having a party in one of the rooms. I persuaded them all to leave, revoking their room privileges on the grounds that not more than three people were authorized to be in the rooms without special permission. One of them looked at me mournfully and said, "Hey, man, it's semester break." He was a big, varsity football type, and for a moment I thought he was going to be confrontational. I told him he should have gone skiing if he wanted to enjoy taking the chance of getting some broken bones. Luckily for him, his buddies pulled him back as they left.

During my solitary floor checks of the hotel and office building, I'd thrown a quick series of punches and kicks on each landing. I figured, besides facing down the drunk and the college punks, I'd gone maybe four rounds total. It helped to assuage my guilt over the missed workout, and I vowed to go in first thing in the morning and let Chappie punish me to his heart's content. As I walked through my final tour of the hotel, I thought about that. And about Elijah Day.

After I finished the walk-through, I went back down and stood by while the airport shuttle bus arrived. As I strolled by the lobby I heard Kathy's voice again, singing "All at Once." I went over to the bar and leaned against it. Sue slipped me another club soda as I listened. After the song there was a smattering of applause. Kathy thanked the patrons and told them it had been a pleasure entertaining them this evening. I stepped over to talk with her as she was folding her music and glanced at my watch. It was almost time for me to pack it in too.

"What happened to 'One More for the Road'? Isn't that usually your swan song for the night?"

"It is, but I figured I owed you your favorite song before I left," she said, smiling. "I haven't seen you very much lately."

"Yeah, well, I been busy training for a fight," I said. "It's gonna be next Friday. If you want to come I'll get you some tickets."

"Oh, I'm sorry, but I'm booked to play here," she said. "But otherwise I'd love to go. Who are you fighting?"

"A big black guy out of Detroit named Elijah Day."

"Is he good?"

"He's the champ," I said. And hopefully next week I'll be, I thought. But I didn't want to jinx it by predicting that I'd win.

I went over to the front desk to see if my relief had arrived yet. Marsha was coming out of the women's washroom carrying a screwdriver and a square piece of white cardboard. I grinned at her and said, "I guess I don't want to know what you were doing with that."

"Just everybody else's job," she said. "I wrote out three work orders about the top toilet paper dispenser not working correctly in the first floor ladies' room. When the bottom roll's gone, the top one's supposed to fall down in place. Well, the damn thing's been broken since before New Year's, but do you think they could get off their asses and fix the damn thing? Noooo. They just keep putting a new roll in the bottom and leaving it. So finally I have to go in and do it. Christ, I'm sick of this place."

"So did you fix it?" I asked.

"Yeah," she said, calming down slightly. "Look at this." She held up the cardboard, which I now saw was a folded coaster from the piano bar. It said Season's Greetings on the front and had a picture of a cocktail glass surrounded by festive ornamentation. "Somebody'd jammed this between the top roll and the bottom one, keeping it from falling down. And this was wedged in between another coaster." She held up a long gold-colored key.

I raised my eyebrows as I took it from her. It appeared to a commercial key of some sort, with a rounded end and a number, 1427, stamped below the hole.

"Know what it's to?" I asked, handing it back to her.

"No. It doesn't look familiar," she said. "I guess I'll just put it in Lost and Found to see if anyone claims it. But I'd like to find out who wedged it in there, and shove it where the sun don't shine."

"My, my, such hostility for such a nice girl," I said as I stepped back. I saw one of the local coppers walking toward me fixing his tie, and knew he must be my relief. And not a moment too soon, I thought as I looked at Marsha's baleful stare. But something about the key being jammed in there bothered me. I didn't know why, but I figured I had enough to worry about for the time being and dragged my sorry ass home.

Chapter 16

Everything was quiet and well lit as I entered the back door and came in through the kitchen. Placing my winter jacket on the back of a chair, I looked through the dining room toward the front of the house. Black and white images of Humphrey Bogart and Ingrid Bergman flashed across the TV screen in the living room. Of all the gin joints in all the world, I thought. Then I heard it: the volume of the TV almost covered the sound of crying. I tossed my sport coat on a chair in the dining room and immediately went to the couch. Laurie was leaning forward, her face in her hands, her back shuddering faintly with uncontrollable spasms.

"What's wrong?" I asked, placing a hand on her shoulder.

She looked up at me, the tears still streaming down her face. Then suddenly she was standing and pressing herself to me, her face buried against my chest, as she muttered, "Oh, Ron."

"What's the matter?"

"That . . . tape," she managed to say between sobs. "It was just so terrible. How could she do things like that?" I patted her back and held her, cursing myself for letting her watch it at all. Peeps . . . I should have really kicked his ass, and then my own for not screening the tape first myself. But I was so anxious to show I was picking up some leads. So damn anxious . . .

Finally her crying became less spasmodic, and I gently urged her back down to the sofa. I went into the kitchen and grabbed a couple of paper towels off the rack and gave them to her. Not as soft as tissues, but they do wonders for a runny nose.

Laurie wiped at her eyes, and then blew her nose, her pretty face looking swollen and puffy. "Are you all right?" I asked softly.

She nodded, her hazel eyes flashing downward. "I guess I thought I'd already gone through the worst part. But seeing her in that movie . . ."

I pulled her to me for a hug and searched for the right words to try and comfort her. As we talked my hands began to make light circles on her back. I suddenly realized that it was affecting me physically. So did she. . . . It had been a while. I hadn't been with anybody since Paula. And I was still under the specter of the pending HIV test. Then Laurie put her arms around my neck and gently kissed my lips.

"Hold me, Ron," she whispered. "Please. Just hold me tight."

Talk about *déjà vu* all over again . . .

It was one of those moments when you suddenly start to slide and realize you should have slowed up about a hundred yards back. I felt the soft swell of her breasts pushing against my chest, but somehow didn't feel totally comfortable in my new role of Shade, the seducer of innocents. Her mouth came to mine again, and this time she opened her lips. I hesitated, still holding her, then kissed her cheek. "Laurie, we're moving kind of fast on this," I said. My words must have hit her like a runaway deer smacking into a fence. I felt her muscles tense.

"You . . . don't want me?"

"No, no, that's not it at all. You're a beautiful girl," I said. "A man would be crazy not to want you. I'm no exception. But things are sort of complicated."

She pushed away from me, grabbing one of the paper towels and wiping at her nose again, her gaze fixed on the floor. I put my hand on her shoulder and felt her shudder slightly.

"You mean because of you and Paula?" she asked through the sniffles.

"Hey, we've got history, kid," I said. "Up until a few days ago, I still thought of you as that little girl in pigtails."

"I'm not a little girl any more."

"Yeah, I've noticed. Believe me, I've noticed." I took a deep breath. I still had to call tomorrow to get the results of my blood test. "I'm just not sure it's the right thing to do right now."

"Yeah, I guess not." She drew herself up straight. "Could you take me back to the hotel now, please?"

"You're welcome to stay here," I gestured toward the couch. "If you'd rather not be alone. We could finish watching the movie."

"I've already seen it," she said. "It's been on TV."

"Hey, it's *Casablanca*," I said. "You can never see it too many times. I get something new out of it every time I watch it. I could narrate it for you. I'll even make you some popcorn."

She showed me a lips-only smile.

I reached over and brushed my fingers gently over her cheek. "You've been through a lot today, and you're emotionally vulnerable right now. Especially tonight. And if anything happened between us now, at this moment, I'd be worried that you'd wake up tomorrow morning and regret it." Eerily, over her shoulder Bogey was giving his "Maybe not today, maybe not tomorrow, but soon, and for the rest of your life," speech to Ingrid.

"Oh, Ron," she said, lurching forward and pressing

against me again. "You're such a special person. So considerate of other people. How did my cousin ever let you get away?"

How did she let me get away? I wondered what twisted version of the story of me and Paula she'd been fed. Ask your uncle, I thought about saying. Instead, I just held her there, feeling her warmth and softness transferring to me, and knowing that if I'd played my hand a little differently, we would have been leaving a trail of our clothes to the bedroom. And I also knew that I could probably still manipulate her in there. But the question remained: If I did, would I be able to look at myself in the mirror in the morning?

The next morning my shoes crunched through some freshly fallen snow as the sky in the east showed a pinkish glow starting to break through the thick velvety blackness. I raced along, hoping not to hear a telltale whistle of any approaching trains. When my alarm had gone off at six, it was all I could do to slip out from under the covers and shuffle around getting my winter running clothes on. Laurie had continued to slumber on the couch, looking warm and comfortable under a thick comforter. Little Rags had wormed his way into the space between the curve of her legs and the back of the sofa. The lucky little bastard. I turned north and headed into the wind, ducking my head to shield my eyes from the onslaught. As I battled the stinging needles of ice, I mulled over the ups and downs of my current situation. I didn't regret that I'd resisted the extreme temptation to make love to Laurie. She was a client, and in a particularly vulnerable state, like I'd told her. And there was still the matter of her cousin's "legacy." How could I tell her about that? Even though I kept telling myself that the test would come back negative, there was still that lingering worry that it wouldn't.

Although I didn't really place much credence in his abstinence theory, at least Chappie wouldn't be pissed off at me. But he was probably still mad about my missing that workout last night. And chances were that he'd never know how nobly I'd handled myself last night anyway.

Why weren't things ever easy for me, I wondered, as the icy wind tore at the exposed skin around my eyes. I lowered my head and continued onward. I wondered if that applied to this case too. If I kept looking under rocks, more sordid stuff about Paula would probably come out. My guess was that asshole Peeps knew more than he was telling. I'd have to wait to see what George uncovered about him. Maybe that would shed some light on things.

I reached the end of my third mile and began the long sweep back toward my house. It was getting lighter out now, and as I shifted direction, the wind was blowing mostly at my back and I was able to put my head up. The dark, heavy clouds to the north looked ominous, and the snowflakes were getting more substantial. An oncoming car cruised slowly by me on the snow-encrusted street, and the driver held up his hand with his index finger pointing toward his temple. He whirled his finger in a circle as he passed, staring and grinning at me.

Yeah, I thought, I was probably pretty close to certifiable, putting myself through this. But in another week I'd know if it was worth it.

The snow had slowed me down considerably and it was almost seven-thirty when I trudged up the steps of my back porch. The odor of freshly brewed coffee greeted me. Laurie sat at the table sipping from a cup. She had on her same clothes from last night, plus one of my sweatshirts. Even without makeup, her face looked fresh and pretty. And young. Real young.

"Hi," she said with a smile. "I woke up and figured you'd be out running. You want me to fix you some breakfast?"

"Sure," I said, heading for the bathroom. "But I'll need to grab a quick shower first. Everything you need should be in there." I pointed toward the refrigerator.

"Okay," she said. "Scrambled, right?"

"Right," I said. "You've got a good memory." I stripped off my running clothes and shoved the wet mass into the hamper instead of just hanging them on the line down in the basement for another few runs. Then I hopped in the shower and lathered up, letting the hot water run over my back to ease the kinks. I finished about ten minutes later. The smell of the bacon and eggs was inviting. I drew the towel around my waist and walked quickly into the bedroom. If Laurie saw me, she didn't say anything. The phone rang while I was slipping into my jeans and a sweatshirt. I glanced at the caller ID. It was Chappie.

"You up?" he said.

"Just finished my run," I said.

"Oh, really?" he said in an exaggerated tone. "That's strange since you been disregardin' everything else I been tellin' you to do."

I didn't try to argue with him. After a moment's silence, he said, "So you gonna grace us with your presence for a workout today, or what?"

"Just tell me when you want me there," I said.

"Nine o'clock," he said quickly. "Sharp. I got some sparrin' partners lined up and don't want to pay 'em for sitting around doin' nothing. Again," he added.

"I'll be there with bells on."

"Just get your white ass in here for a workout or the only

170

bells you'll be hearing be the ones in your head," he said and hung up.

I grinned. Good old Chappie. He always went the extra mile trying to goad me into the best shape before a fight. But it had been such a long road to get this title shot, and I didn't want to let him down most of all. From the sound of his voice, though, I knew that this morning's workout was going to be a ball buster.

When I went back into the kitchen Laurie had already put my eggs, bacon, and juice on the table. She popped two slices of wheat bread out of the toaster and asked if I wanted butter on them.

"Yeah," I said, sitting down. She set a fresh cup of coffee in front of me and began buttering the toast.

"So what's our plan for today?" she asked.

"First I'm going to enjoy this great breakfast you've made for me," I said. "You did fabulous. Thanks."

"My pleasure."

I sampled some of the eggs, and then nodded my head in appreciation. She smiled and sat down across from me, biting into a slice of toast.

"I absolutely have to get a workout in this morning," I said. "That was Chappie on the phone. He's still ticked off about last night. Then I'll get a hold of George and see if he's found out anything on the stuff I left with him. But—" I paused.

Laurie looked questioningly at me.

"I probably should tell you that if I keep on digging, more unpleasant stuff might come out. And it may not be real pretty."

The hazel eyes darted away from me momentarily. "Yeah, I know. I'm prepared for that. Well, at least I think I am."

I nodded.

"And . . ." She tossed her hair back and caught it with her fingers. "If you wouldn't mind, I'd like to accompany you to the gym. I could use a good workout."

"You work out?" I asked. It came out sounding more skeptical than I'd intended.

"Yes, I work out," she said with a mixture of embarrassment and mild hostility. "I go to the gym at school all the time. Just because I smoke doesn't mean I don't work out."

"Sorry. I didn't mean that the way it sounded."

"That's okay. My kind of working out isn't anywhere near your class. But I thought I did see some aerobics and weights there, right?"

"Sure." Good sublimation, I added mentally.

"Great," she said. "Ahhh, and also, if you wouldn't mind, I was thinking that I'd just go check out of that hotel after we're finished eating. That is, if the offer of your couch is still open."

"Sure," I said, thinking about the old saying that living with temptation could make you stronger. Or could it?

"Thanks," she said. "It's so expensive. And this way I'll have more money to pay you with, right?"

I smiled as I shoveled in some more scrambled eggs. "Plus we can watch *Casablanca* a couple more times," I said. "Remember what I told you: the more you see it, the better it gets."

"I'm beginning to see what you mean," Laurie said, looking at me over the rim of her coffee cup. But there was something in her eyes that I found unsettling.

Chapter 17

It took us longer than I'd planned to get to the gym. First I had to take George's truck over to the gas station and top it off. I wanted to be ready for his standard "Is it on empty again?" inquiry when I talked to him later. With Laurie following me in The Beater, we drove to George's house and dropped the truck off. His wife wasn't there, so I just parked it in front and kept the keys. Then we went to the Holiday Inn to get Laurie's car. Unfortunately, the combination of the cold and the inactivity had taken its toll, and the damn thing wouldn't turn over. I rummaged through my trunk and found jumper cables. We sat huddled in The Beater while her battery charged up and the misty snow that I'd run through earlier started to solidify into heavy white flakes. When we finally got her car started, there was a layer of one or two inches on the hood and roof.

After parking her car in my garage to warm up awhile, we headed for the gym without further delay. I would have preferred a bit longer to rest my legs, but I knew that Chappie would have my head if I showed up too late. As it turned out, I missed the mark by only twenty minutes or so, and he didn't seem pissed at all. At least not until he spotted Laurie. One look at her and he gave me what I've come to know as the long, cold stare.

"So glad you could make it," he said.

"Sorry. The weather, you know. Been waiting long?"

"Shit no," he said. "I told 'em not to get here till after ten, figuring you wouldn't be rolling in till then anyway, since I told you nine, and you always do what I says."

"Say, you remember Laurie, don't you?" I put my arm around her shoulder and ushered her forward. She smiled and nodded shyly.

"How you doin'," Chappie said.

"Laurie wants to get a workout in too," I said.

"Glad somebody's interested in workin' out," Chappie said. "Maybe some of that will rub off on some other people. People who have important fights coming up in less than a week."

"I'll get her set up," I said.

"Yeah," he muttered. "And I'll go check on the mad Russian."

"Alley's here? How's he doing?"

"He's one crazy white boy," Chappie said. "Wants to fight again this weekend. I told him it be too soon. Got to let that cut heal. But he was insisting till I told him that your fight's comin' up then. Don't know what's with that boy." He shook his head. "Enjoy your workout, Miss."

I showed Laurie where the women's locker room was, gave her one of the locks we kept in the office, and found Brice, who was working the weight room. He looked pretty impressive in his tank top and sweats.

"Darlene here?" I asked him.

"Huh-un," he said, straining out his last few curls with a pair of fifty-five-pound dumbbells. The muscles seemed ready to jump out of his skin.

"I brought a good friend of mine here," I said. "Can you take her around and show her how to operate the machines and stuff?"

"Sure, Ron," he said, setting down the dumbbells. "Ahhhh, is she yours?"

I frowned. Mine. Brice could be an idiot in the way he

looked at women sometimes. "Let's just say that she and I are very good friends."

"Okay, I get the picture," he said, holding his hands palms outward. "I'll look, but won't touch."

I nodded a smile and headed for the locker room. It wasn't that I was jealous of the possibility of them hitting it off or anything. Well, maybe I was a little, but I just didn't want Brice messing around with Laurie. It wasn't right for either of them. She was such a sweet kid, and he had a bodybuilding contest coming up. That meant that he'd probably be increasing the dosage of his usual series of injections and he'd be prone to some unpredictable behavior.

I didn't mind Brice messing with all the steroid and growth hormone stuff that he did, as long as it didn't affect me or Chappie. Once, when the euphoria of the chemicals had gotten the better of him, he'd let a couple of his bodybuilding buddies talk him into getting in the ring with me. He suddenly found out what speed and timing were all about and that taking punishment from a quick series of jarring combinations was a whole lot different than dishing it out. Or thinking that you were invincible because you could bench press 400 pounds. His chin wasn't what he'd imagined it to be, either, and he'd quickly ended up on the mat, with a healthy respect for me ever since.

I dressed quickly in my usual sparring outfit: sweats, cup, and T-shirt. After slipping on my foot-protectors and shin guards, I wrapped some tape around them. Out on the floor Laurie was looking petite and sexy in spandex tights and a form-fitting sweatshirt as Brice showed her how to use various machines. She smiled as I walked by.

At the doorway of the boxing room, I heard the steady rhythm of a speed bag being pounded. Alley stood in front of one of the three speed bags, working away with an intent expression on his face. I tossed my bag of gear down beside him and began taping my hands. When the timer bell sounded, he stopped and grinned at me.

"Ron, hi." He looked exhausted.

"How's the cut?" I asked. He canted his head to let me inspect it. A track of black stitches wound jaggedly over his left eyebrow.

"Is okay," he said. "I want fight Friday, but Chappie say, no can do. You fight then." He punctuated the sentence with one of his broad, guileless smiles.

"You should let this heal more," I said, pointing to the cut. "Don't fight too soon."

He shrugged, his mouth pulling into a taut line.

"You want to hold the pads for me?" I asked.

"Oh, no," he said, shaking his head and grinning again. "I have to sleep. School tonight, then work."

"Busy man." I slapped him on the shoulder. "You get some rest now."

He nodded and gathered up his stuff. As I watched him drag himself toward the doorway, I wondered if I was going to look that tired after I finished this morning's workout. Brice stuck his head inside and called to me.

"Some guy called here for you. Wanted you to call him back as soon as possible."

"Who?"

"Never mind who it was," Chappie said, stepping into the room. "You got a workout to do." Then, turning to Brice, "What you mean tellin' him something like that to distract him beforehand? You be gettin' his head all messed up. Lord knows it be messed up enough already." He turned to me and grabbed the tape. "Let me do that."

As he wrapped my hands with rote skill, he began his standard lecture about how women before a bout are a fighter's worst enemy. Once again, he proceeded to tell me the familiar story about the unscrupulous promoter who set him up with a prostitute once on the eve of an important match. Although I could probably have recited it by heart, I just let him tell it, figuring I had it coming for missing last night's workout. Like listening to the priest going through the litany to grant you absolution.

When he'd finished I said, "Chappie, I'm not sleeping with her."

"Un huh," he said dubiously. "I can tell that by the way you two been stealing lovie-dovie glances at each other."

I sighed heavily.

"What you want me to do?"

"What do I want you to do?" he snapped. "That's easy. Just keep away from her till after the fight."

"That's kind of difficult," I said. "She's staying at my house for a few days."

He rolled his eyes and snorted disgustedly.

"And you tellin' me you two ain't messin' around?"

I nodded.

"Well, I guess it don't matter none no how. You don't never listen to what I tell you anyway," he said. "Just re-member, you got the biggest fight of your career coming up and you gonna jeopardize it all if you . . ." He didn't com-plete the sentence. After a deep breath he said, "Look, Ron, this ain't gonna be no cake walk. I called some people I know up around Detroit and they told me that Elijah Day be trainin' his heart out. He remember what you did to him last time and he out for redemption."

"I know that," I said. "But he ain't gonna get it."

Chappie smiled slightly, then told me to go warm up. "I want you sweatin' just like before a regular fight," he said. "We go real hard today, but it'll be your last hard workout.

Then easy to moderate till fight night."

I nodded and started stretching and loosening up. After about twelve minutes Chappie came back with three black guys. I knew two of them. Melvin Prodder, who was about my size, and Jessie Wilson, who was taller than I was but about thirty pounds lighter. Chappie introduced the other guy as Demetrius Wall. He looked about the same weight and build as Elijah Day.

"Demetrius from Miami," Chappie said. "Friend of mine down there told him to look me up."

I nodded a hello and continued shadowboxing. Chappie gave them each helmets and sixteen-ounce gloves, and then slipped a pair on my hands. After knotting them and pulling a helmet over my head, he motioned for me and Melvin to get up into the ring.

"Okay," he said. "This is what we lookin' for." He gave me a rundown of what he'd heard Day was doing. He told me he wanted me to stick and move, to take the fight into the later rounds. "Day's got that big, muscle-bound build. He gonna get tired after about four or five, then we gonna put him to sleep. So we goin' a full twelve today."

A full twelve meant that we'd be going a full three minutes each round, like boxing, instead of the standard two-minute rounds of kickboxing. As I slipped through the ropes I thought that I had thirty-six minutes of hell in front of me. Forty-seven if you counted the minute breaks in between.

Melvin always earned his money. He had quick hands and picked up extra money as a journeyman boxer and professional sparring partner. I used my jab to pick him apart and set up a couple of good right hands.

"Get them damn kicks in!" Chappie yelled. Kickboxing regulations required that each fighter throw a minimum of seven hard kicks per round. A light meter was set up on the ring posts, keeping track of them. If you missed your standard quota, you had to make it up the next round or be disqualified. Chappie always hated that rule, but preferred it to the other organization that allowed leg kicks, in the Thaiboxing style. Those could be hell on your knees and usually shortened your career significantly.

I picked it up, throwing several front kicks at Melvin, and caught him with a side kick that knocked him into the ropes. He took a couple of ragged breaths after that and danced away from me. I closed in after him and smacked another front kick into his side. It must have caught him in the liver, because he dropped to one knee. Chappie, who'd been inside the ring acting as sort of an unofficial referee, pushed me toward a neutral corner and began tolling an exceptionally slow count. When he reached eight, Melvin got up and raised his hands. The bell rang as I moved forward.

"Good round," Chappie said to me as he sprayed some water on my face. "But slow down. Our game plan is to draw it out. Dance around a few." He replaced Melvin with Demetrius and told us to get started when the bell rang.

Demetrius, unlike Melvin, was a full-contact karate fighter and had a good arsenal of punches and kicks. He kept bringing his left knee up to block my front kick until I feinted once and smashed a right to his body. After that he was more cautious. Chappie let us go three, which did me good since I wasn't familiar with his style. That meant that I had to figure things out during the round. He did manage to tag me a couple of times before the bell rang, and I realized I was getting tired.

Chappie put Jessie in next. He was adept at using his feet as well, and his lighter weight gave him a slight edge in the speed department. I chased him for three rounds, managing to cut the ring off toward the end of the last one. When I finally trapped him on the ropes I made him pay for all his hitting and running by punishing his body. I kept up my barrage until the bell rang. Jessie's face was slightly contorted as he headed for the corner, but we slapped hands, the boxer's handshake, to show our mutual respect.

Melvin came back in for two. Chappie kept yelling for me to "Stick and move," so I ended up dancing and letting him chase me. Toward the end of the last round he ran out of gas and remained crab-like on the ropes while I pummeled him. But the quick pace had taken its toll on me as well. I felt exhausted, my arms and legs feeling like they had lead weights attached to them. Chappie must have been planning on this because he sent in a freshly rested Demetrius for the last three. It was his test to see if I was really in top shape or not. And I knew if I could win these remaining rounds against a fresh opponent I'd really stand a good chance of taking that championship belt away from Elijah Day.

Demetrius became Day in my mind's eye. I started after him with a fervor and determination to make every shot count. He countered beautifully, using that leg-block effectively at first. For two rounds we dueled, give-and-take. He caught me with a couple of shots that rang in my head. I countered and caught him with a left hook that made him wince. When the bell rang signaling the end of the eleventh, we both staggered over to our respective corners. Chappie checked me over first, massaging my shoulders and putting more Vaseline over my face.

"You good for one more?" he asked.

I knew he was testing me.

I nodded.

He strode across the ring and administered to Demetrius. I had time to take in two deep breaths before the bell rang.

At this point I felt the surge of adrenaline that I always got knowing I was going into the last round. We moved to the center of the ring and exchanged kicks. Circling, he tossed, I followed. Each of us pushed, trying to land solidly on the other. I missed with a left hook and he came over the top with a right cross counter that knocked me back, then down. Chappie was standing over me and swinging his hand counting. I was up at five, telling myself that it was more of a slip than a knockdown. "Dance and clear your head," I heard Chappie saying. My legs felt rubbery for a few seconds, then seemed to come back. Demetrius, grinning widely, moved forward, intent on delivering a knockout blow. I danced away instead of trying to meet him. Been there, done that, I thought, and let him chase me. I bounced around on my toes while he plodded forward. When he came in close to punch I feinted with the front kick again. His left came down involuntarily in an instinctive block, and I had my opening. My right hand caught him in the jaw and he crumpled like a bag of dirty laundry.

He showed guts getting to his feet after a very long eight count. I moved in quickly and blasted a combination to his body, then his head. Reeling, he lurched toward the ropes, covering up. I followed, throwing a few light front kicks, then a couple more hooks. I heard him grunt, and he had that glassy-eyed stare of a guy on the verge of being knocked out. I glanced for Chappie, who was standing a few feet away. I tossed a couple more punches then stepped back. I knew I could have finished him right then and there, but didn't. Instead I danced back to the center and let him follow me on his rubbery legs. He was still on queer street. The bell rang a scant twenty seconds later. Chappie moved forward and jumped between us. He glared at me and then took Demetrius' arm and escorted him to the corner.

"Set that stool in there for this boy," Chappie yelled at Melvin. After he sat Demetrius down and sprayed some water over him, he came over to me.

"You had him there," he said, squeezing a steady spray over my face. "Why didn't you finish him?"

"Ah, gym wars," I said. "Who needs 'em?" I opened my mouth and he directed the spray into it.

"That kind of thinkin' ain't gonna win the big one for you," he said. "Not finishin' a man when you got him . . . It's a bad habit to get into."

"I didn't want to hurt him."

"He paid to take a beatin'," Chappie said. "You think he wasn't trying to impress me by knockin' your head off?"

My arms felt so tired that I propped them up on the ropes. I was too exhausted to argue with him, but I knew I could have finished it with a knockout. That was the difference. I looked across the ring and saw Demetrius leaning forward now, his elbows on his knees, head down. He knew too. Beyond him Melvin and Jessie sat toweling off. Jessie raised his hand and gave me the thumbs-up gesture. Over by the doorway, her back against the wall, Laurie stood watching all of us.

Chapter 18

I hobbled over to Laurie and leaned against the wall.

"Wow," she said, brushing some hair away from her face. "Brice suggested that I come and watch you spar. You looked great, but . . . It was pretty brutal. Will the fight be that bad?"

"Worse," I said. "This was a cakewalk compared to what I have in store next Friday." She was still in her spandex and was looking very svelte. "I need to get some steam to unkink before I shower."

"Oh?" She smiled. "That sounds nice."

"They just have a sauna booth on the women's side," I said.

"Oh, too bad it's not co-ed. So how long will you be?"

"I'll need about twenty-five minutes total."

"Well, I usually need at least twice that long to shower and fix my hair." I rolled my eyes and she quickly added, "But I'll bet I can beat you."

I told her I'd race her and appreciated her musical laugh as she moved toward the locker rooms. Something I regretted a few moments later when Chappie walked by and said, "Un huh."

I frowned and grabbed my ditty bag.

The steam room was way too hot, so I decided on the sauna instead. We had both on the men's side. After stripping down and drinking copious amounts of water, I went inside and sat on the wooden bench leaning forward. I felt the gentle embrace of the heated air sweep over me and immediately started to sweat again while mulling over the case. And our next moves. I watched the droplets fall to the floor and wind their way between the dark tiles toward the center drain.

Ten minutes was about all I could stand. I went to the fountain, then hung my towel on the hook and hit the shower. Usually nothing feels quite as good as a hot shower after a hard workout, but today I really felt drained. No second wind today, I wearily thought after drying off. I took my time getting dressed then stuck my head out the door to see if Laurie was done yet. I didn't see her, so I fished out some coins and called George from the pay phone. He answered after three rings.

"Detective Grieves."

"Yeah, it's Ron. You busy?"

"Not at the moment," he said guardedly. "Why?"

"It just took you a long time to answer."

"It's an old police rule. Never answer the phone before the third ring," he said chuckling. "If you do, the people on the other end think you're sitting around with your thumb up your ass. What's up?"

"I just wanted to tell you that I dropped off the truck in front of your house," I said. "Ellen wasn't home so I still got the keys. And, yes, it's got a full tank."

"Well, thanks for telling me, but I figured it would," he said. "You probably still need a favor or two from me this week."

"Hey, you're starting to sound like a real honest-to-God detective. How about I drop by in a little while and give you the keys?"

"Make it later on this afternoon. Doug and I were just about to grab some lunch," he said. "Anyway, you sound beat. Where you at?"

"I just finished my last hard workout before the fight." I rotated my shoulders, which were beginning to feel stiff and sore.

"Hell, don't worry about the keys. I'll get 'em tomorrow. I got an extra set."

"You sure?"

"Yeah, we might take off early tonight ourselves. This snowstorm's keeping people off the streets." He laughed. "Tomorrow we'll catch hell 'cause everybody will be shooting each other from being cooped up together. But at least those kind are easy to clear."

"Such cynicism from a dedicated public servant," I said with a chuckle. "Say, did you find anything on those phone numbers yet?"

"Not yet."

"Well, how about that Peeps guy?" I asked. "Anything come back on him?"

"I ain't had time to run him yet."

"You just said you were sitting around doing nothing."

"Doing nothing!" he snorted. "You don't know how lucky you are to be your own boss. Not to have some prick breathing down your neck all day. Oh shit, here comes the L.T. Check with me later." He hung up abruptly, and I knew that my old buddy Bielmaster must have been prowling in the station.

I fished another quarter and some nickels out of my pocket along with the card from the medical clinic. It was Friday and I had one more call to make that I'd been putting off. I fed the change into the payphone and dialed.

After about twenty rings the receptionist answered and immediately put me on hold. The computerized operator broke the silence periodically by telling me that I had to deposit "ten cents more please, for the next one minute." I dropped two more dimes into the slot, wondering if I'd have enough change.

Finally a nurse with a Draconian voice came on the line and asked if she could help me.

"I hope so," I said. I gave her my name and told her I was calling for the results of my blood test.

She put me on hold again. This time, at least, the background was some radio station, but it sounded like Yanni's greatest hits. After dropping two more dimes in the slot, the nurse finally came back on the line.

"Mr. Shade?"

"Yes."

"I'm afraid you'll have to come in for those results," she said. "We can't give them out over the phone."

"Why not?" I asked, suddenly feeling a chill creep up my spine.

"It's standard procedure for that type of test. We're not even allowed to open the envelope until the patient is present."

"Can't you just hold it up to the light and look through it to give me a hint?"

"I'm afraid not, sir."

I sighed.

"Okay, I'll be right over," I said, and hung up.

I tried my best to look nonchalant when I walked out of the locker room. Laurie was standing by the office talking to Chappie.

"See, I told you I'd beat you," she said, punching me lightly on the arm. Chappie eyed this action closely, then let his quiet gaze settle on me.

"Keep him straight now, Laurie," he said with a grin. But he sort of squinted when he glanced my way.

"Hey, Ron," Brice called from the other room. "There's

some guy waiting in front to see you."

I told Laurie to wait and went to the front reception room. A big guy in a tan coat and a dark fur hat stood stamping the snow off his feet. When he looked up and smiled, it took me a moment to place him. The whiskers of his beard and mustache were frosted with ice.

"Father Dilousovich," I said. "How are you?"

He extended a hand, after withdrawing it from a worn mitten, and we shook.

"Ah, Mr. Shade, I am flattered that you remember me," he said. "But please, call me Boris."

"Only if you call me Ron," I said. "I'm afraid Alley's already left for the day."

"I know." His entire face creased into a frown. "But it is you I came to speak with. May I buy you lunch?"

"Well, I'm kind of beat right now," I said, thinking about that damn envelope in the care of the truculent nurse waiting for me over at the clinic.

"Mr. Shade, I'm very sorry to impose on you like this," the priest said. "But it is imperative that we talk. Please."

I noticed him slipping a bus transfer from his mitten to his pocket. The poor guy had taken the CTA all the way from the North Side just to try and see me.

"Okay, as long as it's a quick one."

"Oh, my car is in for repairs," he said. "Otherwise, I would offer to drive you."

"We can take mine," I said. I went and got Laurie and introduced them.

Outside the snow had really started to accumulate. I started up The Beater, got out, and swept off at least three inches of fluff from the hood, windshield, and roof. I usually don't let people see me driving it. When you work for yourself, the kind of car you drive is an inevitable indication of your level of professionalism. People will assume, if you're driving a shit-car, that you must be a loser. And who wants to hire a loser to help them solve their problem? Probably the same people who would go to a dentist with a beat-up '57 Edsel. I made a mental note to go looking for a new car as soon as the weather broke.

After three attempts to get out of the parking spot, I finally succeeded. We sped down the alley and headed out onto Western Avenue. I shot down to 111th Street to a nice place called Leona's, glancing at my watch the whole way. A lot of coppers from the Morgan Park Station eat there regularly. Boris ordered chicken kiev, and Laurie a burger and fries. I ordered some broiled chicken and a salad and drank three glasses of water. When the waitress passed I asked her to bring me another one.

"A strenuous workout today, Mr. Shade?" he asked.

"My last hard sparring session before the fight," I said. "It's next Friday. Want to come?"

"Certainly, I will try to make it." The waitress came by and filled our coffee cups. Boris took a long sip, then wiped his mustache with a napkin. He inhaled deeply before he spoke.

"Ron, you must forgive me if I seem to take advantage of our acquaintance," he said slowly, "but Allyosha speaks very highly of you and Mr. Oliver."

"I'm glad to hear that." I canted my head to steal a glimpse at my watch.

"Well, I'm rather worried about him." Boris took another sip of coffee and seemed to weigh his next words carefully. "You have met Smershkevich, Allyosha's sponsor?"

I nodded.

"Then you have seen the problem." He sighed and drank some more coffee. "That is not his real name, of course.

The man is very bad. He is, for lack of a better term, a gangster. In my country before, he did many terrible things."

"He sort of gave me the creeps," I said.

"He is not even a true Russian," Boris said, the cords in his neck starting to bulge out. "He's half Georgian and half Chechen. A *vory v zakone* . . . a professional criminal." He paused and sort of composed himself. "You must pardon me. We Russians are an emotional people."

"I guess that's why you write such great operas," I said.

He smiled slightly.

"Can't Allyosha dump him?" I asked.

"It is not possible," he said. "In order for Allyosha to come to this country, he had to borrow money. A lot of money. Smershkevich provided the passage and sponsorship, but in exchange . . . It was like making a deal with the devil."

"Yeah, Chappie told me that the kid wants to fight again this month. Before his eye has had a chance to heal."

Boris nodded emphatically. "Yes, yes, that is Smershkevich. He's pressuring Allyosha. Every week that goes by, the interest on the debt grows. Soon it will be impossible for Allyosha to ever pay it off."

"That sounds like some kind of extortion," Laurie said. Although she hadn't said much, she'd been listening intently to the conversation.

I took a sip from my own cup and looked down at my watch. One-forty-five.

"Father . . . Boris," I said. "I feel badly for Allyosha, but . . ."

"I know, I know, Mr. Shade," the big priest said, starting to become more animated again. "There is little either you or I can do. We are not wealthy men, nor would I

189

ask you anything of the sort even if we were." He glanced around, then leaned closer over the table. When he spoke his voice was barely above a whisper. "My concerns are of a different nature. I have been told that you are a private detective."

"That's right."

"Perhaps you would consider looking into the affairs on Mr. Smershkevich." The dark eyes shot around the room. "In a professional capacity. I would pay you, of course."

Coming from a guy who rode the bus and wore rag-tag mittens and a jacket that had patches on both elbows, I figured on how much he could pay.

"I'm involved in another case right now, Father," I said slowly. "I'd like to help, but I'm not sure exactly what I could do."

"But this man is involved in many criminal activities," he said. "If enough evidence could be collected, perhaps the authorities could intercede."

"It's possible," I said. "Why don't I talk to a friend of mine on the police force and see what I can find out?"

"You will need a retainer, of course," he said, leaning and pulling out a long cloth change purse from his jacket pocket.

"Let's just hold off on that for now," I said. "Like I mentioned, I'm pretty much booked up at the moment. But I can make a few discreet inquiries."

He nodded, but set the purse on the table.

"In the meantime," I said, taking out my pocket notebook, "you can give me whatever information you know about Mr. Smershkevich."

After lunch we drove Father Boris to the 95th Street bus stop. Despite a new round of stinging flurries, he insisted that he would be fine, and thanked me profusely for my help. As we were driving away, I noticed Laurie looking back toward the bus shelter.

"Don't worry," I said. "Your case is still my top priority."

"Oh I'm not worried about that. I just felt so sorry for him, that's all. He seemed like such a nice man."

She has a lot to learn if she wanted to be a lawyer, I thought. But the reality checks were coming fast and quick, the longer she stuck with me on this case. I glanced at my watch again.

"Are we late for something?" she asked. "You keep looking at your watch."

"I've got to pick up some test results," I said. "Prefight stuff."

"Oh, okay. You looked so tired that I thought you'd want to go home and rest," she said. "I was going to offer to fix dinner for you."

"That sounds good."

Laurie smiled and watched as we cruised past some workers trying to clear the rapidly falling snow from in front of a restaurant. It looked like they were fighting an unwinnable battle.

The nurse turned out to be pretty much as I'd pictured her on the phone. Middle-aged, with stiff brown hair and hefty shoulders. Two stern lines descended from either side of her nose to the scarlet coated border of her lips. Dark eyes peered out at me through thickish lenses encased in old fashioned plastic frames. Holding the envelope in her right hand as we sat in the small office, she looked like the malevolent nurse who tortured Jack Nicholson in that old movie about the cuckoo's nest. Slipping the edge of a razor blade letter opener under the flap, she deftly sliced open the top, unfolded the paper, drew her lips into a tight line, and looked at me.

"The test was negative," she said, turning the sheet so I could see a bunch of writing, at the bottom of which read: SAMPLE NON-REACTIVE.

"What's that mean exactly?" I pointed to the capital letters, resisting the urge to address her as Nurse Ratchet.

"It means that at this time, there is no trace of the virus in your blood." She flipped open the folder, punched two holes in the top of the paper, and fastened it into the metal-pronged clips. "Your tests were also negative for STD's and any of the hepatitis viruses."

I felt a surge of relief. Even though I had been relatively confident of this, it was still good to hear it.

"Why couldn't you have told me that over the phone?" I asked. "I've been on pins and needles all day."

"Well, Mr. Shade," Nurse Ratchet said. "Just whose fault is that?"

I didn't answer.

"But actually, it's the law," she continued. "We're not allowed, for reasons of privacy, to open the envelopes without the subject being present. And the news is so potentially serious that we have to be ready to deal with extreme reactions if necessary."

I nodded, and stood to leave. She gave me a stern look that froze me in place and said, "Just a moment, sir. I'm not finished yet."

I sat back down in the chair. Behind her a life-sized plastic version of a cut-away human head with half its face removed stared back at me from a shelf.

"I have to give you several admonishments," she said. "First, even though this test was negative, there is still a chance that you may have contracted the virus through your last unprotected sexual contact."

"Huh? I thought you said it came back negative?"

She took a deep breath and raised her eyebrows, as if she were rebuking a rebellious child.

"Let me finish. Basically, that means that you were free of the virus at the time of the contact," she said. "It can take as long as six months to establish a traceable presence in your system. Which is why you're going to have to continue taking precautions. Condoms, refraining from donating blood, proper disposal of all bodily fluids. And you'll have to be tested again in six months to be absolutely sure."

Great, I thought. Six more months of living on the edge.

"Do you understand the instructions, sir?"

"Yes, thanks."

"That's quite all right, Mr. Shade," she said. "Is that young lady waiting out there with you?"

"Yeah."

"Well, will you discuss the proper procedures that I've outlined with her?"

Oh, right, I thought. Tell her that we're concerned Paula might have given me . . .

"Perhaps we should make an appointment to test her also?" she asked.

"No," I said. "She's just a friend." And a client, too, I thought.

She stared at me with the same kind of doubting, scornful look that Chappie had given me at the gym.

"Very well, Mr. Shade. You can make your next appointment at the information desk if you wish."

I didn't wish, but if I did, it would be not to have to come back here. I grabbed my jacket and stood up.

"Just remember to take the proper precautions," she said, flipping the file closed. She focused the dark eyes on me again and added, "There's no substitute for responsible behavior."

Chapter 19

Responsible behavior were the buzzwords that kept running through my mind on the drive home. Traffic was slower than normal from the storm, but luckily the clinic wasn't that far from my house. I felt totally spent. Worn out, but whether from the ball-busting workout or the stern lecture from Nurse Ratchet, I wasn't sure. The build-up of salt glazed the windshield with a film of white, so I pushed the washer switch and watched as the wipers and solvent cleared everything off.

If it were only as simple to clean the slate in life, I thought.

Laurie seemed to be taking the lousy weather in stride and just sort of glanced over at me and smiled wearily. I tried to make sense of what everything meant so far. The fight with Red at the hotel, Paula not wanting to go home, her abrupt exit from my house early that next morning by cab, the *8AM* number scrawled on my pad, her death, the drugs, Red having old Mr. Turner call him, the clone phone, Peeps . . . It seemed like a gigantic jigsaw puzzle with all the pieces spread out in front of me on a table. But I was missing an overall picture to know how to put them together.

A car braked hard in front of me and we skidded slightly, almost rear-ending him. Laurie snapped to alertness, reaching out and grabbing the dashboard.

"Oh, my God, I thought we were going to hit him," she said.

"Yeah, me too." I decided to give the puzzle-solving a rest and concentrate on just getting home safely. I was doubly glad that George had told me to wait until tomorrow to return the pick-up's keys.

The snow in the alley wasn't too deep, but I still had to spend a couple of minutes with the shovel clearing off the cement apron in front of my garage. By the time I backed The Beater into the second car spot next to Laurie's little Nissan I felt stiff and tired.

It must have showed. As soon as we were inside, she looked at me and said, "You look exhausted."

"I am kind of beat." I rotated my arms and shoulders a little. "That workout this morning was a real killer. I feel like soaking in a hot tub."

"Why don't you relax and let me fix something to eat," she said. "What do you have?"

"There's some chicken breasts in the freezer," I said. "And maybe a baked potato, or something." All three of the cats had come out of hiding and were walking in little circles on the kitchen floor. Georgio let out a mournful-sounding cry.

"Say no more." She placed her hands on my chest and pushed me toward the bathroom. "You just go in and take a nice hot, relaxing bath, and I'll have this fixed up for you in a flash. I'll feed them too." She motioned toward the cats.

I grinned at her.

"That sounds real good, Laurie," I said. "We can watch *Casablanca* together, if you want."

She began to busy herself in the kitchen while I got some clothes. Before going into the bathroom, I took out one of Kathy Daniel's CDs and put it in my stereo.

"This is my friend," I said. "She sings at the hotel where I work."

I closed the door and stripped down while the water got hot. When the tub was half-full, I settled down in it and let it wash over me. The only problem with being six-one is you have to fold your legs into a yoga-like position in the tub if you want to submerse yourself, but I managed. When the water was nearing the top, and good and hot, I used my foot to press the faucet closed. I lay back, with just my face and the tops of my knees sticking out of the water, and tried to relax. But the pieces of the puzzle kept swarming back to me. Finally, I told myself that I'd just have to wait to see what George came up with and I listened to Kathy sing. I'd missed most the songs on the disk mulling things over, and I knew that this was the last song in the collection. It was another of my favorites that she did: "Wind Beneath My Wings."

The water had turned cold and I sat up and pulled the stopper. Standing, I grabbed a towel just as Laurie knocked gently on the door and said that dinner was ready. When I came out after toweling off and dressing, she had both places set on the kitchen table. It was dark outside and a crust of snow had adhered to the storm window.

"Your friend can really sing," she said. The CD had gone back to the beginning.

"Yeah, she's pretty good," I said, sitting down. "Makes working at the hotel bearable sometimes."

"Are you two seeing each other?" she asked as she sat down.

"Kathy? No," I said. "She's married. We're just friends."

"All I could find in the way of drinks was this cranberry juice."

"That's pretty much it until I get to the store to buy more." I took a bite. "Mmmmm, you're a great cook."

She smiled and began to eat as well. We talked and

laughed, and Laurie kept jumping up to get me more to drink, or some more butter. Finally I told her just to relax and eat. Afterward we each took a cup of hot tea and moved into the living room, and I put *Casablanca* into the VCR.

"Too bad you don't have any wine," she said. "I always enjoy a glass after dinner."

"I think I do have a bottle somewhere, but it's not chilled," I said. I started to get up. "I'll see if I can find it."

"Oh, that's okay," she said, holding up her mug of tea. "This is fine."

We started watching the movie, but after a while I found myself dozing. When I'd snapped awake a few times, she smiled at me and suggested that I hit the sack.

"Like I said, you looked exhausted before." She leaned forward and gently brushed her hand over my forehead. "You're so sweet, always helping everybody. Me, your friend Alley, that Russian priest . . ."

"I'll have to change into my Superman costume in a minute." As I sat up, I groaned and rotated my head to try and unkink my back.

"What's wrong?"

"Oh, I must have been sitting funny, or something," I said. "My back feels a little stiff, that's all."

"Here, lie down on the floor and I'll give you a massage."

"I'll be okay."

"No really, I'm pretty good at it," she said. "Come on." She stood and pulled off my sweatshirt, then practically guided me to the rug. I lay on my stomach, folding my hands under my chin. Laurie knelt beside me and began working her fingers along my shoulders and back, like she was kneading bread.

"Feel good?"

"Yeah, great," I said. "Where did you learn how to do this?"

"I worked in a massage parlor part-time," she said with her musical giggle. Then quickly added, "Not really. When I graduated from college my aunt and uncle sent me to the Alps skiing as a reward. They had this masseuse there, and every morning I'd get a steam and massage. I loved it."

"I can see why," I said.

"You ain't seen nothing yet." She straddled me, concentrating on my neck and upper back. "Here, straighten out your arms a little," she said, making the adjustment. The feeling of the warmth of her hips on me was starting to affect me.

"I don't know about this," I said.

"Shhh." Her touch had become more gentle now, almost as if she was just running her fingertips along my skin. She traced her nails over my arms, then along my neck, and over my face, all the while pressing down with her hips, her legs snug on each side of me. I felt myself on that slippery slope once again, and knew that this time there was nothing to hold onto. On the TV Laszlo had just gotten Rick's orchestra to play "La Marseillaise" to drown out the Nazis' "Die Wacht am Rhein," and I knew that later on that night Ingrid would brave the curfew to come and see Bogey.

"Laurie," I started to say. But she leaned down and kissed the back of my neck, and I felt a white hot shiver go down my spine and settle in my groin.

"Turn over," she whispered, and as I did, our mouths met. Still straddling me, she touched my face, my head, her fingers running through my hair, around my neck, down to my chest. I ran my hands over the solid sleekness of her hips, up to her back, pulling at her blouse. Fumbling with the buttons, she arched to give me better access. Then the blouse was open and I felt the soft smooth skin of her upper body, exploring its softness and fine texture. My fingers moved up her back, searching for the clasp of her bra. But all I felt was the expanse of elastic and cotton. Her mouth broke apart from mine slightly, and she raised up, her hands moving away from me.

"It's in front," she whispered, undoing the hooks.

Sleep kept eluding me the rest of the night. We lay together, our bodies entwined, Laurie's thigh resting on mine, the skin-to-skin contact feeling warm and wonderful under the thick blankets. Her head was cradled on my shoulder, her breathing slow and regular. I knew she was asleep, so I tried not to move. Or feel bad about what had happened.

After things got so hot on the living room floor that I began to worry about rug burns, I'd picked her up and carried her into the bedroom. I remembered the lush beauty of her body as it had looked in the soft glow of the moon and streetlights streaming through the window. The wetness of her anticipation as I explored her, the flash of a triangular patch of pubic hair, her lack of reaction as I slipped on the condom. Afterward, as we'd cuddled, she thanked me for being so sweet, so considerate.

"It's always best to be safe," she said. "Even with people you feel you've known all your life."

An awkward subject approached very forthrightly, I thought. Safe, considerate . . . that was me. Lucky she didn't meet the Ron Shade of last week. When Paula had.

I took in a deep breath and suddenly wondered how we'd gotten to where we were. I certainly hadn't planned on it. Maybe it was inevitable once I asked her to stay at my house instead of the hotel. Or had she asked me? I couldn't remember. Chappie had been right, giving me his evil stare and lecture. But hell, how could this be any more tiring than that ball-busting workout he'd put me through this morning?

Shade, the seducer of innocents, I thought. Then Laurie stirred and I felt her breasts press against me. The stirring in my groin started again.

No, it had been her just as much as me. That god-damn massage. Almost like she'd practically engineered it. Or maybe things just sort of happened. Kind of like in *Casablanca*, when Bogey embraces Ingrid, even though he knows he shouldn't. And where he didn't know what he was going to do right up until the end. I remembered reading that the actors themselves hadn't even known how the movie would turn out due to the constant rewriting of the screenplay. And that spontaneity helped make the movie so great.

Laurie's hand rubbed over my chest. She was awake now too.

"Mmmm," she said. "Can't you sleep?"

"I was just thinking about you," I said.

Her hand traced down my stomach.

"Oh? Let me see."

Laurie, I thought, in my best Bogey imitation. I think this is the beginning of a beautiful friendship. But I also remembered something else . . . something that I'd learned from my own experience. Just like with me and Paula, once two people have crossed the line into intimacy, nothing is ever quite the same between the two of them again.

Chapter 20

Out of guilt as much as dedication, I got up at six and went for an abbreviated run. Abbreviated because Chappie had told me to scale it down to three miles a day this week. And also because the accumulated snow made it feel like I was running through cement. It was Saturday, and traffic was fairly light. I tried to stay on the road as much as possible, except the few times when I was forced by an oncoming car to jump back into the drifts alongside of the streets.

But the temperature was definitely on the upswing. I could feel it in the air. And with each step. The snow was heavy with moisture. Good packing, we used to say when we were kids. Children would be making snowmen later on when they got up, as reluctant daddies fired up the snowblowers. I resisted the temptation to stop and toss a couple of snowballs at an obnoxious driver who tooted his horn at me. I just kept raising my feet up high as I went along.

When I got back, Laurie was up and dressed, standing with a cup of coffee and a cigarette on my back porch. She smiled brightly at me and said she'd fix breakfast while I showered. Mornings after can be difficult sometimes, but this one wasn't tempered by the overindulgence of alcohol to mitigate any regrets.

No, this had been two mutually consenting adults sliding purposefully down that slippery slope toward intimacy. At the time it had seemed completely natural, aside from the condoms, of course. Spontaneous. But as I stripped out of my running clothes and tossed them in the clothes basket, I found myself wondering if it had been the right thing. I'd sort of compromised my Private Investigator's Canon of Ethics in getting involved with a client, but, hell, I'd done that before. But this time the edginess ran deeper. Maybe because I'd known Laurie from before. But the little pig-tailed girl of my past certainly wasn't the same mature woman that I'd held in my arms last night, right? Or was I just deceiving myself, trying to rationalize that I'd made still another bad move in a history of missteps?

I stood naked under the nozzle and twisted the faucet, letting the ice-cold blast hit me in sobering fashion until it transformed into the warming spray.

When I finished my shower Laurie had a fresh stack of pancakes ready for me, as well as coffee, orange juice, and wheat toast.

"What's our plan for today?" she asked me.

"We're just going to have to wait to see what George can come up with on those phone numbers," I said. "If we get another lead, I can check it out through a friend of mine, but I'm sort of hoping that something will pop up that will attract George's attention."

"So we really can't do much then?"

"Laurie," I said, taking her hand, "I told you at the onset that this ain't like TV or the movies. Sometimes all I can do is poke around the edges and try to overturn a rock to get the police interested."

"I know you told me about not being too hopeful," she said, looking down at the tabletop. "I guess I'm just too anxious."

"Unfortunately something like this takes time to develop."

"What have you got planned for this morning?" She

glanced back at me with a smile.

"Well," I said, picking up my mug of coffee, "I'll have to go out and shovel the walk, then do some laundry. I probably should go in and take a light workout at Chappie's. The fight's coming up in just six more days, so I have to stay sharp. Want to come along?"

"I think I'd better go through the rest of Paula's things," she said. "I'd like to mail them off today. I should try to find some movers, too. But I'll help you shovel the walk first if you want."

"Nah, that's okay. Good conditioning exercise."

By the time I got the walk done, it was getting close to nine. I figured to hit the gym and then get hold of George in the early afternoon. I hadn't had the chance to ask him yesterday about checking on that Smershkevich character either, but that was on the back burner anyway. I stowed the shovel in the garage and came back inside.

Laurie had cleaned up the kitchen, and had several of the bags of Paula's clothes on the floor. She was opening the stack of envelopes that Turner had given us. I told her not to throw anything away until I'd had a chance to look through it. Before she could say anything, my beeper went off. It was George's work number with a 911 after it. I went into my office-room to call him back.

"Got your beep," I said, when he picked up. "What's up?"

"A couple of things."

I heard him sigh.

"First off," he said, "I got the results back on that blood test I asked the doc to run at the morgue. On Paula."

"Yeah?" I could feel the tightening in my gut.

"She was clear. Nothing at all."

I felt a wave of relief, even though I'd suspected as much.

"But there's another problem. That guy. Peeps," he said slowly. I could tell from his tone that something was wrong. "I started nosing around, and it turns out he was a homicide victim. From the looks of it, he was killed a day or two ago."

"No shit?"

"Yeah," he continued. "They found him in his office yesterday. Ron, exactly when did you say you talked to this guy?"

"It was Thursday."

"In his office?"

"Right."

"What time?"

"Late afternoon." I explained that I had to get to the vet's, pick up The Beater, and get to the hotel by six-fifteen.

"Did you tell me before that you roughed him up?" he asked.

"Not really. He took a swing at me, so I just gut-punched him and twisted his arm a little. Persuaded him to give me the file of pictures that he had of Paula. Why?"

"I made a couple of discreet inquiries. One of the uniforms in the First District told me it looked like he was worked over real good." His voice sounded grim. "Do you think your prints are gonna be showing up at the crime scene?"

The familiar twisting grabbed hold of something inside my gut again. I tried to think what I'd touched and what I hadn't touched.

"What are you saying, George? Am I a suspect or something?"

"Look, god-dammit, I'm just trying to get a handle on this fucking thing," he said. "Think about how this looks for a minute, will you? I'm doing you a favor, nosing around about this guy and suddenly he turns up whacked.

It left a computer trail right back here. Now I gotta explain why, you know? And if your fingerprints are all over the place, how do you think that'll look?"

"Well, for Christ's sake, don't you think if I did ice the bastard I'd have wiped the place down before I left?" I said, my voice rising. Laurie dropped the envelope she was holding and came to stand beside me, her brow crinkling.

"It don't matter too much what *I* think," he said angrily. I heard him blow out a breath, then he said, "Look, Ron, before we go assuming the worst, let me get a hold of the investigating dicks over at Area Four. They already called here checking because they seen that I ran Peeps' name on the computer yesterday."

"Okay," I said. "You gonna get back to me then?"

"I'll beep you. Maybe it'd look better if we went up there, and you made a pre-emptive statement."

"Whatever you want," I said. "But should I bring my lawyer?"

"Don't be a smartass," he said, his voice still tight.

I tried to laugh. It came out sounding more like a weak cough.

"Say, did you get anything back on those phone numbers I asked you about?"

"Huh? Oh, yeah," he said. I heard the sound of papers being rustled. "The one turned out to be a new cellular account registered to Peeps. Just opened a few days prior to that call. The Mail Boxes, Etc. on that Regis guy's card came back with an address for some outfit called Lothar Industries. It's another P.O. box." He read it off to me. "Oh, that cloned cell phone you give me was entered in the computer as being stolen, too."

"Thanks, buddy," I said. "Give me a beep when you find out what's up."

I gave Laurie a quick run-down of what George had told me. She looked like somebody'd gut-punched her.

"Oh, God, it's all my fault, getting you mixed up in this," she said.

I put my arms around her and gave her a gentle hug.

"Hey, I've been there before," I said. "It's sort of an occupational hazard with me."

"Really?" she said. "You're not worried?"

"Nah, I ain't got anything to be worried about. The cops aren't really out to frame innocent people, despite what O.J.'s Dream Team would have had us believe. When you get to be a full-fledged lawyer you'll know that."

She smiled weakly.

"Now I'd better get my ass into the gym or Chappie will go ballistic." I slipped on my jacket and picked up my gym bag, trying to look more self-assured than I felt. "You okay?"

She stood and put her arms around my neck.

"You're so special, Ron," she said, kissing me softly. "All this trouble swirling around you, and you're more concerned about me than yourself."

At the gym Laurie's heroic perception of me gave me one more thing to wonder about. Did I want this unexpected relationship to develop into something serious? With all the past history we shared, I suddenly wasn't quite sure. But I did know that I really liked her, and the last thing in the world I wanted to do was hurt her if it turned out bad. Like it had for Paula and me. But we were two different people, weren't we? Or would Paula's ghost somehow intrude? The questions kept flipping over and over in my mind, as I was starting to begin to regret what had happened last night.

Luckily, Chappie was putting me through an easy

workout doing some sit-ups, medicine ball, a little on the bags, and a little with the focus mitts. He seemed almost subdued as he took me through the paces. When we took a break, he asked me how I was doing.

"Fine. Why?"

"How's your head?"

"Still attached."

"You seem distracted."

"Nerves."

He nodded and grinned.

"I know the feelin'," he said. "Ain't no cure for them. Not till you step inside them ropes and get it on." He put his hand on my shoulder and squeezed. "But you ready, I know that. You in great shape, and you got the fight plan down, and you done did it before. The only thing different this time is that it be for the championship."

I smiled and he told me to hit the steam for a little while.

"Take an easy run tomorrow morning, then we'll meet over here and just do another light one," he said as we walked toward the locker room. "After that, we can slip over to my place and watch the football game. Darlene gonna fix something real good."

"Sounds great."

"You can bring your new girlfriend, too, if you want," he said. "What's her name? Laurie?"

"Thanks. I'll do that."

"Just be sure you get a good night's sleep Thursday night." He paused and glanced up at me. "You know what I mean. Then rest all day Friday, okay? We in agreement on that?"

"Sure thing, boss."

"You sure nothing else bothering you?" he asked, squinting slightly.

"No, I'm okay," I said, not wanting to burden him with my latest extraneous array of problems. "It's just nerves, that's all."

I tried to put the Peeps problem out of my mind as I sat in the steam room. It would eventually be clear that I had nothing to do with his murder, but I was also sure that his death was connected to all this somehow. But how? The scattered pieces of the jigsaw puzzle seemed to loom in front of me again. I just had to figure out how they all fit.

I tried putting it all in chronological order, going back to my seeing Paula that first night. The airport shuttle bus had just arrived. Red was dragging her out and they were in some kind of an argument. What the hell had he been saying to her? I strained my memory but couldn't remember exactly.

He'd claimed that she was his girlfriend, which Paula denied. And she said she didn't know him. Also probably a lie. So they were associated with each other in some way. What way? And what about the message she'd left on my machine that morning? She'd said something about being in a jam and wanting to stay at my place . . . And there was something else . . . That she was picking up her car. But the Lincoln Estates cops had told me that the car had been towed as abandoned. The trunk punched. It was cold. Maybe she couldn't get it started . . . Or maybe somebody like Red had been waiting for her. . . .

I got up and stood in front of the shower nozzle, doused myself with a blast of cold water, then sat back down as the heat engulfed me again.

I thought back to that night. Paula not wanting to go home . . . Did she really want to go with me, or was she just trying to avoid Red?

I exhaled, jumping to the morning after. Me out running. Paula awake and using my phone. She calls a taxi . . . No, she calls Peeps at his place first, then she calls a taxi. Then writes down the number for his cellular phone . . . *8AM*. . . .

I suddenly realized that I had it wrong. It wasn't an eight, it was a hastily scribbled "S." *SAM*, for Samuel Peeps. But why write down this number if she knew his other number by heart?

George had said that it was a relatively new cell phone, issued a few days prior. That meant that she didn't know the number. So she'd probably been out of contact with Peeps for a couple of days. Out of contact . . . Out of town? The shuttle bus . . . Was she coming in from the airport? I remembered seeing some airline luggage stubs in her purse when the cat knocked it over. Paula had apparently left her car at the Lincoln Estates Holiday Inn, which a lot of people do when they're taking the shuttle bus to the airport. There's no parking fee, and you can take the bus back out to the hotel when you return. But there were a lot of hotel stops much closer to her apartment. Why come all the way out to Lincoln Estates from the city instead of choosing someplace nearer? What had Red said? Something about Paula not thinking that he'd be able to find her. And what the hell happened to her car? Who broke into it, and why hadn't she picked it up? That's what she'd said she was going to do on that message she'd left on my machine. She'd also hinted that she was in some kind of trouble.

The steam was starting to get uncomfortable, so I got up and went outside. I cooled down, took a couple of drinks of water from the fountain, and went in the sauna booth for some gentler heat.

The pieces of the puzzle still swarmed in front of me, almost coming together to make some kind of sense for a moment, then jumbled again.

If I assumed correctly that Paula and Peeps had been mixed up in something, and that she'd been out of contact with him for at least a couple of days, that's why she'd written down the new cell phone number. She'd come to the hotel on the airport shuttle bus. But I still didn't know why she'd go way out to Lincoln Estates when she lived in the city. To pick up her car? Or maybe to meet Peeps? And how would Red know where to trace her? He must have known she'd be coming from the airport . . . Been expecting her . . . She didn't show up as planned, so it would be a simple task of checking the shuttle bus routes. She could have just as easily taken a taxi, but the bus was more public and less traceable.

I blew out a slow breath. The sauna heat was starting to feel hot now, too. Standing, I pulled open the door and went to the showers. My ruminations continued: I leave a message on Paula's answering machine, and then my place gets burglarized a couple of hours later. So does hers. Somebody looking for something . . . Red was involved somehow, leaving that clone phone with old Mr. Turner to keep tabs on Paula's place. But something was still missing. And whatever it was, Red wanted it bad. Peeps too. Both of them taking elaborate measures to try and find it. Something that Paula had. Something that he figured she might have left with me? And I still had no idea what it was.

I was missing too many pieces of the puzzle. It was like trying to catch steam with your hands. Or maybe I just wasn't looking at the whole picture in the right way? My gut told me that I was getting close. And what I'd eventually find, I probably wouldn't like.

Chapter 21

My session in the steam had given me a clue for at least one part of the puzzle that I could check on. After getting dressed, I went up to Chappie's office and looked up the number for Island Cab Company in the yellow pages. A bored-sounding dispatcher answered, and I asked for the manager.

"He ain't in right now," the dispatcher said.

"Well, he was supposed to look up some records for my partner, Detective Grieves out of Area Two." I gave him my address and the date Paula had called them.

"Oh, hell, I can look that up for you," he said. "Hold on a second."

He put me on hold, then came back on the line. I could hear the rustling of papers as he spoke.

"You said that was December twenty-eighth, right?"

"Yeah."

"Okay, here it is." He paused to grunt slightly. "Call came in at five-forty a.m., unit picked up female passenger six-oh-four, drove her to Lincoln Estates Holiday Inn." His voice had a hesitating lilt to it. Like he had suddenly remembered something else.

I waited to see if he'd offer anything. People will do that sometimes if you don't rush them.

"You know," he said. "Seems to me that there was somebody else asking about this. Some guy demanded to see the manager."

"Oh yeah?"

"Yeah," he said. "Somebody wanting to know where the fare was picked up."

"Do you normally give out that information?"

"Well, not normally, no," he said. "But this guy said he worked for a lawyer. Said he could get a subpoena if he needed to. A real fast talker."

"What did he look like?"

"Maybe fifty, fifty-five. Gray hair, heavyset."

I was starting to get a clearer picture. "Did he look like a drinker?"

"Huh?"

"Did he have an English accent?" I asked.

"Come to think of it, he did sound like a Brit."

Peeps, I thought. "Did you give him the address?"

"Well, now that I don't know," he said. "He spoke to Mr. Williams, the manager."

"Let me guess, was this the same day? The twenty-eighth?"

"You know, I believe it was," he said. "How'd you know?"

"I'm psychic," I said, and hung up.

So now I knew how Peeps had gotten my address to break into my house. Paula hadn't given it to him. He'd gotten it from the damn cab company. Probably by flashing a "subpoena" with Andrew Jackson's picture on it. But how had he known that I was involved? The message I'd left on Paula's machine? I'd used my business number rather than my home TX, but if she'd had caller ID it would have been on there. Peeps must have had access to her apartment, listened to the answering machine, and gotten my home number. Now I was sure he did the burglary to my house, and probably the one at her place too, although that one had somehow seemed more vicious. But what the hell had he been looking for?

I grabbed my stuff. Poking my head in the gym area, I spied Chappie talking to Alley. I couldn't hear what they were saying, but Chappie had his hands up on each side of Alley's head.

"Hey, I'm taking off," I said.

Chappie glanced over toward me and motioned with his head for me to come over.

"I don't like the way this looks," he said. He kept his hands up, moving them back and forth. "You see my hand now?" he asked.

Alley shook his head, then nodded.

"I see some . . . like fire sometimes," Alley said.

"I'm gonna have take to him in and have his eye looked at," Chappie said. "That motherfucker Ross must have been thumbin' too."

I nodded. Alley, who'd just gotten in from his night maintenance job, looked confused.

"What?" he asked.

"I'm takin' you to the doctor," Chappie said.

"No," Alley said, shaking his head. "No doctor. Please. No money."

"I pay," Chappie said.

Alley shook his head again.

"No doctor," he repeated.

"Alley," I said. "Don't argue with Chappie. If he says you go, you go. He's your trainer. Your boss."

Alley looked at the floor.

"You want me to drive you?" I asked.

"Nah," Chappie said. "I'll just have Brice watch the place. I gotta be sure they check this out right."

"What do you think it is?" I said.

"Don't like the way he seein' them flashes," Chappie

said. "And his peripheral vision seems off. I'm worried about that eye more than the cut now."

"Great." In between breaks in our workout, I'd told him about my talk with Father Boris concerning Smershkevich. "Just what the kid needs. More shit to worry about."

When I got home I found Laurie on the back steps shivering as she stood smoking a cigarette. As soon as I walked up, she took one more drag and pinched the ember off, letting it fall into the snow. I waved my hand in front of my face trying to dispel the odor of the smoke as I went up the stairs. We went into the porch and then the kitchen.

"Sorry." She opened the garbage can lid and dropped the extinguished butt.

"No problem. You been cutting down?" Since she'd been staying at my place I really hadn't noticed her smoking very much. I silently hoped she was trying to quit. But then again, maybe she was just picking her smoke breaks more carefully.

My kitchen table was covered with several groups of papers in various stacks. Georgio was curled up on a chair opposite, and slumbering Shasha had her back arched against the heating vent. Rags was meandering about the floor exploring everything.

"Oooh, I wish," she said, then gestured toward the piles of paper. "This is going slower than anticipated. Paula was not the most meticulous person. Her checkbook was a mess. I'm still not sure how much money's in her account. And a lot of her bills went into collections before they were paid."

Live fast, party hearty, and let the bills fall where they may, I thought. Apparently, Paula hadn't changed much since high school.

"But anyway," she continued. "I've been trying to organize things into three major piles. Bills that need to be taken care of, those that really don't matter anymore, and stuff you might be interested in." The third stack was by far the smallest, but I made a mental note to look through all three of them. I told her that.

"Oh, sure," she said. "Whatever you feel is best. You're the professional." She beamed a smile at me. "Say, I used your phone to make a call up to Michigan."

"Home?"

The question seemed to catch her off-guard.

"Ah, no . . . This was just a friend that I was supposed to call," she said. "I'll call home tomorrow, if it's okay. Maybe I should look into getting a phone card."

The way she said "friend" made me immediately think "boyfriend." I wondered if she did have somebody up in Michigan waiting for her. And if she did, where did that leave us?

After making a quick protein shake for myself, I took Laurie out for lunch. We ended up going to a fast-food place where she munched down a salad and I had a coffee. Then we checked out a couple of moving outfits. She settled on the most reasonable one, and they agreed to meet her at Paula's apartment Friday morning.

"That's okay, isn't it?" she asked, turning to me. "I mean, it won't interfere with your fight?"

"It should be all right."

It was already getting dark when we left the moving place, and the temperature seemed to be dropping as fast as the sunlight. Whatever snow had melted during the day's thaw was now rapidly turning to ice. The salt trucks were out in force.

"Chappie invited us to dinner at his house tomorrow afternoon," I said. "Interested?"

"Oh, wow, that's sweet of him."

"It's sort of like a tradition," I said. "The Sunday before I have a fight, we usually meet, eat, and go over our fight plan once more."

"Your fight plan?" she asked. "Is that important?"

"Yeah. You got to have a plan to follow, or you'll end up being lost."

"I can imagine," she said. "But it still sounds pretty scary."

"Life," I said, exaggerating my voice, "is pretty scary. If you let it be. Now why don't we go down the street to the multiplex theater and see a movie? Or would you rather eat first?"

She smiled. "Anything you want, Ron. I just like being with you."

I was thinking how much I liked her smile, and how pretty she looked there in the fading light, that for a moment, I could almost forget that she was the little cousin of a girl I was once in love with a long time ago, maybe with a boyfriend in Michigan. And that she was also a client.

Sunday's early morning run wasn't so early. After the movie Laurie and I had grabbed a late dinner at a restaurant, then stopped by a near-by night club for some dancing and drinks. Actually, she had the drinks while I just had club soda. At close to midnight we'd gone home and things got romantic again. It all seemed so natural that for a moment it was as if she'd been a regular part of my life for a while. And would be for the future. But then reality crept in.

Semester break . . . I wondered how long it would last. Not forever, that was for sure. Then again, had I ever expected that it would?

When I got home, Laurie was watching TV and sorting out whites and colors from a stack of dirty clothes.

"Why don't I do the laundry while you're at the gym?" she asked.

I told her she didn't have to ask me twice.

I met Chappie for our scheduled "quick" workout, and he put me through the paces with the focus pads, the bags, and shadowboxing. He kept saying that I was looking "as smooth as silk" throughout the session, but at this point I wasn't sure if he really felt that way or was just trying to bolster my ego. I mean, I was probably in as good shape as I was going to get, so it wouldn't really help to push any more. And I didn't believe the time I was spending with Laurie was all that detrimental either. As long as I got some rest in between. What it really boiled down to was peaking at just the right moment now, and I hoped that it would be Friday night. But I felt in my bones a sort of indefinable dread. A feeling that even though I'd prepared for this fight harder than I'd ever trained before, something unexpected was coming to knock me off the track.

"Nerves," Chappie said when I told him how I felt. "You just got to trust yourself when the time come."

Trusting myself, I thought. Something that I wasn't doing very much of lately.

Chapter 22

The January thaw continued its steady rise, melting the snow and leaving the streets slick-looking. Most of the huge drifts and piles had shrunk substantially, allowing me free rein on the parkways and road shoulders as I sped through my three-and-a-half miles. After the pleasant dinner at Chappie's the day before, and the nice cozy night with Laurie as we just relaxed together in a warm embrace, I was almost ready to put all the troubles and concerns about the case behind me and just concentrate on worrying about the fight.

My quasi-euphoria, as it turned out, was short-lived. When I walked in the back door I heard Laurie in the shower and I wondered if I should knock and ask to join her. Save water, and all that. But my beeper was doing that intermittent chirping of an unanswered page. The screen lit up with a Chicago exchange and George's badge number behind it, followed by 911. I went back into my office-room and called him.

He answered on the first ring.

"Yeah," I said. "What's up?"

"Where you at?"

"Home. Just finished my run. Why?"

"Me and Doug are over at the morgue on a case, but this Peeps thing's starting to heat up."

"Oh?"

"Yeah," he said. "I ain't got all the details yet, but it might be a good idea to go make that pre-emptive statement we talked about."

"All right."

"So why don't you figure on meeting me up at Area Four, at Harrison and Kedzie," George said. "And, Ron, try not to show up looking like a bum, will ya?"

By the time I hung up, Laurie was out of the shower, standing there with a towel wrapped around her, trying to run a comb through her dark hair. She smiled at me and asked how my run had gone.

"The run was fine," I said. "It was the phone call afterwards that sucked."

After explaining to her that I had to go in and give a "pre-emptive statement" concerning Peeps, she insisted on coming with me. Not wanting to look like a bum, I changed into my gray sport coat, dark slacks, and power tie. Laurie picked out some dressy black slacks and a purple sweater. In an effort to hurry, she'd let her hair dry naturally and it seemed to be missing its usual flip and body wave. It made her appear younger than she was, but she still looked like dynamite.

I tried to persuade her to stay there, but she kept insisting she could corroborate that I hadn't been alone with Peeps for long. Finally, tired of arguing, I agreed, and we went out to The Beater. The drive north in the mid-morning traffic wasn't bad, taking only about thirty minutes. I parked in the lot, and we went into the brick stationhouse. But George wasn't anywhere in sight. I knew I probably should have waited for him, but I was anxious to get this over with.

The desk sergeant told us to wait and we sat down on the metal bench. Presently a blond guy with thinning hair came out. He was thick around the middle in dress pants, a blue shirt, and loosely knotted floral tie. A Chicago star was clipped to the left side of his belt, and a snub-nose revolver in a holster was on the right.

"Mr. Shade, I'm Detective Reed," he said. "Would you come this way please?"

We followed him upstairs and he put each of us in separate interview rooms. After waiting about twenty minutes, Reed appeared at my doorway with another guy who was carrying a yellow legal pad. They entered and smiled.

The other guy was tall with kind of an aging athlete's build and a bushy gray-black mustache. When he turned I noticed that the hair at the crown of his head had thinned out too, but not as bad as Reed's. His shirt-sleeves were rolled up over big muscular forearms, and he regarded me with cold brown eyes.

"Mr. Shade, this is my partner, Detective Randecki," Reed said. "We'd like to talk to you about a few things."

"That's what I'm here for," I said.

"Detective Grieves from the Second District," Reed said. "You know him?"

"Yeah," I said. "Practically my whole life."

He and Randecki looked at one another, then Reed said, "So I take it he helps you out from time to time on cases you're working on?"

"Well," I said, trying to stall. The last thing I wanted to do was to say something to these guys that would get George's tit in the wringer. "Not really. If I get something, some information that he can use, I give it to him. He does the same if he hears something that I may be interested in, as long as it doesn't compromise any police business."

"So do you have any idea why he was nosing around about a guy named Samuel R. Peeps?" Randecki asked.

"You probably should ask him that," I said.

"You know Mr. Peeps?" Reed asked.

"I met him once during the course of a case I'm working," I said.

"You ever been to his office?" Reed said.

"Yeah."

"When?"

"Last Thursday."

They both looked at each other, which I didn't take for a good sign.

"It was the first and only time I ever saw him," I said. "Although I think I talked to him on the phone a couple of times."

"That so?" Randecki asked, matter-of-factly.

I was starting to get a little perturbed by their tactics. I expected them to lurch into good-cop, bad-cop any minute.

"And what was the nature of this visit?" Reed said.

"I went to his office to question him about some photography work he did on a client's relative," I said.

"Who's your client?" Randecki asked.

I looked up at him to slow the tempo a bit. It was none of their business who my client was. It was privileged information and they knew it. But still, I was here to cooperate, and it probably wouldn't hurt.

"The young lady in the next room," I said.

"And who's the relative?" Randecki asked. "What's her name?"

"Look, why don't we quit playing cat and mouse here," I said. "Are you guys on a fishing expedition, or what? 'Cause I'm getting a little tired of this bullshit, and I do have a lot of things to do."

"Don't get smart with me, wise-ass," Randecki growled.

Ah, I thought, the bad cop finally rears his head. I played with the end of my power tie.

"Joe, don't get sore," Reed said in an easy tone. "Ron here's just trying to make a living."

"Guys," I said, holding up a finger for each of my statements. "I went to Peeps' office a couple of days ago. I questioned him about some pictures he took of a Paula Kittermann." I spelled her name for them. "He did a portfolio. She was killed December twenty-eighth by a hit-and-run driver. Detective Grieves called me on the case to make the ID. I'm a friend of the Kittermann family, and they asked me to look into the accident. End of story."

"I hear you're a kickboxer, Shade," Randecki said.

"Yeah."

"A real rough-ass." He stared at me with a challenging sneer.

I didn't say anything.

"So you must know how to take care of yourself pretty well, Ron," Reed said.

I nodded.

"You have any type of problems with Peeps when you saw him?" Randecki asked.

"Peeps," I said, "was an asshole."

Reed leaned forward in his chair.

"Why do you say that, Ron?" he asked.

"You run a background check on him?" I asked.

"We'll ask the questions," Randecki said.

"I'd be interested to see if Peeps had a rap sheet," I said.

"I'll bet you would," Randecki said. "Is that the kind of information that Grieves gives you?"

I didn't respond.

"You own a pistol, Ron?" Reed asked.

"Sure," I said.

"What kind?"

"A couple of 'em," I said. "Why?"

"You ever own a twenty-two?" Reed asked.

"I did. It was stolen in a burglary about a week or so ago."

They exchanged looks again, then Randecki spoke, "How convenient." He moved toward me, emphasizing each phrase with his extended index finger. "So what are you saying. Shade? That you can't account for the whereabouts of this particular weapon of yours?"

"I'm saying that if you find my twenty-two, I'd like to have it back," I said. "It's sort of a family heirloom. My uncle left it to me when he died. The serial number should be listed in the computer as stolen."

"You know that Peeps is dead?" Randecki said.

"I heard," I said.

"He was beat up pretty bad. Like somebody used him for a punching bag." Randecki leaned forward. "You mind showing me your hands?"

I held them up.

"Looks like you mixed it up with someone," he said.

"Several people actually. I've been training for a fight."

"Did you know a twenty-two was the murder weapon, Ron?" Reed said.

"Was it your twenty-two, Shade?" Randecki said, leaning closer to me now. His breath smelled like stale cigarettes and strong coffee.

I looked up at him, resisting the temptation to shove his leering face away with the palm of my hand.

He must have sensed something, or maybe had planned it that way.

"You want to take a swing at me, Shade?" Randecki said. "Well go ahead. But I gotta tell you, you don't look so tough."

"Looks can be deceiving," I said.

"You know, I think I could take you myself."

"Come by the gym and try," I said, leaning back slightly. "I can always use another sparring partner. Look, find the person who burglarized my house, and you can ask him about the gun."

"Shade, I told you before," Randecki said, his face stopping an inch or so from my nose. "I don't like smart-asses."

I knew he was trying to get me to take a poke at him. Then they could hold me, and really shake me down. It'd give them the standard seventy-two hours to assemble some charges. Maybe get a warrant to search my house, and sweat me some more. I was debating the prudence of another smart-ass remark when the door abruptly opened and George stuck his head in.

"What the hell's goin' on here?" he said.

"Butt out, Grieves," Randecki said. "This ain't your district or your case."

"I told you guys to wait till I got over here," George said, stepping into the room. His voice had that certain edge it got when he was about to explode.

"We figured we'd better get started," Reed said, standing up. "Your lieutenant over in the Deuce told us that you were real tight with Ron here. Figured it might be hard for you."

"You back-doored me with the L.T.?" George said, scowling. He looked at each of them, then said, "You low-life sons of bitches."

"Fuck you, Grieves, we don't have to take none of your shit," Randecki said.

George shot forward more rapidly than I'd ever seen him move and shoved Randecki up against the wall with a resounding thump. The mustached detective tried to squirm away, but George leaned his weight forward, pinning Randecki to the wall, and clamped a big hand over his face, squeezing the other man's lips into an exaggerated pucker.

"Listen, asshole," George said, "you ain't seen shit yet. I

told you on the phone that this guy was family. And I expected him to be treated as such. I asked him to come down here to help out the Department with a murder investigation, and you two jokers go double-teaming him without even showing me the professional courtesy of an invitation." Randecki tired to squirm away again, but George's big fingers crushed the puckered lips together more, making them look like purple licorice twists. "And then you dime me out to my boss . . . Why, I oughta kick your fuckin' ass just on general principles."

"Hey take it easy, Grieves," Reed said, trying to pry the two men apart. "Come on, let him go."

George released Randecki, who immediately gave George a hard shove. Both men balled up their fists, and Reed and I both jumped between them and pulled them back.

"You just wait, Grieves," Randecki said.

"Any time, pal," George said. Then emphatically to me, "You ain't got nothing else to say, right?"

It was actually more of a statement than a question.

I shrugged and shook my head.

"Hey, just a minute," Reed said. "I thought you wanted to cooperate, Mr. Shade."

"I told you he wanted to voluntarily come down here," George said. "He admits to being in the office, and the gun's reported stolen in a burglary back in December. You two guys ain't got shit to hold him, and you and I both know it. Now we're leaving, unless you want to really fuck up big time and hold him for nothing, in which case I'll personally make the call to OPS."

"You'd bring those assholes in?" Randecki said.

"Yeah," George said. "Plus the ACLU, Johnny Cochran, and anybody else I can think of."

Randecki massaged his jaw and looked malevolently at

George, but didn't say anything. Reed seemed to ponder momentarily, then said, "You're free to go, Shade. You got a number where we can get in touch with you if we need to?"

I gave him one of my cards. George walked out of the room and I followed. We found Laurie sitting in a break room down the hall drinking some coffee from a Styrofoam cup. She stood up and smiled at us as we entered.

"Everything okay?" she said.

"It is now," I said. "The Lone Ranger here rescued me from the evil clutches of two assholes."

Laurie's eyebrows raised. George's face scrunched up and he made a dismissive gesture with his hand.

"Come on," he said. "Let's get the hell outta here."

"Yes, Kemosabe," I said.

"Will you knock that shit off," he said through clenched teeth.

"I mean it," I continued as we walked down the hallway toward the doors. "I'm gonna get you a white hat and a mask for Christmas next year. Then we'll trade in your pick-up for a big white horse. I ain't never seen anything like it."

He snorted, but the slight remnants of a smile danced over his lips. We turned from the long hallway and started toward the front doors of the stationhouse.

"But just tell me one thing, okay?" I said.

He nodded.

"Were you really gonna hit that jerk?"

"I was thinking very seriously about it."

We pushed through the glass doors and the cool January air engulfed us.

"Man, that's a relief," I said. "The way you were squeezing his lips together like that, I was worried you were thinking about giving him a big old kiss."

I'd run almost to the car before he gave up chasing me.

Chapter 23

George had a pensive look as his big fingers held the ceramic coffee cup. He worked his mouth like he was going to say something, glanced across at Laurie and me, then took a swig of the steaming dark brew. Laurie sat hunched in the corner of the booth, staring down at the table in stunned silence, stirring her cup with an almost detached look. I was the only one who didn't seem extraordinarily fazed by the unexpected turn of events, other than the fact that nobody had seemed the least bit impressed by my power tie.

"I hope this ain't gonna get you in trouble with your boss," I said finally.

George shrugged and looked like he was trying to act nonchalant. It didn't work.

"Don't worry about it," he said. "Won't be the first time." He took another sip. "Besides, those two assholes will get what's coming to 'em. I called them earlier and told them you were family." He squinted reflectively as he looked over at me. "And they don't even show me the professional courtesy of waiting till I got there. . . . Word will get around." He shook his head. "The pricks."

I waited a half a beat then said, "So will you finally admit that I was right?"

"Huh?" he said, his face scrunching up as he set down his cup.

"That there are just too damn many coincidences in this thing for it all not to be tied together somehow," I said, leaning forward. Out of the corner of my eye I could see

Laurie perk up and stare at me. "I mean, first there's Paula's hit-and-run, the burglaries to my place and hers. Red showing up with Paula at the hotel and again at her apartment with a cloned phone. Peeps knowing Paula, and now him getting iced. Christ, this thing's as rotten as a month-old watermelon."

"Yeah, yeah," George said. "You made your point. Now we just got to get the right breaks."

"Did you ever do that check on Peeps?" I asked.

He sighed. "I was just starting that when the son-of-a-bitch turned up dead. And I don't imagine those dicks are gonna be too cooperative now." The waitress came by and filled his cup.

"I'd be mighty interested to see if any of his prints showed up on the latents that they got from my burglary," I said. "Or at Paula's."

"I'll have to call the morgue and see if I can get an extra set," he said. "But if he was Paula's boyfriend, that doesn't prove much if they show up at her place."

"The guy that called me on that set-up had an English accent," I said. "Peeps had an English accent."

"So does bonnie Prince Charles," he said. "Want me to call him and see if he has an alibi?"

"Dammit, you know what I mean," I said.

He smirked and drank some more coffee.

"Yeah, just giving you back a little of the shit you been handing me," he said. Then, looking at Laurie, he added, "Sorry."

She smiled.

"Anyway," George continued, "one thing is perfectly clear. I got to solve this Peeps thing before those other two assholes do."

"Now you're talking," I said. "And this Red guy's tied

into it somehow. I know it. If we can just figure out who he is and what his connection is."

"Hey, can that 'we' shit," he said, pointing his big index finger at me. "You're in enough trouble as it is. Just let me handle it from here on out, okay? You want to come by and look at some mug shots, that's fine. But otherwise, butt out."

"What do you mean, butt out? I started this whole ball rolling."

"Yeah," he said. "And you've done a real good job rolling yourself right into the Most Likely Suspect category. I don't want you monkeying around in this anymore. If one of those pricks goes to the Grand Jury, they could get an indictment against you with what they got already."

"That doesn't mean squat," I said. "They could indict the Pope in that kangaroo court if they wanted to."

"Yeah, but they ain't after him this week," he said, giving me one of his patented authoritarian stares. "I'll crack this thing as soon as I can run down some leads."

"You even wouldn't have any leads if it wasn't for me."

"If it wasn't for you," he said grinning wickedly. "Sometimes I fantasize about that and try to imagine how peaceful and uncomplicated my life would be."

I frowned and drank some coffee. It tasted as bitter as I felt.

"Okay, but will you at least check out some of the stuff I told you about?" I said.

"I'll check the street name file for a guy named Red, but there's got to be a whole lot of 'em," he said. "Plus we're not sure if he even goes by that. It's just what you been calling him for lack of something better, right?"

I nodded. "Remember I told you his name might be Regis Phillips. Can you check on that too?"

He shrugged. "It's worth a shot I guess. And he's a white guy with red hair, which kind of narrows it down some. But I want to concentrate on finding out about this Peeps character first." He picked up his cup and squinted at me. "In the meantime, you concentrate on keeping out of trouble. Remember, you got a fight coming up in a couple of days, and I might even bet some money on you. This time."

I smiled back at him, but I didn't want him to know that the facetious tone of his words had really stung me.

The drive south was your typical Monday afternoon fiasco. Slow motion shuffling from one traffic jam to the next. Bumper-to-bumper all the way south. Plus the double team interrogation tactics of Dumb and Dumber seemed to have had a delayed effect on me. By the time I hit the I-94/I-57 split, I'd felt like I'd been ten rounds with a 400-pound gorilla. I glanced at Laurie, who seemed equally drained.

"You want to go get something to eat?" I asked. "Maybe go to a movie or something?"

"Sure, if you do," she said. "But I'd just as soon grab something and relax in front of the TV."

"You're sure?" I asked. "Don't you want to go out dancing again?"

She smiled that wonderful smile of hers.

"Oh, Ron, the weather's so bad, and it's cold, and you must be exhausted after all you've been through. It's okay. Really."

"You're sure?"

"I'm sure," she said.

"Well, I am feeling kind of beat. Maybe a nap would be nice."

"Now that," she said, reaching over and squeezing my arm, "does sound inviting."

It turned out to be anything but a restful nap. The tension of the afternoon was like a coiled spring and I kept tossing and turning. Eventually, I fell asleep and when I awoke I heard Laurie talking in muffled tones on the phone. Stretching, I listened to her voice as it carried from the other room.

"Yes, I know, Uncle Larry, but things are okay. He's really making some progress." She paused. "No, he's not." Another pause. "You're wrong about that. . . . Because I know. You don't. Well, that was a long time ago. Anyway, I have to go now. I'll call you back later in the week and let you know about the movers. I'm fine, really." Her voice was argumentative. "Okay. I will. Love you too. Bye."

I could hear her lower the phone softly back into its cradle. Then I saw her approaching shadow in the wall mirror opposite the door as she came toward the bedroom.

I closed my eyes and waited to feel the familiar weight of her body getting back in bed. But it didn't come, and I suddenly had the feeling that she was standing at the door watching me. A few seconds later I heard her turn and leave the room, then the sounds of her going through her purse.

I heard the click of a lighter, then the quick padding of her footsteps as she headed for the back porch. She must have thought the smoke would bother me, and she was right.

But what bothered me more was the overheard conversation that convinced me that as far as good old Uncle Lar was concerned, even after all these years, I was still the same asshole who'd knocked up his daughter.

Chapter 24

During my Tuesday morning run, the 138th consecutive day of training, I decided that it was time to go on the offensive in the case as well as the fight. Maybe it had been going over the game plan again with Chappie, or getting slapped around, albeit metaphorically, by those two assholes, Reed and Randecki, but as I rounded the final corner and did my customary finishing sprint, I knew it was time to start making the other guy sweat for a change. And to do that I had to gain the upper hand.

I couldn't wait for George. It was just like Chappie had told me at the gym. "If you want to win it, you gotta go and take it. You can't just lay back and expect somebody to hand it to you." He'd been talking about the fight, of course, but the message was clear: I had to take charge of the case, too, and clear myself.

After a quick shower and breakfast on the run, I grabbed Laurie, got in The Beater, and headed back downtown.

"What's our next move?" she asked me.

"To take the mountain to Mohammed," I said. She raised her eyebrows quizzically and leaned back in the seat.

I swung onto Lake Shore Drive and continued north past McCormick Place, Soldier Field, the museum, and Buckingham Fountain. On our right we were treated to the sight of the cold gray waves splashing over the beach. I cut over left and made the turn that took us to Michigan Avenue. The pre-lunchtime traffic was limbering up, and I must have driven around for at least twenty minutes looking for a vacant parking space. Finally, figuring that I'd used up just about all of George's largess as far as parking tickets went, I turned into a parking garage near the County Building.

"Where are we heading?" Laurie asked, tossing her hair over her collar as we got out. The weather had warmed considerably, and some of the huge stacks of dirty gray snow were starting to melt, but it was still January in Chicago.

"The Hall of Records," I said. "This will be good practice for an aspiring attorney."

She smiled at me and grabbed onto my arm as we walked. Just then the knife-edge of the chilly wind swept around the corner of the buildings and engulfed us. Like I said, it was still January in Chicago.

Inside we went to my usual clerk and asked for help finding the corporate ledger books. The woman seemed to take delight in helping me every time I came in. She smiled and shoved the appropriate request form across the counter. I took out my pen and printed LOTHAR INDUSTRIES, INC. in big block letters. She took the form, smiled again, and vanished among the stacks of long binders. Presently she came back with one, and Laurie and I went to one of the high tables. Paging quickly, but carefully, to the L section, I ran my finger down the printed page. When I found the listing, I took out my notebook and began scribbling.

"What exactly is this going to tell us?" Laurie asked in a hushed whisper. Being in the noisy office was somehow akin to being in a library. Maybe it was all the reference books.

"This," I said quietly, "is the name of the company that rented the post office box for that Regis Phillips character."

"Oh," she said. I admired the fine bone structure of her face as she tilted her head back.

"Look at this." I pointed to the list of corporate officers. "See how many of these names here list the same address?" She nodded. "What do you want to bet that the names are phonies? You've got Regis Phillips listed here, and another person with the same P.O. box address here."

"What should we do?"

"This name here as president is interesting," I said. The name was Akeen Emanuel. "And the fact that he's listed as the top dog is even more significant." I closed the book and returned it to the nice lady. I then went to the computerized telephone information computer and waited until the three people ahead of me had looked up their numbers. After sitting down I typed in "Akeen Emanuel" and found no listing. I tried reversing the order of the names and found a listing with the same address as the one listed in the ledger. After writing this number down, I went to the row of near-by pay phones and dialed it. After three rings, a voice came on and said, "You have reached Lothar Industries. Please leave a message." The voice had a somewhat British sound to it.

Another Limey, I thought, and hung up without saying anything. I looked at Laurie.

"I'm pretty sure this Lothar place is a front," I said. "I'm just not sure for what."

"How does this all fit in with Paula?" she asked.

"That's the other thing I'm not sure of." I sighed and glanced at my watch. I had a workout to get in at Chappie's tonight, but it was still pretty early. Fishing out some more coins, I dropped them into the slot of the pay phone and began dialing.

"Why don't you just use your cell phone?" she asked.

"We're too enclosed in here. Too much iron and steel and tall buildings. Usually you get too much static unless you're outside."

She nodded and I finished dialing. Big Rich answered on the third ring.

"Stafford."

"Hey, buddy, it's Ron. How you been doing?"

"Ron Shade. Hey, dude." His voice was like the rumble of a tank. "I'm cool, man. You?"

That was Big Rich . . . always striving to stay on the cutting edge of current slang.

"I'm working on a case and I'm bouncing off a brick wall," I said. I gave him a quick rundown of Lothar Industries, Akeen Emanuel, and the addresses.

"So is there a story in all this for me, or is this just going to be another line added to the long list of favors you owe me?" he said. He punctuated the question with a deep, resonant chuckle which quickly developed into a cough. I could see his big, 300-pound body hunched over his desk, with one of his smoldering cigarettes hanging from his mouth.

"You know I always treat you to a fair amount of scoops," I said. Big Rich was a reporter for the *Chicago Metro*, a smaller competitor of the *Tribune* and *Sun-Times*. We'd worked together on numerous stories before and had sort of a mutual backscratching pact. Big Rich had an enormous amount of contacts on his computer system, as well as one of the most comprehensive stockpiles of information anywhere in the city. "Besides, this is really important."

He must have picked up on the urgency in my voice because he dropped the wisecracks and said, "Give me about fifteen and get back to me."

"I'm downtown," I said. "I'll come over."

"Okay. See you when I see you." I could hear the clicking of the keyboard over the phone as we spoke.

Since the *Metro*'s offices were sandwiched in one of the

lesser buildings over near the Tribune Towers, I figured it was a little bit too far to walk with Laurie. Leaving The Beater in the parking lot, I hailed a cab and we rode over as the meter kept clicking away. The cabbie, a Third World type, smiled brightly at us in the rearview mirror. Laurie seemed fascinated as we drove over the Michigan Avenue Bridge.

"Oh, Ron, look at those statues," she said, pointing to the Indian and the Army officer.

"Yeah, this used to be Fort Dearborn many moons ago. Site of a real bloody battle. If this was summer I'd take you for a boat ride."

"Maybe I'll come back for it."

The cab dropped us off in front of the building and I paid the fare, wondering if it might be better to leave her at the *Metro* and jog back to get The Beater instead of taking another cab. Inside the *Metro* waiting room was a gigantic pinography machine, surrounded by numerous pictures that described the history of how newspapers were printed. Laurie ran her fingers over the smooth metal surface as we walked past.

"This is really neat," she said. "I've never seen one of those before."

"Wait till you see Big Rich," I said with a grin.

We took the elevators up to the sixth floor and found all 300 pounds of him leaning back in his overstuffed chair, puffing away on a cigarette, and talking to a solidly-built black guy.

"Hey, Rich," I said, holding out my hand. We shook and I introduced Laurie.

"Pleased to meet you," he said. Rich had long brownish-blond hair and thick glasses, but these seemed perfectly in proportion with his oversized body. If he'd stood, he would have dwarfed us in height as well as girth, but for such a large, obviously overweight man he appeared exceptionally well groomed. His drooping, unkempt mustache and the ash-laden necktie were the only lapses in his appearance. He held out his palm.

"This is Mike Marsh, of the *Chicago Reader*," he said, then smiled. "And, the second-best reporter in the city."

Marsh smiled as we shook hands.

"Guess we don't need to ask who the best is, huh?" he said with a wry grin. He shook hands with Laurie and then said he was late for an appointment. We watched him walk away.

My nostrils flared at the cigarette smoke and he immediately crushed the one he'd been smoking into an overflowing ashtray.

"Thanks," I said.

"Don't mention it," he said with a grin. He took out another cigarette and held it between his fingers, but didn't light it. "I remembered that you're supposed to be in training. The fight still on?"

"This Friday," I said, trying not to think about it too much. The nerves were starting to wear on me.

"You're getting me tickets, right?" he asked.

"Absolutely," I said, thinking that if everyone I'd promised free tickets showed up at the gate expecting to get in for nothing, they wouldn't have any seats left to sell.

"Good," Rich said, picking up a stack of printouts. "Now, onward and upward. Lothar Industries is a dummy corporation. All I got is that it's connected to this guy named Akeen Emanuel, who also appears to use the name of Ganiyu Olijede." He paused and spelled it out. "Your guess is as good as mine as to how to pronounce it. Looks like he runs some kind of an import/export business called, get this, Trader Horn." He grinned. "Remember that old movie? Anyway, same guy, or at least he appears to be. Formed the corporations about a year ago."

"What kind of a name is that?" I said. "African?"

Big Rich nodded. "My bet is Nigerian," he said. "Now I didn't find anything in our police report files, but there's a Nigerian crime organization that operates in the Midwest." He fingered the cigarette like he was thinking about lighting it, but didn't. "To the tune of smuggling, drugs, credit card scams, clone phones, you name it."

"You got any more info on him?" I asked.

"Just what's there," Rich said, leaning back. He placed the unlighted cigarette in his mouth and clasped his hands behind his head. "Now suppose you give a little."

"I can't right now," I said. "But I promise to let you in on anything that turns up."

"What kind of bullshit is this, Ron?" Rich said, unhooking his hands and leaning forward. He looked at Laurie. "Pardon my French, Miss." Then back to me. "This mystery stuff doesn't sound like our usual arrangement. You came here asking for help, remember?"

"My cousin was killed," Laurie said. "Ron's been looking into it for me."

Her sudden admission seemed to startle the big man momentarily.

"I'm sorry for your loss, Miss," he said.

"We're not sure how this part fits into it yet," I said, "so I'm gonna pass on any further comments right now, okay?"

Big Rich licked his lips and nodded. "Okay, but keep me apprised. But watch yourself dealing with this Olijede guy. Looks like he's pretty well oiled."

Chapter 25

When we left the *Metro* building, Laurie asked if we could walk over to get the car instead of taking a cab. "At your own risk," I told her. She lit up a cigarette while we walked, holding hands. So much for her quitting, I thought. As we strolled over to the corner of the Michigan Avenue Bridge we paused, with our backs to the wind, to look at the greenish water and out toward the lake beyond it. I watched the smoke, coming out with her frozen breath, drifting from her lips.

"I always like to look at the lake," she said. "It's almost like an ocean."

"Just about as cold and unforgiving too."

"But it's still beautiful," she said, gripping my arm tightly. "Looking at it here I can almost forget about this whole tragic situation. About Paula being dead and you getting into so much trouble trying to help me."

"Hey," I said. "I'm getting paid for it, remember. It comes with the territory, and I'm used to it. Getting hauled in for questioning is pretty much standard operating procedure for me. Besides, it helped light a fire under George's ass, and he's the one who's ultimately got to solve it."

"You're so sweet," She stood on her tiptoes to kiss me. Her nose and cheeks were becoming red from the cold. "I just wish it was different for us right now."

I put both my arms around her waist and we stared at the river some more. In front of the Wrigley Building some guy was working on an ice sculpture. The chainsaw ground off huge chunks from the block.

We watched his artistry for a few minutes. Laurie seemed serene, but a troubling thought started to intrude on me. Becoming personally involved with a client, much less the cousin of a former girlfriend . . . Was this the only private investigator work ethic I was going to break on this case? The jostling crowds continued to brush by us. For all they knew, we were just two young lovers on a sight-seeing tour. And for all practical purposes, that's what we were. I certainly couldn't claim that we were a professional private investigator and his client. And how much, when the time came, would this degree of personal involvement affect my ability to make the right decision? I hugged Laurie closer for a moment, hoping that I wouldn't have to find out. Because deep down I knew that being a professional was all that separated me from the rest of the amateurs in this crazy line of work. And that was all that had kept me alive in the past.

"You know," I said, giving her a gentle squeeze, "I told you before, this thing's probably going to get worse before it's over. Some things might come out that might not be too pretty."

"I know that already," she said. "But we've come so far. And I need a sense of closure on all this. I'm still not sure what I'll tell Uncle Larry and Aunt Louisa, but I have to know the whole truth in order to put my own feelings to rest."

Full speed ahead, then, I thought. The block of ice was beginning to take on some kind of form, but exactly what, I wasn't sure. I hoped the artist had a clearer image in his mind's eye than I did as I struggled with my own problematic block of icy questions.

"You ready?" I said. "I have to make a couple of phone calls."

She took a final drag on her cigarette and tossed it over the side of the bridge.

We walked part of the way back, then the cold started to get to us so we went into a small coffee shop. I bought us two hot chocolates, set hers on the table, took out my cell phone, and dialed the gym. Brice answered.

"It's Ron. Put Chappie on, will you?"

"What's up?" he asked when he picked up the phone.

"I need to get a hold of Young Dick Tiger," I said. "You know if he's still driving a cab?"

"Yeah, I think he is," Chappie said. "Lemme see, I got his work and beeper numbers here in my book."

"He's from Nigeria, right?"

"Yeah, just like the original," Chappie said. "Why? You looking to brush up on your African culture?" he said with a laugh.

"In a manner of speaking," I said. He read off the numbers and asked what time I was coming in for my workout. I told him I'd be in later and hung up. I dialed the work number first and got a dispatcher. She said that Dick was out of the office and asked if I'd like to leave a message. I identified myself as Ron from the gym, and asked if she could relay my beeper's number as soon as possible. She said she would.

Dick's real name was something long and unpronounceable. I'd known him for about seven years from Chappie's, and had even worked his corner on a few of his fights. He'd come over from Nigeria with very little money and, as they say, "a fierce determination to realize the American Dream." Unlike the crime ring that Big Rich had spoken of, Dick worked two jobs, trained, and fought as a light heavyweight for a number of years. He used the name of Young Dick Tiger after the great Nigerian middle and light heavyweight champ of the early sixties. In his late thirties now, he'd slipped to a journeyman status as a boxer, but he still worked just as hard at it. I sipped my hot chocolate and chatted with Laurie until my beeper went off.

I used the pay phone again and heard Dick's familiar African-accented English as he asked me how I was doing.

"Does Chappie have a fight for me?" he said anxiously.

"I don't know about that, Dick, but the reason I'm calling is that I need your help on a personal matter."

"Oh? How may I help you, Ron?"

"It's in regard to a case I'm working on," I said. "Where you at now?"

It turned out he was downtown as well and agreed to meet near Michigan and Washington in about ten minutes. Laurie and I began walking, sipping our hot chocolate through the holes of the plastic lids of the cups. The walk took us past the rest of the Magnificent Mile and as we neared Grant Park I saw the cab sitting by the curb at the next intersection, Dick's familiar profile behind the wheel. We hurried up to it and I rapped on the window. Dick smiled and leaned over to open the back door.

"Ron, how are you?" he asked. He looked toward Laurie and I introduced them. After pulling forward and flipping down the Not For Hire sign on his visor, he turned into the alley behind the row of buildings on Michigan, leaving the meter off.

"I must admit," he said in his clipped tones, "that your phone call has me very, very curious."

"I'll bet," I said, handing him a slip of paper with the African-sounding name Big Rich had found for us. "Can you tell me if that's an African name?"

"Olijede," he said. It sent a quick jolt through me when he said it. "Yes, it is Nigerian. He is a Yoruba."

"Wait a minute," I said. "How did you pronounce that?"

"Olijede." He laughed, then said it slower. "Oh-liejah-day."

"Oh, for a minute I thought you said Elijah Day. That's the name of the guy I'm fighting this week."

Dick laughed again, then asked, "What is it you wish to know?"

"I was just more or less curious about the name," I said. "It's come up in connection with a case I'm working on."

"Ah," he said. "I take it that it involves something illegal then?"

"Yeah," I said. "How'd you figure that? Ever heard of the guy?"

He smiled, then said, "No, I do not know of him. But you are a detective, and he is a Yoruba. They are notorious for doing bad things. They are very stingy, crafty, and their faces are round, like a pie."

"I've never seen the guy," I said.

"The Yoruba are from the southern section of Nigeria," Dick said. "When oil was discovered in the eastern part of the country, President Balewa wanted to give it to the Ibo and Efik tribes, so they could prosper. But the Yoruba and the Hausa realized that they could be rich, and seized control of the country. The military took President Balewa from the palace and executed him." He paused to shake his head sadly. "The tribes from the area known as Biafra tried to break away to form their own country. It started a civil war between them and the rest of the tribes that lasted many years and cost many, many lives."

"What's your tribe?" I asked.

"I am an Ibo," he said. "The Yoruba are the sworn enemy of my people. Many Ibos were massacred during the conflict."

"So you say that a lot of Yorubas are up to no good?" I asked.

"Yes. Many, many come to this country to become involved in smuggling, drugs, counterfeiting . . ." His voice trailed off and he shook his head slowly. "And the saddest part of it is that my country has many, many talented people, but the corruption has become so rampant that now the only outlet for them is to use their talents in bad ways. If I had enough money, I could go back to my country and obtain forged documents that would say whatever I wished them to say." He laughed again, less humorously this time. "I could get them saying I was the mayor of Lagos if I wanted."

I asked him if he'd ever heard of a guy named Akeen Emanuel, or a couple of companies called Lothar Industries or Trader Horn.

"The name sounds like a phony," he said. "Akin is an African name. Sometimes it is pronounced to sound like Akeen. The other two, I have never heard of."

"Could you kind of nose around for me?" I asked. "I'm trying to get a line on this guy Olijede. But be discreet. And careful."

"I will see what I can find out, Ron," Dick said, smiling. "Now, where can I drop you?"

"We're parked in a lot over by the County Building," I said.

Dick put the car in drive and took off. He zigzagged through the streets with an expert's ease and we were in front of the lot in a matter of minutes. I noticed that he still hadn't put the meter down, so I took out a twenty and shoved it at him. He shook his head and held up his vertical palm.

"An old African custom," Dick said. "We always help our friends."

"An old American custom," I said, letting the twenty fall to the front seat. "We never ride for free. Take care, buddy."

He grinned, then grabbed at the sleeve of my coat. "Ron, one more thing."

I paused.

"The Yoruba can be very, very ruthless," he said. "They are known as the warrior tribe. It is you who should take care."

As we made our way south on the moderately crowded expressway in The Beater, Laurie asked me what it all meant.

"It's sort of like a jig-saw puzzle," I said. "We've got a bunch of pieces, but we're not sure exactly how they fit together yet."

"And our next move?"

I considered that for a moment. I knew I had to contact George and see if he'd come up with anything new on Peeps or Red. I'd also ask him to check out this African connection. But until I had something solid, or a way to start putting all the pieces in order, there was nothing to do but play the waiting game.

"Sooner or later something will break," I said, trying to sound positive.

Her lips compressed into a thin line.

"You know," I said slowly, "I told you before that this whole thing might not turn out to be very pretty."

"We've already turned up such sordid elements," she said. "What are you asking me, Ron? If I want to keep going?" She turned and looked at me. Her face flashed with intensity. "I have to. Like I said, I have to be able to put Paula's ghost to rest. Then I'll figure out what to tell my aunt and uncle."

"That's a pretty heavy burden."

"That's why I'm glad I have you to lean on right now."
She reached out and touched my arm.

We rode the rest of the way in silence.

Chapter 26

It was still early afternoon and I opted for a quick protein shake rather than a heavy meal, knowing that I had to make my workout at Chappie's. Laurie asked if she could taste it, so I poured her a glass and went in to change clothes. There was no sense wearing my good clothes so they could get further rumpled in the gym locker. I hung up my slacks figuring I might be able to get another day out of them, but my shirt was sodden under the arms. I slipped out of it and my T-shirt, then glanced up and saw Laurie standing in the doorway looking at me over the rim of the glass. The chalkiness of the protein drink coated the inside of it.

I turned and smiled. "Did you like it?"

"Yeah," she said. "It was almost like a milkshake. But it's all stuff that's good for you, right?"

I nodded.

"You know, you've got such great abs," she said, moving forward. "Could I get abs like that from drinking this stuff?" She held up the glass.

"Sure, if you throw in about two-hundred sit-ups a day," I said. "But your abs are fine the way they are."

"Do you really think so?" She was standing against me now, staring around my shoulder to look at both our reflections in the mirror. "But I really like yours."

Her hands roamed over my stomach, then my shoulders. Before I knew it our mouths were locked together and I was pushing her toward the bed, fumbling with her clothes, this time remembering to check in front for the clasp.

We were still like newlyweds, unable to keep our hands off each other. She seemed to be driven this time, seeking only to please me. Afterwards we lay together, tangled in the sheet and under the heavy blanket, our bodies still flushed from the effort. I was silently counting that the fight was now only about seventy-four hours away when she pulled herself on top of my chest.

"Are you sure it's going to turn out okay?" she asked me.

"What? The fight?"

"No. You know. This thing with you getting hauled in by the cops."

"Aww, hell, that was nothing. Besides, George won't let them railroad me."

"I feel like I've gotten him in trouble too," she said. "First you, then him. All because of my stupid cousin. And you've both been so nice to me."

I put a finger gently over her lips.

"Ahhh, it'll be fine. George will come out smelling like a rose after he solves the case, and I'll be all right."

"You're sure?"

"Yeah. Positive." I squeezed her slightly.

She smiled and snuggled close to me. I looked over and glanced at the clock. It was after four. Georgio jumped up on the edge of the bed with an introductory mew, and stared at us. His new protégé, Rags, followed, trying to make the leap, but not being able to. He used his claws to pull himself up. Laurie laughed.

"They don't hesitate to intrude, do they?"

"Only if I interrupt their afternoon nap times," I said. "But I have to get up pretty soon anyway. I promised Chappie that I'd get in there early for my workout."

"Maybe you should tell him you've already had yours today," she said with a smile.

* * * * *

Laurie declined to go along, saying that she wanted to finish going through all the mail and papers that we'd gotten from Paula's apartment. And that was okay with me. I silently felt it was best if we didn't show up at the gym together and face more of Chappie's rebukes. As I slipped on my coat and grabbed my gym bag, I reminded myself that his admonishments about women weakening legs was just old boxing mythology.

But when I got to the gym I really began to wonder. I seemed to have a little trouble getting into the rhythm of the workout. Perhaps the only good thing about having a fight coming up is that after you finish all your sparring, the last few days leading up to the match you just do your regular workout. Shadowboxing, bag work, skipping rope . . . all the things you normally do in addition to the sparring sessions. At this point you're probably in as good a shape as you're going to get, and hopefully it'll be enough. The enemy now was nerves. Thinking about stepping between those ropes and getting it on against another man who was equally well conditioned and intent on knocking your block off. It was always tiptoeing on the edge of your consciousness. Plus, this time the championship was at stake. Possibly my last shot, and I'd pursued it for so long.

Whether it was a result of nerves or my previous amorous activity, I didn't feel sharp and fast. The workout dragged along, and after Chappie and I had finally gone through about five rounds with the focus pads, he slapped them together and told me to hit the sauna.

"You looking good," he said. "Best I ever seen you."

I was surprised he'd said that, but didn't know if it was what he really felt.

"Hell, I should be after all this training you've put me through."

He grinned. "You gonna kick that motherfucking Elijah Day's ass then?"

"Damn straight," I said.

I sat on the edge of the ring and began stripping off my gloves and pads while I assessed myself. Overall, I did feel pretty confident, but couldn't help but wonder if Chappie really felt that way too, or if he was just blowing smoke to help me keep the nerves away.

"I'm worried about that damn Alley," Chappie said, sitting down next to me.

"Why?"

"I took him over to see the doc the other day, but he run out of the office before they could check him," Chappie said. "Tellin' me he had to go or something."

"Well, he does have a couple of jobs. He's going to school too."

"That's all fine and good. But I'm still worried about that eye. He need to have that checked out if he gonna be fightin' for me. And he missed his workout today, too."

"Maybe he was too tired."

"Or maybe he starting to pick up your bad habits," Chappie said with a laugh. "Why don't you see if you can talk some sense into him? I know he look up to you."

"I'll see what I can do."

I spent about five minutes in the sauna while I pondered things some more. When I got out, I showered quickly and then fished some change out of my pocket and went to the pay phone. I tried George's home number first. Ellen answered and told me she'd get him.

"Yeah," he said, sounding sleepy.

"What the hell, were you taking a nap?"

"I guess," he said. "I just sat down on the couch for a minute and, man, the next thing I know I was dreaming."

"Was it a good one?"

"Yeah, I dreamed I was kicking Bielmaster's ass all the way down the hallway."

"He give you a hard time when you got back?" I asked.

"Nah," George said. "No more than usual. Those pricks from Area Four did call him, though. I owe those bastards. Both of them."

"You find out anything?"

"Let's see," he said slowly. "Peeps had no local records out of Illinois. I faxed a copy of his prints to the Feds and told them to expedite." He chuckled. "I hope my request gets there before Randecki's."

"How about Regis, AKA Red?"

"Didn't find nothing solid."

"Well, I did some checking too," I said. I gave him the rundown on Lothar Industries, Trader Horn, and Ganiyu Olijede.

"Who?" he asked.

"Ganiyu Olijede." I spelled it for him.

"Oh. For a second there I thought you said Elijah Day," George said. "You know, the guy you're fighting."

"I'm trying not to think about him anymore until Friday night. Can you run some checks on that stuff?"

"Sure," he said. "Might be a connection with that clone phone. A lot of Nigerians are into that kind of scam. Let's meet tomorrow for breakfast and you can give me what you got before I go in. Probably be better than you dropping by the stationhouse since Bielmaster's got a hair up his ass about all this."

"Okay," I said, then thinking of Alley, added, "I got one more thing."

"What's that, another parking ticket?"

"No. I wonder if you can run a check on a guy named Smershkevich."

"What the hell kind of a name is that?"

"Russian. Georgian, probably."

"Georgian," he said chuckling. "Ain't that the place where they used to live to be a hundred years old from eating yogurt?"

It was good to hear him laugh again.

"What's his first name?"

"I'm not sure," I said. "But how many Smershkeviches can there be?"

"You'd be surprised," he said. "Anyway, how's he tied into all this?"

"Well, he's not," I said. "This is a separate matter." I started to explain about Alley.

"Jesus H. Christ, Ron," he said, interrupting me. "We're working on a homicide, you're in shit up to your knees, and you want me to waste time checking on some fucking Rooskie?"

"I think he might be into some kind of extortion scheme with some of the local Russian immigrants," I said. "I was talking to this priest, and he told me that this guy's strong-arming people. Might even be using a false name, so he's probably wanted or something. Maybe, if he used a false name, he's an illegal alien, or something."

"Didn't you hear what I just got through saying, god-dammit?" George said. "We got other priorities right now."

"Yeah, yeah, I know, but I thought that maybe, if he came up shady, you could call INS."

"Nahh," he said angrily. "You been watching too many movies. Immigration don't want to mess with no illegals unless they're gangbangers or into major league stuff. Drugs, or smuggling, or something."

"Okay, then," I said, "want to meet at Karson's at seven?"

He grunted an okay and hung up. I figured maybe I'd better wait until this was over before trying to help Alley and Father Boris. Plus I had the fight to think about. George had a point. There was a danger in spreading yourself too thin.

I dropped in some more coins and called my house. When Laurie answered, I told her I was on the way back and that I'd stop and pick up some chicken dinners for us. She said that sounded great. I grabbed my stuff, went up front, and said good-bye to Chappie.

"Remember," he said. "Get a good night's sleep."

His reproachful stare stayed with me as I walked to The Beater. The phone call with George had set me thinking on things again, but there were still too many pieces of the damn puzzle to sort out. I needed some kind of break and was depending on George to get it for me. Ironically, his ass was on the line too, and he was also depending on me to turn something up. All this and Elijah Day lurking just around the corner. Could any of this have come at a worse time?

But, I reminded myself, is there ever a good time for bad things to happen?

I sat in the car and opened one of the two cans of apple/cranberry juice that I'd brought. While I waited for the heater to kick in, I drank the juice in a few long swallows and popped the second one. The temperature had continued to rise, leaving the piles of dirty snow sitting on top of puddles of water. If this kept up, a lot more would melt, which would be good. But then again, with the temperature hovering right around freezing, if another storm blew in, it could mean a lot of snow on top of ice. A dangerous combination.

I pulled out and looked at the long line of streetlights illuminated in the grayish darkness. The days were starting to get longer now. Noticeably so. Maybe there was a light at the end of the tunnel after all.

I went to the drive-up at Brown's Fried Chicken and got eight pieces and an order of fries, figuring that I could watch Laurie eat the potatoes. In ten minutes I was backing The Beater into the garage and figuring that I was in for the night. When I got inside, Laurie was waiting with two glasses of juice poured and plates and silverware all set up. All three cats had also assembled in a line by the table. Georgio bellowed a deep greeting and looked up at me as I set the bag of chicken on the table. Rags moved forward with a clumsy intrepidity, while Shasha, ever the coquette, brushed against my legs.

"I was standing on the back porch with a cigarette when I saw your lights," she said.

I grinned, thinking that I could get real used to having her around. Except for the smoking. But maybe she could quit again. There were good law schools in Chicago, too, and lots of job opportunities. I started to think about what might happen as opposed to the way things were, and wished I hadn't.

But it was time for a reality check, Shade.

She was a client, and she lived in Michigan, she was in law school, and she was just down here for semester break. Plus she was the little cousin of a girl I once loved, whose parents hated me. And she was just a kid in a lot of ways. Sure, she was a grad student and only about eight years separated us chronologically. But in terms of experience we were light years apart. It was just like Harrison Ford said in one of his old Indiana Jones movies: It wasn't the years, it was the mileage.

Who was I fooling? Besides myself? Some major questions still loomed, and I wasn't sure how it was going to turn out in the end. Nothing to do now but keep moving forward, I thought.

We ate together and watched "Entertainment Tonight" on the small TV in the kitchen. I alternately broke off small pieces of meat and dropped it down to the waiting felines. Georgio and Shasha got most of them, but little Rags did manage to hunch over a few pieces and hiss protectively.

"Do you always have this audience when you eat?" Laurie asked me, smiling.

"Only when I have chicken," I said. "They're not too big on salads and pasta."

When we finished, she wiped her hands and got up first. She went in the other room, brought back three stacks of papers, and set them down on the tabletop.

"You said you wanted to look over everything, right?" she asked as she was clearing the plates.

"Yeah." I wiped my hands on a paper towel and started examining the three stacks.

"That one is mostly bills," she said. "And that one's junk mail stuff. The other's some things I thought might be important." I picked up that stack first. "There's a letter from a bank there saying that the payment for her safety deposit box is due."

"We'll have to try to get a look-see in that," I said. "We'll probably need the death certificate."

She nodded.

"What's this one?"

"Looked like some kind of storage rental fee," Laurie said, leaning over my shoulder. I felt the warmth of her touch on my neck. "See at the top."

It said Security Storage Facility—Twenty-Four-Hour Access. The address was in Alsip, which was not too far from the hotel where Laurie had stayed. But something else caught my eye: a set of numbers written in across from the dollar amount. Fourteen twenty-seven. I'd seen them before, I just couldn't remember where.

Then it hit me.

I went to the phone, quickly dialed the hotel, and asked for Marsha. I waited for what seemed like an eternity until her husky tenor voice came on the line.

"Hi, babe, it's Ron," I said. "You still have that key you found taped to the Christmas coaster in the women's washroom?"

"Yeah," she said. "Why?"

"I might know how it got there. What were the numbers on it?"

"Just a minute," she said. I listened to her fumbling through what must have been an assortment of junk in the Lost & Found drawer. "Okay, here it is," she said, coming back on the line. "Let's see, fourteen twenty-seven."

"Thanks," I said, looking at Laurie and winking. "You're a lifesaver."

Chapter 27

We parked in back, near the door, and I used my card to enter the locked employee entrance. Laurie asked me if this was the hotel that I normally worked at as we strolled through the back corridor that ran along behind the restaurants and banquet rooms. A couple of housekeeping workers nodded a hello to me.

"Yeah, this is it," I said, thinking that this was also the place where I'd run into Paula that last night. We went through some swinging doors and entered the main lobby area of the hotel. I steered Laurie toward the piano bar and saw that Kathy was just setting up. She waved to us.

"Hi, Ron," she said. "Working tonight, or just out having fun?"

"A little of both," I said. I introduced her to Laurie.

"Your singing is great," Laurie said. "Ron played one of your CDs for me."

"Oh, thank you so much," Kathy said, smiling. "I was just getting ready to start a set. Is there anything in particular you'd like to hear?"

I excused myself and went to the bar. I ordered my usual club soda, and got a diet soft drink for Laurie. I put the drinks on a table near Kathy's piano, and told her I'd be right back. As I walked over toward the main desk, Kathy started singing that Shania Twain song, "From This Moment On." I wondered if that was the song that Laurie had requested.

I used my passkey to open the door behind the front desk and told the switchboard operator to page Marsha.

She picked up her walkie-talkie and talked into it. Marsha's voice came on a few seconds later, saying that she was en route. I leaned against the wall and waited. When the door opened, Marsha came in and gave me an exasperated look.

"So you really know whose key this is?" she asked, going toward the file cabinet where we kept the lost and found items. She took out her ring of keys and slid one into the oval lock. The drawer came open with a rasping sound, and Marsha reached in and pulled out the key, which was still taped to the Christmas coaster. "Well, tell her all the problems she caused me by sticking it in the toilet paper dispenser," she said, handing it to me. "Why the hell did she do that, anyway?"

"That's what I'm trying to figure out myself," I said smiling. I studied the key again, more convinced than ever that I had found a major piece of the puzzle.

After thanking her I went back to the bar. Kathy was just finishing up another song. Laurie saw me coming, took one last drag on her cigarette and stubbed it out just as I sat down, and took a sip of my club soda. She turned her head and blew the smoke away from me. A few people applauded Kathy's song.

"Wow, she sounds even better in person," Laurie said, glancing up at Kathy.

"She sure does." I looked at her. "Are you about ready?"

"Yeah. Where we going?"

I exhaled slowly before I spoke.

"I think I may have put a couple of things together," I said. "But I'm not sure exactly where it's gonna lead. I'm starting to get sort of a strong hunch, but I'm not totally sure I should be taking you along at this point."

"Meaning?"

"Meaning that I told you before this whole thing might

turn out . . ." I shrugged as I searched for a word.

"Ugly?" she said. "You've only mentioned it about a hundred times."

I nodded. "But I'm probably not going to be able to proceed without your help."

She reached out and wrapped her fingers over my hand and squeezed.

"It's okay," she said. "I told you before. I can handle it."

She talked a good game, I thought. But now it was time to walk the walk.

I told her to finish her drink.

The office next to the high cyclone fence was brick, as were the rows of squat-looking buildings behind the fenced-in area. I'd laid the key on the counter and the older guy behind the counter scrutinized it while Laurie related the long sad tale about Paula. The wall behind him contained a panel of glowing lights, buttons, and several television screens depicting the various lanes of the storage facility. I glanced up and saw that we were being videotaped, too. The old guy's eyes went from the key, to his file, to the copy of the death certificate, to Laurie's ID. Finally he shrugged and pushed his glasses up on his rather bulbous nose. The base of it was streaked with a network of broken blood vessels.

"Well, my condolences on your loss, Miss," he said, looking at Laurie. "My record shows that she was last here on December twenty-seventh at nine-forty p.m." He rubbed his nose, then set the file card back down on the counter. "If you want to sign the card, it'll put you on the access list."

Laurie leaned forward and signed it. Her writing looked very similar to Paula's. That might come in handy later, I thought.

"Ron, why don't you sign it too," she said, handing me the pen.

"You want him on it also?" the old man asked.

"Yes," she said.

The old guy shrugged again and watched me sign my name. "Fill these out, please," he said, shoving two file cards across the counter. "Just so there's no mix-up the next time."

The cards requested the standard information like name, social security number, etc.

"So I take it that other fella's not allowed on the sign-in roster?" he asked.

"What other guy?" I said.

"A couple of weeks ago," he said, scratching his jaw. "This guy came in asking about this locker, but he didn't have a key. Told me it belonged to his wife, and asked if I could help him out. He mentioned your cousin by name, and claimed to be her husband." He licked his lips. "I thought something was funny when I asked him for ID, and right away he started hedging. Then he said he wasn't really her husband officially, but her fiancée. Couldn't give me any of the identifiers, like mother's maiden name, or anything, so I told him to bring her back or have her call. He got kinda irate with me till I threatened to call the police. Then he left. Ain't seen him since."

"What did he look like?" I asked.

The old man pursed his lips.

"Kind of a big guy, but not big as you," he said. "Older too. Maybe around fifty. Had gray hair and a mustache."

"Let me guess," I said. "Did he have an English accent?"

"Come to think of it, he did talk kinda funny. Started off sounding normal, then, once he got excited, he did sound sort of like a Limey."

Peeps, I thought.

"Do you remember the date he came in?" I asked.

His lips curled up again as he pondered. "It was after the twenty-seventh," he said. "Maybe the next day or the day after. Before New Year's though."

"Thanks," I said. "I'm glad you're so diligent at doing your job. That guy was a crook, trying to take advantage of the tragedy. An old ex-boyfriend."

The old man nodded with satisfaction at the compliment.

"You want us to sign out when we leave?" I asked.

"Nah," he said. "Just toot the horn twice when you're ready and I'll open the gate." He reached over and pressed a button. "This one deactivates the electronic locking system for that unit," he said. He pushed a second button. "And this one the alarm." He punched a third button and outside the heavy metal gate began to slide open. "You see, we have a state-of-the-art security system here." He grinned.

"Impressive," I said.

We went out and drove The Beater through the gate.

The aisles had been well plowed, showing black asphalt around bases of concrete. The smaller lockers were in the first two rows, each looking to be about the size of a large closet, judging from the size of the doors. Hooded cameras sat watch on steel poles at each juncture. I was going to have to remember to ask him how long they kept their videotapes. Perhaps they still had the late Mr. Peeps trying to gain access. But at this point I wasn't sure if that would be useful.

The next row of structures increased to the size of small brick garages with corrugated metal overhead doors. Number 1427 was emblazoned above the door frame in block style. A crust of snow covered the bottom of the door, indicating that it hadn't been open recently. I hoped it wasn't frozen shut. We got out and I slid the key that Marsha had given me into the lock on the jamb. It went in kind of rough. I twisted, but the lock wouldn't turn.

"Oh no," Laurie said. "Is it the wrong one?"

"No," I said. "Give me your lighter."

She dug a plastic disposable out of her purse and I adjusted the flame to high and held it up to the lock. After a few seconds of applying the heat, I tried the key again and this time I felt the lock turn. I reached down and gripped the handle and then pulled up the door. It raised fairly easily, despite the cold weather and disuse. Inside, the storage compartment was about ten by twelve. It was practically empty except for four suitcases and a black leather traveling case. A single bulb was attached to a fixture on the ceiling. The switch was on the wall near the door.

I turned on the light and looked at the suitcases. They were all identical. Full sized, light blue plastic. The scuffs and scratches along the sides told me that they'd made more than one trip somewhere and back. There was no heat and the wind whipped inside the compartment like the sides weren't even there. I went over to the door and pulled it down.

"Careful. Don't lock us in," Laurie said.

"I won't," I said, watching the door as it went down. "Anyway, you have to turn the key in the lock outside to secure it."

She pretended to smack herself on the head with her palm.

I went back and grabbed one of the suitcases, flipping the catches up. It popped open, exposing a lot of female type undergarments. All lace and nylon. There were a few skirts, blouses, and bikinis rolled up along the bottom. I closed it and opened the second one. Same thing. Undies, slacks, shorts, blouses, a pair of pumps in a plastic bag. The other two were practically identical.

"She certainly had enough underwear," Laurie said.

"Is that about normal?" I asked.

"Well, it's a lot more than I would need, given the amount of regular clothes in there. I mean, she could have changed three times a day."

I closed the last suitcase and went to the travel case. It was black leather with a zippered top and several compartments on the side and heavy enough to tell me it was full. Opening the top one first, I pulled the sides away, exposing stacks of cash. I pulled one of the bundles out and looked at it. All twenties, rubber-banded together. Probably around a thousand, I estimated.

"Is that all money?" Laurie asked incredulously.

I nodded, replaced the sheaf of currency, and opened the side compartments. Paula's IDs, ATM card, safety deposit box key, credit cards, and passport were all inside. I thumbed through the passport and found the pages littered with visa stamps. Thailand, the Philippines, Taiwan, Jamaica.

Laurie looked at me, the space between her eyebrows furrowing.

"What does all this mean, Ron?"

I sighed, slipped the passport back in the case, and zippered it closed.

"Let's load this stuff in my car and we'll look it over at the house," I said, pretending my shiver was from the cold. "We'll make sense of it there."

But I already had a pretty good idea.

Chapter 28

In my gut I knew what it all meant when we were still in the storage compartment, but didn't want to tell Laurie just then. I figured it would be better at the house. Maybe she had it figured out too, because she didn't look very surprised when I got some tools and began taking the lining out of one of the now-empty suitcases. With the hollow sides and bottom, they had been able to fit a substantial amount in each one. I didn't bother taking each one apart. I just dumped their contents and tested their weight against the one I'd already emptied.

"Is that what I think it is?" she asked.

I smelled one of the packages. It was bitter and acrid even through the plastic.

"Heroin probably," I said.

"But wouldn't those narcotic dogs smell it through the suitcase?" she asked. "They show them walking through airports all the time on TV."

"What they don't show are the tremendous crowds that go through O'Hare every day," I said. "Plus, after September eleventh, most of their efforts have been on checking people getting onto planes, not off. There're so many people, they'd need to put a dog at every corner. So they usually operate less conspicuously. Certain types of people who seem nervous, or fit a certain profile. Then they bring in the dog. If Paula was cool, calm, and collected . . ." I stooped and picked up some lacy underpants. "And what customs agent is going to spend a lot of time fingering through this stuff looking like a pervert, when some ninety-two-year-old grandmother is standing next in line watching?"

"And all the money?" she said, her face looking ashen. "Is that where it came from?"

I didn't say anything. I didn't have to. She shook her head, her mouth compressing in on itself. "That idiot," she muttered. "That stupid, stupid idiot." But in another moment the tears welled up in her eyes. I gently patted her back and walked her over to the couch, sat her down, and got her some tissues. She thanked me and blew her nose. Her face was red and puffy around the eyes.

"Oh, Ron, how—how could she?"

I searched for something profound to say, but came up empty. I muttered that I didn't know and put my arm around her. We sat like that for awhile until the phone rang. I gently extricated my arm from her shoulders and went over to answer it.

"I found Alley," Chappie said. "He down at Cook County."

"What?" I said. "Jail?"

"No," he said. "Hospital. I couldn't understand him no way, so a nurse got on and talked to me. That Russian priest got beat up real bad. Might not make it. Alley's been down there praying."

"Ahhh, shit," I said. I saw Laurie glance over at me. "What room's he in?"

The walls were painted a dingy shade of green, and the white polyester curtain that had been pulled around Father Boris's bed like a make-shift wall did little to shield the conversations of the people talking to the patient in the next bed. A loud TV blared some sitcom, and the canned laughter came at regular intervals.

Father Boris had tubes coming out of his nose, more tubes coming from under the sheet, and casts on both of his arms and on one of his legs. The dark bruises under each of his eyes were turning purple, and from the swelling of his nose, I knew it was broken too. He swallowed dryly and said something to Alley in Russian.

Alley, who looked like he'd been in a train wreck himself, seemed to protest, but the priest only closed his eyes and softly repeated himself. Alley stood, tears welling up in his eyes as he looked at Laurie and me, and left.

I watched him go out the door, then heard Father Boris say, "I told him to go get something to eat in the cafeteria."

"What happened, padre?" I asked.

He swallowed again, and licked his lips.

"If you could get me a sip of water," he said. Laurie went to the night stand and fitted the straw from his water bottle to his lips. With much effort, he seemed able to pull up a trickle of liquid. Then he nodded and managed a weak smile. "I went to Smershkevich myself," he said. "Like a fool, I thought I could reason with him. Appeal to his sense of Russian compassion." He exhaled softly. "When that didn't work, I tried to imply a threat of going to the authorities." Boris closed his eyes and his face seemed to quiver slightly. I realized that he was trying to laugh. "Obviously he was not intimidated."

"Did you make out a police report?" I said. "He can be arrested for this. I got a buddy on Chicago PD. I can call him if you want."

Father Boris shook his head slightly, his eyes still closed.

"He did not do this himself," he said. "He has many hired thugs to do his bidding. Anyway, he made it clear that they would harm Allyosha if I called the authorities."

"But you can't let him get away with this," I said.

"Mr. Shade, he already has."

We stayed for about fifteen more minutes, then a nurse came by and said that visiting hours were ending. Father Boris made me promise to talk to Alley and convince him not to try to go after Smershkevich himself. I said I'd do my best, and when Alley came back up the priest told him to go with me. Outside the temperature had continued to warm up, but a cold, drizzly rain had begun to fall. We ended up driving Alley to his night maintenance job. He sat in the back seat looking like the weight of the world was on his shoulders. I asked him if he'd had any sleep, and he shook his head.

"Tomorrow you sleep," I said. "Then call me." I gave him one of my cards.

He nodded and put the card in his pocket. When we dropped him off, he shook my hand and tipped his hat respectfully at Laurie.

"Oh my God, Ron," she said after he'd left. "He looked awful."

"Which one?" I asked, swinging The Beater back out into traffic.

"Both of them. What are they going to do?"

"I don't know. I was hoping that George might be able to get something on that Smershkevich guy, but this sorta ups the ante."

"I'll say."

We rode on in silence a few more blocks, listening to the windshield wipers squeaking across the glass. Then she said, "What about our case?"

"Well, it's pretty clear that Paula was mixed up with some bad people," I said. "We have to establish a tie-in to them and the drugs we found, then I can turn it over to George and let him make the arrest."

"But what about the Peeps thing?" she said. "Aren't you worried that the police are after you for that?"

"It's obvious that Peeps was in on it. Otherwise, how would he know to show up at the storage facility? My guess is that him and Paula had some kind of side deal going. Red, or Regis, was after Paula that night I bumped into her. He probably caught her the next day." I paused to let the obvious sink in, then said, "He probably killed Peeps too, looking for the stash."

"I still can't believe it," Laurie said, shaking her head. "That she'd do something like that."

"Well, she must have fallen in with the wrong crowd," I said. "And the financial motivation was obviously very good. Those kind of people like to find young women who are susceptible to the lure of easy money so they can take all the risks. They offer them three, four, maybe even six grand to fly to Bangkok, the Philippines, or maybe even Puerto Rico, pick up a suitcase or two, and bring them to a rendez-vous place in the States. It's pretty tempting."

"But why did they have to kill her?" Laurie asked.

I hesitated before answering, then figured I'd have to tell her my hunch sooner or later. It might as well be sooner.

"I think, from the looks of it, Paula wasn't exactly a neophyte in all this," I said. "The amount of cash in that bag shows that she made more than one trip. We don't know what we'll find in her safety deposit box. Maybe she and Peeps planned to keep the money and the dope this time and split."

"Do you really think so?" she said. Her gaze sank to her lap. When I didn't answer, she said, "Yeah, of course. She tried to double-cross them, and they killed her. That's what happened, isn't it? Can we do anything?"

Luckily my answer was delayed by my getting on the ex-

pressway. We clattered through a couple of invisible pot-
holes filled with black water as I pressed the accelerator
down and The Beater's big engine swung us into the entry
lane way ahead of a swarm of approaching cars.

"Like I told you, babe," I said, "all we have to do now is
figure out a way to hook 'em up and George can reel 'em
in."

Chapter 29

I took the luxury of sleeping till six, then got up for my early morning run, taking my time on this one. I wanted to draw it out to think, and also didn't want to risk tripping in the dark and getting hurt with the fight so close. The rain had greatly reduced the snow, allowing patches of green to show through wherever the big dirty piles hadn't been substantial enough to endure. I whimsically hoped that it was some kind of omen: things obscured before, now coming into view. But as I ran across the park, several times my shoes sank into the murky grass with a sucking sound. So much for omens. I stayed to the asphalt and streets as much as I could.

When I got back, Laurie was waiting for me dressed in jeans and a sweatshirt. Her face had a freshly scrubbed look, and she held a small mirror in one hand and a mascara brush in the other as she sat on one of the kitchen chairs with her leg curled under her. The back porch had the smell of a recently smoked cigarette.

"You're up early," I said.

"Couldn't sleep. Want me to fix you something to eat?"

"No thanks. I'm supposed to meet George for breakfast. I'd better run some things by him to bring him up to speed."

"Okay," she said. "I'll keep myself busy doing some cleaning around here. If that's okay, that is." She smiled.

"Sure," I said, "it's the maid's day off." After giving her a quick course on using my ancient vacuum cleaner, I showered. In fifteen minutes I was walking out the door and steering The Beater toward Karson's Restaurant at 111th

and Western. When I walked in, George was already sitting at a booth reading a copy of the *Sun-Times* and sipping from a cup of dark coffee.

"Morning," I said, slipping in opposite him. He grunted and drank some more coffee. The bags under his eyes made his skin seem more sallow than usual. "You look like shit. Didn't you get any sleep?"

"Some," he said. "Kept waking up." He yawned, blinked twice, and managed a weak grin. "You didn't bring that damn cat with you this time, did you?"

"No."

"How's he doing?"

"Real good," I said, "Except I think he was disappointed that I didn't name him George Jr."

He frowned.

The waitress came and we made our standard orders. Eggs over easy for him, scrambled for me.

When she'd gone I gave him a quick synopsis of what we'd found in the storage compartment last night and the theory that I'd come up with. His face brightened as I gave him the details.

"This changes things," he said. "A lot. So you're thinking that Paula was a mule for this Olijede guy, and that her and Peeps tried a rip. They found out and killed her. But why'd they take so long to ice him?"

"Maybe they didn't know he was involved in the rip-off part of it," I said. "Or maybe she was planning on cutting him out. The phone records show that Paula called Peeps from my house that last morning, right? Obviously they were gonna meet. She must have told him something about me, because I've pretty much confirmed that he was the one who set me up on that wild goose chase and then burglarized my house. Probably Paula's place too."

"Looking for the key to the storage locker," George said.

"Right," I said. "And when he couldn't find it, he went to the storage place and tried to bluff his way in. Only the old guy who runs the joint wouldn't let him in without a key. So that means he knew about the locker, but not where she'd put the key. Which means she didn't trust him completely."

"Or she was planning on cutting him out, too," George said. He took a long sip of his coffee, and set the cup down in its saucer. "So you figure that she called Peeps from your place to set up a meet?"

"Or maybe to explain why she'd missed one," I said.

"Then what?" he asked.

"Then she called a taxi and went back out to the Lincoln Estates Holiday Inn," I said. "Probably to pick up her car, which she'd left there. I figure that she was originally supposed to be met at the airport by Red, but she must have taken an earlier flight. She took the shuttle bus to Alsip from the airport, and dumped the suitcases in the storage facility. It's not that far from the shuttle bus stop. Then she took the next shuttle to Lincoln Estates. Her car had previously been left there. Maybe by Peeps with some decoy suitcases in it. She had the original luggage tags in her purse. I saw them. Attach those tags to the decoy suitcases, and she'd have some breathing time before the switch was discovered. But Red must have figured out the double-cross when she didn't show, and traced her to the hotel. Probably through the car being there. Maybe some more of Olijede's goons saw Peeps drive it there."

"And they grabbed her the next morning when she went back to get her ride?" George said.

"Right. And remember the coppers out there said the trunk had been punched?"

He nodded.

"Well, I figure that maybe Red did that, found the decoy suitcases, and figured he had the stuff." I took a deep breath, trying not to extrapolate about the next part. "Then when Paula showed up out there, they grabbed her, thinking that they had the stuff and . . ."

"They decided to tie up their loose end right then and there," he said. Pausing, George ran his tongue over his teeth. "But why did she go back for her car? She had to figure that Red might be watching."

"Remember that she'd left the key to the storage locker in the ladies' room at the hotel," I said. "Plus, she called me back and asked if she could lay low at my place. They must have grabbed her right after she left that message and before she could retrieve the key."

"And they obviously wanted to make her death look like a hit-and-run to divert suspicion. It wasn't until later, when they checked the suitcases, that they discovered that she'd stashed the dope," he said.

I glanced down at the table, trying not to think too hard about that portion of it.

"But that still don't tie in Peeps' murder to all this," he said. "And that's what we really need."

"Unless old man Turner, the building super, had called Red and tipped him that we were in Paula's apartment that afternoon I caught him with the clone phone," I said. "If Red was lurking close, he could have followed me to Peeps' office building . . ."

"And whacked him after you left," he said. "Makes good sense, Ron. Especially if they knew that Peeps was connected to Paula."

"I'm sure they did," I said. "She must have been using her modeling assignments as a cover to travel out of the country. Peeps probably went along as part of the scam on at least a couple of them."

"Might even have avoided X-ray detection by claiming that his undeveloped negatives were in the suitcases," George said. "So where's the shit at?"

"Everything's still at my place," I said.

"Well, hell, you've got to make arrangements to turn it in," he said. "We can inventory it, then get started on re-opening the investigation of Paula's death."

"What about the bag of money?" I said.

"Ron, it's evidence," he said. "And you'd better check out that safety deposit box too. If there's more cash in it, that's a federal offense."

"I'll have to talk to my client about that first," I said.

He frowned. "You ain't thinking about keeping it, are you? How you gonna explain that to the IRS?"

"It's not mine to keep," I said. "But I'm just not sure that turning it over to the state is the right answer either."

"It's fucking drug money, for Christ's sake."

"It's also what Paula died for," I said. "Maybe her family should get something out of all this besides a lot of bad memories and shattered illusions."

He exhaled loudly through his nostrils. "All right, god-dammit. But at least let me confiscate the dope. You definitely don't want to get caught holding any of that shit."

"Yeah," I said. "But where do we go from here?"

"Well." He raised his eyebrows and rubbed his jaw. "We got some leads to explore. Maybe the best thing would be to see what came back on those names you gave me yesterday. Then pull a couple of them in for questioning. The main thing is we can probably introduce all this stuff and it'll be enough to get those two pricks Reed and Randecki off your back."

I stared at him. The waitress came and set down our

plates. When she'd gone I said, "I been thinking."

"Oh no," he said, spreading some strawberry jelly on a piece of toast. "That's always a danger sign."

"Suppose I contact this Olijede guy . . . Offer to sell him back the dope for a finder's fee."

He blew out another slow breath as he dipped the toast into the yoke of his eggs.

"I don't know, Ron. You been making a real mess out of things as it is, and that sounds kinda risky."

"Hell, everything's risky. And what do you mean, I been making a mess out of things?"

He smirked. "I mean that it's time to leave this to the professionals." He bit into the jelly-covered toast.

"Thanks a lot. So what's your idea to tie all this together?"

He considered this for a moment.

"It's gonna entail some major planning," he said. "We got to move real cautious on this. Plus, whatever it is, I'll have to sell it to the brass."

After breakfast I picked up Alley from his midnight maintenance job. His head shot up when I tapped the horn, and he smiled wearily as he trudged over to The Beater, looking like he'd been run over by a truck. I took him home, over his protestations, and told him that Father Boris had made me promise to make sure he got some sleep. He finally acquiesced. As he got out of the car at the house where he rented a room, he moved with the stagger of exhaustion. I wondered, with all the problems I had going at the moment, what I was going to be able to do to help him.

Laurie wasn't there when I got back to my house. I found all of my laundry stacked and folded in the red plastic basket, and a note written in her flowing script on top.

Dear Ron,

Gone shopping!!! Be back later with enough groceries to fix you a very special dinner. Go for your workout and I'll see you later this afternoon. Took your spare keys.

Love you,
Laurie

Love? I wondered if that meant she was thinking seriously about staying. I re-read the last lines. Pretty soon we were going to have to sit down and have *the talk*. I glanced over at the four light blue suitcases sitting in my living room and remembered George's advice: "You don't want to get caught holding that shit." He was right. My house wasn't the best place for them. I'd decided to take them back to the storage facility for the time being when the phone rang. It was Chappie.

"What you doing?" he asked me. I sensed a tone of subdued excitement in his voice.

"Just getting ready to go out," I said. "Why?"

"Saul called," he said. "Some dudes from ESPN are coming over to do an interview with you and maybe some filming of you training. What time can you get here?"

"Give me an hour," I said.

"Okay," Chappie said. "Saul was real excited. Figures this will really hype the fight."

"I'm surprised that they're paying this much attention to a kickboxing match," I said.

"Yeah, me too. But I guess they was up at Detroit last night for a Red Wings game, and Elijah Day was there doing some woffin'. Now they want to get you doin' some too."

"Good," I said. "I'm in a woffin' mood."

Chapter 30

Before hitting the gym I shot over to the storage facility and dropped off all of the suitcases. I figured the cash would be safe enough there, and I certainly didn't want to take the chance that Reed and Randecki would unexpectedly show up with a warrant to search my house and find a large stash of money and dope. That would just about guarantee my future. As it was, I wasn't worried about being framed for the Peeps murder. I mean, I wasn't overjoyed about being number one on their hit parade, but I had faith that George would be able to clear things up, especially the way they were falling in place.

Still, I didn't want to take a chance. I had enough to worry about with the fight now only about fifty-five hours away. I pondered the situation as I drove to the gym for my fifteen minutes of fame.

Inside a crew of three guys was there. One guy to interview me, one guy with a camcorder, and another guy who set up a small TV to monitor everything. They asked me to take off my shirt, then let Chappie and me watch the tape of Day shooting his mouth off at the hockey game the night before. On the small screen, standing next to the diminutive announcer, Day looked as big as a house, his dark, shaved head glistening under the stadium lights, along with the thick gold rope around his neck.

"The Red Wings are kicking butt, just like I'm gonna do Friday night in Chicago," Day was saying. A Bundini

Brown-type sycophant stood just behind him, echoing everything Day said like some poor man's version of a Greek chorus.

"Yeah, we gonna be kicking butt," the sycophant said.

"Now, correct me if I'm wrong," the announcer said, "but didn't Ron Shade beat you in your previous fight?"

Day shot the smaller man an intimidating glare, causing the announcer to edge away slightly.

"Nah, that ain't true," Day said. "I didn't even train for that fight, and I still gave him all he could handle."

"He didn't even train," echoed the chorus.

"I been training harder than I ever trained . . ."

"Harder than he ever trained."

"And now," Day said, grinning into the camera, "I'm the champion."

"We the champ, we the champ," said the chorus.

"So you're predicting a victory then, Elijah?" asked the announcer.

"I'm predicting that I'll take Shade out," Day replied, holding up his massive fist. "Shade's gonna think it's Friday the thirteenth, and I'm that dude in the hockey mask. What's his name? Jason?"

"Yeah, Jason," the sycophant said. "Friday the thirteenth!"

The announcer started to wish him luck, and Day and his chorus began to mug some more for the camera by saying in unison, "Remember, always bet on black."

I wondered what Wesley Snipes was going to say if he heard Day was stealing the line from *Passenger 57.* "Shut that motherfucking thing off," Chappie said. "We gonna really have to kick that boy's ass now, after he be woffin' like that."

The guy who held the microphone smiled as he came

forward. He looked to the cameraman and asked if they were rolling. The cameraman nodded and focused on the face of the other man. The twin globes of the camera lights felt hot and blinding. I canted my head so I wouldn't have to look directly into them.

"This is Todd Tracey and we're at The Beverly Gym in Chicago where Full-Contact Karate fighter Ron Shade is training for his match Friday night for the Heavyweight Championship against titleholder Elijah Day." He paused and turned to me, holding the microphone between us. "Ron, how long have you been preparing for this fight?"

"It seems like forever," I said.

"You look in pretty good shape. Do you feel ready?"

"I'm ready." I saw Chappie standing in back of the cameraman frowning and jerking his raised thumb up and down, which was his signal for me to elevate the hype. "I've trained for this fight harder than any match I've ever had. I've beaten Day before, and I'll do it again."

"That's right, you did win your last match up," the announcer said. "Do you feel his style will present a problem for you this time?"

"Day's a good fighter, no doubt about it," I said. Chappie frowned and started with the thumb again. "But he keeps forgetting that I didn't just beat him last time. I knocked him out."

The announcer winced and drew his forefinger across his throat. The cameraman stopped.

"Ron, we'd rather you didn't mention that you knocked him out," the announcer said.

"Why the fuck not?" Chappie asked. The announcer smiled.

"It's a matter of marketing," he said, almost apologetically. "We're trying to promote this bout as a potential war, an even-money match-up. If people think that Day was knocked out last time, it diminishes his stature, and hence, the fight will be seen as a cakewalk."

"A cakewalk?" Chappie said. He snorted in disgust. "You ain't never stepped inside them ropes for real, has you?"

The announcer smiled again. More nervously this time.

"No, sir," he said. "Nor would I. But, gentlemen, if you please, time is the network's money." He flashed his smile again.

"Maybe you could pan around the gym some and do a voice-over?" I said. "Give the place some publicity?"

"Sure, we'll get it in," the announcer said. "Now let's take it from the point where I asked you if his style will present any particular problem for you. Okay?"

I nodded. Chappie grinned.

"All I can say is," I said, glaring and holding my clenched fist toward the camera, "Day's gonna wish he *was* wearing that hockey mask he was talking about once he steps into that ring, regardless of whether it's Friday the thirteenth, or not."

It went on like that for about twenty more minutes, then they interviewed Chappie a bit. I silently wondered how much of the interview would be edited out, and asked them as they were packing their stuff.

"Don't know," Todd the announcer said. "Depends on how they want to run the spot." He shot me the high voltage smile again, and added, "We'll send you a cassette of it."

Yeah, I thought. I'm not so sure I'd want one after they'd butchered it, but it might be nice for posterity.

When they'd gone, Chappie told me to change into my

workout clothes and we'd go through a quick one. I nodded wearily.

"What, that bullshit that Day was spoutin' get to you?" he asked.

I shrugged.

"I just want it to get here," I said.

He smiled.

"I know the feeling," he said. "But you can't rush it. It'll be here soon enough. Then you got to remember our strategy. You set up the bait, and let him come to you." His fists shot out and snapped a quick three-punch combination in the air. "That the way to win."

Set up the bait and let him come to you, I silently repeated. Sounded like a formula for success.

After my workout I spent ten minutes in the steam, then jumped directly into the shower. As I let the cold water sluice over my body, I pushed the pictures of Elijah Day out of my head, and thought about the other Olijede. I didn't even know what he looked like. But I knew Red.

And maybe it was time to start baiting the trap for them as well.

After I dried off I took my time getting dressed and pondered my next move. It wouldn't do any harm, I figured, to start the ball rolling a little bit. That way I could go to George and hand him the whole thing with a ribbon around it. He'd told me to sit back and do nothing, but I was tired of just taking punches. What the hell, I had to take some definitive action myself for once, right? I gave myself a mental affirmative and fished out a couple of coins from my pants pocket and went to the pay phone in the locker room. I figured it was safer using that one just in case Olijede had a caller ID box; it would just come across as The Beverly Gym.

I paged through my pocket notebook until I found the number I'd written down for Lothar Industries and dialed it.

It rang three times and the same recording as before came on and said to leave a message.

"This is for Mr. Olijede," I said. "I've recovered some property of yours, and I'd like to speak to you about my finder's fee for returning it. The name's Shade. You can reach me at . . ." After hesitating, I left my beeper number then hung up. What the hell. I had to give them a way to call back.

I clapped my palms together, feeling strangely good that I'd taken some small step toward getting to the end of this mess. The bait was set.

Laurie was back by the time I got home. It looked like she'd practically bought out the grocery store and the whole kitchen table was covered with bags, foods, and other stuff. Plus, the cats all sat around the table dutifully watching her. She smiled at me as I came in.

"Hi," she said. "I thought I'd splurge a little, since you're being so nice and letting me stay here and all."

"It's been my pleasure."

"So I bought all kinds of good things. I checked your refrigerator before I left. You needed them."

"Thanks," I said.

"What would you like me to fix?" she asked.

I glanced at my watch. It was close to three-fifteen.

"Before I decide," I said, "you still got that receipt and key for Paula's safety deposit box?"

"Yeah. Why?"

"I was talking to George this morning and he suggested that we turn over everything to him."

"Okay," she said slowly.

"Now if we turn over the suitcases, he'll be able to re-open the investigation on Paula's death," I said. "Or at least come at it from a different angle."

"Good," she said.

"But it'll also mean that you'll lose everything. All the money that she had."

"I don't care about that," she said, shaking her head.

"Maybe you don't. But we have no way of knowing exactly how much money she earned legitimately, either. And I'd like to see you and your family come out of this tragedy with a little more than a lot of bad memories."

"But is that ethical?"

"To hell with what's ethical," I said. "Your cousin's dead. Let's do some good with what's left as we pick up the pieces. It's better than the state or the feds taking everything, right?"

Laurie looked at the floor. Georgio stepped forward and rubbed against her leg. She reached down and stroked his arching back.

"It's your choice, Laurie."

"Okay, Ron, what should we do?"

"Let's go check out her safety deposit box," I said. "And do it now, while we still have time. Before the cops and the DEA clamp a lid down on everything."

Laurie sighed. "If you say so."

God, I thought, she's got a lot to learn about the real world soon if she's going to become a lawyer.

The bank was downtown. All ATMs, busy tellers, ringing phones, and smiling personnel. A uniformed security guard stood watch near the front doors. He told us the safety deposit boxes were on the basement level. The escalator glided downward, leaving us off at a T-shaped corridor. Off to the right a rather plump-looking black girl sat behind a long countertop going over papers. We presented the key, a copy of the death certificate, and Laurie's Michigan driver's license.

"I'm not sure if I should do this without authorization," she said.

"Come on, Miss," I said, turning up the voltage in my smile a few watts. "We're down here all the way from Michigan to settle her cousin's affairs. We'd really appreciate a little help here."

She bit her lower lip.

"Okay," she said. "You've still got the key, right?" Moments later she led us into the vault and slipped the flat keys into the two holes. The drawer, which was one of the large size, pulled out slowly and felt substantial in my hands. Inside the privacy room, we sat down and lifted the metal lid, and saw several stacks of currency wedged into the box. Laurie looked over at me, and I held a finger to my lips.

"Just put as much as you can in your purse," I whispered. "I'll take the rest."

Anticipating that there might be a lot to carry, I'd brought along a collapsible nylon gym bag. We managed to stuff all the money into it, and then returned the empty drawer to the bank girl.

"There wasn't any currency in there, was there?" she asked. " 'Cause then you'll have to make out a declaration."

"Just family heirlooms," I said, holding up the bag and smiling. "And photographs of old friends."

As I drove home, Laurie counted. The rush hour traffic made it slow going, so she was glad to have something to do. I was anxious to see how much Paula had stashed away for a rainy day myself.

"Fifty thousand, Ron," Laurie said, turning to look at me as we crept toward the right lanes as we neared 95th Street. "This is so unbelievable."

"Yeah," I said, thinking we knew for sure now that Paula hadn't been a neophyte. But then again, I never thought she was.

"This means that she was pretty heavily involved, doesn't it?" Laurie asked, seeming to read my thoughts.

"It kind of removes any lingering doubts."

She compressed her lips and let her hands fall to her lap.

"I don't think I even want to know who killed her anymore." A depressed resignation had crept into her voice. "And I don't want this damn drug money either."

"Like I said, that's a decision you need to make later. Right now . . ." I paused as I swung over to get on I-57 south as the Ryan Expressway ended. "We need to finish tying this thing up. I was going to wait to give you a written report, but maybe it's better to just run it by you now."

I told her my best estimation of what exactly had happened, from Paula's involvement with Peeps, to the probable double-cross. When I'd finished, she was silent for the rest of the ride home, and I wondered exactly what effect my words had on her. When I pulled up in front of the house she glanced over at me with a tentative smile and said, "Okay, what's our next move?"

Our next move turned out to be rushing to my bank and having her open a safety deposit box account in her name using my address. I was on it as secondary signer. After we'd deposited the recovered funds discreetly inside her new box, we turned and left. As we walked to The Beater

Laurie hugged my arm.

"You of course read that part on the agreement about not storing cash in the safety deposit box, correct?"

"Yeah," I said. "But it beats filling out a declaration when it comes time to draw out more than ten thousand."

"Roger, wilco," she said, saluting. "See, I've been practicing."

"Practicing what?"

"My para-military skills so I can help you catch this Nigerian guy when we spring the trap on him."

"Wrong." I stopped walking. "We don't spring the trap. I do. Along with George."

"But—"

"No buts," I said, interrupting her. "It's too dangerous for you to get involved."

"Aren't I already involved?"

"Yeah, I guess you are. But it's going to be kept to a minimum from this point on."

"We'll see," she said, flashing a lips-only smile.

When we got home, I sat back and let Laurie fix the spectacular meal of roasted chicken and baked potatoes she'd been planning. She even fed the cats. I watched the news, then we ate together in the kitchen. Silently I wondered about the note she'd written earlier and signed, *Love you, Laurie*. Was this breach of client/private investigator ethics going farther and faster than I'd intended? Obviously the answer was yes. . . . But what exactly had I been intending? And how far should I let it go? That and other imponderables weighed heavily on me as we went into the living room to watch *Casablanca* again. It had been a few nights since we'd seen it and Laurie wanted me to explain all the nuances and references in it.

"What's the significance of that song?" she asked as

Laszlo fires up the band to play the French National Anthem to foil the Nazis.

By the time Ingrid snuck off to meet Bogey, we were snuggling, and when he said, "We'll always have Paris." I was carrying her off to the bedroom.

"What about the tape?" she murmured, her lips pressed to mine.

"You know how it ends."

Later on, as we lay tangled together under the covers basking in the afterglow of passion well spent, I wondered if my comment on the movie's unhappy ending had been more appropriate or prescient.

Laurie shifted on top of me, lifting her head, which had been resting on my chest.

"So is Chappie right?"

"Chappie's always right," I said. "Just ask him."

She giggled. "No, silly, I mean about this weakening your legs."

"I'll be all right as long as I can rest up Friday," I said. "But we probably should cool it tomorrow night, though."

"Okay. I just don't want to be detrimental to you in this fight," she said. "I don't want you blaming me afterwards in the unlikely event that you don't win."

"You won't have to worry about that. 'Cause I'm gonna win."

And if I don't, I thought, I know who to blame.

Chapter 31

Thursday turned out to be more of the waiting game. My beeper never went off, making me wonder if Olijede even got the bait set-up I left. George called and I filled him in on my actions thus far. He was silent at first, then relented, saying that he was having a harder time than expected trying to reason with Reed and Randecki.

"Those two pricks couldn't find their assholes with both hands," he said. "But I'm working on things. Just keep the stash where it is for now and get hold of me right away if that guy contacts you."

I said I would.

"Maybe I can get some guys in Narcotics interested in helping out. Then we can take him down ourselves and not worry about them two jerks."

"Okay, brother."

"And, Ron . . ."

"Yeah?" I figured he was going to wish me luck on the fight but instead he said, "Just don't try to do anything else by yourself, all right? Just let us pros handle it."

"Okay," was all I said, even though the anger over his dismissal of my abilities burned in my gut.

So I was pretty much relegated to sitting around watching the clock and thinking about Elijah Day. I did call the hospital to check on Father Boris, who was resting comfortably with Alley at his bedside. Then picked up Paula's Firebird from Big Ed's, who replaced the damaged trunk lid for us. We also touched bases with the movers to make sure everything was set for the next day and found out they'd tow the Firebird up to Michigan for an extra fee. Laurie agreed and I followed her up to Paula's old apartment parking lot.

Initially we'd figured to leave the Firebird there for the next day, but Laurie waved to me as I began pulling into the reserved spot.

"Ron, I don't think the insurance is still valid on her car," she said. "You don't think it would get broken into or stolen here, do you?"

I glanced around the neighborhood.

"No one to watch it real close," I said. "We could leave it at my place tonight, and drive it down in the morning."

"Maybe that would be a better idea," she said.

It would also be smarter just in case Red or Olijede was still keeping watch on Paula's old digs, I thought. But the chance that they were going to take my bait was getting doubtful. Maybe they realized the jig was up, and decided to cut their losses and run for the border. Or at least out of the area for a while.

So we left Laurie's Nissan in the spot instead of the Firebird. We managed to put most of the stuff that she wanted in the boxes the movers had provided, and left the rest of the stuff for them to pack. We even called old Mr. Turner to tell him the apartment would be vacant after tomorrow.

"Suit yourself," the old man said. "You ever find out about that phone?"

"Yeah, it was hot," I said. "The cops have it. That guy ever call back asking about us?"

"Nah," he said, and hung up.

What an old grouch, I thought. He probably didn't have anybody to call with the damn phone anyway.

I drove the Firebird back, appreciating the smooth acceleration of the engine as I stepped lightly on the gas.

"This baby reminds me of my Camaro," I told Laurie as we cruised along at seventy in the express lanes.

"You had another car besides The Beater?"

"A black Camaro. It got stolen."

"Oh, that's too bad," she said.

After sticking the Firebird into my garage, we both got our bags and headed to the gym for a light workout. As we were getting into my car, Laurie told me that she'd only had two cigarettes all day.

"That's great," I said.

"You seem to be having a salubrious effect on me," she said.

"What's that mean?"

"That you've been good for me." She leaned over to kiss me.

Right, I thought, but will you still think that when semester break's over and it's time to get back to your other world?

It seemed strange not to have to run Friday morning when I woke up. The day's first light was just starting to nudge its way between the slits of the blinds as I lay there with Laurie entwined next to me and the three cats each curled up in one of the folds of the heavy quilt. True to our word, she'd kept her panties on all night and we'd abstained. But now I found myself feeling restless. Maybe it would have been better not to vary our routine after all, despite my promise to Chappie. But he'd pulled me aside and practically begged me to rest up until the fight.

"Nothing even remotely strenuous," he'd said. "Please." With a request phrased like that, what could I do?

But now I almost felt like getting out of bed and going for my run. Work out the kinks. Break a sweat. But I didn't. Chappie was right. If I wanted to win, I had to conserve my energy today. I was going to need all of it tonight.

"Don't waste a minute doing nothing that ain't restin'," Chappie had stressed. "Don't even get up to go to the bathroom lessin' you really have to."

"Why would I do that if I didn't?" I said. But I knew what he was trying to say. Conserve and conquer. Elijah Day was the one who had that long drive or flight down from the Motor City. That put the home court advantage in my corner.

By seven-fifteen I just couldn't stay in bed any longer anyway. My alarm clock rang a few minutes later. Laurie had to be up at Paula's by eight to meet the movers, so I said I'd drive her.

"No, don't be silly," she said. "You rest. I'll just take the Firebird up and drive my Nissan back, once they get everything started. I need to make a few stops on the way back anyway."

"No, I've got to do something, or I'll go crazy. I'll follow you up in The Beater in case you have problems or anything."

We stopped at a coffee shop and got two toasted bagels with cream cheese and coffee. Plain for her and whole wheat for me. Then we shot over to the expressway and headed north. Unfortunately, when we got to Paula's old place, the movers were nowhere to be seen. She pulled over to the curb ahead of me, stopped, and came back to my car.

"Where are they?" Laurie asked, looking at her watch. "It's eight-fifteen. They were supposed to be here by now."

"Call them." I pulled out my cell phone and handed it to her.

She dialed and spoke to someone who said that the truck was on the way and that traffic must be heavy or something.

"I guess we'll just have to wait," she said. "Sorry."

"That's okay," I said. "Chappie wanted me to rest anyway."

At nine-fifteen the truck finally showed up. A crew of five Mexicans got out of a van behind the truck and they all headed for the apartment. I honked my horn and waved at them.

"Where you guys been?" I asked.

"*Lo siento, senor.* Un, I am sorry, Sir," a swarthy guy who looked to be the foreman said, rolling his head apologetically. He spoke to the group in rapid Spanish, then turned back to me. "We got all tied up."

"Yeah," I said, figuring I'd leave my run-for-the-border/immigration jokes for another time. Or unless I needed to light a fire under them. But then I could always call up Raul and ask him to come over. He'd know exactly what to say to light a fire under their asses.

Laurie told the honcho the apartment number, and we all started over to the building with them. Just then my beeper went off. I quickly checked to see if it was Olijede, but it was the number for the gym. I dialed my cell phone and got Chappie on the first ring.

"Yeah, what's up?" I said.

"I called your house and got no answer. You supposed to be resting."

"I am. I just had to get out of there for awhile."

"You feel up to doing another interview?"

"Sure," I said. "Who is it this time?"

"Outfit called Reel Sports."

"Never heard of them."

"Me neither. Supposed to be a new show on cable, or

something. Called me at eight saying they wanted to set up an interview with us. I said okay, then they called me back a couple of minutes ago wantin' to know if we was good to go this morning at ten sharp. Guess they doing a show on the sport of kickboxing and was interested in making you their feature attraction. But this morning they only gonna be in town a short time."

"Maybe they ought to wait till I win," I said, laughing.

"Yeah, well, they backing it up. Offered to pay us a grand just for doing the interview before the fight."

"For that kind of money I'll even put on an exhibition for them."

"No, you ain't," he said. "I probably shouldn't even be letting you do this."

"Chappie, I'll be fine." I glanced at my watch. Nine-twenty-three. "See you at ten."

When I turned to Laurie, she looked quizzical. I explained things and asked if she'd mind watching over the group of movers for an hour or two till I got back.

"Not at all," she said. "You go ahead."

"Okay," I said, watching the amigos unload their dollies from the big truck. "I'll be back as soon as I can."

"Don't worry. I can take the Nissan back. I'll be fine." She leaned forward and planted a gentle kiss on my lips. "Honest."

I had an uneasy feeling in the pit of my stomach. Nerves, I thought. Just waiting for the big moment to arrive.

Chapter 32

I thought I was doing all right at first, getting to the gym by about two minutes to ten. I knew Chappie would be waiting, so I parked in a hurry on the backside of the building and began a hustling trot around to the front entrance. That's when I saw my old buddy Red leaning along the side near the section of glass brick windows. I slowed my steps and scrutinized him. He was wearing a wine-colored leather coat that hung down over his waist, and a white scarf wrapped artfully around his neck with just the right length left dangling. Sort of like a hoodlum's version of a male model. Looking right at me, he smiled. You wouldn't really call it a smile, though. More of a smirk. The same kind of smirk that he'd had right before I'd kicked his ass that night in the hotel.

"Hey, Shade," he said. Both of his hands were in his jacket pockets. The right one looked bulky. Like he was holding something.

I instinctively pulled my coat around and felt for my gun which I wore in a pancake holster on my right hip.

"Suppose you just let me see your hands," I said. "Nice and slow."

"Sure," he said, moving his arms with extended deliberation. He held up his open palms. "Satisfied?"

I did a quick glance around. No one else seemed to be with him. The standard rush of cars went back and forth about a hundred feet in front of us along Western Avenue, but the side street was deserted. I relaxed slightly, letting my hand creep around to the side of my leg.

"You want something?" I asked.

"Yeah, you might say that."

"Well, I'm in a bit of a hurry," I said.

"For a Reel Sports interview?"

I felt a sudden sinking feeling. How the hell could he know about that unless the whole interview thing had been a ruse? I hated to think I'd been had. Again. But I tried to cover it with a quick smile of my own.

"Is that why you came by?" I said.

"Actually I came by to give you this," he said. Red started to reach into his right side coat pocket, but he hesitated. "Relax, will you? I'm just gonna get a cell phone out of my pocket, okay?"

"That's all it better be," I said. My hand went back to the comfort of the Beretta's grip.

His head rocked slightly, back and forth, as he withdrew a cell phone from the pocket, just as he said he would, flipped open the speaker flap, and pressed the recall button. Winking at me, he raised it to his ear and then spoke moments later.

"Boss? I'm with Shade now." He paused, listened, then extended the phone toward me. "It's for you."

I took the phone with my left hand, keeping my right on the Beretta. Pressing it to my ear, I said, "Yeah."

"Ah, Mr. Shade, I presume?" a voice said. It had a distinctly British inflection, but with enough of a foreign sounding pitch that I knew it had to be Olijede. "I am very, very glad that we are finally getting the chance to speak to each other directly."

"Me too. I take it you got my message?"

"Oh, but of course," Olijede said. He laughed. It was one of those forced, foreign sounding laughs that seem to rise up a few octaves on the second syllable. Like the sound of somebody laughing at something that wasn't really funny. "I must say, you are a very, very clever man, Mr. Shade."

"So you want to discuss my finder's fee, or what?"

"Actually, I had something slightly different in mind," he said. "I thought that perhaps an exchange of property would be more in order."

"I'm listening."

"Very good, because there is someone with me now that I wish you to hear." I heard a muffling sound with the phone, then seconds later a terrified hello from Laurie.

"Laurie, are you all right?"

"I'm okay, Ron," she said. Her voice sounded far away, like she was standing at the other end of some long dark tunnel. I mentally cursed myself for letting her drift into harm's way. It must have shown on my face because Red suddenly got a bigger smirk on his face.

"Have they hurt you?" I asked.

"No, I'm all right. Just kind of scared, is all."

"It'll all be okay," I said, trying to sound as reassuring as possible. "Where are you now? Can you tell?"

"Not really," she said. "We're in some kind of black limousine with tinted windows."

Before I could say anything else, her voice and breathing stopped coming from the phone and Olijede came back on the line.

"Ah, Mr. Shade, I trust the brevity of that conversation will suffice. Now, here are my terms. You shall take my associate to the location of my property and turn it over to him. This shall be done immediately. When he calls me back to acknowledge that this has been done, you will be told where to pick up your friend." He paused for a mo-

297

ment, then asked, "Is this perfectly clear?"

"Yeah," I said. "But make sure this is perfectly clear too. If you hurt her in any way, I'll track you down and kill you."

He responded with the irritating up-and-down laugh again. It was really starting to grate on me.

"Mr. Shade, believe me, this is not the appropriate time for threats and bravado," he said. "Now do as you have been told, and all will be well. Please hand the phone back to my associate at this time."

"Just remember what I said." I extended the phone toward Red, who was still grinning at me.

He mumbled into the phone a few times, and pressed the END button. Stepping over to the curb, Red stuck out his arm like he was hailing a cab. But instead of a cab, a small, green Ford Taurus pulled out from an adjacent alleyway and screeched to a halt in the street in front of us. Two tough-looking guys sat in the front seat. One black and the other white. The black guy was behind the wheel, and the other guy was pointing a gun at me. Red paused and jerked his head toward the Taurus.

"Let's go," he said. I saw him withdraw a snub-nosed pistol from his jacket pocket too.

I moved over toward the car and Red opened the rear door. As I started to get in, he placed a hand on my shoulder.

"Not so fast, buddy," he said. I felt his palms begin to pat me down, lifting the rear end of my jacket and unsnapping the Beretta from its holster. The search was quick and thorough, and when he'd finished, Red punched me hard in the kidney which doubled me over. He shoved and I bumped the side of my head on the door frame as I slid inside the rear seat area. Red got in behind me.

"Nice piece," he said, hefting my weapon. "Lots better than your little shit twenty-two. But that did the job, I guess."

My breathing was coming fast and sharp, the pain in my side just starting to ease. I glanced at the white guy in the front seat. He had short blond hair that had been cropped in a buzz-cut and a fat, jowly face. He grinned at me as I sat hunched over, obviously enjoying seeing me in pain. His teeth were very bad.

"So you did Peeps?" I managed to say.

Red showed me his smirk again as he pressed the ejector button and checked the magazine. He then replaced it and pulled back the slide slightly to verify that there was a round in the chamber.

"Yeah, shortly after you softened him up," he said. "But he had it coming. Him and Paula tried a rip-off." His eyes drifted over toward me. "But she was a lot more fun to do than him, right, Leon?" He slapped the black guy's broad shoulder. I could see the other man's thick lip curl up under his bushy mustache. "Which brings us to our next subject. Where's the stuff at, Shade?"

"Is this the part where I'm supposed to say, 'What stuff?' "

"Only if you want to make things difficult for your little girlfriend," he said. "Nice looking babe. Almost as juicy as Paula was. You fucking her?"

I said nothing. If I told them where the stuff was, they had no reason to keep me or Laurie alive. I mentally searched for an angle to play.

"Look, Shade, I'm gonna have to call the boss back in a second or two here, and if I don't got nothing to tell him, you're gonna be listening to the broad screaming till you talk."

"Okay," I said with a sigh. "The stuff's in some blue suitcases."

"No shit," he said, letting the sarcasm seep into his tone. "Now quit fucking around."

He obviously knew I was trying to stall, but it was just as obvious that short of some miracle, I was out of options.

"They're in a storage facility on 115th Street, just past Cicero," I said. "But it's a place that you have to sign in and out of with high-tech security. Peeps wasn't on the authorization list. That's why he couldn't get in."

"What about you?" Red asked.

I quickly debated saying that it was only Laurie on the list, but then they could shoot me and dump me in some alley.

"Yeah," I said. "I can get in."

"And the key?"

"I got it on my ring."

Red nodded, then took out the cell phone again. He pressed the RCL button and I watched the yellow numbers flash across the screen.

"Yeah boss," Red said into the phone. "He says the stuff's in some kind of storage facility and he's got the key." He paused and listened, then his lips stretched into that smart-ass grin again. "Okay, boss," he said and hung up.

"Lucky for you, your story's the same as hers, Shade," he said. "Now, show me the key."

"It won't do you any good," I said, reaching in my pocket for my keys. "Like I told you, you got to sign in and out."

"But you're on the list, right?" He grinned. It was more of a statement than a question.

I nodded. The pain in my back had pretty much subsided, but my ear still felt sore where it had smacked against the metal of the car frame.

"Where's this place at now?" Leon, the driver asked.

I told him the address, measuring my breaths like I was still in pain. Let Red think that he'd hurt me more than he had. Maybe it would cause him to drop his guard. The car began to roll up toward Western. I had maybe ten or fifteen minutes tops before we'd get there. Time enough, I hoped, to figure a way out . . . for myself and for Laurie.

As we got to 111th Street, Red told Leon to hang a right and pull into the alley behind a row of small businesses. Leon carefully signaled, then made the turn. We proceeded south in the alley for about twenty yards when Red spoke again.

"Okay, this is cool. Paulie, get out and get in the trunk."

"Huh?" Paulie said. His mouth hung open like he didn't know if Red was kidding him or what.

"I said, get out and get in the fucking trunk," Red repeated.

"What for?"

Red reached forward and slapped him. It wasn't a hard slap, but had just enough force to spur the lethargic Paulie into action.

"Aww, man, I don't want to get in no trunk," he pleaded.

"Shut up and do it," Red said. "We're gonna have three guys driving into the place, and three guys driving out."

"And none of the rest of you gonna pass for me," Leon said with a grin. I noticed the ease with which he and Red related to one another. Like they'd worked together a long time, each knowing the other guy's moves.

Red told Leon to give him the keys and to keep me covered. Leon pulled a chrome-plated snub-nosed .38 out of his pocket, transferred it to his left hand, and turned slightly so he could point it at me. Red and Paulie got out. Moments later I heard the trunk lid raise up and felt the suspension shift as Paulie apparently stepped into the trunk.

Three men in, three men out, he'd said. That meant on the return trip I'd probably be the one riding where Paulie was now. The only question was, would I be alive?

Chapter 33

It was a different guy behind the desk at the storage facility. Red stood beside me with his hand conspicuously placed in his right side coat pocket. And I knew he wasn't holding the cell phone either. I signed the register card, and the clerk took it to the ledger to verify the signature. Satisfied, he slid the card in an automatic stamping machine and then pressed the three buttons. Through the windows I saw the heavy gate beginning to retract electronically.

"Just beep your horn when you're ready to leave," he said.

I nodded, wishing he hadn't made the departure so easy. Red and I went back outside to the Taurus.

I got in the front passenger and Red jumped in behind me.

"Which way?" Leon asked.

"Fourteen twenty-seven," I said, looking at the seven-foot-high cyclone fence with the barbed wire on top. It was a dubious place for a break. I was effectively trapped, like I was in maximum security, and Red seemed to sense this. His tone was more relaxed as he spoke.

"I hope you're not trying to pull a fast one on us, Shade," he said. "Paula thought she could, and Peeps, too."

"And I know what happened to them," I said.

He grinned. "Right. So I'm gonna just verify that the stuff's where you say it is before I make the call back to the boss about your girlfriend."

"It's there," I said. But silently my mind was racing. If he had been lulled into a state of semi-complacency, and he wanted to check for the drugs, it meant that he might be a tad lax and preoccupied. Maybe. But what other chance did I have? I knew that once he had those suitcases, and I replaced idiot Paulie in the trunk, it would be all over for me. And for Laurie, too.

Leon stopped in the aisle in front of the storage locker. He glanced around. No one else was anywhere in sight.

"Cameras," he said, pointing to the one mounted on the pole at the end of the aisle.

Red nodded, then said, "Shade, get out real slow and open the fucking door." He removed the Beretta for emphasis.

I got out, jiggled loose the key, and inserted it in the keyhole. The door began to raise. For an instant I considered doing a quick roll under it and trying to lower it quickly, but Red and Leon both were getting out now. Plus, that would only trap me inside. The door continued its elevation, curling into the top section of the storage locker just under the ceiling. Reaching around, I flipped up the light switch. Inside, the four suitcases sat along with the black leather case containing the cash. Red smirked and stepped inside, the Beretta held loosely now down by his leg.

"Get Paulie out of the trunk and give me the tire iron," he said.

Leon snapped the car keys between his dark fingers.

"What's in that bag?" Red asked.

"Money," I said, moving toward it. "You can have it. Let me show you."

"Hold it," he said, raising the Beretta and waving me over by the door, half watching me, and half watching the bag as he edged around. To my side Leon was opening the lid and

Paulie was clambering out of the trunk. Red knelt, holding the pistol loosely, and he gripped the leather material with his left hand and placed two of the fingers of his right on the tab of the zipper.

I knew it was now or never as I made my move, rushing toward him and snapping a kick at Red's right elbow. I felt my instep connect and saw the Beretta go flying, skittering across the bare concrete floor and smacking against the brick wall. Leon and Paulie began their rush, and I did a quick skip-step sideways, slamming a low side-kick into Paulie, who was closer. He doubled over, as I had hoped, and I shoved him the rest of the way to the floor, causing Leon to trip. I saw Leon's right hand bringing up the .38 as he fell, so I clipped him right on the point of his chin as he crumbled. The gun discharged, searing the left side of my face with a flare of light and heat. My hands grabbed for his wrist as he hit the floor, and when I felt the cool solidness of the metal I ripped and twisted the weapon away from him.

Paulie swung his arm in an arcing motion, hitting me on the calf just below the knee, and sending a bolt of pain right up my leg. I glanced down and saw that he had the tire iron. Out of the corner of my eye I noticed a blur of movement and knew Red was getting to his feet. Dancing backward, ignoring the screaming pain in my leg, I snapped my head back just as the tire iron smacked the side of my head. Paulie's feral teeth flashed. I pointed the revolver at his face and pulled the trigger.

I heard his convulsive grunt, or at least thought I did. The explosion of the round going off in the muffled, shell-like structure made my ears ring. Swiveling, I tried to draw a bead on Red, who was moving toward the opposite wall. Before I could fire, Leon grabbed my left foot and pulled. The .38 discharged as I felt myself falling forward, the round cracking against the concrete floor and ricocheting off somewhere.

My elbows took the brunt of my fall. Scrambling up, I lurched forward toward Red like a defensive lineman and slammed him into the heavy brick wall. The air seemed to go out of him and I followed up instinctively with a three-punch combination, keeping the gun in my hand as I hit him.

More movement flashed and I turned to see Leon's dark face glistening with sweat, the frosty breath expelling from his mouth like smoke, the tire iron cocking back over his head. Just pointing and pulling the trigger, I felt the .38 explode in my hand again. But Leon kept on coming. Could I have missed? I squeezed the trigger twice more, seeing him jerk slightly with each shot, the front of his dark jacket suddenly slick with blood. The arm with the tire iron lowered slowly and he staggered forward on drunken legs. I was set to put another bullet in him when Red bounced off the wall and slammed into me.

We went down in a twisted heap, the shoulder of my coat rubbing coarsely over the concrete. I felt the rear of my head bounce once off the floor, Red's forearm pushing forcefully downward under my chin. His fist smashed into my cheek and jaw several times. Bringing the .38 up under his armpit, I pulled the trigger but nothing happened. Had I fired six already? I squeezed the trigger again, but no discharge. Then I adjusted my grip and brought it down on the top of Red's head a couple of times. He grunted and rolled, using his arm to trap mine. Then his fist slammed into my jaw. I whipped my left hand into his side as many times as I could, but without the leverage of my legs, they were just arm-punches.

We rolled together, like unlikely lovers, each trying to

whip in blows on the other with our free hands. His body mashed my right hand, which still held the .38, against the rough floor. I kicked with my legs, rolling us over once more, leaving the revolver in our wake.

I found myself on top and managed to free my right arm. I swung at his head, but missed. He managed to connect with a punch to my side and grabbed for my balls. Struggling to block his hand, I had a sudden recollection of our first encounter. I had been correct to remain on my feet in that confrontation. He was stronger than I was. Heavier too. And he seemed to have some sort of grappling experience.

I connected with a left to his temple. Blood was streaming down his face from the welts I'd opened with the gun. Shoving off with my legs, I struggled to regain my footing, but Red grabbed my leg and I fell on my left side, hitting hard. He was scrambling to get on top of me, but I managed to do a few snapping flutter kicks which kept him off. Breathing hard, I scrambled to my feet and swung a left hook at his rising figure.

He slipped the punch, though by design or luck, I wasn't sure. But the momentum of the blow swung me off balance, and I felt Red's powerful weightlifter's arm encircling my waist. Certain that he was going to try to body slam me on the concrete floor again, my left arm swooped down and snared his neck. A scissor-choke, they called it in judo. Tucking my forearm in just under his chin, and clamping my biceps over the back of his neck, I clasped hands and pushed backwards with all the strength my legs could muster. Combined with Red's forward motion, we went down, with me landing on my back and his body sailing over me. He struck the floor beyond my head and shoulders with a horrendous slapping sound. But I'd gripped his neck so hard that it didn't travel the same way as the rest of him. When I rolled to my feet and grabbed his lapel to label him with a right cross, his head lolled backwards at an almost ludicrous angle. I delivered the punch anyway, and felt the looseness when I connected. His neck was broken.

Dropping him, I staggered over and searched for my Beretta. It lay in the far corner. Gasping like I'd just sprinted a half-mile, I staggered over and pressed the switch lowering the overhead door. Still no one else in the surrounding aisles. The door lowered as Red's dead eyes stared up vacantly at me from the floor. Neither Leon nor idiot Paulie had moved during the struggle. Twin puddles of dark, thickening blood were spreading from under each of them. I slowly let my back hit against the wall, then squatted to lower myself to the floor.

Chapter 34

It took me a few minutes to get my breathing back to normal and figure out what to do next. As far as I could tell, I wasn't injured other than a few cuts, scrapes, and bruises. But where did I go from here? That was, as they say, the million-dollar question. After putting the suitcases in the trunk of the Taurus, I went through the pockets of the three dead guys. They yielded very little. Leon and Paulie both had wallets with petty cash in them. Red's wallet contained several hundred dollars, numerous credits cards, and various IDs in the names of Regis Phillips, Regis Werner, and Regis Brill. It would probably take the cops several hours to get his real identification by fingerprints, and I didn't have a couple of hours.

I replaced all their personal property except for Red's cell phone. After leaving them, and the .38, in the storage facility, I raised the door enough to slip under, then lowered it again. The temperature had been dropping again and I figured the cold would keep them on ice, so to speak. I got into the Taurus. It felt like I'd gone ten rounds in a meat freezer. The left side of my head had a large lump that was dripping crimson from the center. My right cheek and eyebrow were bruised and starting to swell. I pressed the recall button and watched the last number called flash across the screen. Then I hit SEND. It rang twice before Olijede answered.

"This is Shade."

"Ah, Mr. Shade," he said. His voice was hesitant, uncertain. "How nice of you to call."

"I want to talk to Laurie," I said as calmly as I could.

"I am afraid that is not possible at the moment. May I trouble you to speak with Regis?"

"Regis can't come to the phone right now," I said. "Well actually, I could bring it to him, but he couldn't talk into it. Neither could any of the three other identities he had in his wallet."

"I see," Olijede said slowly. "Mr. Shade, it seems that I have badly underestimated you."

I could tell by his tone that I'd caught him flatfooted.

"So did your three stooges," I said. "Now listen, you want your stuff, and I want Laurie. I'm willing to trade, no questions asked. We got a deal?"

"A deal?" he said. He was stalling for time, trying to figure out what to say.

"Yeah, a deal. Now let me speak to her."

Several seconds of silence, then he said, "Just a moment."

After a couple of minutes, Laurie came on the line.

"Ron?" she asked.

"Yeah, it's me, babe. Are you still okay?"

"I'm all right, Ron, but I'm just real scared." Her voice broke.

"I know. It's okay. Can you tell where you're at?"

"I don't know," she said. "We're at some kind of house, but I don't know where it is."

"Listen, I'm going to get you out of this," I said. "Everything will be all right. Believe me. Just do what they tell you for now."

"All right, Ron. But please . . . hurry."

Olijede came back on the line before I could say anything else. I knew he was still holding the better hand, since he had Laurie and I didn't know where the hell he was. I didn't even know what he looked like.

"Mr. Shade, I have considered your offer and agree," he said. "But you must follow my instructions to the letter. Do you understand?"

"As long as the instructions include me physically exchanging the suitcases for Laurie," I said.

He laughed his lilting, up-and-down laugh again.

"I'm sure we would agree that you are in no position to dictate terms," he said.

"I ain't dictating nothing," I said. "I'm telling you like it is. We're each holding something the other wants, and you don't trust me any more than I trust you."

"And your point is?"

"That you won't see your stuff unless I see Laurie, safe and sound, when we make the exchange," I said. "You can name the place. Take your stuff and we both can walk away."

"And what assurance do I have that you won't contact the police?"

"Yeah, right," I said. "I'll want to tell them about the three dead bodies I left in the storage locker, won't I?"

He laughed again.

"Very well, Mr. Shade. You have your deal." He was speaking slower than he normally did. I took that to mean that he was scrambling. "You shall proceed to the O'Hare Oasis with my property and I will call you back in precisely forty minutes on the cell phone and give you further instructions."

"I'll need more time than that."

"Absolutely not," he said. "I will expect that you will be there in a timely fashion then? Good-bye, Mr. Shade, and please keep in mind that we will be watching you at all times."

The connection went dead. I glanced at my watch. Five to one. If I was supposed to be up by the airport in forty minutes, I'd have to hustle. I slammed the gear shift into drive and took off. I honked twice at the gate and the attendant opened it without looking outside. After driving through, I stopped and jotted down the number to call Olijede back, and quickly dialed George. All I got was his voice mail, which meant that he was out of the station. After leaving a quick message and telling him to beep me immediately, I pressed END and then got the number to Red's cell phone by pressing RCL and #. I wrote that number down, too, then dialed George's beeper. The clock was ticking, but there was no way Olijede could tag me until I got to the oasis. I stepped on the gas and headed over toward the tollway, gripping the cell phone in my left hand and waiting for George to call me back.

Red's cell phone rang again precisely forty minutes after I'd last spoken with Olijede. I'd spent the time trying to deal with the discomfort of my aching head, and wondering if he did indeed have someone watching me. They knew what Red's car looked like, but did Olijede really know me by sight? Of course, other than him being a Nigerian, I didn't know him either. Or any of his henchmen. I let the phone ring two more times before I answered it.

"Ah, Mr. Shade, I see you have followed my instructions."

"Yeah, now let me talk to Laurie."

"I am sorry, that is not possible at this time."

"Bullshit," I said. "Let me know she's all right or I don't fucking move."

He sighed. "Very well. Miss."

She came on the line again.

"It's Ron. Laurie, just say yes or no. Are you okay?"

"Yes," she said.

"Are you near the airport?"

"Yes."

"In the limo?"

Before she could say anything else, I could tell the phone was being taken from her. Olijede came back on the line.

"Very well, Mr. Shade. You have your assurance that she is all right. Now, are you ready to proceed?"

"Yeah."

"Very well," he said. "But let me take the time to remind you that you are being watched as we speak."

I wondered if that was really true, jamming the car into drive and leaving the parking lot, checking the mirrors. Two cars took off behind me. One was a dark Chevy Caprice with two guys in it. I had a pretty good idea who they were.

"You will proceed back on the tollway and proceed north toward the airport," he said. "You will be given instructions as you drive."

"Okay, I'm northbound," I said. "Where do I go from here?"

"Move to the right side lanes," he said.

I purposely stayed where I was to see if he'd correct me. If he did, I'd know he had a tail car.

"Mr. Shade, do you understand the instructions?"

"Yeah," I said. The split in the tollway was coming up, with the lanes I was in heading off northwest toward Rockford. The exit to the airport was to my right.

"Then exit at the airport, please."

I glanced in the rear-view mirror. The Chevy had dropped back a few car lengths. The traffic was way too heavy for me to tell if anyone else was tailing me. And they knew the Taurus. No long dark limousines stood out. I signaled and veered right.

"Very good," Olijede said a few moments later. The timing of his remark made me feel that he was either behind me, or, more likely, he had someone else reporting to him on a separate phone.

"I took the airport exit. Now what?"

"Continue onward," he said. "I will tell you where and when to stop."

"Remember you ain't getting your stuff till I get Laurie."

He made no reply. I was on the airport road now, going over Mannheim and heading toward Bessie Coleman Drive. The signs above the lanes announced that Terminals One, Two, and Three were straight ahead. Outside parking and hourly parking had their designated lanes also.

"I'm going toward the terminals," I said into the phone. "Where the hell am I supposed to head?"

"Continue toward the main terminals."

I did. Up ahead, the lanes split again, this time for departures on the upper level and arrivals on the lower.

"Arrivals or departures?" I asked. "Up or down?"

"Proceed to the lower level, Mr. Shade," he said. "That's right. But do not stop until I direct you to."

"You expect me to stop in the middle of the road, or what?"

"No, no, no," he said. "Continue around the circle."

I coasted past Terminal One. To my left was a parking lot. I saw the listing for the airlines: Lufthansa, United, United Express. Terminal Two was next: Air Jamaica, America West, America Trans Air, Continental, Northwest.

"Where do I pull over?" I said into the phone. "I'm coming up on Delta now." Delta was in Terminal Three.

"Pass the terminal and then take the small extension road and go around the circle again," he said. "This time pull into Parking Lot B. Do you understand?"

"Pull into Parking Lot B," I repeated. The black Chevy shot by me.

"That is correct," he said.

I swung the Taurus around and entered the perimeter road again. This time when the sign came up for the lot, I exited. At the end of the ramp was an automatic parking tab dispenser. I stopped before I entered the drive. A car behind me honked. I stayed where I was.

"Where do I go?" I asked. The obnoxious guy behind me continued to lean on his horn, just as I'd hoped.

It took him a few seconds to reply. I strained to listen for the blaring horn over the cell phone, but I could discern nothing.

Olijede told me to pull forward and take a ticket. I did, reasonably certain now that he didn't have an eyeball on me himself. He most likely had someone in a car behind me relaying my movements.

"Okay, now where the hell are you?" I asked. "I know you have someone following me, but I want to see Laurie."

"Mr. Shade, your perception continues to amaze me," Olijede said. "You will now pull into the lot and find an inconspicuous parking space."

I studied the cars in back of me. The idiot with the horn shot around me and went screaming off in the opposite direction. A nondescript-looking blue Buick LeSabre turned my direction and stayed far enough back so that I couldn't see the driver.

"Is that your guy behind me now?" I asked. "In the blue LeSabre?"

Olijede laughed. "Mr. Shade, I see now that I did very much underestimate you before. It is a mistake that I shall not repeat."

I slowed in the aisle. The LeSabre hung back too. The lot was pretty full, but I passed up several parking spaces. Scanning the lot as best I could, I still didn't see any limos.

Finally Olijede said, "Mr. Shade, any of the spots you have passed will do."

"Okay," I said into the phone. "I'll grab the next parking space that I see, all right?" I pulled into the next open space I found. It was near the edge of the lot and butted up against a taller parking garage structure that went up several stories. A tall cyclone fence and a steep embankment separated them.

"Now what?" I asked, keeping an eye out for the blue LeSabre.

"Remain in the vehicle, Mr. Shade, and my associate will approach you."

"Stay in the car so I can get shot?" I said. "No way."

I got out and locked the Taurus, stepping into the aisle and conspicuously stuck the keys in my pocket as the Buick slowly drove by. The guy behind the wheel was staring at me and talking into a cell phone. I put my phone down by my leg and grabbed my Beretta with my right hand. I ran toward the LeSabre. The driver's eyes widened and he tried to shoot forward, but had to jam on the brakes as a black Chevy Impala screeched to a stop in front of him. I leveled the Beretta at the guy's face and motioned for him to open the driver's door. He immediately tried to jam it into reverse and back away, but another dark Chevy pulled up and tapped the LeSabre's rear bumper. I smashed a round-house kick into the driver's door window. The glass exploded in a myriad of shards, and I swept the jagged edges away with the barrel of my gun. I reached inside and ripped the door open and dragged him out.

"Where is he?" I yelled, pressing the barrel of the Beretta into the man's forehead.

"I don't know," he screamed as he dropped the cell phone.

"Bullshit!"

George suddenly appeared, his big, stainless Smith & Wesson .45 pointing down at the driver. He and the rest of the cavalry had been shadowing me since I'd left the oasis. I grabbed the phone from the ground. I just had to hope that wherever the big man was, he didn't have a direct view of what had happened.

"Olijede," I said into it. "You want to tell me where Laurie is now, or do I put a hole in another one of your goons?"

"Mr. Shade, I see you are not following my instructions," he said. "This could have dire consequences for your lady friend."

"You touch her and you're dead," I said. George motioned for me to cover the mouthpiece and he brought his radio up to his lips.

"We locate that limo yet?" he said.

"Got a couple of them on the upper level, Sarge," a voice came back.

"Well, run 'em, dammit," George screamed. "Lothar Industries. See if any of 'em come back to Lothar Industries."

I brought the Beretta down hard on the top of the guy's head. A huge cut opened up and the blood followed. He collapsed to the asphalt. I thought about rubbing his face in the shattered glass.

"I'm waiting, Olijede," I said into the cell phone. I began walking in a diagonal direction toward Terminal Three. It was at least a football field away.

"Ron," George said in a whisper as he trotted up beside me.

I covered the mouthpiece again.

"This ain't going according to plan," he said. "You were supposed to let him get control of the dope."

"Look, Olijede," I said into the phone again. "Tell me where and I'll bring you the shit myself. Your guy can drive off in the Taurus as soon as I have Laurie."

"Mr. Shade," he said. "Please put my driver back on." I glanced back at the driver. The plainclothes narco boys were already slipping on the bracelets. One of them was removing a gun from the guy's waistband. George shrugged.

"All right, wait a minute." I suddenly heard the sound of a plane's takeoff drowning out Olijede. Looking around, I spied a jet ascending from the northwest leaving huge white vapor trails against the darkening sky. I pointed emphatically to George, who spoke quickly into his radio. Running back to the now-handcuffed driver, I screwed the pistol into his ear and held the phone down by my leg. The tone of the conversation had led me to believe even more so that Olijede was in the airport somewhere, but not close enough to see us.

"Not one word," I whispered, bumping the Beretta against his ear for good measure. "Understand?"

He nodded. The blood was cascading down his face and mixing with the thinner streams of sweat.

I held the cell phone up close to his face, and leaned in like a lover so I could hear it too. George twisted his lips into a ferocious looking snarl and rubbed the barrel of his revolver against the driver's groin. The man seemed to turn an extra shade of gray.

"Yeah, boss," he said.

"Herman, are you all right?" I heard Olijede's voice say over the phone.

Herman gulped. "Yeah, boss."

"Very well," Olijede said. "Remove the suitcases from

the trunk of the Taurus and place them in the rear of your vehicle."

"Okay, boss," Herman said.

I held the phone down again.

"The son-of-a-bitch is too damn smart to handle the dope himself," I said. "He's just going to drive off."

George raised his radio again. "What's taking so long on finding that damn limo?"

A static-laden reply came over saying something about Terminal Three. The boys from Narcotics were busily placing the suitcases into the trunk of the LeSabre. I leaned in close to my boy Herman again and whispered softly.

"Tell him you're done, or my friend here will blow your balls off."

George grinned malevolently.

"It's done, boss," Herman said into the phone.

"Good, now instruct Mr. Shade to get into the passenger seat. When he does, you will drive out of the lot and back to the perimeter road again."

Herman said okay.

We tossed him into the back floor area, and George got in after him, leaning down like a protective parent. I got into the driver's seat as the black Impala moved out of my way. The uniformed officers who had been blocking the aisle we were in immediately held up the stream of cars to let us by. The guard raised the gate in front of us and I went through.

As I pulled onto the perimeter road, I spoke into the cell phone again.

"When do I see Laurie?" I asked.

"Very, very soon," Olijede said.

I figured that he'd be waiting to put a bullet in both of us as soon as he determined the coast was clear. I circled around the angular curve and saw the limousine up ahead, idling by the curb in the livery section. A marked police unit began to creep up along side of me, then zoomed across. The limo lurched away from the curb a few seconds later, sideswiping a yellow cab and careening out into the main traffic lanes. I floored it and shot after them. The marked unit pulled alongside the limo and tried to angle in front of it, but the bigger car veered left and smashed into the squad. Metal crunched against metal and then both vehicles straightened out.

"What the hell you doing?" George yelled.

"It's blown," I said. "He's running."

"Stop that damn limo!" George yelled into his radio. "We got a hostage inside it."

The marked squad steered directly into the left front fender of the limousine, which careened into the side of a departing taxi. I was going too fast to stop and crashed into the left rear. The airbag exploded in my face in a cloud of foul-smelling dust. Scrambling to open the door, it took me three tries. As I crawled out, I saw the rear door of the limo open and a lean-looking black guy jumped out, pulling Laurie by her long brown hair. It had to be Olijede. His right hand held a wicked-looking automatic.

I reached for the Beretta and hit the pavement on my belly. Olijede pointed the automatic at the police car and fired several rounds into the rear windshield. Cars were screeching behind us, and people who had been lining the edge of the sidewalk began to scream and run. Olijede tried to drag Laurie with him, but she twisted and turned in his grasp, her long legs kicking at the asphalt. He pointed the pistol at the top of her head.

"No!" I screamed.

He looked up at me and hesitated, smiling maniacally, and seemed about to pull the trigger when his head jerked back in a crimson mist. I looked up and saw George holding his Smith & Wesson in both hands, a wisp of smoke trailing upward from the barrel.

Olijede's lips twisted into a scowl as he began a slow-motion pirouette, his legs turning to rubber as he curled forward, falling over Laurie's supine figure. The two uniformed officers from the marked unit ran forward with guns drawn. Seconds later they were pulling out a white guy from the driver's door. I scrambled to my feet and sprinted to Laurie. She had a bloody lip that looked like she'd need stitches. But other than that, and the tears streaming down her cheeks, she seemed all right. George came sauntering up, his trusty semi-auto dangling loosely down by his leg.

"Is she okay?" he asked.

I nodded, pressing her to me.

He barked more orders into his radio, the only part of which I heard was the request for an ambulance and a supervisor.

"Officer-involved shooting," I heard someone else saying into a police radio.

I looked up at George.

"Nice shot, Kemosabe," I said.

He nodded.

The sky over the top of the terminal was turning a velvety gray, but remnants of scarlet still edged over the superstructure. George holstered his weapon, glanced at his watch, then shook his head.

"You mighta won that fight," he said. "And I had a hundred bucks bet on it, too."

I just held Laurie close and felt her arms around me.

"I won the one that counted," I said.

He raised his eyebrows and said, "You know, maybe you're finally starting to grow up after all."

Chapter 35

Probably the less said about the fight, the better. Suffice it to say that amidst all the dead bodies and crashed cars, they weren't about to let me go. And the way I'd felt I probably wouldn't have been able to lift my legs through the ropes anyway. So George managed to send someone with lights-and-sirens to the Aragon to break the news to Chappie. Although he managed to get Raul to sub for me as a last-minute replacement, it was immediately changed to a twelve-round heavyweight non-title fight, which was a damn shame. Raul managed to hold his own through the first five rounds, sticking and moving like I was supposed to have done. Then Day got tired, just like we'd figured, and Raul began to peck him to death. Day spent the final two rounds on sodden legs, getting slugged and slugging back. In the end it was ruled a draw only because Raul had missed his required number of kicks in one round. And that was kind. One of the judges must have been blind, or drunk. Or from Detroit.

Elijah was nothing but gracious about what a great fighter Raul was. He even hinted that there could be a re-match. He could afford to be gracious. The belt stayed around his waist. And all I could think about was that I knew I could have won that damn fight, and how I'd let Chappie down. Then again, what choice did I have? He was okay with it, or at least he said he was.

Laurie checked out of the Emergency Room, after getting a bunch of stitches on the inside of her mouth and an icepack for the bumps on the top of her head. Mostly she was just pissed off that she didn't get to see me win the championship, because she knew how hard I'd worked for it. So I told her she could come down for the next one. She ended up staying at my place for another week, letting me nurse and baby her back to health while she relished every moment of it.

And I sort of liked it, too, but it was all tinged with *déjà vu*. The same way you feel when you're enjoying an old movie that you'd seen before, and you know it isn't going to have a happy ending. Sort of like *Casablanca*.

On our last day together winter seemed to release its icy grasp a bit, and even hinted at the possibility of an early spring. But I knew it was not to be. So that night I took her downtown for dinner and a play. I was still too sore to go dancing. We had a great time, and somehow, as we lay in each other's arms afterward, we managed to put the whole thing in perspective.

"You know I have to go back to Michigan tomorrow," she said.

"Yeah, I was figuring that semester break was just about over."

"I'll stay if you want me to, Ron." I could feel her wet tears splashing down on my shoulder as she spoke. "You know, I came down here thinking that you were the person from the past who'd sort of ruined my cousin's life. And then you end up saving mine. You're such a great guy . . . So thoughtful and nice . . . And I really did fall in love with you."

It wasn't that I wasn't in love with her. It was just that I knew there was just too much "past" between us. Too much extra baggage.

"What about law school?" I said. "All the hard work

you've done. And all the plans you have?"

"They don't matter so much anymore."

I heard Bogey's voice echoing in my mind: Maybe not today, maybe not tomorrow, but someday . . .

"I think they do," I said.

I thought about that whimsical saying I'd seen printed on a poster one time about letting something go if you loved it. If it comes back to you, it's yours. If it doesn't, it never was. But I kept the trite saying to myself. Instead, I reached back for something more significant.

"Well," I said, "we'll always have Paris."

When she left the next morning it was overcast, and a misty sleet was stinging our faces. We kissed and held each other, neither of us seeming to want to be the first to let go. But we both knew we had to. After another few minutes of tearful good-byes, and promises to call and write that I knew would probably not be kept, she got in her little car and drove off.

She'd given me Paula's Firebird in lieu of payment, and had agreed to use the remainder of the recovered money to pay for school. To do something good with her cousin's "legacy."

I stood there in the rain watching her until she turned at the end of the block, and disappeared from my life.

Forever? I wondered.

Then I did what I always do in situations like this. I changed into my sweats and went for a long, slow run. Only this time I didn't see Elijah Day at the top of every hill. I saw Laurie waving good-bye. I kept thinking about everything that had happened this past month . . . And about what might have been . . . And what would never be. But I knew it was for the best. I left my regrets behind me as I eked out my finishing sprint feeling almost like a winner. But then again, this run wasn't about winning or losing. It was about putting to rest old ghosts.

George called me later and asked me to work security at the hotel from six to midnight. As usual, he told me that he was in a real bind.

"You're always in a real bind," I said.

"Hey," he said. "You owe me big time anyway."

It was true. Not only had he come through in the crunch for me and helped to save Laurie, but he'd also subsequently tipped off INS to Smershkevich's shenanigans and set in motion the ignoble Russian's deportation back to the motherland.

"Yeah, I guess I do, don't I?" I said. "You really saved my bacon all right."

"What the hell you talking about?" His low chuckle resonated over the phone line. "I'm referring to all that money I coulda won betting that Elijah Day was gonna knock you out."

"Ha ha," I said, enunciating each word.

His voice got serious for a second. "Laurie leave?"

"Yeah." Then, after a few beats of silence, I added, "She wanted me to thank you for her. She said she'll always think of us as her two Windy City Knights."

I heard his low chuckle again.

"See, I told you that name had potential. Maybe you should start calling yourself that when you fight. It has a ring to it."

"Maybe I will. You know how to pick 'em, all right," I said.

For my first appearance back at the hotel, the place, I ironically noted, where this whole damn thing had started, I did my best to keep a low profile. The wrap-around Oakley sunglasses inside didn't help any. Finally, tired of all the peculiar looks, I took them off, displaying my still-battered face. The swelling had all disappeared, but the stubborn purple bruises made me look like a guy who'd come in second in a collision with a freight train.

Marsha was her usual acerbic self, smirking as she looked at me, and saying, "Nice mascara, Ron. But it looks like it's running."

At least Kathy was more sympathetic.

"Oh my God, Ron, what happened to your face?"

"Remember that fight I was training for?"

"Yes. Is that what happened?"

"No," I said. "I never got there, but I took on three guys in a make-shift meat locker."

"So . . . Did you win?"

I nodded my head. "And I'm still a contenda. You shoulda seen da odda guys," I said, trying a poor, at best, imitation of Marlon Brando in *On the Waterfront*.

She smiled, but it was a wary smile. "Oh?"

"In other words, I proved I wasn't just another bum from the neighborhood."

Sue, the bartender gave me my standard club soda, and I sat in a booth off to the side of Kathy's piano.

"Well, I do have a surprise for you," she said, taking out some sheet music and setting it on the rack. Before I could ask her what it was, she began pressing the keys and singing "As Time Goes By."

It brought back a lot of memories. Maybe too many.

I listened as her voice floated hypnotically over the melody. She'd obviously done her own arrangement, and her version was slow and sexy. Much different from the movie, but somehow, just as moving. When she was finished there was a smattering of applause from the rest of the bar patrons, whom I'd hardly noticed before then.

"So, what do you think?" she asked. "I went out and bought the music after you asked me to play it before, and I've been practicing all week. I wanted to surprise you."

"Well, you sure did that," I said. As I picked up my drink and brought it to my lips, I couldn't help thinking about Laurie . . . and Paula. . . . I silently wondered if the world would really always welcome lovers?

Yeah, I figured. I guess it would.

Kathy was setting up another song. I tipped my glass toward her as she smiled at me over the top of the piano. I smiled back, and said, in my best Bogey imitation, "Here's looking at *you,* kid."

About the Author

Michael A. Black graduated from Columbia College Chicago in 2000 with a Master of Fine Arts Degree in Fiction Writing. He also has a Bachelor of Arts degree in English from Northern Illinois University. For the past twenty-five years he has been a police officer in the south suburbs of Chicago.

The author of over forty articles on subjects ranging from police work to popular fiction, several of his short stories have appeared in various magazines and anthologies including *Alfred Hitchcock* and *Ellery Queen's Mystery Magazines*, and *The Mammoth Book of Legal Thrillers*. He has also written two nonfiction books for young readers, *The M1A1 Abrams Tank* and *Volunteering to Help Kids*, which were published by Rosen Press.

His first novel, *A Killing Frost*, debuted in 2002 with rave reviews, and featured blurbs from such modern masters as D. C. Brod, Sara Paretsky, and Andrew Vachss. *Windy City Knights* is the second novel in a series featuring private detective Ron Shade.

Black has worked in various capacities in police work including patrol, tactical squad, investigations, SWAT team leader, and raid team member. He is currently a sergeant with the Matteson Illinois Police Department. His hobbies include weightlifting, running, the martial arts, and bird watching. It's rumored he has five cats.